CHARLOTTE LINK

is one of Europe's bestselling crime writers and has sold more than fifteen million novels in Germany alone. Her atmospheric brand of psychological suspense made *The Other Child* a massive #1 bestseller in Germany and was greeted by rave reviews. Charlotte has been nominated for the Fiction Category of the German Book Prize and her work has been widely adapted for TV, with the adaptation of *The Other Child* transmitted in Germany in 2011.

CHARLOTTE LINK

THE WATCHER

WORLDWIDE®

TORONTO • NEW YORK • LONDON
AMSTERDAM • PARIS • SYDNEY • HAMBURG
STOCKHOLM • ATHENS • TOKYO • MILAN
MADRID • WARSAW • BUDAPEST • AUCKLAND

Recycling programs
for this product may
not exist in your area.

ISBN-13: 978-0-373-18971-7

The Watcher

A Worldwide Library Suspense/June 2015

First published by Pegasus Books LLC

www.Harlequin.com

Printed in U.S.A.

THE
WATCHER

Prologue

HE WONDERED IF his wife had noticed anything yet.... Sometimes she looked at him so strangely. Suspiciously. She didn't say anything, but that didn't mean that she wasn't watching him closely. And drawing her own conclusions.

They had married in April. It was now September, and they were still in the phase where they were careful around each other, trying not to reveal their own eccentricities too clearly. Yet he could see that one day his wife would become a nagger. She was not the type to get involved in a shouting match, throw plates, or threaten to throw him out of the house. She was the type to go on and on at him, quietly moaning about things and driving him around the bend.

But for now she kept a lid on it. She tried to do everything just as he would like. She cooked the food he liked, put his beer in the fridge in plenty of time, ironed his shirts and trousers, and watched the sports shows on TV with him, even though she preferred romantic films.

And all the while, she was keeping an eye on him. At least, that's what it felt like to him.

She had married him because she could not live without a husband, because she needed to feel protected, cherished, and cared for. He had married her because he had been close to the edge: no stable job, little money. He had felt that he had come unstuck at some point. He had already started to drink too much. At that point he had still been able to find a few odd jobs and pay the rent on the unappealing little apartment he lived in. But he was losing courage. He could no longer see a future for himself.

And then Lucy had come along with the little bicycle repair shop that she had inherited from her late husband. He had seized the chance. He had always had an eye for opportunities, and he was proud not to be a ditherer.

Now he was married. He had a roof over his head. He had work. His life was on track again.

And now this. These feelings, this compulsion, the inability to think of anything else. Of anything else except for *her*.

And *her* was not Lucy.

She had blond hair. Not the poorly dyed blonde of Lucy's hair, which was already gray here and there. No, proper blonde. Her hair flowed down to her waist and shimmered in the sun like a cloth of golden silk. She had blue-green eyes. Depending on how bright the light outside was, but also on the color of the clothes she was wearing and of the background, her eyes sometimes looked as blue as forget-me-nots or as green as the sea can be. This intensive play of color in her eyes fascinated him. He had not seen anything like it in anyone else's eyes.

He loved her hands too. They were delicate and slender. Her fingers were long and slim.

He loved her legs. Delicate too. Almost fragile. Everything about her was. As if she were carved from a pale-colored piece of noble wood by someone who had taken a lot of time and effort over her. Nothing about her was ordinary or coarse. She was loveliness personified.

When he thought of her, he broke out in a sweat.

When he saw her, he could not take his eyes off her. That was probably what Lucy had noticed. He tried to be near the gate whenever she came down the street. Normally he would give a bike he had just repaired a test run on the pavement, in order to have an excuse to hang around.

He loved the way she moved. The spring in her step. She didn't move awkwardly; she took large strides. There was so much energy in everything she did. Whether she ran or spoke or laughed: yes, unlimited energy. Strength.

Beauty. Such an overabundance of beauty and perfection that it was sometimes hard to believe it was true.

Was what he felt love? It had to be love and not just greed, excitement, and everything else that came with it, for that only came because he loved her. Love was the beginning, the ground in which his longing grew. This longing that he could not muster for Lucy. Lucy was an emergency solution and not one that he could give up, because without Lucy he would be a social wreck. Lucy was a bitter necessity. Life sometimes demanded that you had to give in to bitter necessity. He had learned long ago that there was no point in fighting it.

And yet everything in him rebelled against it. And then he would be flooded with a wave of overwhelming helplessness. For what chance did he have? He was not attractive. He had no illusions about that. In the past, yes, but now.... He owed his belly to his predilection for beer and fatty foods. His face was bloated. He was forty-eight years old and looked ten years older, especially when he had drunk too much of an evening. Unfortunately, he could not break the habit. He ought to exercise and eat more vegetables, drink water or tea, but it just was not that easy to change thirty years of habit at a snap of the fingers. He wondered whether this elf, this sprite, would still be able to love him. In spite of his belly, the bags under his eyes, and the fact that he huffed and sweated at the smallest exertion. He had inner qualities, and perhaps he would be able to communicate them to her. Because he had known for a while now that he would not be able to do without her. In spite of Lucy and her jealousy and the risk he was taking.

He was a forty-eight-year-old fatty whose body and soul were aflame.

The problem was that she, the elf, the being he longed for day and night, was so much younger. So very much younger.

She was nine.

PART I

Saturday, October 31, 2009

LIZA MANAGED TO slip out of the room unseen just as the man readied himself to give a speech on the occasion of his father's birthday. He had tapped a fork against his glass several times until finally the hundred guests had understood. The background roar of laughter and talk disappeared and everyone's eyes turned to the nervous man who seemed at that moment to regret nothing so much as his decision to make a speech on his father's seventy-fifth birthday.

The speaker was turning alternately red and white. He got into such a muddle over his words that it took him three tries before he really got started. A few men in the audience made jokes to their neighbors. He had certainly managed to attract everyone's attention with his awkwardness.

The moment could not have been better.

During the last fifteen minutes, Liza had worked her way toward the exit. Now she only had to take two more steps to be outside. She closed the heavy door behind her and leaned briefly against the wall, breathing deeply. How peaceful it was out here. How cool. The room had become unnaturally hot because it was so full. She had the impression that no one suffered the heat as much as she did. Everyone else seemed to be enjoying the evening immensely. Beautiful clothes, jewelry, perfume, relaxed laughter. And she was in the middle of it all and yet blocked off from it as if by an invisible wall.

She had smiled mechanically, had replied when someone asked her something. She had nodded or shaken her head and drunk her champagne, but the whole time she was numb. She felt as if she was a puppet and someone else was pulling the strings, so that she herself had no control over her movements. And that is what had been happening for years. Her life was not guided by a will of her own. If you can call what she had a *life*.

A young female employee of the elegant Kensington Hotel, a venue appropriate to the status of the man whose birthday it was, came by just then. She stopped a moment, unsure whether the woman leaning against the wall needed help. Liza supposed she must look the worse for wear, at least if she looked at all like she felt. She straightened herself up and tried to smile.

"Everything all right?" asked the employee.

She nodded. "Yes. It's just…it's pretty hot in there!" She nodded toward the door. The young woman looked pityingly at her and then walked on. Liza realized she had to get to the ladies' and fix herself up. The way the woman had looked at her, she must look pretty bad.

The marble-floored room was bathed in a gentle light, and quiet, calming music wafted from hidden speakers. She was afraid of meeting someone, but it appeared that she was alone. No one seemed to be in the cubicles either. But as there were a hundred guests at the birthday party alone, as well as all the hotel's other guests, this situation wouldn't last long. Liza knew that someone could come in at any moment. She didn't have much time.

Supporting herself on one of the luxury washbasins, she looked at herself in the mirror above it.

As so often when she looked into a mirror, she had the impression that she did not know the woman she saw.

This was even true when she was not as stressed as she was now. Strands of her beautiful blond hair, which she had pinned up at the start of the evening, were hanging messily down the sides of her face. Her lipstick was probably on the rim of her champagne flute; it certainly was no longer visible on her mouth. Her lips appeared very pale. She had been sweating heavily. Her nose was shiny and her makeup smudged.

She had felt it. Guessed it. That is why she had longed for nothing quite so much as to leave the dreadful room and its suffocating crowd of people. She had to get a grip again quickly and find a way to survive this evening. It could not go on forever. The champagne reception was almost over. The buffet would soon commence. Thank God. That was better than a seated five-course meal, which could go on for hours and where anyone who made a quick getaway was immediately noticed—at least by their neighbors. A buffet offered many more possibilities for a quick and discreet disappearing act.

She put her handbag down in front of herself on the marble-topped surface, fiddled nervously and clumsily with the catch, and finally managed to fish out her makeup tube and her compact. If only her hands would not shake so much. She had to be careful not to spill any on her dress. That would be all she needed tonight.

While she tried to open the compact, unsuccessfully, she suddenly started to cry. There was nothing spectacular about how it happened. The tears just trickled out of her eyes and she could not stop them. She raised her head in disgust and saw a face she did not know—a face that had now become a crying face. That made her turmoil complete. How was she to go back to the room with fat, red, swollen eyes?

Almost in a panic, she tore a handful of silky soft tis-

sues from the silver dispenser on the wall and tried to
stem her flood of tears. But it almost seemed as though
the effort to stop them only made them flow all the more
strongly. They just would not stop.

I have to go home, she thought; there's nothing for
it: I have to leave!

And as if everything was not already bad enough,
now she heard a noise behind her. The door leading to
the hall opened. High heels clacked on the marble floor.
Liza could see the blurred outline of a figure through
her tears. A woman who was crossing the room toward
the toilets. She pressed the tissues to her face to make
it look as though she were blowing her nose.

Hurry up, she thought, go away!

Suddenly the footsteps stopped. For a short instant there was complete silence in the room. Then the
stranger turned around and went over to Liza, putting
a hand on her gently trembling shoulder. Liza lifted
her head and looked at the woman in the mirror. A face
full of concern. Inquiring eyes. She did not know the
woman; but, judging by what she was wearing, Liza
guessed she was there for the birthday party too.

"Can I help?" she asked. "Don't think you have to
talk to me, but...."

The warmth and concern audible in the calm voice
were too much for Liza to bear. She lowered the tissues.

Then she surrendered to her pain and stopped trying
to stanch the flood of her tears.

Sunday, November 22

IT WAS LATE on Sunday evening when Carla first became conscious of a peculiar thing about the elevator and its doors. At that point she did not have long to live, but her powers of imagination could not let her see what would happen to her that night.

She sat in her apartment, somewhat puzzled, because suddenly she was certain about what had been going on for a few days now. The elevator would come up to her eighth floor and stop, the doors would open automatically, but then nothing further would happen. No one got out; she would have heard their footsteps in the corridor. Nor did anyone get in; she would have heard footsteps beforehand. She was sure there had been none. If there had been, she would have registered them on some level of her consciousness. The building was not good at muffling sounds. It was a seventies tower, a rather unadorned building with long corridors and many apartments. Families lived in the larger apartments, and the smaller ones were inhabited by singles who worked the whole time and were almost never home. Hackney was one of the poorer boroughs of London, but the area where Carla lived was not all that bad.

She tried to remember when she had first heard the elevator come up without hearing anyone step out of it. Of course that happened occasionally, and had happened since she moved there. If someone pressed the wrong button, realized their mistake, and got out at a lower floor, the elevator would still make the journey to the top floor, open its doors, then close them again and wait until it was called to another floor. But recently it had been happening more often. Unusually often.

Perhaps in the last week? Perhaps in the last two?

She turned the television off. The talk show on TV right now did not interest her anyway.

She went to the apartment's front door and opened it. She pressed the light switch right beside her doorbell, bathing the corridor in a harsh white light. Who had decided on these lights? They gave your skin a deathly pallor.

She looked down the long quiet corridor. Nothing and no one in sight. The elevator doors had closed again.

Perhaps some joker in the building who had taken to pressing "8" before he got out. Although quite what someone would get out of that was a mystery to Carla. But many of the things that drove people, that people did or wanted to do, were a mystery to her. When all was said and done, she thought, she was fairly isolated from society. Alone, abandoned and living on her pension for the last five years. If you got up on your own, spent the day reading or watching television in a small apartment, only occasionally making the effort to go for a walk, and then ate alone again in the evening before sitting down in front of the television, you ended up distancing yourself from normal life. You lost contact with people whose daily life was made up of their jobs, colleagues, spouses, children, and all the related worries, tasks, and—of course—joys. Perhaps she seemed much stranger to other people than she realized.

She closed her door again and leaned against it from the inside, breathing heavily. When she had moved into the building, she had at first thought that she would have a better life there. She had hoped that in this building full of people she would feel less lonely, but the opposite was the case. Everyone here slaved away with their own lives, no one seemed to really know any of the others, and everyone lived as anonymously as possible. Some apartments were also empty. For some time now, no one but Carla had lived on the eighth floor.

She went back into the living room, wondering whether to turn the television on again. She left it. Instead, she poured herself some more wine. She drank every evening, but she had imposed a rule on herself that she was not to start before eight. Until now, she had managed to stick to that.

She jumped when she heard the noise of the elevator again. It was going down. Someone must have called it. At least that was normal life. People coming and going in the building. She was not alone.

Perhaps I should look for another apartment, she thought.

Her finances did not give her much room for maneuver. Her pension was modest. She could not make big changes. Nor was it clear that she would be less lonely elsewhere. Perhaps it was because of the building. Or perhaps it was down to her.

Thinking that she couldn't bear the silence any longer, she reached for her telephone and hurriedly dialed her daughter's number. She did it before fear or shyness could get the better of her. She had always had a good relationship with her daughter; but since Keira had gotten married and had a baby, the contact had started to crumble a little. Young people did not have time. They were so occupied with themselves and their lives.

Where to find the energy to look after a mother whose life had gone down the drain?

Carla could sometimes scarcely believe it herself: divorced after twenty-eight years of marriage. Her husband had been in debt up to his eyeballs. He had lived beyond his means, and over the years the debts had grown and grown. He had skedaddled before his creditors could catch up with him. For years now, there had been no trace of him. Carla was still suffering from the experience. She was often whiny. Keira had escaped the mess into which her father's bankruptcy had plunged the family by finding her own comfortable life in Bracknell, forty-five minutes southwest of the center of London. After getting a math degree, she had found a good job in a bank and married a man with a safe job in the bank's management. Carla knew she should be happy for her daughter.

Keira answered the phone on the second ring. She sounded stressed. Her little boy was screaming in the background.

"Hi, Keira. Mom here. I just wanted to see how you were."

"Oh, hi, Mom," said Keira. She did not sound enthusiastic. "Yes, everything's okay. Johnny's just not sleeping well. He's always screaming at night. I'm pretty shattered."

"His teeth must be coming in."

"Yes, that's it." Keira went silent for a moment, then asked, duty-bound, "And how are you?"

For a second, Carla was tempted to just say the truth: that she felt rotten, that she felt completely alone. But she knew that her daughter did not want to hear that, because everything was too much for her too right then. She would have reacted badly.

"Oh, well, I am on my own rather often," she said.

"Since I retired…." She left the rest of the sentence unsaid. Things could not be helped.

Keira sighed. "You have to find some leisure activity you like. A hobby where you can meet like-minded people. Whether it's a cooking course or a sport that you start doing, you need to be around people."

"Hmm, jumping around with old ladies in aerobics classes for the elderly…."

Keira sighed again, this time with obvious impatience. "It doesn't need to be that. God, there's oodles of options. You'll be able to find something that matches even your expectations!"

Carla was tempted to let her daughter in on the secret that she had been going to a self-help group for single women, but that she had not managed to make any lasting friends there either. Probably she had been moaning too much. Nobody could bear her for long. No, it was better not to let Keira know about that project.

"I think everything just depresses me," she said. "If I go swimming or cook during the day, it just makes me realize I'm not a fully active member of society anymore. That I'm not working and have no family to care for. And when I come home again, then of course no one is waiting for me."

"But you would certainly meet some nice women who you could do things with now and then."

"Most of them probably have a family and don't have time for me."

"Right, because you're the only divorced retiree in all of England," replied Keira sharply. "Do you want to sit in front of your television in your apartment every night for the rest of your life under a cloud of despair?"

"And get on my daughter's nerves?"

"I didn't say that."

"This building is oppressive," said Carla. "No one shows any interest in the others. And the elevator is always coming up to my floor, and then no one gets out."

"What?" Keira sounded irritated.

Carla wished she had not said that. "Well, I just noticed it. That it happens quite often, I mean. Apart from me, no one else lives up here. But the elevator is always coming up."

"Then someone is sending it up. Or that's the way the elevator is programmed. That it automatically goes to the different floors."

"But it only started in the last week or two."

"Mom...."

"I know. I'm getting a little odd. That's what you think. Don't worry. I'll get my life back on an even keel somehow."

"Of course you will. Mom, Johnny is screaming again, and...."

"I'll leave you! It'd be nice if you and Johnny would visit. Maybe one weekend?"

"I'll have a look and see if there's a good time," said Keira vaguely. Then she quickly said good-bye and hung up, leaving Carla with the feeling that she had been an annoyance and a burden.

She *is* my daughter, she thought defiantly. It *is* normal for me to call her now and then. And for me to tell her when I am not feeling well.

She looked at her watch. It was just after ten.

Nevertheless, she decided to go to bed. Perhaps to read something. Certainly in the hope of falling asleep quickly.

She was just about to go into the bathroom to brush her teeth when she heard the elevator again. It was coming up.

She stood in her hall, her ears pricked up.

I really wish someone else lived up here too, she thought. The elevator stopped and the doors opened.

Carla waited. For nothing to happen, no sound, nothing.

But this time she heard something. This time someone left the elevator. There were steps. She heard them quite clearly. Steps outside in the corridor, which was no doubt brightly lit as usual.

Carla swallowed. Her throat was dry. She felt a prickling sensation on her skin.

Now, don't let it get to you. First you got worked up because no one got out, and now you are getting worked up because someone has.

The steps approached.

This way, thought Carla. Someone is coming to my door. She stood paralyzed behind her front door.

Someone was on the other side.

When the doorbell rang, the spell was broken. The bell was normal life.

Burglars don't ring the bell, Carla thought.

Nevertheless, she took the precaution of looking through the peephole first.

She hesitated.

Then she opened the door.

Wednesday, December 2

1

GILLIAN WENT BACK into the kitchen. "That was Diana, Darcy's mom," she explained. "Darcy isn't coming to school today. She has a sore throat."

The telephone's ringing had not been enough to tear Becky out of her lethargy. She was hunched over her bowl of muesli, staring moodily at the flakes and bits of fruit in the milk.

Just turned twelve, thought Gillian, and already as grumpy and listless as a teenager at the height of puberty. Weren't we different back then?

"Hmm," went Becky, showing no interest. Chuck, her black cat, sat on the chair next to her. The family had found him on holiday in Greece. He had been a half-starved bundle of bones on the side of the road and they had smuggled him into their hotel. The big issue for the rest of the holidays had been how to get Chuck out of the hotel without being discovered each day and then, after taking him to the vet, how to bring him back in again. Gillian and Becky had dripped liquid food into his mouth for hours with an eyedropper. For a while everything had suggested that he would not survive. Becky had cried the whole time; but although everything had been so difficult and nerve-racking, she and her mother had been very close as they nursed Chuck together.

In the end, Chuck's will to live had won out, and he had traveled back to England with his new family.

Gillian sat opposite Becky at the table. Now she had to drive her to school. She and Darcy's mother shared the school run, and this week was Diana's turn. But not, of course, on a day when her own daughter wasn't going to school.

"But I did find out something interesting," said Gillian. "You've got a math test today!"

"Maybe."

"No, not 'maybe': you *have*! You've got a test, and I had no idea." Becky shrugged. She had a moustache of hot chocolate on her upper lip. She was wearing black jeans that were so tight, Gillian wondered how she had managed to put them on. Her black jumper was just as skin-tight, and she had a black cloth wrapped several times around her neck. She was trying to look cool, but with the chocolate on her lip she just looked like a little girl in a strange costume. Of course Gillian refrained from telling her that.

"Why didn't you mention it? I've asked you every day if you had any tests coming up. You said you didn't. Why?"

Becky shrugged her shoulders again.

"Can you please give me an answer?" asked Gillian sharply.

"Don't know," mumbled Becky.

"*What* don't you know?"

"Why I didn't say."

"I expect you didn't like the thought of having to study for it," said Gillian wearily.

Becky looked at her angrily.

What am I doing wrong, Gillian asked herself, to make her look at me with so much hate? Why did Darcy's mother know about the math test? Why, probably, did everyone's mother know except me?

"Brush your teeth," she said, "and come. We have to go."

On the way to school, Becky did not say a word: she just looked out the window. Gillian wanted to ask if she felt confident about the test, if she knew the material well, but she didn't dare. She was afraid of a snotty answer and had the nasty feeling that one might make her burst into tears. That happened more and more often nowadays, and she found that she had no way of defending herself. She was unhappy with her life and afraid of her twelve-year-old daughter's provocative behavior. How can a forty-two-year-old woman be so unsure of herself?

Becky said good-bye in front of the school with a few terse words and then loped off across the road on her skinny legs. Her long hair floated behind her. Her rucksack bounced around on her back. She did not turn to wave good-bye to her mother. In primary school, she had always blown her mother kisses and beamed at her. How was it possible that she had changed so completely within just a few years? Of course she felt defensive this morning. She knew that the math test would be a disaster and that it had been a mistake to avoid studying for it. She had to vent her annoyance at herself somehow.

Gillian asked herself if they were all like that. So aggressive. So unreasonable and lacking in empathy.

She started the engine but just drove to the next street, where she parked again. She opened the window a little and lit a cigarette. In the yards all around, a frost lay on the grass. In the distance she saw the river flowing along like a lead ribbon. The Thames was wide here, obeying the rhythms of the tides as it pushed toward the sea. The wind smelled of seaweed, and the seagulls screamed. It was cold. An inhospitable, gray winter's morning.

She had once talked about it with Tom. Almost two years ago now. Or, rather, she had *tried* to talk about it with him. About whether she as a mother was doing something wrong. Or whether all children were like that. He had not known what to say.

In the end, he had said: "If you were more in touch with other mothers, you might know. You would know if you were doing anything wrong. You might even know how to do it right. But for some reason, you refuse to build up a network."

"I'm refusing nothing. I just don't get on well with the other mothers."

"They're normal women. They won't hurt you!"

Of course he was right. That was not the point. "But they don't accept me. It's always as if…I was somehow speaking a different language. Everything I say seems to come out wrong. It doesn't fit in with what they're saying…." She knew how that must sound to Tom, who saw everything rationally. Like nonsense. Complete and utter nonsense.

"Nonsense!" he said promptly. "I think you're imagining it all. You're an intelligent woman. You're attractive. You've got a successful career. You have a husband who is more or less presentable and not without success in his own job. You have a pretty, clever, and healthy child. So why have you got such a complex?"

Did she have a complex?

Lost in thought, she tapped the ash of her cigarette out of the car window.

There was no reason to have complexes. Fifteen years ago, together with Tom she had started a company in

London that specialized in tax and business consultancy. They had worked like the devil to get the company going, but it had been worth it. Now they employed sixteen people. Tom had always stressed that he would never have done all that without Gillian. After Becky was born, Gillian stopped working in the office every day, but she still had her own clients. Three or four times a week, she took the train in to London for work. She had the freedom to work as and when she wished. When Becky needed her, she would not go to the office that day and would catch up with work over the weekend.

Everything was fine. She could have been happy.

She looked in the rearview mirror and saw her deep blue eyes and the strawberry blond curls over her forehead. Her long wild hair never really let her look tidy. She could remember how as a child she had hated her curls and their reddish color. As well as the freckles that inevitably accompany red hair. Then she had gone to college and met Thomas Ward, her first boyfriend, who was to become the man of her life, her great love. He had loved the color of her hair and counted her freckles one by one. Suddenly she had started to find herself beautiful and to appreciate what was special about her appearance.

You should think about all of that, she thought, all the good that's come into your life through Tom. You are married to a wonderful man.

She had finished her cigarette. She wondered about driving to the office. There was a whole pile of work waiting for her, and experience told her that the best way to stop brooding was to get working. She decided to drink one last cup of coffee at home, then get changed and go to London.

She started the engine.

Perhaps she should meet Tara again. Her friend worked as a public prosecutor in London and—according to Tom, who didn't like her much—was a radical feminist. In any case, Gillian's chats with Tara did her good.

The last time they met, Tara had told her, not mincing her words, that Gillian was deep in a depression.

Perhaps she was right.

2

SAMSON HAD STOOD at the top of the stairs listening for a long time and only hurried down in his socks when he was sure that no one was around. He wanted to put his shoes and parka on as quickly as possible and disappear outside; but as he bent over to tie his shoelaces, the kitchen door opened and his sister-in-law Millie appeared. The way she moved toward him reminded Samson of a hawk that has spied its prey.

He straightened up.

"Hi, Millie," he said uneasily.

Millie Segal was one of those women who even before reaching forty merit the double-edged epithet *She must have been pretty once*. She was blond, had a good figure and regular features, but the skin of her face was etched with deep furrows from too much tanning and too many cigarettes. She looked older than she actually was, as well as careworn and strangely embittered. The latter was less a matter of her unhealthful lifestyle than the fact that she was a deeply unhappy woman. Frustrated. Samson had sometimes talked to his brother about it. His brother had explained to him that Millie was convinced that she had been ill-treated by fate. This was not because anything tragic had ever happened to

her, but rather because in the daily little disappoint-
ments and injustices, she saw some larger disadvantag-
ing of her person.

Whenever Gavin, her husband, asked her what exactly was souring her life, she would always reply: "Everything. It's everything."

Unfortunately, Samson knew that he played no little
part in this *everything*.

"I thought I heard you," said Millie. She was not
dressed yet. Because she went to work later on, every
morning she would quickly slip into a track suit and
make her husband breakfast before he left for his early
shift. Gavin was a bus driver. Often he had to get up at
five in the morning. Millie would make him coffee, pop
slices of bread in the toaster, and make him the sandwiches that he took to work. She could display real care,
but Samson was convinced that she did not do it out of
real warm-heartedness. Gavin paid a high price for his
breakfast: he had to listen to her griping and moaning
the whole time. Sometimes Samson wondered whether
his brother would not prefer to be alone at that early hour
with jam on toast and a cup of coffee, reading the paper.

"I'm just going out," said Samson, slipping into his
parka.

"Any news about work?" Millie asked.

"Not yet."

"Are you looking?"

"Of course. But times are hard."

"You haven't chipped in with the housekeeping
money this week. I have to do the shopping. And you
don't hold back when it comes to eating."

Samson fished his wallet out of his pocket and pulled
out a note. "Will that do for now?"

"It's not much," said Millie, but of course she took the money. "Better than nothing."

What did she actually want? Samson wondered. She had not intercepted him just about the money.

He looked at her questioningly.

Millie just said: "Gavin gets back at midday. We'll eat at two. I've got a late shift."

"I won't be here for lunch," said Samson. She shrugged. "Up to you."

As it was obvious that they had said all they had to say for now, he nodded at her, opened the front door, and stepped out into the cold day.

Every meeting with Millie made him nervous, unsure, and apprehensive. He could barely breathe around her. Out here, he started to feel much better.

He had once overheard a conversation between Millie and his brother. Since then, he had known that Millie wished for nothing so much as for him to move out of the house. Of course, he had seen that before, too. Millie had left him in no doubt that she saw him as a fly in the ointment. It felt quite different, however, to hear her talk about it so frankly. Nor had he known until then that she was putting her brother under massive pressure.

"I wanted to have a normal marriage, a completely normal marriage," she had hissed. "And what do we have now? Some kind of apartment-share?"

"That's not what it is," Gavin had replied uneasily. He sounded exhausted, like someone who has had to talk about an unpleasant topic far too many times. "He's my brother. He's not just any lodger!"

"If only he were! Then at least we would be paid rent. But as it is…."

"It's his house too, Millie. We inherited it jointly from our parents. He has the same right to live here as we do."

"It's not a question of rights!"

"Then of what?"

"Of decency and manners. I mean, we're married. One day we might even have children. Be a real family. He's single. He's out of place. Anyone else would notice he is in the way and find somewhere else."

"We can't force him. If he went, then I'd either have to pay him his share of the house, which I can't afford, or we'd have to pay him rent for his part of the house. God, Millie, you know what I earn! It would put us in a tight spot."

"As your brother, he shouldn't accept money from you."

"But he would have to pay rent somewhere else, and he hasn't got a job. How's he supposed to do that?"

"Then let *us* move out!"

"Do you really want to? If so, you can forget about a house with a yard. Nothing against an apartment, but are you sure you'd be all right with that?"

Listening and sweating outside the door, Samson pulled a scornful face. Of course she wouldn't be all right with that. The most important thing to Millie was status, even more important than getting out of the shared living arrangements with the brother-in-law she disliked. Millie was from a simple background. Her marriage to a homeowner had been a big step up the social ladder, even if the home was a narrow rowhouse on a busy road. She loved to invite her friends over and show off the yard, which she had laid out and looked after so it looked very pretty. She would not be able to leave it behind. No, Millie did not want to move out. She wanted *Samson* to move out.

She had not replied to her husband's last sentence, but the silence had been eloquent enough.

Samson shook off the thought of that depressing conversation and set off on his walk through the streets. There was a particular logic and timetable to his walks. Today he was five minutes late, because he had hesitated so long before daring to go downstairs and because Millie had caught him.

He had lost his job in June, six months ago. He had been a driver for a frozen-foods delivery service. But during the current economic crisis, everyone was watching their pennies and orders had gone down dramatically. In the end, the company had been forced to reduce the number of drivers. Samson had seen it coming. He was the last employee to have been hired and the first one to be laid off.

The house that Gavin and he had inherited from their parents was at the end of their street, near to a busy main road. The houses at this end were narrow and their yards were thin strips. In the opposite direction, the street led to the Thorpe Bay Golf Club and showed itself in a rather different light. The houses were larger and were adorned with little turrets and oriels. Their yards were generously sized. Trees towered high above well-tended hedges and the cast-iron fences or pretty stone walls that surrounded the properties. Impressive cars parked in the drives. There was a pleasant peacefulness to the scene.

Southend-on-Sea stretches out forty miles east of London along the north bank of the Thames to the point where the river becomes the North Sea. The town offers everything the heart could desire: shopping, schools, nurseries, theatre and cinemas, the obligatory fun fair down on the promenade, as well as long sandy beaches, sailing clubs, even a kite surfing club, pubs, and restaurants. Many families, for whom London had become too expensive and who, moreover, thought it would be better for their children not to grow up in the giant metropolis, moved out of London to the town. Thorpe Bay was the part of Southend where Samson lived. Much of it was made up of the rolling meadows of the golf course and the many tennis courts opposite the beach. Whoever lived here seemed to have landed in an idyll: tree-lined roads, lovingly tended yards, well-maintained houses. The wind from the river carried the smell of the salty sea.

Samson had grown up here. He could not imagine living anywhere else.

Shortly before he reached Thorpe Hall Avenue, he would always pass the young woman with the large mongrel. She took her dog for a walk every morning. She was already on her way home by this time. Samson had followed her home several times and was reasonably sure about her living arrangements. No husband, no children. Whether she was divorced or had never married, he could not say. She lived in a poky semi-detached home, but it had a big yard. She seemed to work from home, because she never left home during the day, apart from when she went shopping or walked her dog. However, she often received deliveries from couriers. Samson's conclusion was that she worked at home for a company. Maybe she typed up dictation. Maybe she wrote reports or edited text for a publisher. He had noted that she would occasionally go away for several days at a time. During those trips, a friend would house-sit for her and walk her dog. Obviously she had to meet her employer now and then.

A little farther on, an elderly lady was sweeping the pavement in front of her house. He often passed this lady on his walk. Today she was sweeping up the leaves, the last few leaves, that had sailed over the fence from the tree in her front yard. She would often be sweeping the pavement even on those days when anyone else would have said that there was absolutely nothing to do. Samson knew she lived on her own. Even a less observant person than he would have seen that she had a need to do something that gave her a chance of snatching a quick "good morning" from a passerby. She never had visitors. Either she had not had any children or, if she had, then they were not the kind who cared about her. Nor had he ever seen any friends or acquaintances whom she could visit.

"Good morning," she said, rather out of breath, as soon as she had seen him.

"Good morning," he mumbled. It was his unbending rule that he would have no contact whatsoever to the people he watched. It was important that he not stand out. But he could not bring himself to pass this woman without greeting her. In any case, if he had not said anything, he would have only made her remember him all the more. *The unfriendly man who walks past every morning...*. At least this way she would remember him positively.

He had now reached the row of houses opposite a pretty little park. The Ward family lived in one of the houses. Samson knew more about them than about all the other people, because Gavin had called on Thomas Ward's help to sort out inheritance-tax issues after their parents' deaths. Ward and his wife worked as financial consultants in London. Ward had advised Gavin, who was near to despair over the issue, at a more-than-reasonable rate. Since then, Gavin would not hear a word against Thomas, even though Thomas was exactly the kind of guy neither brother liked normally, what with his big car, his fine suits, and his ties that were not showy but obviously expensive....

"You shouldn't judge someone by their appearance," Gavin always said when Ward came up in conversation.

"Ward is all right. Leave it!"

Samson knew that Gillian Ward did not go to the London office every day. He could not see any pattern in her working hours. Probably there was none. But of course she also had to take care of her twelve-year-old daughter, Becky, who often seemed quite withdrawn and difficult. Samson had the impression that Becky could be quite rebellious. No doubt she did not make her mother's life any easier.

He was surprised to suddenly see Gillian's car come down the street and turn into her drive and stop. That was strange. He knew that she shared the school run with the mother of one of Becky's friends and that this week was the other mom's turn. He was sure. Maybe she had not taken the children to school. If not, where had she been? At this early hour?

He stopped. Was she planning to go to the office? She always drove to the station, either Thorpe Bay or South-end Central, and then continued by train to Fenchurch Station in London. He had followed her on a number of occasions, so he knew her route perfectly.

He watched her go inside. The light in the hall went on. The Ward's pretty red door had a lozenge-shaped window, so from the street you could look down the hall and into the kitchen behind it. Through this practical window, he had on one occasion seen how Gillian had sat back down at the breakfast table after her family had left. She had poured herself another cup of coffee and drunk it slowly in little sips. The newspaper lay next to her, but she had not been reading it: she had just stared at the opposite wall. That was when he had first thought *she's not happy!*

The thought had pained him, because he had come to like the Wards. They were not the typical kind of people he shadowed. He preferred single women. He had already asked himself why he was shadowing them so doggedly. One summer evening when he had hung around in the streets and stared into the Wards' yard and watched them laughing and chatting, he had suddenly had his epiphany. They were perfect. That was what attracted him so magically. The absolutely perfect family. The attractive father who earned good money. The beautiful, intelligent mother. The pretty, lively child. The cute black cat. A nice house. A well-kept yard. Two cars. Not rich or flashy, but solidly middle-class. An ordered world.

The world he had always dreamed of.

The world he would never be part of. He had realized that he found some consolation in watching it over a fence.

He went closer to the house, right up to the gate, and tried to spy into the kitchen. He could see Gillian bent over the table. Aha, she had poured herself a cup of coffee. She held the thick mug in her hands and took the same small, pensive sips he had seen before.

What did she think about? She often seemed to be deep in thought.

He hurried on. He could not afford to linger too long in one place, certainly not out on the street like that. He was dying to know what Gillian was worried about, and he knew why: he hoped finding out would calm him down. It had to be something temporary. Nothing, please nothing, to do with her marriage or her family.

Perhaps her mother or father was ill and she was worried. Something like that.

He walked down Thorpe Hall Avenue, past Thorpe Bay Yards, the long stretch of lawns and tennis courts along the seafront, and crossed Thorpe Esplanade to reach the beach. The hectic early-morning traffic was only slowly easing off. The beach lay there cold, abandoned, and wintry. Not a living soul in sight.

He took a deep breath.

He felt as exhausted as others did after a long, hard day at work. He knew why: because he had seen Gillian. Because he had almost bumped into her. This situation, which he had not been prepared for, had caused him such emotional stress that—as he now realized with hindsight—he had marched double-quick to the beach. Anything to get away. To a more peaceful place where he could calm down.

He watched so many people. He memorized their daily routines and habits. He tried to understand how they lived. He would not have been able to explain to anyone what it was that fascinated him so much, but he could not help himself. It was impossible to stop once you had started. He had heard of geeks who built up a parallel life for themselves online in *Second Life*. Those people and what they did seemed close to what he did. Living a second life as well as your own real life. Dreaming your way into other people's fates. Roles you could slip into. Sometimes he was Thomas Ward, the successful man with the lovely house and expensive car. Sometimes he was a cool guy who did not stutter or blush, who asked the pretty woman with the dog out on a date—and of course was not refused. It brought light and joy into his days, and if it was dangerous or disturbing (he had the feeling that a psychologist would have expressed a number of serious doubts about his hobby), it was the only chance he had to avoid the sadness that enveloped him.

But gradually something was changing, and that made him uneasy.

He went a little farther down the beach. It was more windy here than up among the streets. He was quickly frozen to the bone. He had forgotten his gloves and kept blowing into his hands to warm them up. Naturally, that was no reason to deviate from his clearly defined walking schedule. He had even started a file in his computer on the objects of his attention. His sense of duty did not allow him to forget to note down each evening everything he had seen and experienced. But he no longer did it with the same enthusiasm as he had once had. And he knew why that was so: it was because of the Wards, especially Gillian Ward. The Wards had become more and more important to him. They had become *his* family. His daydreams were full of them. There was nothing that he did not know about them, that he did not want to experience with them.

It was probably an inevitable development that his interest in the other people who had fascinated him so deeply was now waning. He had the vague feeling that this was not a good thing. He understood now why right from the start, he had chosen to watch and keep a written record of a large number of people. He had not wanted any individual to become too important. He would take part in lives without being swallowed up by them.

With Gillian, there was a risk he would be.

The wind blowing from the northeast was really cold. Not a day to spend at the beach. Over the summer, it had been fun to stroll through the streets from morning to night, avoiding the heavy atmosphere at home.

Naturally, now in winter it felt different. The only advantage was that it got dark early and that from five, at the latest, he could look into the brightly lit houses. To do so, of course, you were at risk of freezing off various parts of your anatomy.

He lifted his head in the wind, sniffing like an animal. He thought the air smelled like snow. Not that they often had snow here, but he would have bet on a white Christmas this year. Although, of course, a lot could change before then.

Definitely too cold, he decided, to walk any farther along here. He left the beach, and when he came across a food kiosk on the promenade he paused. Unfortunately, he had had to give greedy Millie almost all his money, but after lengthy searches of all his pockets he managed to come up with two pounds. That was enough for a hot cup of coffee.

He drank it standing up, protected from the wind by the kiosk wall. He enjoyed the tickle of heat in his hands as he held the cup. There was a newspaper stand just in front of his nose. He read the headlines, and his attention snagged on a particularly sensational *Daily Mail* front page: GRISLY MURDER IN LONDON!

He bent his neck to try to read the story below the headline. An elderly woman had been murdered in a tower building in Hackney.

The act had been one of extreme brutality. It was estimated that the woman had been lying dead in her apartment for ten days before her daughter found her. There were no clues to the killer's possible motives.

"Ugly thing, that," said the kiosk owner, who had seen what Samson was looking at. "I mean, especially the thing about ten days. That someone can be dead so long before someone realizes. What's become of our society?"

Samson murmured agreement.

"The world gets worse every day," the other one said.

"That's right," said Samson. He finished his coffee. The change from his coffee was just enough for a *Daily Mail*.

He bought the paper and walked on pensively.

3

AT LEAST SHE had finally stopped shaking.

Detective Inspector Peter Fielder from the Metropolitan Police, also known as Scotland Yard, was not even sure that she was ready for questioning, but he knew that time was of the essence. Carla Roberts had no doubt been lying dead in her apartment for over a week before her daughter discovered her. This had given her murderer a massive head start. They needed to act quickly; but at the moment they were getting nowhere with this young woman who was holding her baby tight and shaking like a leaf and who threatened to burst into tears when a policewoman suggested that she hold the baby for a moment. A patrol car had driven her to the hospital the evening before. She had stayed the night under heavy sedation. This morning, she had been driven home to Bracknell.

The officers accompanying her had called Fielder's cell phone to tell him that Keira Jones seemed to be doing better. That was why he was now sitting in her nicely decorated, warm living room, drinking mineral water, with Keira sitting opposite him, as white as chalk but much calmer than the day before. Her husband, Greg Jones, was home. When Fielder arrived, Greg had just fed the baby, changed its diaper, and put it to bed. Now he was standing at the window, his arms folded across his chest. The posture expressed not defensiveness but a need to offer protection. He was clearly devastated by events, but he was trying to stay somewhat calm and collected.

"Mrs. Jones," said Fielder cautiously, "I know it's not easy for you to talk to me right now. I'm really sorry to insist like this. But we really are running out of time. The coroner's provisional judgment is that your mother has been dead for about ten days. In other words, it took a long time to find her…."

Keira closed her eyes for a moment and nodded.

"We have a little boy who demands a lot of attention at the moment, Inspector," said her husband. "For the past few months, my wife has been completely over-stretched. I work all day and can't help her much. My mother-in-law felt a bit neglected by her, but—"

"Greg!" said Keira in a quiet but tortured voice. "She didn't *feel* neglected. I *did* neglect her."

"For goodness' sake, Keira. I work hard. We've got a little kid. You couldn't be driving to Hackney all the time to hold your mom's hand!"

"I should have at least called up more often."

"When was the last time you called her?" asked Fielder. "Or rather: when was the last time you had any contact with your mother?"

Keira thought for a moment. "That was…it was last Sunday: that is, over a week ago. She called me quite late at night. About ten at night."

"You didn't talk to her again after that?"

"No."

Fielder made a mental calculation. "So that was Sunday, the twenty-second of November. Today is the sec-

ond of December. Everything would suggest that soon
after she called you, she…was attacked."

"Was killed."

He nodded. "Yes. Was killed."

"It's dreadful," said Greg Jones. "Just dreadful. Who
could have guessed something like that would happen?"

Fielder looked out the window. In the well-kept front
yard, there were a swing, a sandbox, and a slide. They
were bright, cheerful colors. No doubt the proud father
himself had put them up a little prematurely for his little boy. The Joneses seemed like a happy family. Neither Keira nor Greg seemed cold-hearted or selfish. A
lot of factors had come together: Greg's stress at work,
Keira's stress with their baby, and the fact that the trip
to Hackney was long and awkward, especially with a
little one in tow. The grandmother living on her own
had simply slipped out of sight by accident. Probably
Carla had been on her daughter's conscience, but Keira
had not found a way to make her mother part of her life.

The same as in so many families.

"Was your mother divorced?" asked Fielder. Keira
had already told them that her mother was, during the
first short interview the day before, but Fielder wanted
to hear more about it.

"Yes," said Keira. "For the last ten years."

"Are you in contact with your father? Was your
mother?"

"No." Keira shook her head. "We don't even know
where he is. He had a building-supplies company. We
always lived well and thought everything was all right.
But then it came out that he was massively in debt. Everything collapsed, and he fled abroad—to avoid his
creditors."

"But before he did so, your parents divorced?"

"Yes. When the bankruptcy came out into the open, so did my dad's relationship with a younger colleague. My mom applied for a divorce immediately."

"But you can't be sure your father is still abroad?"

"No. That's just what we assume."

"But you are sure he hadn't been in touch with your mother for years?"

"Yes. She would have told me if he had been."

Fielder made a note. "We'll try to find your father. Do you know the name and address of his lover from back then?"

Keira shook her head. "I think her first name was Clarissa. I can't remember her surname. I wasn't living with my parents at the time.

I was studying in Swansea. I didn't know all the details. I mean—" She suddenly began to cry. "My mom called me all the time back then," she sobbed. "She was in a really bad way. Her life had fallen apart. My dad had been cheating on her for years, and now the money was gone too and the house was going up for auction…. She was feeling rotten, but I often fobbed her off with excuses. I wanted…I suppose I didn't want to have anything to do with it all." Her sobbing grew louder.

Greg stepped over and stroked her hair awkwardly. "Don't blame yourself so much. You were in college. You had your own life. It wasn't your job to sort out your parents' problems."

"I should have been there more for my mom. Then and now. She was lying murdered in her apartment for days, and no one knew! That shouldn't have happened!"

The baby started to cry in the next room. Almost with relief, Greg left the room. The situation was too much for him, which was, thought Fielder, no wonder. Something had broken into the Joneses' lives which they could never have seen coming. They would never really get over it.

Keira reached out for her handbag, pulled out a handkerchief, and blew her nose.

"He works hard, and he wants to relax on the weekends…. You know, my mom was never exactly someone who spread sunshine wherever she went. She was always moaning. Because of the divorce, the bankruptcy, everything. That made her…rather demanding. In my opinion, that was why it was so hard for her to find friends. Most people…just could not bear her after a while. It sounds terrible, what I'm saying, doesn't it? I don't mean to speak badly of her. And anyway, no matter how much she could get on people's nerves, she didn't deserve to die like that. Never!"

Fielder felt for her. He had seen her dead mother, lying in her living room, her hands and feet bound with masking tape. The murderer had stuffed a bunched-up bit of cloth down her throat. A checked tea towel, as it turned out. The first investigation had revealed that it must have made Carla Roberts throw up. She must have been trying to retch enough to force the cloth out of her mouth.

"And normally she would have managed," said the coroner at the scene of the crime. "It looks to me as though the murderer kept the cloth pressed into her mouth long enough until she suffocated on her own vomit."

Fielder hoped that Keira would never ask him for these details. "Mrs. Jones," he began. "Yesterday you said that when no one opened the door after you rang the bell a number of times, you used the spare key to open the door to your mother's apartment yourself. How did enter the building? Do you have a key for the door to the building too?"

"Yes, I do, but it was open downstairs. I rang the bell, but I didn't wait. I just got into the elevator. Up at her apartment, I rang again. And again. In the end, I unlocked the door."

"Were you already thinking that something might have happened?" Keira shook her head. "No. I hadn't told her I was coming, and I just thought she wasn't at home. That she was shopping or out for a walk or something. I just thought I'd wait for her in the apartment."

"Does anyone else have a key to the apartment, apart from you?"

"Not that I know of."

"It looks," said Fielder, "as though your mother let her murderer into the apartment herself. There are certainly no traces of a forced entry. Of course, it is still too early to draw any definite conclusions, but it could be that your mother knew her killer."

Keira looked at him in horror. "That she *knew* her killer?"

"Do you know who your mother's friends were?"

He could see that tears were flooding Keira's eyes again. For the moment, she managed to keep them back.

"She didn't have any, actually. That was the problem. She lived in complete isolation. The evening I… last spoke to her, I even had a talk with her about it. About her sitting at home, about her not making friends, never doing anything…. She listened to me patiently enough, but I didn't have the impression that anything was going to change."

Fielder nodded. That fit the picture he was building up. Someone with an intact social life does not lie dead in their apartment for ten days without anyone noticing the fact.

"How long has it been since your mother stopped working?"

"Almost five years. She found a job in a drug store after the divorce, but she didn't enjoy it. She retired at sixty. Luckily, she had worked early in her marriage, so her pension wasn't disastrous. She got by."

"Did she ever have any problem with her co-workers at the drug store?"

"No. She got along with everyone all right. But she lost touch with them after leaving. I don't think she's still in touch with anyone she met there."

"And apart from that—wasn't there any hobby that meant she sometimes met other people?"

"No. Nothing."

"And in her building? Was there anyone she knew a little bit more closely?"

"No, not even that. Everyone there seemed to live their own little lives without even knowing their neighbors' names. And my mom wasn't the kind of person who could approach people. She was too shy and unsure of herself.

"But she had also never done anyone any harm. She was a good person. A friendly person. I just can't understand how *anyone* could have had such hatred for her. I don't understand...."

Fielder thought of the brutality with which Carla had been murdered. Perhaps the murderer had not had a problem with Carla specifically. She was only a timid, somewhat self-pitying retiree. Maybe the murderer just had a problem with women. A deeply disturbed man. The crime suggested as much.

"Is there anything else I should know?" he asked.

Keira thought for a minute. "I don't think so," she said, then added, quickly, "Yes, there is. I don't know if it's important, but on the night I last talked to my mother, she mentioned something strange…or at least it seemed strange to her. She said the elevator came up to her floor a lot. But no one ever got out."

"She was sure of that? That no one got out?"

"Yes, apparently she was. She would have heard if anyone had gotten out. And as she was the only person who lived on the top floor, it all seemed rather strange to her."

"Since when had she noticed this? Did she say?"

"She said something about one or two weeks. And that it hadn't been like that before. Because I had said that maybe the system was set up so that the elevator went to different floors at regular intervals. But she didn't say any more about it. She realized that I wanted to end the call." Keira bit her lip.

Fielder leaned forward. He felt sorry for the young woman. It was bad enough to lose your mother. That would affect anyone deeply. To lose her in a brutal crime was almost unimaginable. But then on top of that, to carry with you for the rest of your life the certainty that you had been distracted and annoyed when you talked to her last…. That would prove an almost unbearable burden for Keira Jones, he was sure. "Mrs. Jones," he said. "Did you have the impression that your mother felt threatened?"

Keira's eyes filled with tears again. "Yes," she blurted out. It sounded like a sob. "Yes. I think she was afraid. She just couldn't say what she was afraid of. She did feel threatened. And I didn't do anything to help her."

Her head sank onto her lap and she started to scream.

4

DIANA WAS BAKING MUFFINS.

Why are mothers always baking nowadays? Gillian wondered. She felt how her thought was accompanied by the first insistent stabs of a headache. Who was to actually eat all the muffins the millions of mothers were baking every day?

Diana, Darcy's mother, spooned the dough from the large ceramic mixing bowl into the muffin trays. The kitchen smelled of chocolate, butter, and almonds. There were thick red candles on the table and a pot of vanilla-flavored tea. A little bowl of crystallized sugar stood next to it.

"Have some more tea," Diana said.

She was attractive: blond and slim. She played tennis and golf well. She was a fantastic cook. She knew how to give a house a homey feel. Her daughters loved her. She volunteered to help with putting up decorations for school parties, and she liked to be an accompanying parent on school trips. So the teachers loved her too.

And she baked muffins.

However, at the moment, she had one topic on her mind which had little to do with the cozy, Advent atmosphere in her kitchen—the murder of an old lady who lived on her own in London. Apparently everyone was talking about it. Only Gillian had not heard about it yet. Gillian and Becky had come over because Becky wanted to give Darcy her homework. The girls had retreated to Darcy's room, and Gillian had been invited to have a cuppa. She had actually wanted to say no. She had just come home from work, was exhausted, and had only accompanied her daughter because she didn't want her walking around on her own in the dark. But she did not particularly want a chat at all.

But the first thing Diana said to her at the door was: "And? So, what do you think of that *horrible* murder?" Of course Gillian had asked what she meant, and with that her fate was sealed. Diana, who was always keen to find someone for a gossip, had pulled her into the kitchen and told her in minute detail everything she knew.

"Apparently she lay in her apartment for over a week before anyone realized! Isn't that dreadful? I mean, to be so alone that it takes forever for someone just to think you might be dead?"

"It's more dreadful to be murdered in your own apartment, I'd say," replied Gillian. "How did the murderer get in? Do they know?"

"Well, it seems there are no signs of forced entry. People say she let him in herself. So it could be someone she knew. Because no one is so careless that they just throw open the door to the apartment when someone rings the bell—especially if you live on your own!" Diana again turned her full attention to her muffin dough and Gillian drank her tea, thinking about the London murder and perfect mothers. She tried to breathe calmly. Sometimes that helped when she could feel a headache coming on.

Diana had filled the trays. She put them in the oven, set the temperature, and then sat down at the table and poured herself a cup of tea too.

"Apparently she has a grown daughter. That's who found her."

"How horrible!"

"Yes, but until then the daughter hadn't noticed that

her mother hadn't been in touch for ten days. Odd, that. With my daughters, that couldn't happen to me."

Gillian thought about Becky's challenging behavior to her. Would she be able to say the same thing about her daughter with the same convinced tone? *That couldn't happen to me?*

"And how…was she murdered?" Gillian asked anxiously.

"The police haven't revealed that," said Diana regretfully. "You know…so there is knowledge only the murderer would know. And to make sure there aren't copycat acts or false statements. That's what the paper says. But it seems she was killed in an extremely brutal way."

"It must be someone perverse," said Gillian, repulsed.

Diana shrugged. "Or someone who felt an enormous hatred for the woman."

"Yes, but you can hardly hate someone that much. At least, it's not normal if you do. I hope they catch the culprit soon."

"Me too," said Diana fervently.

There was an awkward silence for a moment. Then Diana changed the topic abruptly.

"Are you coming to the tennis club's Christmas party on Friday?"

"I didn't know there was one. A party?"

"Becky doesn't tell you anything!" said Diana, not realizing how painful this truth was to Gillian.

"Maybe she did tell me and I wasn't really listening," said Gillian, but she knew that was not true. She listened whenever Becky told her something. But Becky barely ever did. That was the problem.

"But you're coming?" checked Diana. "Everyone should bring a few biscuits or something. It'll be nice."

"Yes, I'm sure it will." And you'll bring your stupid

muffins! I'll get through it, she thought, somehow I'll get through it! Saying that Tom was about to get home and she had to get supper ready, Gillian finally managed to make her getaway a quarter of an hour later. She felt free when she and Becky were finally on the other side of the road. The cold wind did her good. After a certain point, she had barely been able to stand the festively decorated kitchen, the smell of cooking, and oh-so-perfect Diana.

"Why didn't you tell me that there's a Christmas party in your tennis club the day after tomorrow?" she asked when they were almost home. As usual, they had walked home in silence.

"Didn't want to," mumbled Becky.

"Didn't want to what? To tell me? To go?"

"To tell you."

"Why not?"

Becky walked up their drive silently. Tom's car was parked in front of the garage. He normally drove to London earlier than Gillian and came home later. Gillian had to fit Becky and the housework into her routine, so they had decided to each make their own way to work.

Gillian grabbed her daughter's arm. "I want an answer from you!"

"To what?" asked Becky.

"To my question. Why you didn't tell me?"

"I want my own Internet connection!"

"That's not an answer."

"Everyone in my class—"

"Rubbish! Everyone in your class does not have their own connection, there's no need. The Internet—"

"Is terribly dangerous, full of evil men who try to get to know girls in chatrooms and then—"

"Unfortunately, yes, they do exist," said Gillian. "But

that's just *one* of the dangers. The main reason is just that I think you're too young to spend hours in front of the computer every day without our checking on you. It's not good."

"Why not?" asked Becky.

"Because it's more important for you to do your homework, meet your friends, have some exercise," said Gillian, and even she could hear that she sounded like a nanny.

Becky rolled her eyes. "Mom, I'm twelve. You still treat me as if I were five."

"That's just not true."

"It is. Even when I want to go to see Darcy, you come along because you think something might happen to me on the way. And you absolutely hate talking to her mom. Why don't you let me go on my own?"

"Because it's dark. Because—"

"Why can't you just trust me?" asked Becky. Then she saw her father, who had opened the front door and was standing in the bright light of the hall. Without waiting for an answer from her mother, she ran to him and threw herself into his arms.

Gillian followed her slowly, pensively.

5

SHE JUMPED AS the beam of light slid along the wall behind the television. A moment later, she wondered if she had imagined it. Or dreamed it. She had fallen asleep, in spite of the detective film being exciting. But that often happened to her. She was a morning person. From half past five in the morning, she was awake with lots of get-up-and-go energy. Now, in the evening, it was a different story.... Sometimes she went to bed at eight.

She sat up in her armchair.

She listened for noises outside. She could not hear anything. She had noticed the same thing three or four times recently: that a car came out here, in the evening, in the dark. She had heard the engine. She had seen the headlights' beam glide across the living-room walls. And then—nothing. Not a sound, a light, nothing. As if someone had stopped and turned the engine and the headlights off.

And was just sitting there...*doing what?*

Anne Westley was not a woman who was easily scared. The first time, she had stood up, stepped outside, and even walked down the paved path to the gate. She had tried to make something out, but it was almost impossible out here. The woods grew right up to the edge of her property. Anne knew that a night is never completely black, but out here it was. Almost impenetrably black.

And the position of her house was what made the appearance of a car so strange. There was not even a road anywhere nearby. Some distance away, there was a remote car park, from which location a number of footpaths led into the woods. On weekends, especially in the summer, there was a certain amount of activity there, but in the winter, and especially once it was dark, almost no one went there. Maybe just a couple looking for a quiet spot to make out. But a couple wouldn't go farther into the woods and force their car down the narrow track that ended at Anne's front gate.

She stood up, went to the window, and tried to look out, but all she saw was her own face reflected in the glass. She switched off the little lamp in the corner and the television. The room was now in complete darkness. She strained to see something outside. It was hard to make out anything. It was more that she could sense the yard with its many bushes, high grass, and now-bare fruit trees. In the summer, she had harvested baskets and baskets of cherries, apples, and pears. She had spent weeks making jams and jellies that she poured into big jars that she sealed with elastic bands before adding a sticker and neatly labeling each one.

Making jam, she always thought of Sean. Of how he had always been most excited about the fruit trees and their own jam. And she had known that she had only harvested and boiled up the fruit for his sake. She wasn't a big jam-eater. In her lifetime, she wouldn't manage to eat all the jam stockpiled in the cellar. One day she would die and then, along with everything else, tons of jam jars and their contents would have to be disposed of.

Sean and she had discovered the house eight years earlier when they were out on a walk. They had gone on an outing to Tunbridge Wells, a pretty town that nestled between fields, meadows, hills, and woods on the western edge of Kent. The area was famous for its fruit trees and its endless fields of hops. The summers were warm, and every spring the sweet, heavy scent of the fruit trees' blossoms hung in the air. Sean and Anne had wandered through a wood full of bluebells and anemones, and suddenly the house had appeared before them. It was an old gamekeeper's house or hunter's lodge, by the look of it. It looked pretty dilapidated, obviously uninhabited and not particularly inviting. But that hadn't put Sean off. He had fallen in love with the garden and could not stop talking about it. "It's so big! All those fruit trees. The lilac bushes. Laburnum, jasmine…everything you could wish for. And surrounded by the woods. It's what I've always been looking for. What I've been waiting for!"

She hadn't needed all of that. They had both been sixty years old, and Anne had thought it would be more sensible not to burden themselves at their ages with a large yard which would mean hard physical work. Sean had of course argued the exact opposite. "We can allow ourselves the garden just *because* we will retire in a few years. Then we'll have lots of time and needn't rush the work. We're not the kind of people to sit in an apartment all day and stare out of the window. Come on, let's give it a try! Let's try something new one more time!" They had indeed managed to buy the house. In fact, it hadn't been hard. No one else had wanted it.

And from then on, all their free time, every weekend and all their holidays, had been spent there in the woods, renovating the house bit by bit. It was a laborious task, but to Anne's surprise they had found it very satisfying. They had sanded down old parquet flooring, laid tiles in the kitchen and bathrooms, painted walls, had new windows put in, broken through walls and created larger rooms where previously there had been many small rooms. They had put down a large area of wooden decking for a south-facing deck. It had a wooden railing around the edge and steps leading down to the yard. They had cut down a few trees to let in more light. And Anne had made herself a studio up under the roof. She had discovered painting a few years earlier, and it had become a passion of hers.

She wondered if she should go out; but to see if a car was parked outside, she would have to go out to the gate. The cold outside put her off. And no doubt she wouldn't see anything anyway. Perhaps she had only imagined the beam of light this time. She had been dozing, after all. Perhaps she had even fallen asleep.

But then something had woken her.

She tried to brush away the eerie feeling that had crept up on her. She really was all alone out here. She was fine with that during the hours of daylight, but in the evenings she sometimes had to tell herself to get a grip, to stop all kinds of unsettling thoughts from taking over.

She turned the light on again and went into the kitchen. It was a beautiful kitchen of white-stained wood, with an Aga and a long breakfast bar, opposite the door to the deck, where you could read the paper and sip at a cup of coffee. She poured herself a drop of whiskey, downed it in one, and then chased it down with another. Normally she didn't react to problems with alcohol, but for the moment it seemed to help her calm her nerves.

After Sean's death, she had not once tried to find comfort in drink. She had not sought any help anywhere. In her experience, work was the best medicine for all psychological problems, and so she had plunged into gardening work and painting, thus making it through the hard first year. Now two and a half more years had passed, and she had everything under control. Herself, her pain, and her life out here far from anyone.

Sean had died when everything was ready. In the middle of the summer, just a few weeks after his sixty-fifth birthday. In June he had stopped working, just four weeks after Anne had left her job as a GP and retired. At the beginning of July they had wanted to throw a house-warming party for the new house. They planned to have it in the garden, which seemed to be sinking under a sea of blossoming jasmine. They had invited almost eighty people, almost all of them had said they would come. The day before the party, Sean had climbed up onto the roof, because he had his mind set on tacking Christmas lights to the guttering. Coming down, he had missed the top rung of the ladder and fallen to the ground. It didn't seem too dramatic, however, because he only broke the head of his thigh bone. Nothing worse than that. Of course he was angry and disappointed to be lying in the hospital and have to cancel his party. But then he had contracted a lung infection, antibiotics didn't help at all, and within four weeks he was dead. Anne never had time to really understand what was happening.

She had buried him. Sometime in November she, in turn, climbed up onto the roof and took down the Christmas lights—a stupid, garish chain of lights not worth anything, let alone the damage they had caused.

After a second drink, Anne finally relaxed. She decided that she had imagined the headlights' beam. Something on television had probably woken her up. A scream, a gunshot. That is what you get in detective films.

Still, tonight she would use the safety chain on the front door too, which she normally didn't do. And she would close the shutters on all the downstairs rooms' windows.

That could not do any harm.

Friday, December 4

1

"And? What do you spend your days doing now?" asked Bartek.

It was loud in the pub. Every table was taken. Everyone was laughing, chatting, drinking. Shouting. Samson was not all that fond of the pub, but Bartek always insisted, and as Bartek was his only friend he didn't want to upset him. They sometimes met here on Fridays, if Bartek had the day off. They met up early, at six or six-thirty. Bartek's girlfriend gave him aggro if he spent all of his free evening in a pub with a friend, so they normally went home by eight-thirty at the latest. Samson had come by car, although that meant he couldn't drink. But he was never a big drinker anyway, and taking the bus seemed to him like too much hassle. He had no wish to stand in the cold at the bus stop, let alone walk all the way. As usual, he had spent the whole day wandering around outside. He had had enough of that now.

He had inherited the car from his mother. He knew that Millie held it against him. Even now, after all these years. She could never get over it when other people got what she herself wanted.

"Well, I don't just sit around at home, if that's what you mean," Samson replied to Bartek's question. "I'd get bored. And this week, Millie's shift starts in the afternoon, so she'd be around half the day and…well, you know. I can do without her company."

Millie worked in a care home for old people. Samson knew that she hated her work. When he heard her talking about her patients, he shivered at the thought of one day being old and completely at the mercy of someone like her.

"I don't know how you can stand it," said Bartek. "Still living with your brother and sister-in-law! You're much too old for that!"

"But the house is mine too!"

"Then let them pay you your share as rent, but find somewhere else. You're treated badly there!"

"I'm afraid of growing old alone, if I live on my own," said Samson quietly.

Bartek raised his eyebrows. "How old are you? Thirty-four! It's time you found a woman to live with! Don't you plan on marrying one day and starting a family?"

Samson took a sip of his alcohol-free beer.

Bartek had touched on a delicate point. They had talked about it from time to time: marriage, having children, living a normal life. Bartek, who had had a steady girlfriend for years, did not find the topic easy either. His girlfriend had wanted to get married for a long time now, but Bartek, although he was almost forty, was afraid of the commitment. Samson had never wanted to admit that he had different issues and had hidden them behind a fear of commitment that he did not in fact have. On the contrary, he longed for nothing so much as for a wife. A house, a yard, children, a dog…. He could picture it in his mind, and often he thought he would give everything for it to become reality. But the embarrassing—and in his mind, perverse—truth was that he had never even had a girlfriend. Neither at school nor since. Never. So he had never even come close to the whole issue of *marriage*.

"Well…" he answered evasively. "It's not like you meet a woman every day who you want to marry!"

"My girlfriend's got me to that point now," said Bartek, and he did not look all that unhappy at the thought of it. "She gave me an ultimatum. Maybe that was good. Next summer we're going for it. There'll be a big party, everyone's coming. You're invited too, of course!"

"Nice," said Samson and tried not to sound too envious. Bartek was always lucky. Always, in every way. They had met before Samson did deliveries for the frozen-foods company, when he was working for a chauffeur-services company. Bartek worked there too, but unlike Samson he had not been let go. Someone like Bartek never lost his job. Everyone liked him too much, from his boss to his colleagues to the clients. When a car was booked, they often asked specifically for Bartek. *Can we have Bartek? Can we have the really nice Pole?*

Bartek spoke perfect English but with a charming East European accent that went down well, particularly with women. He knew how to keep people entertained with a few stories from his life, which were normally completely made-up but told in a way that hooked his listeners.

Samson, who would lie awake at night and go over and over in his mind why women constantly ignored him and why he was always the first to be let go when a company needed to make cutbacks, had often wondered if it was because of his grotesquely boring biography. What did he have to tell people about? Or perhaps it was his name. Who is called Samson? If there was one thing he could not forgive his late parents, then it was that they had given him that name. His mother had read a book during her pregnancy in which someone was called Samson, and she had liked the name. Samson's brother, who was two years older than him, had been luckier. Gavin was a name that did not attract teasing all through school.

"You have to start to get out more, be around people," said Bartek. "Else you'll never find the right woman. So, what was it you said you do all day, if you're not sitting around at home?"

I haven't yet said what I do, thought Samson in irritation. Sometimes Bartek did not really listen to him. After all, he never had anything particularly impressive to talk about.

He hesitated briefly, wondering whether it was wise to tell Bartek what he did. He wanted so much to tell someone, and there was no one else apart from Bartek. "In a way," he said mysteriously, "I do spend my whole day around people."

"Really? What do you do?"

"I look at other people's lives."

"Huh?" went Bartek.

"I walk around the streets. At set times. And it's really interesting…you find out a lot about people in their own surroundings. How they live. Whether they are alone or have a family. Whether they are happy or unhappy. That kind of thing."

Samson suddenly thought that he had probably made a mistake. It was stupid of him to open up to Bartek like this. He could see it in the expression on his friend's face.

"You mean, you *stalk* other people?" asked Bartek

after a pause in which he was obviously trying to make sense of what he had heard.

"I *analyze* them," explained Samson.

"What do you mean, you analyze them?"

"I try to find out things about them. For example, why someone is alone. And how the person deals with that."

"And what do you get out of it?"

"I understand things."

"Yes, but why? I mean, what exactly do you want to find out?" Samson saw that there was no point. Bartek would not understand. Perhaps the whole thing was incomprehensible.

"Well, I'm alone too," he tried, nevertheless, to explain it. "And I often wonder why I am. And so I try to figure out why other people are in the same boat as me."

"Yes, but—now, don't take this the wrong way—but it's a completely...well, pretty disturbed way to go about it! Why don't you look on the Internet? There are thousands of people there with the same problems as you. There are tons of forums where you can talk to people about it."

"I do that too," admitted Samson. "But it's so anonymous. I often feel doubly alone, if I've spent the whole afternoon chatting to someone five hundred miles away who I don't even know, just because he too couldn't find a partner."

"So is your main issue about finding a woman?"

"Yes. That too."

"So do you think you're going to find a young, single woman by wandering the streets and spying into other people's houses?" asked Bartek, who was obviously trying hard to bring a certain structure and logic to a situation that seemed grotesque to him.

"Not exactly."

"So what the hell makes you do it, then?"

Samson shrugged his shoulders. "Doesn't matter."

"No, it does. Don't take this the wrong way, Samson, but it sounds pretty crazy to me. If you ask me… being unemployed isn't good for you. You're starting to do some odd things."

"I didn't choose to be jobless."

"No, of course not. But are you trying to find something? You're still young! You can always drive a taxi… something. But creeping around after other people all day—that's not going to help!"

"It's interesting."

Bartek shook his head. "God, Samson, really…. Have you at least found a woman who *could* be right for you? So there's been some point to all your walking?"

Samson had to admit that there was not an abundance of single young women that he had his sights on. "Most are quite a bit older, of course. A lot older than me. There is one woman in my…schedule. She is my age and obviously lives on her own. She works at home as a freelancer and has a big dog."

"And? Have you ever talked to her?"

Samson realized that Bartek did not understand a thing. He would never talk to the women he shadowed.

"No."

"Invite her out for coffee."

"Yes, why not," Samson said, but only to keep Bartek happy.

"You can find women on the Internet too," said Bartek.

"I know, but—"

"No buts. You shouldn't just always talk. And dream. You have to *do* something!"

"There is one family," said Samson hesitantly. He

did not want to draw Bartek deeper into his confidence, but he suddenly had the feeling that he should correct the impression that he had only been targeting women. Bartek seemed quite shocked, and he did not want to leave it like that. He did not want his only friend to see him as some kind of sex offender.

"They live at the other end of my street. Right by the strip of green, opposite the golf course."

"Okay. And what about them?"

"He's a business consultant. He helped Gavin once. She's very attractive. And they have a charming daughter. She's about twelve." Bartek was not looking any less perplexed than before. "Right, and what do you want with *them*? Nab the yummy mommy?"

"No, of course not. They are just so…so perfect, you know. A dream family. The family I'd like to have one day!"

Bartek was looking very uneasy now. "Samson, my impression is that you've lost touch with reality a bit. You dream about other people's lives, but you don't change your own at all. It seems like you're fleeing something!"

And, thought Samson, don't people need that sometimes? The chance to escape?

"I'll be okay," he said. Why had he started? He was sure that Bartek would latch on to the topic like a terrier and not let go.

"Let me see if I can sort something out for you," said Bartek. "There must be a woman for you somewhere! You don't look bad, you own a house…well, half a house…you're not stupid and you have no disgusting characteristics. It would be easy if—"

"Look, I'm jobless."

"All the more reason to start to really look for a job."

"I'm looking like mad." That was not true. Samson had not even signed on at the Job Center. He knew that was a mistake. Things could not go on like this. Without income of some kind, his savings would soon dwindle. But as soon as he signed on, he would need to write heaps of applications and he would need to keep bringing proof that he was trying to find work. How was he to fit that in with his other activities? Many days he had thought to himself: tomorrow I'll start to think about the future! Tomorrow I'll sign on, and then I'll deal with the problem!

But he never had. His desire to continue to observe the people in whose lives he took such interest—an interest so much more intense than he could ever tell to Bartek or anyone else—was simply too great. His life without this activity seemed pointless to him.

"If you really work on it, you'll find something," said Bartek optimistically. To Samson's great relief, he then changed the topic and turned to his own plans for the future: his marriage plans, his wish to buy property for himself and his soon-to-be wife, the difficulty of obtaining a mortgage, and, and, and.... Samson let it all wash over him. He had not eaten since breakfast, and his finances did not even allow him to order a burger now, the cheapest item on the pub menu. But that did not matter. He felt a pleasant dizziness. Everything around him seemed somehow dulled, lacked sharp outlines, had a nice haziness: people's voices, their laughter and chat, the clinking of glasses, the cold air that swept in when someone opened or shut the door, Bartek's prattling on, everything.

He was thinking of Gillian Ward.

2

IF ONLY I could leave without anyone noticing, thought Gillian.

But of course she couldn't. She could not go without Becky, and that did away with any chance of an unnoticed exit. The tennis club kids were running around the hall. Becky in black leggings and a pink T-shirt was one of the wildest of them. Impossible to extricate her. The parents, mainly mothers, sat in a café area separated from the actual sports hall by a glass wall. The café was part of the club, and this was where committee meetings and parties took place. Christmas decorations were up and Christmas songs were booming from the stereo. The bar was serving coffee, tea, or champagne. The parents had brought food themselves and set up a buffet on a long table. There was an abundance of Christmas biscuits, Christmas pudding, and home-made cakes, as well as many salads, two cheese platters, and bowls of nibbles. There was no way it would all be eaten. Gillian had baked a chocolate cake and put it with the other food, but no one had yet taken a slice, as she could see out of the corner of her eye. To her own surprise, this fact upset her in an almost childish way. Her cake looked pretty good. Of course, there were two almost identical chocolate cakes right next to it, which could explain why it had so far been untouched.

At the last minute Diana had canceled, because Darcy's throat infection had gotten worse. As Gillian had never talked to any of the other people here, she had sat completely on her own for the first half hour. She had to do something if she was not to just stare stupidly at the wall. All the other mothers seemed to be friends with each other, judging from the impenetrable wall of sound—shouts, laughter, and talk. Everyone felt comfortable here, everyone was happy.

Everyone except Gillian.

In the end, a mother had sat down next to Gillian, but only because she had arrived late and not found another seat. She put a tray down on the table in front of her, laden with various salads, cheese, and a big glass of bubbly.

"God, I'm hungry," she said. With a glance at Gillian's empty coffee cup and the two half-nibbled biscuits on her saucer, she added, "Aren't you?"

"Not really," said Gillian.

The other mother tucked into her food with relish, at the same time telling Gillian in detail about her son, who had suffered from eczema since early childhood and had a number of other allergies and food intolerances. She had visited any number of doctors with him, had tried everything, advised strongly against cortisone based on her own experience, but could recommend various balms and globules and was quite an expert in the field.

"Does Becky have allergies too?" she asked.

"No," said Gillian and swallowed the answer that was on the tip of her tongue: I think she's allergic to me. Recently there hasn't been a single civil word between us. I wish it were something else: an allergy to grass pollen, dust mites, or a lactose intolerance. Then I'd know where to start. But like this, I'm completely lost.

She did not say it, but she felt how close she had been to saying the words and it scared her. This woman was a complete stranger whose only connection to her was that their daughters played tennis together, and she had been so close to confiding in her all the pain that she had almost sunk underneath these past weeks.

Get a grip, she ordered herself. She decided to call

her friend Tara Caine later that evening. Tara was loyal and reliable, and Gillian knew that she would not gossip about anything Gillian told her.

The other mother—Gillian still did not know her name—took a swig of her champagne and finally changed the topic. "Doesn't Burton look fantastic again today?" she asked in a low voice.

Gillian looked around the room and spied John Burton, the trainer, leaning on the bar and surrounded by a horde of mothers. No doubt he was answering questions on the children's progress. If the situation was proving stressful, he did not let it show. Of course, it was nothing unusual for him. Every time Gillian took Becky to team practice, she could see how the mothers surrounded him. That might of course be because they wanted to be informed about everything to do with the team. No doubt Burton's effect on women had something to do with it too. He was good-looking and, even more importantly, he had the aura of a mysterious past.

People said he had been in the police force and had risen rapidly through the ranks before leaving at the young age of thirty-seven under mysterious circumstances. Then he had founded a private security firm that now employed a good two dozen employees. Its services included guarding both people and buildings. He lived and worked in London, but twice a week he came out to Southend to train two young people's tennis teams. He had made an effort to recruit some of the players from disadvantaged parts of town. He considered sport, particularly team sports, to be the most effective preventative measure against young people's slipping into criminal activity, as Gillian had once heard by chance, when he was explaining this to a couple of mothers who hung on his every word. Particularly for the well-to-do women he was a hero, a fighter. Gillian could imagine how much they romanticized him.

Probably he is not at all what they see in him.

But she had to admit that he was attractive. "Yes," she finally answered. "He's pretty good-looking."

"Pretty good-looking? I always have to stop myself having indecent thoughts when I see him. Strange that someone like him doesn't have a wife."

"Maybe he has a lot of girlfriends."

"But then we'd have seen one of those girlfriends, coming to watch or collect him or something. It's odd. I've never seen him with a woman."

"He wants to keep his private life separate," said Gillian. She could understand that. The women here are like vultures, she thought.

"I still find it odd," insisted the woman. "Like much about him." Gillian did not want to know what she meant by that and did not reply. Gillian's silence did not of course stop her neighbor from sharing her opinions.

"I'd really like to know why he had to leave the police. He was in Scotland Yard. That's not a career you just throw away! And then he comes out here for these sessions. He lives in London. So why come all the way out here? Maybe no sports club in London wanted to have him. Why not?"

Gillian had the distinct impression that she would not be able to bear listening to the woman's detailed thoughts on the trainer's private life on top of the story of her son's maladies. She looked into the smug face with its crude features and stood up abruptly.

"I'm sorry. I just have to have a smoke." She tried to make her exit a little less impolite. "This damned addiction…."

Dear God, don't let her be a smoker too.

The woman smiled sourly. It was clear that she was offended.

Gillian thought about what Tom would say now. *You see, that's why you're always alone! When someone tries to get close, you immediately brush them off.*

She pushed her way through the crowded room and breathed a sigh of relief when she was at the cloakroom. The voices in the main room sounded muffled now. Gillian put a hand to her forehead. It felt hot.

It took five minutes for her to find her coat among the piles of coats and put it on. Then she stepped out into the dark evening. It was cold, but it was not as windy as it had been in the last few days. Fog was rolling in from the river. It wrapped itself around her head like a damp, cold cloth. She fished out a cigarette, lit it, and sucked on it greedily. As always, the nicotine relaxed her immediately, although she also felt guilty at once. Tom hated it when she smoked. All his arguments against it were correct. Like every year, her New Year's resolution would be to stop.

Like every year, she would not manage.

She massaged her temples gently with her left index finger. There had been no air in the room, she realized that now. There was no way she could go in again.

I'll stick around out here for half an hour and then tell Becky that we have to go, she decided. Another reason for her to hate me. Perhaps she should not be so surprised that her daughter did not get on with her. Perhaps her strange ways got on Becky's nerves far more than she realized.

Just when she was stubbing out her cigarette in an empty planter, she saw John Burton step outside. He had put on a black jacket and slung a scarf around his neck. He smiled when he saw her.

"Doing the same as me?" he asked. "Abusing your lungs?"

She nodded. "I'm afraid so. In any case...." She did not finish the sentence because she did not want to hurt his feelings, but he seemed to understand what she wanted to say.

"In any case, it's a good chance get away from all of that," he nodded toward the sports hall. "Unbearable."

"You think so too?" she asked in surprise.

He got out a pack of cigarettes and held it out to her. She took one. While sticking a cigarette in the corner of his mouth, he tried to get a steady flame from his lighter, but it kept going out before either of them could light their cigarettes. Burton cursed. Gillian got out her lighter. Hers worked, and she lit their cigarettes.

"Thanks," he said.

They smoked in silence. In the end, he said "I saw you go out. You looked like someone escaping something."

"I'd been hoping no one would notice," said Gillian.

"Apart from me, I doubt anyone did. They don't notice other people, at least not like that. But I had the feeling the whole time that you didn't feel good here."

Gillian swallowed. It was extraordinary what an understanding comment and a tone of sympathy can trigger. She had the feeling that she was on the point of tears—and that was, of course, terrifying. She would have found it awfully embarrassing to bawl her eyes out here on this foggy winter's evening outside a sports hall next to her daughter's tennis trainer.

"I was told all the illnesses someone's son has," she said. "Every detail and allergy. The woman just wouldn't stop. There came a point where my head was hammering. Perhaps that is why I seem a little pained."

"Yes, that was Philip's mom," said John. "He's a nice

bright kid. In my opinion, he doesn't have any allergies. He has his mother and that's his problem."

He said this so calmly that Gillian had to laugh. She was surprised at herself. He had not been that funny, after all. But the laughter came from deep inside herself, from her belly, and bubbled up. She laughed freely, without holding anything back, and thought that she had not really laughed properly, from deep inside, for ages. At the same time she realized that something was not right because she was laughing more than was right for the situation. She was close to hysterics, and it seemed to her that John Burton was looking at her in surprise too. "But…what's the matter?" he asked and put his hand on her arm. Only then did she realize that she was no longer laughing but crying, and that she had not noticed how one had become the other. The tears were pouring down her face. Her skin had already been wet from the fog, and now it was wet and salty too.

"I don't know," she sighed. "I'm sorry…I just don't know." To her dismay, she realized she could not stop crying.

"Oh, God," she moaned.

Making a quick decision, Burton stubbed out his cigarette, took Gillian's cigarette out of her hand and put it in the planter too, then took her arm.

"Come on. Before other people see you out here…. You don't want to give them material for a month's gossip."

She could not say anything. She just shook her head. Without any will of her own, she let him lead her across the car park and got into a car whose door he held open for her. She registered that he then got in from the other side and sat down next to her. She was still crying, but she did at least manage to open her handbag and rummage around for a tissue.

"I'm so sorry," she sobbed.

Burton shook his head. "Stop apologizing. I was watching you this evening and saw how unhappy you were—and you know what I thought?"

"No."

"I thought: she's going to start crying sooner or later. And I hoped it wouldn't happen to you in there. I'm glad it happened here in my car instead."

She finally found a tissue and gave her nose a good blow. Tears were still falling, but the wild burst of despair had passed.

"Frankly, I prefer that too," she said. "Thank you."

"Feeling a bit better now?"

"A little. But I can't go in yet."

Burton thought for a minute. "There's a pub near here. If you like, we can go for a quick drink of something strong. That sometimes helps."

"Good idea. I hope I'm not too much bother."

He turned on the engine and steered the car out of its bay. "Do you think I'm excited about the company back in there?"

"Hard to imagine."

"Exactly."

A few minutes later, they reached the Halfway House. It was on Eastern Esplanade, right by the beach and with a direct view of the river, although you could only guess at it now with the fog and darkness. The windows were brightly lit and music was pouring out into the night.

"Not the best pub in town," said Burton as they got out. "But it's nearby. And you probably won't meet anyone here who knows you." A hubbub of voices and loud laughter met them as they went in. Gillian saw that the pub, with its many tables and chairs, was full of people. There were no pictures on the plastered walls, nor plants on the window ledges. The place could hardly have been more spartan, although that did not seem to make it any less popular. A variety of age groups mingled. Gillian realized that John was right: it was not the kind of place Tom would frequent. Nor anyone from her circle of acquaintances.

Burton spied a free table with two chairs and opened a path through the crowd. "What would you like?"

"Any shot is good. A double would be better."

He nodded and pushed his way toward the bar, while Gillian took off her coat, hung it over the back of the chair, and sat down. It did her good to be here. To have bawled her eyes out. She took her compact mirror out of her handbag and appraised the damage. It was clear she had been crying. Her skin was blotchy and her eyelids swollen. Her nose was red. Well done. Typical of her. She had managed to end up in a pub with a desirable man and she looked like a tearful schoolgirl. In fact, it would have been a step up if she had looked like a schoolgirl.

I look at least ten years older than I am, she thought wearily. Now I really look like a woman you could take pity on.

She glanced around the room in the hope of seeing the door to the toilets. Perhaps splashing her face with a little cold water would help. Because of all the groups of people standing in the room, it was hard to make out where things were. Suddenly her eye was caught by a man who looked familiar to her. He was younger than she was, in his mid-thirties at the most. He was sitting and drinking a beer with another man. He was staring at her. Then she remembered. He lived on the same street as she did, just at the opposite end. He lived there with his brother and sister-in-law. Tom had helped his brother once to sort out an inheritance. Afterward Tom had said that they were rather strange people. She smiled at him rather uncertainly. Oh, great! So much for not meeting anyone she knew. How wrong you could be. Her face was tear-stained, she was sharing a table in a pub on a Friday night with a man who was not her husband, and she had immediately met one of the neighbors. Sometimes nothing went right.

The young man smiled back at her shyly. He seemed surprised. You could not really blame him.

John Burton returned to the table armed with two full glasses. "I was as quick as I could be," he said apologetically, sitting opposite her. "Have you acclimatized?"

"Yes, thanks. And realized that I look terrible. I'm really sorry."

"We had agreed that you were not going to say 'sorry' anymore."

He raised his glass. "Cheers!"

She took a long sip. And then another. The whiskey burned her throat, sending waves of heat through her stomach. It was probably wrong to drink it, especially this much of it. This was no double: it must be at least a quadruple. And she had not eaten much all day. Afterward, she would pick her daughter up and drive home, pretty tipsy. She brushed aside her misgivings and took the next sip. For the moment, she only wanted the relaxation that alcohol brought her. Distance from everything. From her worries and fears and her sadness. "Would you...would you like to talk about what's upsetting you?" asked John after a while.

Why not?

"To put it simply, my daughter rejects me because

she feels I make all her decisions for her and don't give her enough freedom. And my husband no longer notices me. So, just the usual, I suppose." She gave a forced little laugh.

John Burton did not join in. He looked at her thoughtfully. "I can't say anything about your husband. But I know your daughter quite well. I like Becky. She's sporty, ambitious; she's a team player. She has a strong and independent nature. Yes, she's also pigheaded and difficult sometimes. But she might just be going through a difficult phase and hurting the people who are closest to her. Don't worry too much: it will all work out in the end."

Surprised by the clarity of his pronouncement, she said "You're sure?"

He nodded. "I'd bet on it."

"Thank you," she said. She was amazed that in a few words he had managed to give her a feeling of relief. It was not that all her problems were solved immediately, but she did feel better. He had taken her seriously and also tried to provide her with some comfort. Unlike Tom, who normally just said that she was imagining it. Unlike Tara, who immediately created such complex psychological scenarios that she felt quite dizzy. Unlike Diana, who, whenever Gillian complained, only insisted on how happy she was with her own low-maintenance daughters.

For the first time, Gillian had the impression that someone had really helped her.

"You understand a lot about children," she said.

"I understand something about sports. And you find out a lot about people when you watch them carry out a team sport. Whether they are children, young people, or adults. They basically all act just like they would in real life."

She looked at him with curiosity. "Is it actually true that you used to be in Scotland Yard?"

His features hardened. "Yes."

It was obvious that he did not want to talk about his former career and, above all, about the circumstances that had led to his leaving it. So Gillian turned the conversation in another direction.

"What do you think about the terrible murder of that old woman in Hackney?"

"There's not much I can say. I know no more than what's in the papers."

"But you used to be involved with things like that."

"Yes, but in this case I can't tell much. The police are keeping quiet about how the victim was killed. It seems it was done in some unusual way that they are not revealing now, that could help them convict the culprit later. I just read that she was neither robbed nor raped. So it wasn't for the money or sex, at least not the main motive."

"Main motive?"

"If she was killed in a particularly sadistic way, then sexual motives may have played a role."

"Do you think it will happen again? That there will be another victim?"

"Possibly. It's not clear what the motive was. Perhaps there was a personal issue between the murderer and the victim; but even then, someone who is capable of such a crime is a ticking time bomb. It's certainly not the usual way to sort out quarrels or disagreements."

"It's scary," said Gillian. "Whenever I read such things, I think that just getting through life halfway unharmed is a miracle."

"It will all be sorted out. Most crimes are, in the end."

"But not all of them."

"Not all of them," he admitted.

She risked touching on his past again. "Is that why you left? The police, I mean? Because it was unbearable to be confronted with terrible violence and not always be able to see justice was done?"

Again his face hardened. "There were many reasons," he said evasively, emptied his glass and looked at his watch. "I'm afraid we'd better be getting back to the club. Not that I'm anxious to go; but if they realize both of us are missing, they might get silly ideas in their heads."

She realized she was staring at him. She was not just looking at him in the way you normally look at the person you are talking to, but she was completely fixed on him. All the people and the sounds around them had retreated into the background. They were there, but it was as if there was a thin wall between Gillian and John and the rest of the world.

It must be the whiskey, she thought. I knew it was too much. "And what ideas would they be?" she asked, surprising herself with the challenging tone of her voice. It was not like her to flirt. It was not what she did; she never had. She thought it was too easy to look stupid when you did.

"I think you know," said John and stood up. He had not responded to her tone, and she was sure he was angry with her. Or at least annoyed. Maybe he thought she was too obvious. Maybe she had been too nosy when she asked about his previous work. In any case, the wall that had isolated the two of them for a short time was no longer there. Once again, they were part of the overcrowded pub along with all the people standing elbow to elbow and the innumerable voices. They were part of the laughter, the clinking of glasses, the smells of alcohol, sweat, and damp coats.

As they pushed their way toward the exit, they passed close by the table where the man from her street was sitting. Now she remembered his name: Segal. Samson Segal.

"Goodbye," she said.

He nodded to her, gazing at her. Just as he had when she had first seen him.

She wondered uneasily whether he had been like that the whole time.

Whether he had stared at her like that the whole time.

Saturday, December 5

IT WAS SATURDAY, but the investigation had to go on.

Detective Inspector Fielder had promised to go into town with his wife to do some Christmas shopping, but then he had been called to the scene of the brutal murder of Carla Roberts once again. It was clear to him that he would have to disappoint his wife. Every minute counted now. His wife's pursed lips as he asked her to bear with him suggested a difficult weekend to come. There would be at least one serious talk about their relationship. There was no way around it.

His colleagues had gone over Carla Roberts's building with a fine-tooth comb. They had talked to the other residents and had left phone numbers in case someone remembered something. It had all turned up very little. In fact: nothing at all. No one had known Carla personally. The people who did remember her described her as a quiet woman who lived very much on her own. She was rarely seen in the stairwell. She always said hello in a friendly manner but was obviously too shy to befriend anyone.

"I think she rarely left her apartment," said a man on the sixth floor. "She was too self-conscious and full of inhibitions. Completely isolated, if you ask me. No one gave a damn about her."

Fielder wondered if that was just what had made her a victim. Perhaps it was her isolation, which had not only made it easy for the culprit to murder her but also gave him a head start before the police investigation got under way. Anyone who knew a little about Carla Roberts's circumstances could have figured that her body would not be found too quickly because it would take a while for anyone to miss her. That was invaluable for the perpetrator of a crime. Every day that went by before the police got into gear was a day's advantage for the criminal—and a disadvantage for the police.

As he had thought the previous Wednesday in Keira Jones's apartment, Fielder thought: This criminal has nothing against Carla Roberts personally; he just has a problem with women. And he chooses the ones who are easy prey.

And this possibility was in some ways the worst. For if there was no personal connection whatsoever between Carla and her murderer, no matter how far back in the past, then the search for the murderer would be blind guesswork.

There was just one clue. She had obviously let him into her apartment herself. That was a gleam of hope. It was the only indication that she might have known him, however fleetingly.

Detective Sergeant Christy McMarrow walked over to Fielder once he had finally found a parking space and gotten out of his car. Fielder liked Christy because she was dedicated. She gave her job a high priority in her life. Christy was available day and night. She was ambitious. And passionate about her work.

He also found her incredibly attractive, but he knew that he should not be thinking that.

"The caretaker called us," she said. "I think you should take a look."

The caretaker was a small, stocky man with an unhealthy red flush to his face. He was standing outside

the door to the building and was almost hyper venti-
lating. Fielder already knew him. Right after his chat
with Keira Jones, he had asked the caretaker about the
elevator. Apparently it was not possible for the elevator to go to a floor without its having been sent there.
If Carla Roberts heard the elevator unnaturally often
on her floor, then someone must have been sending it
up there.

Or gone up in it. Without getting out. Fielder did find
that very strange.

"I found out that something isn't right about the door,
Inspector," said the caretaker as soon as he caught sight
of Fielder. He pointed to the glass door to the building.
"And I can't understand how I didn't notice it before
now. Somehow…well, it could just be pushed open the
whole time. When I'd noticed it once or twice before, I
thought people were being careless, not closing it properly; but today I realized…that it wasn't just carelessness. And so I called your colleague."

"That was the right thing to do," Fielder assured him.
He examined the door. He thought about what Keira
Jones had said: the front door had been open when she
came to visit her mother.

"Why was it today that you realized it couldn't just
be carelessness?" he asked.

The caretaker looked embarrassed. "Because I started
to think. I mean…after the terrible incident you can't
help wondering…. Well, suddenly I thought it shouldn't
have been like that. With the door. It has a spring, so
after you've opened it, it closes behind you and locks.
Every time. You have to be really careful to keep it from
happening. You know what I mean? I realized how stupid I'd been. The door was never locked, as if everyone

who'd gone through had just gently rested it on the lock. And why should people do that? That would be crazy!"

"It certainly would," said Fielder. "So the spring mechanism is broken?"

The caretaker nodded. "Yes. The door closes so slowly now that it doesn't lock anymore."

"Since when? Or rather: when did you notice it?"

"Not long ago. Maybe…four weeks ago?" Fielder turned to Christy.

"We'll need someone to check what caused the defect. Whether it was just wear and tear or helped along by someone."

"Right."

"Let's suppose someone did it. From then on, they can get in and out without any problem, can observe Carla Roberts, torture her psychologically by getting the elevator to go up to her floor now and then. Then one day they go up to her door, ring the bell, and she lets them in…. Would she have done that? All alone up there?"

"Maybe she had met her murderer once or twice in the building," said Christy. "Without knowing that it was just someone who crept in and hung around sometimes. She might have thought the person was one of the other tenants. You'd open the door to someone from your own building, wouldn't you? Although in a building where people barely know each other, there's no guarantee of anything." Fielder nodded distractedly. There were too many open questions. They still had not managed to find Carla Roberts's ex-husband. And if he really had disappeared abroad years ago, possibly to the other side of the world, then the search was not going to be easy. Of course, in that case he was probably not involved in his ex-wife's death either.

The investigations concerning his former lover had also proven fruitless so far. Her identity was now known, but she had not lived at her last known address for years. Fielder speculated that she had gone abroad with her lover.

He rubbed his cheek tiredly. "We have to try to find out about Carla Roberts's private life. It's impossible that there was absolutely no one she talked to or went to the cinema with. Have you got any leads?"

"Not yet," admitted Christy. "The daughter knows so little about her mother's life that she can't help us at all. I've got the dead woman's address book. There are a few names in it that I'll go through. According to the daughter, the names are mainly staff at the drug store where her mother used to work. That might help a little."

"Have a go," said Fielder.

For some reason, he did not hold out high hopes. Carla's colleagues at a workplace that she had left years ago—what help could that be?

He could not afford to make the case even more complicated by de-motivating his most capable colleague.

Monday, December 7

"Have you ever really tried to talk to Becky properly?" asked Tara. "I mean, in a way that shows that you take her seriously. She obviously feels you're boxing her in— and so she rebels against that. It'll only get worse in the next few years. So you two should find a way to avoid letting every day become a battle of wills."

"Tara, maybe I do treat her like a child, but she *is* a child. She's twelve! I know she *thinks* she's grown up, but I'm afraid she's wrong."

"Twelve-year-old girls today are more mature than we were when we were that age. Not that I'm saying you should just let her do what she wants all the time, just that you shouldn't pooh-pooh the issues she brings up."

"I don't. And by trying to explain my point of view to her, I'm trying to engage with her," explained Gillian. "Unfortunately, she doesn't show the least willingness to see things from my point of view. That's where we always get stuck."

"And could you do that when you were twelve?" asked Tara. "Put yourself in your mother's shoes— know what she felt, what her worries and needs were?"

They were sitting in Gillian's kitchen. It was late on Monday afternoon. Becky had gone to Darcy's house straight from school. Gillian had worked until early afternoon. She had had to deal with a particularly unpleasant and unhappy client. Then she had driven to the supermarket and had just gotten back, and flung all her shopping bags full of food, cat food, and cat litter on the kitchen table, when Tara called. Tara had just talked to a witness living in Shoeburyness. She said her witness was vital to the case on her desk right now, and as her journey back went right past Gillian's house, she asked if she could drop in for a cuppa.

Not long after, she was standing in the doorway. As ever, she looked stressed but also fresh and elegant in a dark-blue trouser suit with leather boots and a matching coat. Gillian hurried to unpack her groceries and feed Chuck, who was already acting vexed. Jittery as she was, she once again felt inadequate beside her friend.

"How does Becky get along with Tom?" asked Tara.

"With Tom? Great," said Gillian. "But that's no surprise. He's barely around; and the little time he does spend with her, of course he can be the dream daddy who lets her do what she wants and plays along with every idiocy. I have all the day-to-day routines to deal with, and they are full of traps."

Tara looked at her carefully. "And how are things between the two of you? Between you and Tom, I mean."

Gillian took a deep breath. "Not great. But not bad, either. It's not like we fight. Actually, we don't talk much to each other. As I said, he's barely ever here. He lives for our company and for the tennis club. That doesn't leave a lot of time."

"So he's still as crazy as ever about sports?"

"It's getting worse. He comes home, changes, and off he goes. Other men drink a few beers after work to wind down. He has to work it off. Honestly, I'd rather he had a few beers at home. But it's not just sport. Naturally, he has to network too. There are committee meetings and other meetings, and preparations for competitions. They meet up socially every Tuesday night. If I were in my death throes, I don't believe he'd miss his Tuesday meetings. I don't even know if he really likes to go, but it's just part of being a member. Apparently people raise their eyebrows if someone doesn't go one week."

"You could always go with him, couldn't you?"

"I could. But I don't play tennis, and they only talk about tennis. Anyway, I don't like to leave Becky on her own. At least not in the evenings."

Tara smiled. "You fuss like a mother hen." It sounded affectionate. Gillian smiled back at her.

Tara and Gillian had met five years earlier in London at a French course the two of them had taken. Gillian had wanted to polish up her schoolgirl French and so had signed up for the course. Tara had worked as a lawyer in Manchester for many years. She had then applied to a London court and been taken on. In her very first case there, her lack of French had been a problem. Typically for her, this experience had immediately driven her to take a French course. The two women had sat next to each other and had taken an instant liking to one another. They had remained friends ever since.

"Surely Tom—now, don't be annoyed if I ask.... Surely he's not having an affair, is he?"

"Tom? Never!" replied Gillian in horror. At that moment, two things happened simultaneously: the telephone rang, and the Christmas lights, which were strung up in the kitchen window and connected to a timer, came on.

"Oh, good Lord," said Tara with a grin. She found Christmas pretty ghastly.

"Excuse me," said Gillian and walked over to the phone in the hall. "Gillian Ward," she answered it.

"Hi, it's John Burton. Am I disturbing you?"

She wondered why the tone of his voice gave her

a funny feeling in her stomach. Something inside her knotted up in a way she had not experienced for a long time. Out of the blue, she remembered what the woman at the Christmas party had said: *I always have to stop myself having indecent thoughts when I see him.*

Why does that come to mind right now? Gillian wondered. "No," she said. "You're not disturbing me at all."

"I just wanted to ask if you got home all right on Friday night."

"Oh, yes, thanks. Yes, here I am." She waited. It seemed to her as if her voice had an unnatural sound to it. And she knew that Tara was listening carefully.

"And then," Burton continued, "I wanted to say that I'll be in the Halfway House this Wednesday. If you'd like to meet again, I'd like that."

She was surprised. On Friday she had drunk too much and made an embarrassing attempt to flirt with him. She had thought she'd annoyed him, but over the weekend she had come to the reassuring conclusion that she need never be in close contact with him again, even though he was Becky's coach. Until now, she had avoided chatting with him when she dropped off or picked up her daughter. It was never difficult, in fact, as Burton was so completely surrounded by other mothers that she could hardly have gotten near him. And that is what it would be like in the future. Friday had been a one-time mistake. It would soon be forgotten. She had bawled her eyes out, she had drunk too much, she had flirted with him. It all went together. Burton would see it for what it was. And if not, that was his problem.

"This Wednesday," she repeated.

"Yes, I'll be there around seven. After coaching the young people's group."

Becky was still, just barely, in the children's group. She would not be there on Wednesday.

"I...I'm not sure."

"You can think about it," said Burton. "I'm going anyway. You can decide at the last minute if you like."

She could only think of one question. "Why?"

"Why what?"

It was hard to speak in Tara's presence, but Gillian had no wish to carry on talking in monosyllables. John Burton must think that she was not able to form complete sentences.

"Why do you want to meet me?"

"I find you interesting," said Burton.

She went quiet. How, for Christ's sake, were you to deal with such a situation?

"I'll think about it," she said in the end.

"Okay," said Burton. She had the impression that he was fairly sure that she would come.

"All right, until then, maybe," she said. He replied "Until then!" and hung up. He had left off the *maybe*.

You're pretty confident, thought Gillian.

"Who was that?" asked Tara straight away. "I don't mean to embarrass you, but you had a rather high-pitched voice and your cheeks are red. What is it?"

"It was Becky's tennis coach. John Burton."

"And?"

"He wants to meet me on Wednesday evening."

Tara looked at her with curiosity. "Is there something you want to tell me?"

Gillian stopped where she was. She felt her face flush. "Not yet. There's nothing I *could* tell you. Whether there will be, one day...no idea."

"Hmm," went Tara. She did not seem convinced that the situation was as harmless as Gillian wished to convey, but she understood that she would not get any more out of her right now.

She looked at her watch, reached for her handbag, and stood up. "I'm afraid I'd better get going. I've got one more appointment today."

"Difficult?"

"It's all right." She looked closely at Gillian. "Are you going? On Wednesday?"

Gillian shrugged her shoulders. "I still don't know. Just in case...could I tell Tom I'm meeting you?"

Tara smiled. It looked a little malicious. "Of course. I'll give you an alibi any time. Just let me know."

Gillian showed her out. She wondered if this was the first step toward cheating and whether she had just taken it: asking her friend to cover for her, because she was going out with another man.

It was dark outside. And cold. All the houses in the street were competing to have the shiniest and brightest Christmas decorations.

"Don't let the situation with Becky get you down," said Tara. "I'm no psychologist, but I can imagine that she is struggling with the situation at home too. Anyone can feel how unhappy and discontented you are. She doesn't want that for you. Children want happy moms."

"But...."

"But moms can't always be happy. And children learn to deal with that too."

"I hope so. I think a little distance will be good for us. Becky is going to my parents' again from after Christmas until the New Year. So we'll have a little break from each other."

It was what they had done for years. Becky went to her grandparents' in Norwich from Boxing Day. The habit was from the time when Gillian and Tom still took part in New Year's Eve parties or went off on a short break. They had not done any of that for years. "Don't just think about her. Think about yourself too," suggested Tara. In the light of the porch lamp, Gillian could clearly see her friend's face. She looked rather worried.

A man went by the yard fence, glancing at the two women as he passed.

Tara shook her head. "Him again!"

"What do you mean, again?"

"He was hanging around here when I came."

"Are you sure? It's dark, after all."

"I know. But I could see his face clearly. He was hanging around here earlier."

Gillian looked at the receding figure. "It could be Samson Segal," she said. She sometimes ran into him when she left her house, and she thought she recognized his gait even in the dark. "He's nice. Harmless. He lives at the other end of the street." *And goes to the wrong pubs and saw you with John Burton!*

"Think about all the crimes that happen each day," warned Tara. "There are tons of screwed-up characters on this planet."

Gillian had to laugh. "If I was in your line of work, I'm sure I'd think that too!"

"Just be careful," asked Tara, unlocking her dark-green Jaguar. Gillian watched her go. Then she pulled on her winter boots with a sigh and slipped into her coat. She would go and pick up Becky, even if that once again made her daughter annoyed with her. Was she overdoing it with her caution and care? In Becky's eyes—most certainly. But the world was a dangerous place, Tara was right about that. And she would know.

Better not to take a risk. She started walking.

Tuesday, December 8

1

HE HAD BOUGHT sausages and some dog biscuits and had actually managed to divert the dog from its usual course. He knew their route well, and he was not disappointed this morning. The dog ran down the hill before its owner was in sight. Samson knew that he only had about a minute before the young woman appeared behind the trees. He crouched down on the edge of the strip of park, half hidden behind the leafless bushes, and held out a bit of sausage and tried to attract the dog's attention. "Here, doggie, doggie! Here! I've got something yummy for you!"

Unfortunately, he did not know the dog's name. He had never heard its owner call it. He had to make the dog curious and let the smell of meat do the rest.

Indeed, the dog did come bounding over and greet him like an old acquaintance. It wolfed down the sausage without chewing it and then followed the stranger expectantly. Samson made a loop and entered the park again at another spot. He could not afford to be seen with the dog.

In the distance, he heard her calling: "Jazz! Hey, Jazz, where are you?"

So, Jazz. Finally the big shaggy dog had a name. Jazz pricked up his ears and turned his head. Samson took out another sausage.

"Jazz! Nice sausage!"

Jazz's greed won out, and he bounded over to Samson. After a while, Samson dared to grab the dog's collar and lead him along. They reached the end of the strip of park and crossed the road in order to walk up, alongside the golf course, back toward where the dog and woman had come from. Samson guessed that Jazz's owner would look for him down at the river, because that was the direction she had seen her dog go. No doubt she would be worried that he might try to cross the Esplanade and be hit by a car. Samson planned to hang around the golf course for a while and then go back to the beach later.

He had a long, cold day ahead of him. Of course, December was not the best month for such a plan, but should he waste valuable time by waiting until summer? He had taken the chat with Bartek to heart. He did not want to end up a madman with no grip on reality, given over to absurd daydreams. He had to *do* something. He had to make a move. Bartek was right.

He had thought up the plan with Jazz two nights ago. He thought it was genius. Dognap him, hang around with him for most of the day, and then bring him back to his desperate owner. Explain to her that he had found him somewhere. She would express her gratitude and relief, maybe ask him to come in for a cup of tea. That might lead to more.

Jazz had eaten the second sausage and all the dog biscuits, and he was getting restless. It was clear that he wanted to go back. In the end, Samson took off his belt and slipped it under the collar, improvising a leash. He talked to Jazz in a calming voice.

"We'll go back to your home. Don't worry. Yes, she'll look for you and get pretty worried now. I'm as sorry about that as you are. But just imagine how happy she'll be when she opens the door to us. She might even really like me. A woman has never really liked me, you know that?"

Jazz listened carefully to him and wagged his tail. Samson found it nice to talk to a dog. The dog looked at him with such concentration that it seemed he could really understand what it was all about. And you could be sure that he would not tease you or laugh at you, whatever you confided in him. Nor would he tell the secret to anyone else.

"I also wanted to have a dog," said Samson. "But first my parents were against it. And now Millie is."

When he said her name, he could feel the hatred like a small, hot flame in his stomach. Millie, who was so dissatisfied and so cold. Who showed him every step of the way what she thought of him: that he was a loser, a burden, unnecessary. Someone who had done nothing with his life.

"Millie decides everything in our house," he told Jazz. "Although the house belongs to my brother and me. But unfortunately, he's completely under her thumb. I just can't figure out how he could marry such a poisonous piece of work. Well, she used to be pretty attractive…."

Gavin had never had difficulty with women. He was not a man who all the women flew to, but neither was he someone they all avoided. Everything had always been pretty normal with him. Nothing to attract attention. Gavin was average, in every way. Samson knew that most people would be annoyed to be considered average. But they had no idea what it felt like to be someone who did not get anything right and was constantly used as a doormat. Someone, in other words, who was below average.

"I think your owner is pretty," he said to Jazz. "I don't like her as much as Gillian, but unfortunately Gillian is married."

Jazz gave a little *wuff.*

He stroked the dog's shaggy head. "Your owner has not even noticed me yet. But that might change today. You needn't be afraid at all. You'll see her again tonight."

They had reached the golf club's clubhouse. There was only one car in the car park. Apart from it, the place was deserted this cold early morning. Since it was, Samson dared to walk around the building. There were no lights on in the windows. No one was inside. A large poster at the front door announced a black-tie Christmas ball. It was to be held that coming Saturday in the clubhouse. As the poster said in particularly large and bright red letters, the famous London lawyer Logan Stanford had organized it. The climax of the evening would be a prize drawing whose proceeds would go to help street children in Russia.

Samson knew Logan Stanford. Not personally, of course, but from the gossip rags that Millie liked to read so much and left strewn around the house. Stanford was an extremely successful lawyer with first-class connections to the rich and powerful of the land—even to Downing Street, it was whispered. He had oodles of money and influence. And he was known for constantly organizing charity events up and down the country. His nickname was "Charity Stanford," and he did his best to live up to it. He collected huge donations and made sure they reached the most needy of this world. Nevertheless, Samson could not help but have reservations about him whenever he saw him on the colorful pages of *Hello!* yet again. He thought Stanford looked rather smug. And his guests too…all those lifted faces rigid with Botox, lavish evening dresses, sparkling jewelry. Champagne by the bucketload. High society was celebrating itself in the first instance, but the end result was money for people who were much less well off than the British upper class. "So what?" Millie had once said when he expressed his unease. "What's the problem? At least they're doing something. If they have fun at the same time—who does that hurt?"

He himself could not really say what it was about it that annoyed him. Perhaps it was the feeling that these people were less concerned about the misery in the world than their own self-aggrandizement. Perhaps he had trouble reconciling the issues faced by Russian street children with the artificially enhanced wives of the top ten thousand people in England.

But perhaps that was silly of him. Perhaps the important thing really was just the end result and not whether everyone involved had a pure heart and undertook their charity activity out of utter conviction. Millie was right about this: at least they were doing something.

Samson hung around the clubhouse and car park for quite a while before finally daring to go down toward the river. Of course there was the risk that he would meet Jazz's owner, no doubt hysterical by this stage. It would not be a problem. He could claim that he had just found the dog and was taking it back home.

He reached the beach without having been seen. The sand was wet and heavy. The fog hung in heavy clouds over the water, muffling the cries of the seagulls. It was no longer as cold as it had been a few days ago, but Samson found the dampness in the air almost worse. It crept under your clothing and into your bones. It not only froze your body, it hollowed it out.

They walked along the beach, past the empty, closed-up bathing huts with their colorful fronts and the carved wooden decorations on the roofs. There was nobody at all around. Jazz seemed to have gotten used to the situation. He jogged along beside Samson, occasionally sniffing at the stinking flotsam that the river had washed up and, when it smelled particularly interesting, lifting his leg. He seemed to be in a good mood.

Samson could have kicked himself for not having thought to park his car somewhere nearby. If he had, he could have warmed up now and then. He was an idiot. He had planned to wait until late afternoon to bring Jazz back. Jazz's owner would be at her wits' end by then and so all the more grateful to him. But by then he would have caught a cold.

Very clever of me, very clever. Typical.

After what seemed like an eternity to him, they reached the spit of land where the Thames became the North Sea. Here at Shoeburyness there were wonderful beaches and meadows, dotted with the old fortifications built to defend Britain from a German invasion during the War. Samson knew the area. He and Gavin had often played here as children, although it was a fair distance by foot from Thorpe Bay. Gavin had taken his friends there, and Samson had been allowed to play with them. Because their mother insisted. The other children had grumbled but reluctantly put up with him. Samson had learned then what it meant to be unloved. Not to be accepted.

He thought about what he had said to Jazz at the golf club. It felt like hours ago. That he found Jazz's owner pretty. Why had he thought he had to tell Jazz? Because it was not what he really felt?

Well, you couldn't say that she was *not* pretty. But to

be honest, her appearance did not get his heart racing.
And she was not the woman around whom his thoughts
circled when he lay in bed at night and stared at the
ceiling, just able to make out its lines in the weak light
cast by the street lamp outside his window. It was just
that she was the only woman in the neighborhood who
was roughly the same age as he was. And who was not
obviously in a relationship. Of course, Bartek would
raise his eyebrows and ask him why on earth he did not
look more widely, why the one suitable woman whom
he had stumbled across on his walks now appeared to
him to be the only possible woman for him in the whole
world. Bartek would mention the Internet again and all
its opportunities. Very clever of him. As if Samson had
not figured that one out on his own. He had even met
several women that way. He could remember how awkward, even torturous, the dates had been. He had no idea
how to fascinate a woman; and every time, after just a
few minutes, he had realized that his date was starting to get bored. That of course made him stutter and
start to talk about the stupidest things. And once the
women heard that he lived with his brother and sister-
in-law, they quickly made their excuses and fled. Now
he was unemployed, too, which would hardly improve
his chances.

They had left the beach, crossed the big car park,
which was jam-packed in summer and was now completely empty, turned inland, and reached Gunners Park,
a large open space. In spite of all the paths that criss-
crossed it, it had not been developed. It was still meadows, fields, copses, and expanses of scrubland, where
the wind coming in off the North Sea flattened the grass.
Part of the park was a nature reserve, closed to the public
but a paradise where innumerable kinds of birds nested.

The locals loved to come on outings to the rest of the park. Samson remembered school walks that had ended in a sausage roast in the park. Everyone whittled a stick to a point, spiked a sausage on the end, and held it over the flames. The Tupperware containers full of carrot sticks and dips were opened, and the cartons of apple juice. And everyone had fun and enjoyed the day. Samson was the only one wishing for it to end soon, because he felt isolated among all the happy people. He would sit there on his own with the rucksack that his mother had lovingly packed for him. From the way she equipped him for school outings, Samson had seen how much his mother loved him and how much she wanted him to enjoy himself. But her power had shrunk over time. When he was still a small child, she had still been able to force the other children to look after him. But by the time he was in secondary school, that no longer worked. Certainly not by the time he was a pimply teenager. And she could not help him at all when it came to girls.

He sat down on a bench. Jazz crouched down at his feet. The fog enveloped them from all sides, leaving them as good as blind. The sea had disappeared somewhere in these thick, wet veils.

Samson thought about Gillian Ward.

In fact, for a while he had only been thinking about Gillian Ward—and, what is more, in a way that was quite inappropriate, considering that she was a married woman. The day before, he had crept around her house. He had seen her friend come and then leave, managing to catch a glimpse of Gillian herself too. He spent almost all his time on Gillian.

"I'd never try anything with her," he said to Jazz. "She's married and has a child. The Wards are an ideal family. A family like that shouldn't be destroyed."

Jazz cocked his head to one side in an effort to understand what Samson was telling him.

An ideal family....

Samson had had the shock of his life when he saw Gillian enter the Halfway House on Friday night. Why was she there? Without her family? And who was the man accompanying her? Samson did not know him, had never seen him with the Ward family. He took an immediate dislike to the man, although he tried to analyze his feelings objectively. Was he just jealous? Or was he envious of the man himself? It was obvious that this was a man who only had to snap his fingers and any woman he wanted would jump into bed with him. Or was there something about him that justified Samson's suspicion? Something dishonest, shady, insincere?

That is how Samson would have described him, but perhaps he was being unfair. The man had taken to a pub the woman Samson would have loved to take out—at least in his dreams. In reality, he died a thousand deaths just at the thought of it. For it would be impossible for him to sit down at a table with her and chat over a glass of wine without her realizing how pathetic he was, that he was neither entertaining nor witty nor exciting. And that he often stumbled over his words, stuttering and messing up every punch line, should he even get close to delivering one. He had noticed how women sitting with him would try to look at their watches inconspicuously and, with greater or less success, suppress a yawn. It had made him come out in a sweat and filled him with despair. He could not let that happen with Gillian. He had the feeling that a similar reaction from her would make him suicidal.

So he had to focus on Jazz's owner. Perhaps something would come of this plan. If only it would not take so long! He looked at his watch. Nine in the morning. He did not want to turn up at her house before nightfall.

He cursed his idea. No doubt it would all lead to nothing anyway.

2

WHEN MILLIE'S SHIFT finished at noon, she immediately set off for home. She never stayed a second longer in the care home than she absolutely had to. She could barely stand the smell of the place. And the sight of all the old fragile people. The meaningless blather of those who had dementia. The long corridors, the horrible linoleum on the floors. The sight of the trolley on which lunch was wheeled around to the rooms long before lunchtime. Millie found the food in the home so disgusting that she often lost her appetite for the rest of the day. The thought of the contents of those plastic plates and feeding cups would keep her from eating when she got home.

At least that helped her to stay slim—perhaps the only good thing about her job. She was getting old so fast, she thought, but at least she still had a nice figure. Sometimes she turned this way and that in front of her bedroom mirror to stop herself from falling into a depression. In tight jeans and a low-cut top, her body was still capable of spreading some happiness.

She had to take the train from Tilbury to Thorpe Bay. Gavin and she could only afford one car, and normally Gavin used it. Otherwise he would have to get up even earlier for his early shifts. It infuriated Millie that Samson had his own car and that it was normally left unused. She wondered what had brought her late mother-in-law to leave her car to such a loser. Gavin had explained to her that his mother had had a very close relationship to Samson. She had always felt the need to look after and protect him more than Gavin. "He was the problem child. He was always on his own, always in his shell. Whatever he did, it never went well. He was clumsy and never able to function well socially. Never. Even back in nursery school. When our mom was dying, her biggest worry was for Samson's future."

Just remembering this conversation made Millie pull a face. It was so unfair! Gavin had a job. Gavin had a wife. Gavin was normal. And who got the car? His little brother, who just annoyed everyone around him.

The train was taking forever again. Millie had to force herself not to think about how quickly she could have gotten home by car. If not, she would have only gotten more angry, and she knew that it was this rage that was etching the deep lines in her face and giving her an embittered expression.

The rage was making her old.

She strutted down the streets toward her house. It was a good distance from the station. Every morning and evening, the Christmas lights sparkled from the houses, but at this midday hour there was only the dreary atmosphere of a leaden, foggy December day. In the autumn, leaves had glowed red and golden in the yards, but now the bare branches rose up jagged and black against the gray sky.

The fog was not as thick on the ground anymore. Perhaps it would dissipate by the afternoon and even let in a few rays of sunlight. But as it got dark so early now, that was little help. Millie hunched up her shoulders. If she ever had the money, proper amounts of money, she would emigrate. Somewhere where it was warm and sunny.

She had not consciously registered the woman coming toward her, although she was the only other person on the street, so she jumped when the woman suddenly addressed her.

"Excuse me!" A high voice, a little shrill. Desperate.

"Yes?" Millie stopped.

"I'm looking for my dog." The woman's eyes were bulging, her hair a mess. Drops of sweat were glistening on her nose, suggesting that she had been running around the neighborhood for a long time. She was warm. She seemed distraught.

"Jazz. Part Alsatian. Quite large, long-haired. You haven't seen him, have you?"

Millie was not particularly fond of dogs. "No. I've just come on the train from Tilbury."

"He ran away this morning. It was still rather dark and…I don't understand. He's never done anything like this before."

Millie noticed with annoyance that although the woman was about her age, even in her desperate state she looked much fresher, younger, and less wrinkly than Millie. No doubt she had a job that she enjoyed.

"I haven't seen a dog. If I notice anything, I can let you know, Mrs….?"

"Miss Brown. Michelle Brown." The young woman got a bit of paper and a pen from her coat pocket and scribbled some numbers down. "My phone number. Please, if you…you know, he's everything to me."

So, not such a happy life after all, thought Millie. She put the piece of paper in her pocket, nodded at Michelle, and carried on home. It was not likely that she would come across the dog.

Samson's car was in the drive. He had left the house that morning and once again left his car. She had asked him about it once. He had said petrol was too expensive.

That was a fair point, she had to admit, particularly for someone without a job.

She unlocked the front door. She did not expect her brother-in-law to be home. For the last few months, he had been leaving home early and returning late. That was, essentially, fine by her, but it also made her suspicious. What the devil was he up to all day?

She did not believe his assertion that he was looking for work. If he had been, he would not have needed to be outside from morning to night. To her, job-hunting meant writing piles of applications. It was true that he was often on his computer late at night, but why should he do something at night that he could do just as well during the day? And if someone was looking for work and not finding any, that normally involved rejection letters, which came by post. Some might come by e-mail, but not all of them. And it was often Millie who was the first downstairs after the postman had been there. Nothing had come for Samson for months. All right, one or two bits of direct mail from companies that he had ordered things from in better days. But nothing that looked at all like it could be a rejection letter.

She looked at her watch. A quarter past one. Gavin would be home for lunch in half an hour. His shift ended a little earlier today too. But she had time to get something out of the freezer. One of the few advantages of having Samson in the house was that while he had had his job delivering frozen foods, they had had a discount on the company's products.

Making a quick decision, she climbed the stairs. She had snooped around in Samson's room a few times when he was not there, justifying it to herself by saying that he was obviously mad and that it was important for Gavin and her to know a little more about him. Gavin had grown up with Samson. He was used to his brother. He could not see that his brother had a screw loose, but she had felt it from the first moment. When Gavin presented Samson to her, her first instinctive thought had been "there's something funny about him." And every year since that day, her conviction had only grown that she had been right. She called his name, and, as no one answered, she pushed open the door with determination. Although she had known his room for years, she still shook her head in disapproval. It was a teenager's bedroom, not that of a man in his mid-thirties.

The narrow bed in which he had slept as a little boy. The football club pennant above it, although he had never played football as far as Millie knew. Adventure books on the shelf. The flowery curtains that his mother had sewn.

The room was meticulously tidy. There was not a speck of dust to be seen. The bedcover was pulled up neatly on the bed. She had tried but never achieved such perfection with her and Gavin's bed.

She looked at the bookshelf, now and then glancing out the window. The bedroom faced the street, so she would see Samson if he came back unexpectedly. She did not expect him to arrive before the evening.

She opened the door of his wardrobe. The classic children's bedroom wardrobe in pine. It contained neatly folded pullovers, a few shirts and jeans. All of it plain and respectable. Millie was not at all amazed that he never managed to get a girl. Apart from his nature, his shyness and his tendency to stutter and blush, it was also his clothes. He looked like a little boy. It had not surprised Millie to hear that most of his clothes had been bought or made by his mother.

However, the computer on Samson's desk was what

most interested her. Samson had bought it himself when he was still working as a chauffeur and earning quite good money. Flatscreen. Quite big at that. The computer was the only thing that gave this old-fashioned room a more modern look.

Samson sat for hours at the computer. Millie had never managed to find out what exactly he did on it. A few times, she had surprised him by coming in without knocking, but she had found that he could react remarkably quickly on those occasions. Whatever he was looking at, he had clicked it away before Millie could see what it was.

She knew that what she was doing was out of order, but she excused herself by saying that it was important for Gavin and her to know what Samson spent his time doing. After all, they all lived under the same roof. You had to be careful. What if he was browsing on sites that showed child pornography? Gavin and she wanted to have children one day. It was her duty to get to the bottom of this.

She turned on the computer and heard its quiet hum as it booted up. A quick glance out of the window. Still no sign of Samson. The screen went blue. As she had feared: a box asked for a password.

Of course, he was not completely stupid. Millie thought quickly. Most people use the name of someone close to them as their password. Children, spouses, pets. Unfortunately there was no one like that in Samson's life. His brother was his only living relative. She tried out *Gavin,* but it did not work.

He will hardly have used my name, she thought. Damn it, who else does he know?

That was not an easy question when you were talking about someone as socially awkward as her brother-in-law. On the other hand, at least it reduced considerably the number of candidates.

There was that friend of his from the chauffeuring service. The one he sometimes met on Friday in the pub by the river. What was his name? Bartek. She typed in *Bartek*, but that was rejected too.

She did not want to give up. It was the first time that she had gone this far: attempting to get into his computer. She had to think. If he was not using a made-up word or a combination of numbers, then it must be possible for her to crack his damned security.

She looked around the room, as if the white walls and the clean gray carpet might offer some hint. The wardrobe was full of jumpers knitted by his mom. Mom had sewn the curtains too. Mom had bought him the adventure stories on his shelf that he no longer read. That was what the room told her: of the powerful love between Samson and his mother. A love that had survived her death. It told of the limitless care of a woman for her difficult, suffering son. And of the pain that the son still carried with him after having lost the only person he could relate to.

Millie's mother-in-law's first name had been Hannah.

She typed in the name. The computer opened with a melodic sequence.

"What on earth are you doing?" said a voice behind her.

Millie spun around. Gavin was standing in the doorway, looking at her in horror.

She immediately turned off the computer and stood up. As she believed attack was the best defense, she hissed at him, "Do you have to creep up on people?"

"How can you root around in my brother's computer?" asked Gavin, looking uneasy.

She shrugged. "I think it's necessary for our security."

"Security? Why security? Samson wouldn't hurt a fly!"

"How do you know? Do you have any idea what he spends hours doing every evening? Perhaps he downloads violent games. Or watches porn."

"He's a grown man. He can watch what he likes."

She pushed past him and started down the stairs. Gavin was forced to follow her.

"I don't agree," she explained. "He's disturbed. You have to keep an eye on people like that. And on what they do. Or do you want your brother one day to run amok in a school or whatever?"

"Why would he do that?"

They had reached the kitchen. Millie opened the freezer, took out a TV dinner, and banged it down on the table. Gavin flinched. "Either you don't read the papers or you don't understand them. Most of the time, when someone suddenly flips and mows everyone down, the relatives explain afterward in astonishment that they would never have imagined it of the person. But when the journalists drill down a little, they find out that the guy had always acted a little strangely and if the others had paid more attention, then the catastrophe could have been avoided."

"But Samson—"

"It's just a matter of being careful, nothing else," said Millie. How stupid she had been, to let Gavin catch her, she thought.

If he told Samson about it, Samson would change his password immediately and next time he would choose one that she would never be able to crack. However, instinctively she knew that Gavin would keep his mouth shut. He shied away from conflicts more than anyone else she knew. He would think twice before pouring fuel on the already-volatile relationship between his brother and his wife. "So, do you want to carry on griping, or would you like me to cook you something to eat?"

It seemed that he wanted to say something else about the problem, but he decided not to. He looked tired. His day had begun at five in the morning. He had transported screaming kids and raucous teenagers to school in his bus. He felt completely exhausted. She could read in his face how he had closed the topic because he didn't have the energy for an argument.

"I'd like to eat," he said obediently.

3

TUESDAY, DECEMBER 8, 10:10 P.M.

SHE'S NOT BETTER than other women. Not at all. Michelle Brown. Now I know her name and what she is like. She's arrogant, just thinks of herself, and is ungrateful. Nor is she particularly pretty. At least, not when you're standing next to her. She looks better from a distance. Her face was blotchy and tearful. Her mascara was smudged. If I compare her to Gillian Ward! Recently in the Halfway House it was obvious that she had just been crying, but that didn't take anything away from her beauty. It made her ethereal, tender. You wanted to take her in your arms and protect her. Whereas I would never want to hold Michelle Brown in my arms. She's not my type at all. Even so, there was absolutely no reason to treat me in such a dismissive fashion.

I'm sitting here and have wrapped a woolen scarf

*around my neck. I've got a big mug of hot lemon juice
and honey in front of me. I can feel a cold coming on.
I feel like death warmed up. It looks like the price for
my Michelle Brown adventure is going to be a case of
the flu.*

*I was at her place at half past five. At half past four
I had started on the way home. I wouldn't have been
able to stick being outside in Shoeburyness any longer.
The cold had crept into all my joints. I had the feeling I
could only walk like an old man. I was desperately hungry too, but it was too far to walk to the center of Shoeburyness and in any case I didn't know where to find a
supermarket. In the summer you can buy sandwiches
on the beachfront, but not in December, of course. I
should have thought of making myself a sandwich that
morning. Millie does always say it's painful to see how
stupid I am. She's probably right. I still had a little piece
of sausage left, but it was for Jazz. Even though I was
feeling funny, I couldn't bring myself to eat his tidbit.
Especially as he had been so good and patient. It was
touching to see how he let everything just happen, even
though he was freezing too and maybe also afraid he
wouldn't see his owner again. I felt really bad for him.
So he got the sausage. Just the smell of it made me feel
faint. I had been so nervous that morning, I hadn't really had any breakfast.*

*I hung around at the beach for a while. There was ab-
solutely no one there but me. If it hadn't been so cold, I
would have enjoyed it. It was dark and the waves breaking on the shore were black and mysterious. The fog was
lifting and you could see that behind the wetness in the
air, a beautiful day had been waiting to come through.
I even experienced the end of the sunset. A fiery red
winter sun was sinking into the yellowy-gray fog over*

London. The river was in the foreground. A tugboat was gliding slowly toward the estuary. Whenever I turned around, I could see in the last light of day the high, pale grass slowly swaying in the quiet wind. There was a wonderfully melancholic atmosphere. I wished so much that Gillian was around. I wished I could share this special mood with her.

At half past five I rang Brown's doorbell, after having dragged my tired bones all the way back along the beach to Thorpe Bay. She threw open the door and stood in front of me, looking at Jazz, who wagged his tail like mad. Then the two of them were in each other's arms—or rather, she crouched down and he whined and wriggled and licked her tearful face. She did not pay me any attention at first. Finally she got to her feet again. She looked even more ruffled than before and seemed somehow...embarrassed.

I don't know what I had been hoping for. I think I had imagined at times during the previous night that she would hug me spontaneously. Beaming. Overflowing with gratefulness. Instead she was inhibited. Perhaps now that she had her treasure again, she would have really liked to slam the door in my face. But she was too polite to do that, of course.

"Where did you find him?" she asked.

I made a vague gesture toward the river. "I'd gone for a walk. A long way toward the sea, almost to Shoeburyness. Suddenly he came up to me." As I spoke I felt the color rising up my neck. I hoped that Michelle didn't notice my embarrassment.

She looked at me in confusion. "What was he doing there? I don't understand...I don't understand why he ran away. He's never done that before!"

"Perhaps he smelled or saw another dog somewhere and followed him," I conjectured.

She did not look too convinced, but naturally she did not guess what had really happened.

"How lucky that he has a tag on his collar with my address and telephone number," said Michelle. "Otherwise you wouldn't have been able to find me easily. Although I have already registered him as missing with the police and an animal-rescue center. They could have told you who his owner is." She had no idea how well I knew her already. Her comment hurt. For over half a year, when she walked her dog early every morning, we had passed in close proximity to one another and she obviously had not seen me at all. She did not exclaim something like "Oh, aren't you the one I always see in the morning?"

Instead, she thought I was a complete stranger. It was typical. Women do not notice me. And if they notice me, then they forget me again the very next second. I am a man they do not waste more a second thought on—and their first thought is one of scorn. That is how it is. In my despairing moments I know that nothing will change.

"Well, I'm glad I found him and could bring him back to you. He's a lovely dog!"

"He's like a baby to me," said Michelle in a soft voice.

I was so cold, chilled to the bone, and I thought: you could at least invite me in for a coffee. Of course she did not know I had spent the day outside, but I had brought her "baby" back, after all! Wasn't that worth a coffee?

We stood there, facing each other a little embarrassedly, and then Michelle said, "So, thanks once again, Mr....?"

"Segal. Samson Segal."

"Mr. Segal. I'm Michelle Brown. I'm so relieved.

It was a terrible day. I was imagining Jazz run over or captured for animal testing. I was seeing horrible things...."

"Then I can only wish the two of you a nice evening now," I said and turned to go. She did not stop me.

She called out one more thanks as I went out the gate.

And then that was it. When I turned toward the house from the street, the door had already closed.

And there I stood. Freezing. Hungry. Completely exhausted. For nothing. The worst thing is that I always think such situations only happen to me. That it is my fault and no one else's. I imagine what would have happened if Bartek had taken her dog back. Bartek with his black hair, his dark-brown eyes, his piercing stare, and his slight accent. Bartek, who can really dazzle a woman. Who can be witty and charming and to whom people are immediately drawn. She would have invited him in. Probably they would have toasted the dog's happy return with a glass of bubbly, and perhaps Michelle would even have lit a few candles or the fire, if she had a fireplace. Bartek would not have had to drag himself home like a bedraggled poodle.

Of course, her behavior said a lot about Michelle Brown. She would have thrown herself at a man like Bartek; she got rid of me as if I were a bothersome salesman. As if I had tried to sell her a newspaper subscription. It says something about women in general. Most of them are pretty superficial. A strand of black hair casually falling across the forehead, an East European accent—and hey presto, you can have your way with them. Bartek is not a bad guy, but there's not much to him, he just does what's in his own interest. Whereas I am deep. I could give a woman much more warmth and emotion than he can. I just need women to give me *a chance to show that. Mom used to say that too. Samson is a man you see when you take a closer look. He has a big heart, but it's not obvious at a first glance.*

But women don't take the time. They see a shy man who blushes easily and who cannot come up with witty comments. When they hear I'm unemployed too, then it's decided. Women are gold-diggers. Michelle too, no doubt. She examined me. She noticed that my clothes are not expensive and are rather worn. That was it for me. I was just good enough to catch her dog and bring it back. But she was not up to inviting me in, even for a moment.

She is like all the others. All those damned women who show you as a man what you are in their eyes: trash. A nobody.

I think I hate Michelle.

I hate everyone who hurts me.

Wednesday, December 9

1

EVEN THE LONGEST NIGHT, thought Anne, finally reaches an end.

It was six in the morning when her tension finally abated. It was still black as pitch outside and would remain so for the next two hours, but Anne had always gotten up at six; on weekdays in order to go to the clinic, and at the weekend to have two undisturbed hours in which to paint before she prepared breakfast. Whether it was light or dark outside, she started her day at six. She liked to be awake while others were still sleeping. Although now that she lived all on her own in this house in a wood, little remained of her feeling of moving in a luxurious silence through a sleeping world. The noises, voices, and whispers of the wood sounded different in the night than in the day, and yet it was not the same as looking out on dark silent houses. In her solitude out here, there was the danger that day and night, waking and sleeping, would melt into each other. Especially in this dark time before Christmas.

Anne had spent the last night in the living room. Wrapped up in a warm blanket, she had drunk hot milk in little sips and tried to calm her tattered nerves. She had gone to bed that night at half past ten, had read for half an hour and then quickly fallen asleep, but then in the night she had been startled out of her sleep and for a split second had seen the beam of a headlight slip across her bedroom walls and heard the purr of an engine. Then the engine cut out and the light went out.

Somewhere out there in the cold winter's night was a car, with someone sitting in it and…and what, exactly? What was someone doing in this clearing far from any village, watching a single house in the middle of no-where surrounded by an orchard of bare fruit trees? Why?

She lay in bed, her heart racing, and hoped that she had just dreamed it, but she knew it was no dream. Nor her imagination. It had happened too often recently. She had to start to take it seriously, although she did not have the slightest idea what the *it* was.

The luminous numbers on her bedside radio clock had shown her that it was almost half past midnight.

In the end she had pulled herself together and stepped over to the window. These upper-floor windows had shutters too, but she did not close them. She moved about carefully so that she would not be seen and peered out. Pale moonlight from behind the clouds. She could not recognize anything—not a car or a person. But she knew someone was out there, breathing, waiting.

For a moment she had considered calling the police. *I live in a wood, in what used to be a hunter's lodge. Maybe ten minutes by car from Tunbridge Wells. There's a car outside. I think someone is watching my house. It's been going on for weeks. I see the beam of the headlights when the car approaches over a rough dirt road. That road is all there is here. Then the light goes out. The car must be there somewhere. And I don't know what the driver wants. What he wants from me.*

Her hand had reached out twice to the telephone. Twice it had twitched back. She thought it all sounded like the mad ramblings of a batty old crone. She could imagine the impression she would give: an elderly woman, almost seventy, strange enough to live in a god-forsaken place far from everyone else, an unsociable widow, a painter of wild and colorful pictures. And now she sees lights and hears car engine noises.

Finally she pulled on a pair of tracksuit bottoms and went downstairs. On the ground floor all the shutters were firmly closed. In the past, Anne had normally left them open, but she did not dare to do so anymore since these odd things had started happening.

At least no one outside could see her. She turned on all the lights and the television. For its voices, to listen to someone, to reassure herself that she was not alone in the world.

She heated up the milk. Surprised that she was so bitterly cold, she wrapped herself in a woolen blanket. She would not be able to sleep any longer this night, she realized that. Awake, she alternated between look-ing at the wall and the television, while someone else sat outside and was no doubt staring at her house. She knew that lines of light shone out through the chinks in the shutters. Whoever the mysterious stranger was, he could see that she was awake. Although she could not say whether that fact had any meaning for him.

In the morning, the nightmare lost its sharp edges. Anne planned to drive into town and take a few Christ-mas parcels for friends to the post office. She knew that by then, at the latest, everyday normality would have put the fears of the night to flight, making them seem almost unreal. She was happy that she had not called the police and made a laughingstock out of herself. And she was even happy for the long night she had just had, because it had helped her make a decision: she would move back to London, where she had spent most of her life. And where people lived whom she still knew from earlier times.

She had gone back and forth over it in those nighttime hours that had not seemed like they would ever pass. She had experienced again all the pain she had felt after Sean's death. And the determination with which she had put a lid on her feelings of loneliness and fear. Above all, she had thought about the promise she had made to herself and to him in the first moments after he had fallen asleep forever in the hospital. *I'll carry on with your dream. With the house you loved so much. With the fruit trees and the balmy summer evenings on the balcony and the silent winter's nights, when the whole wood is covered in hoarfrost. I'll live all of that for you.*

That morning she gave herself permission to retract her promise. Not just because some madman was wandering around the wood and could possibly become a danger to her. Whoever it was and whatever the person's motivation, that was just the trigger for her decision.

She had understood something this night. She really was living Sean's dream. But that had nothing to do with her own wishes, desires, longings, and ideas of what life should be like. As a couple, life here had had its charms. For a single person, it could become a nightmare.

She was tired but also electrified. Joyful. Relieved.

She went into the kitchen, turned the coffee machine on, boiled an egg, and took out two slices of bread. She hummed quietly to herself. After going to the post office, she would look for a real estate agent. Perhaps one could look at the property in the next few days and tell her what kind of a selling price to expect. And then she would dive into her own house-hunting. For example, for a pretty two-bedroom apartment with a large balcony for plants. In a house with other people who might become her friends. In the evening, the lights of the city would be around her. She realized she was almost crying as she imagined it. How difficult it had become to bear this isolation. Now that she was aware of it for the first time, she understood how unhappy she had been. How much she had been living in opposition to her own dreams.

She hummed away to herself.

The most beautiful thing was that she was sure Sean was nodding at her in encouragement.

2

"And?" asked Peter Fielder when Christy stepped into his office. It was still early in the morning and not much was happening yet in the offices and corridors of the Met. Peter liked to get to Scotland Yard at the break of day, when he would not be approached constantly and disturbed. He could get a lot done then, before the day's usual hustle and bustle took over and colleagues rushed in and out, phones rang all the time, and unplanned conference calls popped up.

Christy McMarrow felt the same, and it was probably this match in the way they worked, thought Peter, that made them such a well-oiled team.

His "And?" referred to his certainty that Christy was bringing him new information. She never just came by for a coffee or a friendly chat.

And yet she did not look exactly happy. Whatever she had found out, it did not seem to have brought them closer to a breakthrough. "I talked to two of Carla Roberts's former workmates yesterday, from the drug store," said Christy. "Both of them described Carla as a nice, friendly, but very reserved woman. Apparently she was quite hard to get close to, although she was always ready to help and warm-hearted. Both of them exclude the possibility that she could have had enemies there. Of course, I'll still talk to the manager, but my instinct says that this isn't a hot lead."

"Hmm," went Peter. "Anything else?"

"I've gone through Carla Roberts's address book, but there are almost no entries in it. Apart from her colleagues from the drug store. After she retired, it doesn't look like she's written down anyone else. Either she made no new acquaintances, or she just didn't write them down. I've managed to find one other person she used to know, from when she was still married. Eleanor Sullivan. She was a casual acquaintance of the Robertses. I went and visited her."

"And what did your instinct tell you there?" Peter was not being sarcastic. He had learned to trust Christy's instincts a lot in the last few years. It may have had something to do with his admiration for her as a woman.

"Nothing to get excited about," Christy had to admit reluctantly. "Nothing at all, really. It doesn't look to me like Carla's murderer is someone she used to know—unless there are some dark secrets no one knows about. Mrs. Sullivan remembers Carla well and describes her just like the others did: shy, reserved, but very friendly. She says that to her knowledge, Carla never got into problems with other people. She said that Carla was far too quiet and inconspicuous to get into a fight with anyone. She must have been an extremely unassuming person who avoided conflicts and rarely provoked anyone."

"Hmm," went Peter again. "It makes you despair! She didn't even have a computer. There are no e-mail contacts, no chat forums, no Web site visits to give us a clue. We're completely in the dark here!" The characteristic that had made Carla Roberts's life difficult, her shyness and plainness, was now also an obstacle that hindered them in ascertaining the causes of her violent death. She was a woman with no rough corners, who had never had a run-in with anyone. And yet who then died in a gruesome way. This harmless nature must have triggered some horrific aggression in someone. "There must be something in her life," he said; "there must be *something* that drove the culprit to this brutal crime. It's one thing to shoot someone down from a distance. It's a completely different thing to tie someone up and stuff a cloth so far down their throat that they are sick. And then to ram it farther down and wait until the victim chokes horrifically to death on their vomit. There was a lot of hate behind that. Why did Carla Roberts trigger that? She just slipped through her days like a shadow you barely notice, and she had a friendly face too."

"Unless the murder had nothing to do with her as a person," said Christy. "But just with the fact that she, being all alone, was a suitable victim. For a man who has some basic problem with women. After all, that was the first thought that went through our heads when we saw what had been done to her."

"Still, we have to stick to her life, because we don't have any other clues." He suppressed a yawn. He was so tired. "Did this Mrs. Sullivan say anything about the Roberts marriage?"

"Yes. It was a pretty normal marriage. No major highs or lows. Her husband worked hard, was always at the office. Carla was devastated when she heard of the financial disaster and of the fact that he had been cheating on her for years. What was most distressing for her was the fact that she never guessed at any of it. Mrs. Sullivan phoned her at the time and apparently the only thing Carla said on the phone was that cliché *Why didn't I see it? Why didn't I see it?* She could not get over that."

"Was her husband ever violent toward her?"

"No. In a boring, unspectacular way it really was a happy marriage. In general, he was seen as a calm and rather staid fellow. According to Eleanor Sullivan, the divorce went smoothly. She did not take him to the cleaners financially—there was no money to fight over. And anyway, he disappeared pretty quickly, never to return."

Regarding his work, Fielder would not have thought in terms of his instincts, but he did have the distinct feeling that they would be wasting their time tracking down her ex-husband.

He changed the topic. "What about the door to the building? Any news there?"

Here Christy did have some results to share.

"Yes. Forensics says that it was clearly tampered with. The spring that ensures that the door closes automatically must have been pulled out with a pair of pliers. So anyone could go in and out whenever they wanted, without a key."

"Could have been the murderer."

"Yes. But not necessarily. The caretaker says they have a lot of vandalism. Hackney is not exactly the most genteel part of town. A youth could have just been having some fun and our murderer took advantage of that."

Peter Fielder rubbed his eyes. He needed something now. A thread to follow in the fog of this opaque case. A trace of a lead. Something to give him an adrenaline rush and chase away his tiredness. But there was nothing. Nothing but the feeling of creeping through a rolling mist and not really taking a single step forward.

Christy noticed that he was deflated. "Hey, boss, chin up! It's almost Christmas!"

"Yes. Christmas soon. And there's a madman running around out there. Christmas won't change that."

"Do you think he'll do it again?"

"Possibly. He might have a problem that won't have been solved with Carla's murder."

"A guy who hates women? And just looks out for good opportunities to act on his hate? That would support the idea of Carla being a chance victim."

"To some extent. Nothing is *only* chance. Somewhere, Carla Roberts's life intersected with her murderer's life. It might have been at such a tiny and apparently insignificant point that we'll have great difficulty discovering it. But I don't think that someone would just have taken the elevator to the top of an apartment building and rung a bell at random and then murdered the woman who lived there alone, without having first heard about her and known how she lived there."

Fielder stood up. He was determined not to let himself be defeated by his depressed mood or his exhaustion. "No, I think the murderer knew Carla Roberts. Knew a lot about her. And that's why we have to examine her life. Down to its tiniest details. We have to look at things that are not immediately of interest. And we have to realize that we don't have much time."

Christy did not say anything.

She knew he was thinking of the next victim.

3

IN THE HALFWAY HOUSE, it was not as full as it had been the previous Friday. There was nonetheless an excited babble of voices from the cluster of people at the bar. The floor was wet and dirty. Everyone had brought some of the miserable damp weather in with them. Somewhere in the background, Christmas music was warbling from a radio.

From the doorway, Gillian made sure that the man from her street, Samson Segal, was not here this time. If he had been, she would have turned around on the spot. There was no need for him to see her having a second tête-à-tête with a stranger. It did not look like he was there, as far as she could tell at first glance. She could not keep looking, as complaints were already being directed her way.

"Close the door, will you? It's not exactly a warm summer's night out there, darling!"

John Burton came up to her just when she thought she was going to chicken out. She had almost hoped that he had already left, as she was three quarters of an hour late. It flattered her that he had waited, although her stomach knotted up too.

"Nice that you've come," he said. He took her coat and put his hand on her arm while leading her to a little corner table on which stood two glasses of wine. "I hope this table is okay?"

"Yes, of course. I'm sorry I'm so late. We don't leave Becky on her own at home yet, so I had to wait for my husband to get in."

In fact, Tom had come home early. She had told him in the morning that she was meeting Tara, and he had kept to the agreement they had without a grumble. In such cases, he would come home as early as possible, so that Gillian could get away in time.

But she had hummed and hawed. And asked herself why she felt so uncertain. John Burton was her daughter's tennis trainer. He had invited her out for a glass of wine. Not in his house, but in a pub—a public house.

Nothing more to it. It was ridiculous to get so worked up about it.

Tara, whom she had talked to on the phone during her lunch break, to get her alibi set, had hit the nail on the head. "If there's nothing more to it, then why don't you just tell your husband the truth? Why do you need me?"

"Tom might start to imagine something."

"And what are you imagining?"

"Tara...."

Tara had laughed. "Listen, darling. You don't have to justify yourself to me. And you can use me as an excuse for Tom. I don't mind at all if you jump into bed tonight with this dream man. Just don't expect it—an affair—to solve your problems. It might give you a nice thrill. Nothing more."

"I'm not jumping into bed with him!"

Tara did not reply to that, but Gillian understood exactly what people mean when they talk about *eloquent silence.*

In the end, she did go. She did not want to look like a coward. She decided to wear jeans and a sweater, to brush her hair neatly and put on a little lipstick, but other than that she was not made up. Burton was not to think that she was making a great effort for him. In any case, she had to ensure that Tom did not suspect anything. She had never gotten all dolled up to meet Tara.

Once they had sat down, they clinked glasses. "They have surprisingly good wine here. And if you are hungry, we can—"

She immediately interrupted him—she really could not think about eating right now: "No, thank you. A drink is fine."

She took a sip. She liked the wine, but more than anything its soothing effect on her nerves was good. She felt a little more relaxed now.

"How's Becky?" asked John.

Gillian shook her head. "Nothing new. She just doesn't get on well with me right now. When I told her this morning that I was going out tonight, she cheered up. She loves eating supper and watching a bit of TV alone with her dad. I try not to think about it, but it does hurt."

"I think that many girls have a phase where they are very close to their dad. Where their mom is in the way. But that will change again. Suddenly *you'll* be the one she's telling all her secrets to, and her dad won't have a clue what's going on. Then one morning the boy who's just spent the night with his daughter will be coming out of the bathroom, and he'll wonder what else he's missed."

"That all sounds so simple when you talk about it."

John shrugged. "People today seem to make such a drama out of bringing up kids. Sometimes they just need to be given some space."

"Sometimes that can be fatal."

"There's not a single right way to do things," admitted John.

Gillian changed the topic. "By the way, officially I'm spending the evening with my friend Tara right now. I've just told my husband that I'm meeting her."

"You lied to him?"

"Yes."

"I get the impression you don't do that often."

Gillian took a quick gulp of red wine and asked herself why she had said so much. *Just don't start to lead him on, or flirt with him or something like that. It's not you!*

"No. Of course not. But I…just didn't want any hassle."

"He would have minded you meeting me, then. That's clear."

"Wouldn't you mind, if you were in his place?"

"I'm not married. Out of choice. So I don't have to deal with such awkward situations."

"It was just easier to say that I was going out with Tara," said Gillian.

For a while, neither of them said anything. In the end, Gillian asked: "Why did you want to meet me? I mean, our last meeting can't have been any great shakes for you."

"Why not?"

"I was crying, mainly. And I told you a few banal problems. Nothing to write home about."

He looked at her, thinking about what she had just said. "I didn't see you as a woman with banal problems."

"As what, then?"

"As a very attractive woman, who has a few problems. And who *doesn't* have a few problems?"

"I had the impression that you were annoyed."

"I wasn't annoyed. Distracted, maybe. You talked about something I didn't want to talk about."

"Leaving the police."

"Right," he said, and his expression changed.

This time Gillian was smart enough not to push him on it. "You still haven't answered my question," she said. "Why meet me today?"

He smiled. "I have. I did answer it." She waited.

"I just said: you're a very attractive woman," he explained.

"That's why?"

"To be honest—yes."

His directness was disarming. Gillian had to laugh. "I'm married."

"I know."

"And where's this to lead?"

"That's up to you," said John. "After all, you're the one who's married. You have a family. You have to pretend to be meeting a friend to meet me. You have to decide how far you want to go."

"Maybe I just want to finish my wine and then go home."

"Maybe," said John and smiled again.

There was something arrogant about his smile, as if he did not believe that she would just go home. John Burton suddenly seemed like an old hand going through the motions, and she had the feeling that she was being manipulated. He was probably just working through a tried and tested routine, cleverly blowing hot and cold, making indifferent comments one moment and then adding a tempting suave smile at the right time. She thought back to the Christmas party at the tennis club, when the other mothers were puzzling over the good-looking coach's love life. He probably did not have a long-term partner in his life, nor was that what he wanted. He seduced whoever crossed his path and whomever he took a liking to, had a brief affair, and then turned to the next object of his desires.

Gillian was aware that she had no exact idea of what she wanted, but at least it was clear to her at the moment what she did *not* want: to be one more conquest notched up by an attractive Don Juan. She drank the last of her wine and refused another glass.

"Not for me, thanks. Nice to have a chat, John. I think I'll drive home now."

He looked surprised. "Already?"

She stood up. "Yes. I've made my decision."

He also stood up, but she had already grabbed her coat off the hook and was out the door before she had time to put it on. After the stuffy air inside, it was wonderful to feel the fresh air outside. Gillian enjoyed the coolness and the quiet outside. The beach and the river were right in front of her. She saw the deep dark water and heard the quiet gurgling of the waves. She smelled saltwater and seaweed. She slipped into her coat. Suddenly a giant weight fell from her soul. What had she been thinking, coming here?

She had almost reached her car, which was parked along the road, when John appeared behind her. He was slightly out of breath. "Just wait," he said. "Good God, you sprint along!"

"I wasn't waiting for you," said Gillian and opened her car door with the beeper. She wanted to get in the car, but John held her arm.

"What did I do wrong?" he asked.

"In principle, probably nothing," explained Gillian. "It's just—I don't want to."

"What don't you want? To have a drink with me? To talk to me?"

"I don't want to lie to my husband and daughter. I don't want to get into anything that would mean I had to."

"You already lied to your husband today."

"Bad enough. I don't need to do that again."

"Wait," he pleaded. "Please. Don't just get in your car and drive off. I'm sorry if I acted stupid and blasé." He batted away something she was about to say. "No, I did. I wanted to look like a real charmer, and probably that annoyed you. Which is understandable. I'm sorry. There's nothing else I can say. Really. I'm sorry."

"That's all right. It's just…."

"…just that you won't give me a second chance."

"John, you've got to understand—"

"Can we sit in your car for a bit?" he asked. "It's rather cold, and who knows who could hear us here on the street."

"Okay," agreed Gillian. She sat down behind the wheel and John slipped onto the passenger seat.

"I find you fascinating," he said. "And I want to see you again. I'm assuming you've realized that. I know that the circumstances are not ideal. Nevertheless, I just can't get you out of my head. I tried this past weekend. I can't."

"I'm sure there are enough women who can be there to comfort you," said Gillian.

He looked right into her eyes. The expression on his face was utterly serious. And honest. "No," he said. "There aren't. Maybe that doesn't match the rumors about me, but it's true. There are no other women."

"The club's mothers think you're an incorrigible seducer."

"Great. But it's not true. My last relationship finished over a year ago, and since then I've been as celibate as a monk."

"You're hardly rusty when it comes to trying to put the make on a woman."

"If I really was in practice, I would have noticed I was coming across really badly. I've already said sorry, Gillian. I just wanted to look cool. It was idiotic of me."

"You try to act all mysterious."

"What do you want to know? I'll tell you!" It almost

looked like he was begging. "I don't want to hide anything from you, Gillian!"

"Why did you leave the police?"

He crumpled up. He lifted both hands in helplessness. "Oh, God. You're persistent about that, aren't you?"

"I'm interested," said Gillian.

"All right," he said, resigned. "Although probably you'll throw me out of the car right now, when I tell you. And take your daughter out of the club."

"Doesn't sound good."

"No. Eight years ago I was accused of sexual assault. The young woman was an intern working for me. The prosecution dropped the case because there wasn't any evidence. I was never charged. But I couldn't stay there, so I went. Happy now?"

She looked at him, shocked.

4

WHEN SHE TURNED into the drive, a shadow moved across the path to the front door. Tom.

"I heard the car," he explained, "and thought I'd…."

She locked the car. "What?"

"I thought I'd come out to meet you," he said and smiled.

Tom's concern for her was touching. She often had the impression that he would rather be married to their company than to her, and that his second choice would be his tennis club. However, there were moments when she felt the warmth that they had shared years ago and which was still there, hidden under the layers of daily life. Yet just tonight she would rather do without it.

She felt Tom observing her from the side.

What was he seeing? she wondered anxiously. What was he thinking?

Similar thoughts were going through Tom's head. He looked at Gillian with her long, somewhat chaotic hair and the fine silhouette of her face. He saw the woman he had known for over twenty years. He had gotten to know her as a student and soon not been able to imagine living without her. It had been a long time since he had felt her presence as intensely as he did this evening. He had felt a sudden uneasiness, which had driven him out of his warm living room into the cold when he thought he heard the engine of their car.

Worried, he wondered why he had been uneasy.

Gillian had been nineteen when she started college, and she had fascinated him from the first moment he saw her. She was different from the other girls—not only because of her eye-catching wild hair. There was also something old-fashioned about her that made her stand out. Gillian was the only child of overly protective parents who had warned her throughout her childhood and youth of the many dangers of the big bad world. Her time at college gave her the feeling of freedom for the first time. She had chosen Glasgow, although she was from Norwich. One single thought had been decisive in her choice, as she later once admitted to Tom: to put enough distance between her parents and herself so her mother could not conveniently come swooping in to check on her.

Gillian had seemed unsure of herself, often hesitant and inexperienced, but the joy she took in life could be felt behind her shyness. Until college, her mother had managed to keep such a good eye on her that no man had ever managed to be alone with her. This behavior by her mother had also undermined her self-confidence.

Most girls had steady boyfriends by the time they were sixteen.

She had no idea whether she even made an impression on men, let alone *what* impression.

But then Tom had come along and pretty much laid siege until she surrendered. Very soon, they were an item. Suddenly Gillian blossomed—not just because of this good-looking young man, the university's star tennis player, but also because she discovered her own strength and what she was capable of. She realized that in spite of her mother's warnings, life was not so much threatening as it was an exciting challenge. She was loved by her fellow students and her teachers, got good grades, and danced away the nights on the weekends. When she got a summer job at a film-production company after graduation, the company did not want to let her go. They offered her a permanent contract and gave her real responsibility. After a little while, she was in charge of all the budgeting for their projects. Gillian seemed to be aglow at that time.

That's changed, thought Tom. And maybe that's why I'm worried. She doesn't glow any more. She doesn't beam.

"And how was it with Tara?" he asked when they had stepped inside. "You went to the pub, didn't you?"

"Yes, why?"

"I can smell it. You're back rather early, aren't you?"

After saying goodbye to John quickly, she had driven to a car park near Becky's school and waited there for quite a while, so as not to return all too soon after leaving. For a moment, she had been tempted to drive to Tara and discuss the disturbing news with her, although that would have meant driving to London. But she had decided for herself that her friend was the wrong person to talk to. In her friend's eyes there would be no mitigating factor for John Burton. Gillian would not be given any peace until she took Becky out of the club. Tara was a lawyer. The fact that proceedings had been dropped and he had not been charged would not have made any difference to her. She knew only too many cases that had a *lack of evidence.*

When Gillian got too cold in the car park, she had started for home, but it was still unusually early for an evening with Tara.

"Tara had someone else to meet," she quickly explained. "You know, she never really has time. We just had a quick chat halfway between here and London."

"I understand," Tom said. He looked at Gillian in the bright light of the hallway. "You look tense. Is everything okay?"

"Of course. Just…well, Tara's work stories can sometimes get on my nerves."

"I don't understand why Tara, of all people—" Tom started to say, but she interrupted him before he could start criticizing her friendship with Tara again.

"Is Becky asleep?"

"She went to bed twenty minutes ago, and I just looked in on her and she's already asleep. Holding Chuck, of course. She's always been so complaisant."

Of course. There were never any problems between Becky and him. The problems were all kept for Gillian.

"We ordered pizza," Tom carried on.

"And ate it watching TV. You know how she likes that—eating it right from the box, sitting on the floor."

She realized she had sounded much sharper than she had intended.

"I wasn't criticizing you, Gillian. Of course this is an

exception. But I'm not often here with Becky on my own and when I am, we can do something special."

She did not herself know what had got into her. Tom was right. Nor did she in any way begrudge him and Becky a lazy evening with pizza and television. She was a grown woman, and it was probably ridiculous for her to feel jealous and unfairly treated. It was not fair, and yet it was probably normal in many families: Tom was the father who rarely had time; but when he did have time, he would turn a blind eye to the usual rules and do something silly with his daughter, which she loved enormously. As the mother, Gillian had to care much more for her daughter and make herself unpopular by putting salad and vegetables on the table, insisting that her daughter do her homework and nagging her when her bedroom started to turn into an impenetrable mess. Her daughter was only annoyed with her, while her boundless admiration was reserved for Tom.

"Maybe I should go to London every day," she said out of the blue. "And work more. Maybe that would do me good."

Tom looked at her in surprise. "I certainly wouldn't mind. You are brilliant at your work. It would be great to have you around in the office more. But then Becky—"

"Becky could do with being alone more. She often feels that I smother her too much as it is. I should let go a bit. I always blamed my parents for hampering me by being so protective—and maybe I'm making the same mistake they did."

"Becky is only twelve," Tom reminded her. "Kids that age can overestimate what they can do."

He went into the living room, stood at the window, and looked out into the darkness. What he saw was mainly the reflection of the room. "Perhaps we should just give it a try," he said.

She followed him in, after she had taken off her boots. "She wants me to trust her more. And I don't want to just ignore that."

He turned toward her. She could see how tired he was, how worn out. At the same time, he was full of a thirst for action. No doubt he would have most liked to be on the tennis court, firing shots over the net that his opponent could not return. In the last few years, he had found it increasingly difficult to turn his revved-up inner engine off after work. It was as if he was constantly pumped up with adrenaline. Running his own business had triggered this development in him. He had lost control over his rpm. He acted as if he was taking stimulants, which was not the case, Gillian knew. He put himself in this state. Gillian regularly asked him to go to a doctor about it. She was afraid he was heading for a heart attack; he certainly had a check mark in all the right boxes for one.

"My heart is fine," he would say whenever she mentioned a doctor.

As if he would know. In all the time she had known him, he had gone out of his way to avoid anything resembling a doctor's office.

She went up to him and put her hand gently on his arm. "It will all be okay again," she said.

"Of course," said Tom.

He did not know exactly what she was talking about, but he had the impression that she was no longer talking about Becky but about something else. It had something to do with the distance between them and the fact that Gillian's eyes no longer shone. With the fact that he worked too much and was fanatical about his tennis and did not spend enough time with his wife. Gillian had never criticized his excessive overtime. After all, his company was hers too, and she saw the problems everyone had since the world had plunged into the worst recession since the 1920s. She was not a woman to moan because her husband fought with all his strength to maintain what they had built up. On some level, she even understood why he played sports so much, realizing that it was a valve to regulate the terrible pressure that he would not otherwise have been able to bear.

But she did not understand why he was no longer really with her. Not even with her when he lay next to her in bed. And that made her suffer.

He himself did not understand. He loved Gillian. He knew exactly when he had realized that he wanted to marry her and that there would never be another for him. During their student days, they had gone hiking in the Highlands one autumn weekend. They had a tent and cooking utensils. It had been glorious sunny weather. All around them was the overwhelming solitude and expanse of the high moors. The hills covered in heather had shone a luscious lilac. In the evenings they had lit a campfire and later snuggled up together in a sleeping bag and warmed each other when the temperature suddenly dipped. When they crawled out the next morning, the weather had changed. It was so misty that they could not even see the tips of their noses. They started to walk back. Climbing up a steep rocky slope, Tom had suddenly slipped and fallen so badly that he—as they later found out—fractured some bones in his foot. Lying on the loose stones in the mist, half unconscious with pain, he had to throw up and felt light-headed. He had no idea how they were going to get out of this deserted spot and make their way back to the car park where they had left his old beater. Gillian had been given the fright of her life, but she did not collapse in tears or sink into a horrified helplessness. She made a splint from branches and gauze bandages to stop his ankle from moving. She shouldered the heavy tent and helped Tom get up. Then she supported him, this man almost six foot three, as they walked along narrow paths, through valleys where the humidity hovered in the air, and over rocky heights where the cold cut through them like a knife. She pepped him up when his pain became unbearable, whispering encouragement, and although a time came when she could barely stand up anymore from exhaustion and the weight that she was bearing, she just kept doggedly on, gritting her teeth and not letting anything distract her.

Back then he had thought: I'll never let her go.

It was not just that she had saved him. She had also revealed her true nature to him: her strength. Her determination to do the things that had to be done.

They had married while they were both still in college.

His feelings had not changed in all the intervening years, at least not at the deepest level. He knew that. Gillian was still the woman he loved, the woman he trusted absolutely. His anchor, his companion. But to show her, he would have had to pause in his scramble to keep the business going for a moment, and he could not manage that. He could not stand still, take a breath, and be the old Thomas again. Life had made him a driven person. He was unable to slow down. He literally did not know how.

"I love you, Gillian," he said quietly.

The rapt admiration he felt looking at her was almost painful. Was it really such a long time since the phrase had last passed his lips?

"I love you too," she said.

He scrutinized her face. She seemed different to him. Something had happened in her, happened in her life, and he did not know what it was.

"I have to tell you something," she began out of the blue. "Today I...."

She hesitated.

Tom looked at her enquiringly. "Yes?"

"Oh, nothing," said Gillian. "Doesn't matter."

An hour and a half before, sitting in the car with John Burton, she had not known what to say after hearing his confession. For minutes, she just sat there dumbfounded. John had fished an old crumpled-up receipt from the glove compartment, taken a pencil from his jacket pocket, and scribbled a number on the scrap of paper.

"Here. My cell-phone number. I won't bother you, but if you want to talk to me, you can call me any time. I've told you what you wanted to know, and maybe you want to find out more or just talk about something else. I don't mind. Just call me if you feel like it." With these words, he got out and disappeared into the darkness outside. It was only later that Gillian realized that she now held the reins. She could call him. She could also try to forget the whole incident.

"Sure?" asked Tom. "Are you sure it doesn't matter?" She nodded.

"Time for bed," she said.

Thursday, December 10

"IT WON'T BE easy to find a buyer for the property," explained the real estate agent. His name was Luke Palm, and in fact he lived in London. Anne had gotten in touch with him on a friend's recommendation. He had come to Tunbridge Wells immediately and come out to the woods. The property market was not exactly booming. As a real estate agent, he would take what there was, even if it meant he had to drive a good distance.

Now in Anne's kitchen, looking around, it was obvious how impressed he was. He had probably not expected to find the old house decorated in such a beautiful and cozy way. Anne felt an almost childish pride, a deep joy, as she always did when guests toured the house for the first time and showed their astonishment. Sean and she had achieved a lot. People valued their ideas, the hard work they had put into the house, and their dedication. The recognition did her good. She just wished that Sean could have been there to bask in the glory too.

"But I have to say," he continued, "you've turned it into a *gem* of a place!"

"It was my husband's dream to buy and refurbish the house," Anne said. "We invested a lot of love and energy in it."

"That's easy to see. And yet…the location…."

"I know," said Anne. After all, there was a reason why she wanted to relinquish this little piece of paradise. "It's far from everything. That's why I want to sell.

My husband and I wanted to spend our old age here, but now I'm alone and…have the feeling that I'm becoming isolated." She still felt the need to justify her step, even to this stranger. Although probably she was saying it for her own benefit. She had not wavered since making her decision the night before last. She was still completely convinced that she was doing the right thing. However, there was a world of difference between planning something in theory and actually taking the first steps toward the realization of the plan.

"I couldn't live here on my own either," agreed Luke immediately. "I think you're making the right choice. It's also not necessarily safe to be out here in the woods on your own."

"What do you mean?" asked Anne. She had not mentioned anything about the headlight beams in the night, about the car and her feeling of being watched.

"Well, out here it would take people a while to realize if anything happened to you. You could fall and be lying on the stairs with a broken leg, unable to reach the phone. There are no neighbors to hear you if you shout."

"Oh, that's what you mean," said Anne and relaxed.

"Apart from the fact that there are enough odd characters wandering around in this world," he continued. "Out here, even I would feel frightened now and again, I expect."

Anne immediately felt uneasy again. As long as she was still living here, she would have preferred to be told that it was utterly silly to be worried. That the probability that there was a criminal out there, targeting helpless women, was one in a million, and that her hysteria was groundless. There was something unpleasant about the fact that everyone seemed to understand her fear. Even the friend she had called to ask about the real estate agent had immediately replied: "I'm so relieved, Anne, that you're no longer going to be out there in the woods on a platter for whoever wants to mug and murder you!"

Thank you, Anne wanted to say. Until I find somewhere else to stay, your words will no doubt ensure that I sleep peacefully.

"This house is right for a large family," said Luke Palm. "Or for people with lots of pets. Or who want an alternative way of living or so on. It's a dream for a drop-out!"

Walking around, he had made lots of notes and taken some photos. He said he would write up all the details. "As soon as interested people get in touch, I'll let you know. There will of course be some viewing…."

"That's not a problem," said Anne. "I tend to be home. Just give me a call first."

They said goodbye to each other. The real estate agent was content and confident. He had feared that he would find some godforsaken hole, and instead he now had a treasure on his hands. As he stepped outside, snowflakes whirled around in the dark. Evening had come. The wind sighed in the top branches of the trees.

"You're a brave woman," he said as he left. "Just make sure you bolt your doors."

"I do. But I'm hard as nails; I'll be fine." She watched him as he disappeared between the bushes that surrounded the path. She had put on a show of being braver than she felt. The previous night, she had not seen lights or heard the noise of an engine—and yet, strangely, that did not let her breathe more easily. She almost felt more *un*easy. She didn't believe that she had imagined it all, nor did she assume that it would all somehow blow over. Instead, it seemed to her as if something was waiting out there. She could not define this *something* at all, and she had no idea what the point of the waiting was. But she felt that she was in danger, and the consciousness of it made her see her familiar surroundings in a completely new light. It was as if the trees were crowding in on her. As if the moaning of the bare branches in the wind had taken on a threatening tone. As if floorboards that she had never heard before had now started to creak. As if the world full of people had retreated further away from her.

She carefully bolted the front door and went back to the kitchen, which was brightly lit. There were candles on the table, and she had hung Christmas lights around the window. From outside, her house with its lights and Christmas decorations must look warm and cozy; but who would be out there anyway?

She pushed aside the thought. That was just what she did not want to think about: about who could see inside.

She put the kettle on and turned to the brochures that Luke Palm had left for her. Apartments for sale in London. She was excited.

"I've got some great options for you," he had said. "Bright, spacious apartments. With beautiful, sunny balconies. Just take a look when you're ready. We can meet as early as next week to view them." My first really independent step, she thought and looked contemplatively at the glossy sheets in front of her. She had been twenty-six when she and Sean married. From then on, they had decided everything together. Her whole life, she had needed to come to a compromise with another person. And now she was going to rent an apartment. Her personal dream apartment, in her own dream location. And she would decorate it just as she saw fit.

She suddenly felt more exhilarated than she had for ages. For the first time since Sean's death, she was gripped by an almost forgotten desire to get going, by a happy expectation and excitement.

She poured the tea and lit the candles. It was going to be a wonderful evening. She would plan her future, look at photos, study floor plans, drink tea, and, perhaps later to celebrate the new start, have a glass of sparkling wine.

She sat down at the table.

And at that moment she heard the noise.

The wood outside and the house were always full of noises, but long ago Anne had filed them away in a separate level of her consciousness. She knew the creaking of the roof timbers, the glugging of the heating pipes, the wind rustling in the trees, and the sounds that the animals outside made. But this noise was different, and it made her jump.

It sounded as though someone was on the deck outside the kitchen.

Her first thought was that Mr. Palm might have forgotten something and come back, but then there was no reason why he would not have rung the doorbell at the front door.

Anxiously, she peered through the panes. It was pitch-black outside and bright inside. She could only see her kitchen, the candles, the pot of tea, and a woman sitting at the table with her eyes wide open.

Why had she not closed the shutters when the real estate agent was still nearby, before she was so desperately alone here?

Why had she not packed her things long ago and stayed at a friend's house or a hotel in the city?

She got up, holding her breath and listening for noises outside. She could not hear anything, apart from the usual noises.

Perhaps I was just imagining it, she thought. My nerves are all shot.

It was vital that she close the shutters. Then she would feel safe. Anyone trying to break in would need a lot of strength and time to break the shutters. That would be noisy too. The only thing was that Anne would have to open the door to the deck and step outside in order to unhook the shutters from the wall.

Don't act like a hysterical old woman, she admonished herself. You heard an unusual noise. At least, that's what you imagined. Maybe it wasn't anything at all. Even now you can't really remember how it sounded. You are going slowly mad out here. You can't afford to let that happen. So go outside and close the damn shutters!

You didn't just hear some noise or other. You heard a car. Often. In the middle of the night. Something's not right here. It's got nothing to do with hysteria and a wild imagination!

She ignored her inner voice.

She had to close the shutters. Then she could think about all the unusual things that had been happening recently. She could give in to her fear and all her gruesome imaginings, once she was safe. For now she could not let herself be paralyzed.

She opened the door determinedly. It was snowing more heavily now. A thin white carpet of snow lay on the grass in the yard. And on the steps that led down from the deck.

She stared at the steps.

Her brain was working strangely slowly. There were footprints in the snow. Big, clumping footprints. Someone in winter boots had stomped up the steps. Not her. She had not used the steps all day. She had been in the yard with Luke Palm, but they had gone around from the front of the house. And the snow was just starting to settle now.

Someone must have been here just now. Sometime in the last ten minutes.

A shadow appeared by the wall. Anne saw it from the corner of her eye. In what felt like slow motion to her, she turned around. She saw a thick parka and a woolly cap pulled down low over a forehead.

In a strangely analytical way, she thought: there's no explanation why someone would be here on my deck in the dark.

At least, no explanation that seemed harmless to her.

She understood that the last thing she should have done was to go outside.

Saturday, December 12

1

SATURDAY, DECEMBER 12, 7: 05 P.M.

Millie and Gavin were downstairs watching the news. Millie has already gotten dressed. Coat, boots. She has the night shift at the care home and has to go in half an hour. She is in a correspondingly bad mood. The evening meal was unbearable. She is always as irritable as a pit bull when she has to work, but on the weekends it is even worse.

During the meal, I was the lightning rod again, of course.

When I helped myself to a second portion of fries, she asked when I was next planning on contributing to the household kitty. The few pennies from last week had been spent long ago. She stared at me as if she were ready to pounce. She said that I got "support," after all.

"You write applications regularly, don't you?" she asked. "And you try to get a job? So you must be getting money!"

"Of course," I lied. I blushed, but as that always happens to me when I say something, it did not attract attention.

I'm worried that she can smell it. Millie is a bitch, but she's not stupid. I'm out and about too much. She's been wondering for ages what I'm up to. She is hardly going to believe that I go from door to door asking for work.

It would be good if I could hang around at home for a few days—just as Millie expects of an unemployed person.

But I can't. I'd go mad.

Money's getting tight. I never buy anything for myself, but I have to pay my share of the food, heating, electricity, and water, and my few savings are evaporating. I even scrounged off Bartek last night in the Halfway House. He complained a little—he's a bit hard up now too: his fiancée seems to be pretty demanding and expensive—but he gave me fifty pounds in the end. I made a big gesture at dinner of getting it out and passing it to Millie.

"Is that enough for now?" I asked, and she nodded, looking confused. It didn't exactly make her less suspicious of me, but she had lost her attacking momentum and she couldn't quickly figure out how to get at me.

As usual, Gavin didn't say anything. He nibbled at his food and hoped that the situation wouldn't escalate.

At lunchtime I saw Gillian, Tom, and Becky. It looked like they were about to go on a walk. I was standing right in front of their house when they came out, so I had to say hi. I had not exactly managed to blend into the background, but I hope they didn't think anything else of it. Perhaps they hadn't noticed that I'd been standing there for some time. Perhaps they thought I had just chanced by. In any case, they said hi back in such a distracted manner that I obviously didn't need to worry. Nevertheless, I resolved to be more careful. These short dark days in December can lead to carelessness, because the twilight lets you feel protected. But you are more visible than you think and what's more, there is still some light. There is daylight, even if it's murky. The summer is as distant as it can be.

At first glance, the Wards appeared to be the happy, intact family that I first saw them as. They were wearing parkas, boots, and brightly colored woolen caps, and you might have thought that they were all looking forward to their outing. But by now I had learned to look more carefully. Something isn't right with the family. Thomas Ward looks terrible. His face is gray. He looks exhausted and at the same time wide awake in an unhealthy way. Too much awake. His whole body is always jiggling. That can't be healthy in the long term.

Becky looks like a teenager in a bad mood. She doesn't exactly look happy, but instinctively I would say that there is no really serious or dramatic tragedy lurking in her. Growing up is difficult. I know that only too well.

On the other hand, Gillian really worries me. It's not that she looks as tired as her husband. You wouldn't be worried about her health. Nor is she just grumpy like her daughter. She is...perhaps the best description would be "restless," although that's not quite it either. "Restless" sounds too weak. She is tense, nervous, excitable. To me she's like someone who is torn inside, and I ask myself: why? What in her life has torn her in two?

She flashes a smile at me without any real warmth. She doesn't really know me. She doesn't know how heavily she features in my thoughts, in my daydreams, and how deep in my unconscious she is at night. How I wish I were near her. Not that I want to destroy her family! Every family is sacred to me. I find it terrible how quickly people today separate, divorce, and plunge into another relationship. As if marriage were some pretty little staging post which you leave when things are not all that *great. That's why I would never try to woo a married woman. I would despise myself just for considering it.*

I just want to be a part of Gillian's life. Of her family. It's a longing to experience something that I myself will never have. I will never manage to start a family. I'll never marry or be a father. I've known that for ages, even when my friend Bartek never gives up hope and yesterday started talking about Internet dating again. It just won't work. I can't do any more than observe other people.

I watched them as they drove off. I stood there in the cold, as the occasional flurry of snow fell, and felt how I went very cold inside too. That had to do with the Wards. Something was going to happen. I could feel it clearly. I can still feel it now.

Then I carried on with my usual rounds, but I couldn't concentrate on it. There was this intense feeling of impending doom…. I'm no clairvoyant, but I sense things. I suddenly remembered the guy who had been in the pub with Gillian. I can't figure it out yet, but I didn't like the guy. Somehow he was part of the whole unfortunate situation that seems to hover now over the family.

Downstairs, the front door lock clicks into place. I hear Millie's steps on the path in front. Angry, energetic steps. She could have closed the door more gently, too. I expect she and Gavin had another fight.

I also expect it was about me.

Perhaps I really should move out. I make Gavin's life difficult and mine too. It's terrible to be so unwanted. At the end of the day, it would be better to be on my own.

Best of all would be not to be myself at all. But someone else entirely.

2

SHE DIALED HIS number before she could lose her nerve. It was after ten in the evening, but she guessed that John was not the kind of person to go to bed early. And the time was not the issue here. The big issue was that she was calling at all. That she was calling a man who had told her how much she fascinated him.

Who was clearly looking to have an affair with her. While she was clearly married.

Tom had gone to bed early. She could hear that the television was on—some sports program or other. They had all gone over to Windsor for the day. They had gone for a long walk and drunk coffee in a country pub. When they had come home, they were in good spirits and had color in their cheeks. Gillian baked garlic baguettes and ate with her family that evening. Afterward, Becky was determined to watch *Twilight* on DVD..Gillian sat down with her in the living room and tried to understand why her daughter and all her daughter's friends were so addicted to this film. The walk that afternoon in the cold air had made Becky tired. At some point, she fell asleep and cuddled up to her mother. Gillian stroked her fingers. It was what she had always done when Becky was small. Becky breathed in and out gently, looking as sweet and rosy as a little girl.

Gillian, who had not been looking at Edward and Bella on the screen for a long time, considered her daughter's peaceful and tender face. Its usual stubborn, angry look had completely gone.

How I love her, she thought.

However, it did not leave her any less restless.

She finally took her drowsy daughter up to bed, carefully tucked her in, which Becky actually permitted, and then went back down to the living room. After two glasses of wine, she felt a little more relaxed. As she rarely drank, a little had quite an effect, and two glasses of wine was almost too much.

The receipt on which John had written down his number was in her jeans pocket. She took it out, fetched the cordless phone from its docking station in the hall, and went back to the living room.

A call is nothing earth-shattering, she reassured herself.

He picked up after the third ring. Gillian could hear voices in the background, as well as laughter and the clatter of glasses.

"It's me. Gillian."

"God," said John. "I was afraid you wouldn't get in touch again." He seemed to have really been waiting for her to call.

"I think I overreacted a little the last time we met. I didn't…want to leave it like that."

"Overreacted in which way?"

"I shouldn't just have gotten up and left. I'm afraid the situation just got the better of me."

The laughter in the background got louder. "Where are you?" asked Gillian.

"In the Halfway House. We had a tournament at the club, and then I popped in here. Can you come? I'm sitting all on my own at a table, consoling myself with a little too much whiskey."

Gillian realized with some astonishment how happy and relieved she was to hear that he was there on his own.

"I can't just come like that tonight."

"When can you come?" asked John.

She laughed. "How do you know that I want to meet you?"

He did not respond as if it were a joke. "You just said: *not just like that tonight.* That sounded to me as if it was a question of timing. Not a complete *No.*"

"You're right." She thought for a moment. "I'd just like to talk. I was shocked when you told me you'd had to leave your job. I'd like to know more about that."

"Just tell me when."

"Next Thursday, Becky has been invited to stay the night for a friend's birthday party. My husband has a meeting at his tennis club. I'm free."

"Thursday? That's almost a week away."

"I know." *Enough opportunity to think twice about this.*

"Okay. 'Take it or leave it.' It looks like it's my only option. Fine. Thursday. Do you want to come to me?"

"To your house?"

"Why not?"

She did not want to look silly. Or stuck-up or traditional. "Well, all right. Do you live in London?"

He gave her an address in Stratford, and she scribbled it down next to his phone number on the receipt.

"So, see you then," she said.

"Looking forward to it," said John.

Thursday, December 17

1

LUKE PALM WAS thirty-eight years old. He had worked for the last eight years as an independent real estate agent. One of his principles was to avoid hassling his clients. Of course he knew the cliché of the smarmy, pushy real estate agent who would keep on at people until they ended up buying properties they had never wanted to buy. Properties whose shortcomings the buyers failed to see, swept along by the unscrupulous agent's eloquent words. He had never wanted to be like that. He had made it a point to be different. He'd been rewarded with success. He had the enviable reputation of being honest and serious. People were happy to trust him.

Anne Westley had also come to him through the recommendation of one of her friends. She was a lovely and clever old lady. He had immediately found a rapport with her. Of course, he was lucky to have a client like her. Not only did she want to sell a house, but she was also looking for an apartment. He would earn two commissions with her. So it was natural that he would make every effort to help her.

He had tried to reach her many times over the past week, but had only gotten as far as her answering machine each time. He had asked her to phone him back as soon as she could, but she never did. He wanted to tell her that he had been doubly successful. He had found potential buyers for her house in the woods, and an enchanting apartment in Belgravia in central London had just entered his portfolio. He was sure it was perfect for her. For both, he wanted to arrange viewings before Christmas.

He could not understand why she was not getting back to him. She had seemed so interested, so determined to finally escape her dubious idyll in the woods. Luke could understand that only too well. It was an enchanting property in its way, for sure, but he would not have been able to stand more than a couple of days there.

The couple that had shown interest had five children and many pets. Luke Palm was convinced that he was offering the family their ideal home. He was getting increasingly nervous because he could not put them in touch with Anne.

He was getting worried.

That Thursday, he had called several times. Each time: just the answering machine. He had not left another message. There must already be five or six identical messages from him. But he started to wonder whether he shouldn't go against his principle of never bothering a client.

He toyed with the idea of doing just that. Of just driving out there to talk to Anne Westley. To find out exactly what was happening.

It was mid-afternoon. He did not have any more appointments, just paperwork. He could do that at home later. He did want to go home and get some deskwork done for a few hours, but he hesitated. Maybe he should drive out to Tunbridge Wells and see Anne right away. He had an uneasy feeling. She was so alone out there. Of course it was possible that she had let drop her plan to move, but he felt that she would have told him. She would not just have disappeared on him like this.

Luke Palm looked at his watch. Just after three. Outside, it was snowing more and more heavily. In the last week, it had snowed a few times, but the snow had quickly melted each time. Now winter was really coming, and everyone was hoping for a white Christmas.

The meteorologists had forecast an extremely heavy snowfall for that evening; but, as Luke did not intend to stay long, he hoped he would be home by then. He just wanted to see her briefly, to reassure himself that everything was fine, and to tell her that there were people interested in viewing her house.

He set off at twenty past three.

The start of the snowfall had triggered the usual hysteria among drivers, so it took him longer than normal to get out of town. It was almost five when he reached the small car park for visitors to the woods near Tunbridge Wells. There was not a single car there. After deliberating briefly, he decided to leave his car there and walk the final stretch on foot. The snow was falling more heavily now, and he did not trust the dirt track leading to Anne Westley's house; he did not like the thought of getting stuck and having to dig his car out.

It was already getting dark. In this wood with its high trees, there was even less light. Luke trudged up the narrow track. It had a romantic Christmassy atmosphere, but was also threatening somehow. The snow made everything so quiet. Peacefully quiet? Or as if you were holding your breath? He did not know. He asked himself again how someone could bear to live like this.

And suddenly he thought with some annoyance that he shouldn't have done that. Westley. Dragged his wife out here to fulfill his own dreams. You can't do that to someone else!

Not that Anne had complained. But Luke Palm was good at reading between the lines. He had understood from what she said that it was her husband who had followed his desires, and that it had not been easy for Anne to follow him. Only her loyalty to him, even beyond the grave, had kept her here until now.

The track led into the clearing in which the house stood. Everything looked the same as it always had. If anything, it looked even more enchanting, with the flakes swirling around and all the trees and bushes as if under a layer of sugar icing. A Christmas fairytale.

I hope she doesn't mind my just turning up like this, thought Luke.

There was not a single light on in the house, but he could see Anne's car, so she must be home. She could hardly get out without her car.

He opened the gate and went up the path between the high bushes. Lilac probably, jasmine in between. The yard must be idyllic in spring and summer. Just that anything could happen out here, and no one would know.

He went up the steps to the front door and rang the bell. He waited.

Nothing.

Of course she could have gone for a walk, to get some fresh air. She did not need her car for that. Actually quite possible. Luke could not have said why he did not believe that. Why instead he was increasingly feeling that this was a dangerous situation. It was so damn isolated here! If he had been crazy enough to live all on his own out here, he would have had at least two mean Dobermans. And as for a woman who was almost seventy, living all on her own here…. Somehow it almost seemed like she was tempting fate.

Rubbish. No doubt he was making a mountain out of a molehill. She had probably just gone into the woods with an axe to cut down a Christmas tree, while he was imagining all sorts of gruesome scenarios in which she fell victim to a cold-blooded killer.

Nevertheless, he decided to just look around the back of the house too. From his previous visit, he knew there was a deck and a second entrance there that led into the kitchen.

He went around the side of the house. In spite of the quickly dwindling daylight, he could see immediately that the door was wide open. On the steps up to the door and on the exposed part of the deck, the snow had started to pile up. Virgin snow. Although the door was open, it was obvious that no one had come in here in the last few hours.

He stopped and could hear his own breath. It was not looking good. Anne must be home, so why were the lights not on? He remembered the Christmas lights that had given the kitchen some cheer on his last visit. This time, not a single light was on.

And now he was sure. The calm around him was not the same as peace. It was an evil lurking thing, hiding a fearful secret.

He felt for his cell phone, but realized he had left it in his car. He really wanted to turn around and run back to the car park, but he forced himself to pause. He had to see what had happened. Perhaps Anne Westley had had a nasty fall and was lying somewhere in the house, unable to move. A life-and-death situation.

If so, why is the door open?

He slowly climbed the steps. He wished it would stay

light for longer. The approaching darkness only made it all worse.

He called out, quietly, "Hello? Is anyone in? It's me, Luke Palm!" There was no reply.

He stepped into the kitchen, which was no warmer than outside. The door must have been open for ages. He felt for a light switch, found one, and, turning the light on, jumped at the sudden brightness cutting through the dark.

He looked around.

Apart from the fact that the walls were cold, the kitchen looked as though it had been left just minutes earlier. A half-full pot of tea and a mug stood on the table. On the table he saw the open brochures he had given Anne on his last visit. Next to them were candles that had burned down to their candleholders. In the sink, dirty dishes piled up. Luke's gaze fell on the tear-off calendar. It was still showing December 10— last Thursday. The day he had looked at the house. No one had torn off a page since then.

He looked at the Christmas lights with growing anxiety. Their wires had been pulled out of the sockets. It looked to him as if it had happened suddenly, as one of the chains of lights had slipped off the window and was wrapped lifelessly around the coffee machine. "Something's not right at all here," said Luke. Hearing his own voice made him feel a little better.

He crossed the kitchen, stepped into the hall, and turned its light on too.

"Mrs. Westley?" he called out in a whisper, simultaneously wondering why he was keeping so quiet. He knew the reason. He was afraid that instead of an accident, something much worse had taken place out here. And that perhaps the person behind it all had not gone

far. That he was still here—either in the dark old house
or in the woods surrounding it.

He really should just get out of there. But first he had
to find Anne. If he just ran away now, he would never
be able to look himself in the face again.

He wondered if it had been a mistake to turn on all
the lights. They broadcast all around that he was there.
But how else was he to see anything? He cursed his
bright idea in coming out here. He could have been at
his desk long ago, with a nice cup of coffee. Instead....

A quick glance out of the living room window showed
him that the snow had started to fall more strongly. To
top it all, he would find it difficult to get his car out of
the car park.

He climbed the stairs. Halfway up, he noticed the
strange smell for the first time.

"Bloody hell," he said out loud.

He was under no illusions. It was the smell of rotting flesh.

He found Anne Westley in the bathroom next to her
bedroom. The old lady was lying on the shower mat in
front of the shower. Her wide-eyed gaze was fixed on
the ceiling above her. Something was stuck in her wide-
open mouth. It was checkered. A cloth or a scarf. Luke
could not tell exactly. Her nose was taped over. Her
wrists and ankles were tied together with the masking
tape too. It was all too clear that Anne had not had an
accident: she had been murdered in a brutal way. Her
killer had suffocated her by blocking off her nose and
mouth. She must have fought hard against the cloth in
her throat—desperately, but in vain.

It might have happened on December 10. In any case,
that was what he inferred from the calendar's date. After

he had left that evening. After he had advised her to lock her door well.

Luke Palm sank down next to the bathtub because he had lost all strength in his legs. For a moment he felt faint and thought he might end up on the floor next to Anne. He broke out in a cold sweat all over his body and on his face. He cradled his head in his hands, trying not to look at the dead woman or to notice the smell. And yet trying to breathe deeply.

His dizzy spell passed.

He raised his head. He saw that the handle of the bathroom door was hanging down at an odd angle and that the lock fitting was out of place. It looked as though someone had broken open the lock.

He groaned quietly as he realized what had probably happened. However Anne's killer had gotten into the house, Anne had obviously managed to get away from him at first and escape into the bathroom, which was a room she could lock. But her pursuer had not given up. He had broken the lock and gotten into the bathroom.

Anne must have felt terrible fear. She was locked in the little room without any way to call 999 or to scream out the window for help. Who would have heard her? And at some point she would have realized that the other person was going to win. That the door was not going to keep him out.

Luke stood up, hoping that his wobbly legs would carry him. He had to call the police. Hopefully the phone was working. As he remembered, it was in the living room. He was still afraid, but he told himself that in all probability Anne had been lying dead for a week and that it was unlikely that her killer was still around. He managed to think calmly and rationally about the situation, although deep down he was surprised at his calm. Only later did he realize that he must have been in shock.

As he crept downstairs he murmured the emergency number to himself, "Nine-nine-nine, nine-nine-nine."

He must not forget that number now.

2

"I MADE A stupid mistake," said John. "In the months that followed, I could have slapped myself for it every day. I was an idiot. She was a student at Hendon Police College. I was a detective inspector with the Met. She was doing an internship with me. No way should I have started something."

Outside, the snow was falling more and more thickly. It looked as though the world was going under. Even here in the center of London, all sounds were muffled. An almost-festive silence hung in the air.

John's bedroom in the spacious but sparsely furnished apartment in Stratford contained a wardrobe and a mattress on the floor. There were no curtains in the windows, no carpet on the floor. A few magazines lay scattered on the wooden floor. In the corner there was a half-drunk bottle of mineral water.

Gillian had thrown back the cover because she was too warm, even though the heating only gave out a little heat. She felt peaceful and relaxed, although she knew that she was getting herself into a heap of problems. One of them, and perhaps the most urgent, was the issue of whether she would manage to get back home, and be there before Tom, now that the snow was falling so heavily. Less urgent, but of long-term significance, was the situation she had gotten herself into: she had started an affair with another man. It was unlikely that this would not lead to one difficulty after another.

After spending so long considering, doubting, and worrying about this meeting for the last week, everything had happened so quickly and inevitably in the end. She had rung John's doorbell and he had opened the door immediately, taken her hand and led her in. He had looked happy and relieved to see her.

"Until right now, I was afraid you weren't coming."

"I couldn't do anything else," Gillian said. She had thought again and again that she would cancel and let the whole adventure evaporate, but now she realized that she had never really had the chance to do that. She was already in it far deeper than she had thought.

He was still holding on to her hand. "Would you like a coffee?"

"Afterward," she said. In the next moment she thought: Oh God, Gillian, you didn't really say that! All your friends would be shocked. It's even embarrassing to you.

He looked puzzled, then he raised his eyebrows. "Okay," he said. "Afterward, then."

He helped her out of her coat and then went to his spartanly decorated bedroom with her. Gillian had not had sex for almost a year. Suddenly she regretted nothing so much as her brazen insistence on going to bed with John immediately. No doubt she would be completely inept.

"Maybe…I *would* prefer a coffee," she murmured.

He smiled. "As you wish."

She took a step backward. Why did she always become someone different than who she was, when she was around him? She flirted, provoked him, went on the attack, giving him the come-on. And then she retreated and felt ridiculous.

"I don't know. I don't know what I want." He looked at her expectantly.

"I'm not like that," Gillian continued. "I mean, not like you've seen me. When I'm with you, I always say and do things that don't suit me. I'm a stranger to myself. I don't know why."

He stretched out an arm. Gently he drew a line with his finger from her chin, over her neck, and down the V of her pullover. Gillian could not stop a shiver running down her spine.

"Have you ever thought that it might be the other way round?" he asked. "That the Gillian who is so frank and direct is the real Gillian? And the other one, the one from your normal everyday life, is the stranger?"

Perplexed, she had nothing to say. Perhaps he was right. Perhaps there was more of the shy, convention-bound girl in her than she would have liked. Perhaps she was still not free of her upbringing which, above all, had taught her to be cautious. Perhaps she would never be completely free of it.

"Of course I don't want to manipulate you," said John.

"I won't let myself be manipulated," replied Gillian.

I've just got this one moment, she thought. If I dodge it, have a coffee and then drive home, I'll never do it again. There will never again be a situation like this one.

"I want to sleep with you," she said.

He wrapped his arms around her. "Lucky me," he whispered. "I would barely have been able to stand anything else."

When it was over, after an eternity, when they were both completely exhausted and had perhaps even fallen asleep for a moment, John opened his eyes and said that he loved her.

Gillian looked at him and realized that he was serious.

She had fallen asleep again and just woken up when John got up and left the room. She watched him come back with two big mugs. They drank the coffee, looking out at the snow falling thicker and thicker. Gillian could see the roof of the house across the road. A Christmas star hung in a dormer window. Above it, the snow was piling up in a powdery crest.

"Why don't you have a real bed, anyway?" she asked.

He shrugged. "If you look around my apartment, you'll see I barely have any furniture at all. I must have some block."

"A block?"

He laughed. "Can you imagine me in a furniture store? Buying wall-to-wall cupboards, a coffee table, and a rug?"

"I think that depends on the pieces."

"Everything I own, I've bought in second-hand shops. It's the bare minimum. If things get too comfily middle-class, it feels wrong to me."

"Was it always like that?"

He guessed what she wanted to ask. "You mean, did it have something to do with my job? Or rather, with the fact that I had to give it up?"

"It was a sudden break."

"But not one that changed me as a person. I've always been like this. Pretty unconventional. If I wasn't, I expect I wouldn't have gotten into this mess."

"You wanted to tell me about it," said Gillian.

He played with her hair, looking at her but miles away in his thoughts.

"Yes," he said, in the end. "I think I can tell you about it."

Then he started to talk about his mistake. The mistake that had changed his life.

"But what she wanted to pin on me, the sexual assault, that just wasn't true. We had a fling. She wanted it as much as I did. Her signals were crystal-clear. It was just stupid of me to go along with it."

"How long were you together?"

"For about four months. We had a good time. She was young and really attractive, and I just really liked being with her."

"How old were you?"

"I was thirty-seven. She was twenty-one. I thought… well, I thought we were just having some fun and then one day she'd meet someone closer to her own age and she'd marry him…. I was just enjoying the moment."

"When did it all change?"

He laughed bitterly. "When she failed one of the exams at the police academy. She was really gifted, actually. She just had a bad day. She screwed up a particularly important piece of work. But it was no big deal, really. She only needed to repeat the module. No one would have given a shit about it later. But…she lost it completely. She couldn't accept it. She implored me to *sort it out*. To speak to the examiner, to make him give her a pass, to revise his grade, who knows what."

Gillian shook her head. "And you couldn't do that."

"Of course not. Even if I had wanted to. That's not how things work. I explained that to her. But she wasn't listening to me." He shook his head. It seemed to Gillian as if he were still shaking his head at this situation in which he had found himself back then. "She had gone bonkers. She threatened to go public with our relationship in the Yard if I didn't help her out. I still couldn't do what she wanted. I couldn't have if I'd wanted to."

"And so how did it come to assault?"

"There was no assault," John stated again. "I just wanted to end the relationship. There was no point any more. Unfortunately, I was stupid enough to…." John stopped speaking.

"To what?" asked Gillian.

"I was stupid enough to sleep with her again. While I was actually trying to end things. It was complicated. I don't know why I did it."

"Probably because she was a pretty hot young woman," said Gillian in a level voice.

He sighed. "Yes. You're right. In any case, that's when she realized that nothing was going to change. That it was still over between us. And then she got completely hysterical. Suddenly she claimed that she had not wanted sex this last time. Screamed *rape* and ran to my boss. There was an investigation. The case even went to the Crown Prosecution."

"And you were in it deep."

"You could say that. It was easy to prove that we had had sex. I never denied it. I just kept on saying that it was consensual. She had given herself injuries and acted just like you would imagine a traumatized woman would act. What was more, I had been her boss during her internship. I had not done anything illegal by starting something with her, but I had broken any number of unwritten rules. I was temporarily suspended from the force."

"But you could prove your innocence, couldn't you?"

"No. In cases like this, you can't *prove* anything. Luckily there were several medical reports that treated the injuries on her body with great skepticism. The reports said that she had certainly given herself some of the injuries, and maybe all of them. She had also contradicted herself a lot in her story. The prosecutor could not find proof enough to bring the case. It never reached court."

"But you still had to leave?"

"I could have stayed. But one thing was clear. I had to take responsibility for all of what had happened. I should never have started something with her. The mistake, the guilt were mine. I resigned pretty soon after that. I knew that the incident would stick to me like a bad smell. And I was just so tired of the whole situation. Of my colleagues' hypocrisy, their pitying or gleeful looks, the gossip...I just wanted to get out. To this day, I'm glad I did."

"Are you? Really?"

"Absolutely—no question! I started this private security firm. I'm independent. My own boss. That's how I like to live. I just can't do the whole servile thing in a hierarchy full of intrigue, favoritism, and arse-lickers. I realized that late, but, luckily for me, not too late." She looked closely at him, asking herself if he really felt what he said, or if he was just saying it to help him deal with his situation.

"Why did you join the force in the first place?"

"Idealism," he said. "I wanted to protect good people and catch the baddies. That was at the start. Of course, after doing the job for a while, you quickly lose some of that attitude. But I suppose that's always the way it goes. In most jobs, I mean."

"The children who you coach...."

He laughed. "Okay. That's what's left of my idealism. I'm convinced that it's possible to take children and young people off the streets, to keep them from just hanging around. Their energies can be steered in better directions. It's boredom and a senseless drifting through the day that can make them susceptible to bad things like drugs and violence and to an inability to live their lives with focus and dedication. In my opinion, sports is the best way to learn that. It's what I can offer them. And it works."

"Why Southend? Why so far out of London?"

"I tried in two London clubs first. There was no end of problems when people found out that I'd been in Scotland Yard, and why I'd left. In the end, I just decided to go a little farther out in the hope that it would be harder for people to know about my past. There aren't as many problem families here. Of course, I also coach kids who are not at risk, but some of them I can really help. And it's good that I can, isn't it?"

He took her mug out of her hand and put it down on the floor next to the mattress. He enveloped Gillian in his arms. "If I hadn't, I wouldn't have met you, would I? And that," he said as he started to kiss her, "would have been a real shame."

They made love once more. It was completely dark outside and in the room when they let go of each other. Gillian realized that she could barely keep her eyes open. Her last waking thought was *Whatever I do, I can't fall asleep again.* And with that, she slipped into sleep. She could not help herself. She was very happy and very tired.

When she woke up, nothing had changed. It was dark, but in the light of the street lamp outside the window she could see the snow falling. She looked at her watch and got a shock. It was half past eight. By ten, Tom would be back home. She only had an hour and a half to get home and have a good shower. Seeing as it had been snowing uninterruptedly for the last five hours, she wondered anxiously how difficult the journey back might be.

She could hear John breathing deeply next to her. She stood up without a sound, slipped into her clothes, and took her handbag. She tiptoed out of the room. There was no furniture in the apartment's long hallway, just a coat rack on the wall for a few coats and jackets. Gillian's winter coat was on top and her boots beneath it.

She was just getting her coat on when John appeared next to her, with a towel wrapped around his waist. "You're going already? I wanted to cook for us. Have a glass of wine with you…."

She shook her head. "My husband is getting home soon. I'm already late. Apart from that, I'm scared I'll get stuck in the snow. It's snowing like crazy out there."

"Should I drive you?"

"No. I'll be all right."

He took her face between his hands. "When will we see each other again?"

"I'll call you," said Gillian.

3

SHE ARRIVED HOME at exactly the same time as Tom, after a nightmare of a drive that more than once looked like it would never end. Snowdrifts, cars blocking the road, gridlock. She had been cursing the whole way as she saw her head start over Tom diminishing to nothing and because she had become absolutely convinced that she needed to shower. She smelled of John. She smelled of sex.

She could not meet Tom like this. When the two of them arrived at the same time, turning into the drive from different directions, Gillian realized that she would have to get through the situation somehow.

It was almost half past ten. Tom was later than usual too. "Where've you been?" he asked, surprised.

"In London," she said truthfully. "Christmas shopping." She realized she was not carrying a single bag. "Well…I didn't find anything. Then I had a bite to eat and wasn't watching the time. Then there was the snow. It's almost gridlocked on the roads."

"And what about Becky?"

"She's at Darcy's for a sleepover. Her birthday party."

They put their cars in the garage and went inside. Chuck came up to them, mewling and rubbing up against their legs. The answering machine was beeping, a sign that they had unheard messages waiting. "I got all jittery in the car and I'm all sweaty now," said Gillian. "I think I'll just have a quick shower."

Tom nodded distractedly and pressed the button on the answering machine. There was only one message waiting.

The voice that filled the room was not one that either of them knew.

"Yes, hello…Samson Segal here. I…I live a few doors down your street. At the end of the street. My brother was your client once. I…well, I wanted to say that your daughter is at my house. She was locked outside your house and in a bit of a state about it, so…I let her come over to my place. You can come pick her up any time." He paused. It was clear that he was one of those people who do not like to talk on answering machines. "So…see you soon." Another pause. Stressed breathing. Then he hung up.

"What?" asked Tom, incredulous.

Gillian had been stopped in mid-track on her way to the shower. She turned around. "No way! She was supposed to be staying the night with Darcy!"

"Why did she go to some complete stranger's house?" shouted Tom in shock and anger. "Why weren't you here?"

"And why weren't you?" screamed Gillian.

"I was at my tennis club. I said I'd be back late."

"You're always back late! If you had your way, I'd never get out. I'd always be here holding the fort. You barely live here now!"

"Do you think this is the right moment to argue about it?" hissed Tom.

Gillian pushed past him and took her coat. "I'm going to fetch my daughter!"

"I'm coming too," said Tom.

A few minutes later, they rang the bell at the Segals' house. After just a few seconds, the door opened and Samson was standing opposite them.

"I…th-thought that it would…be you," he stuttered.

Tom pushed past him into the hall. "Where's our daughter?"

"Sh…she fell asleep w-watching TV."

Without waiting for an invitation, Tom went toward where he heard voices that sounded like a television program. Gillian smiled apologetically at Samson and followed her husband.

The television was on in the living room. Becky was lying on a sofa and sleeping. Gavin Segal sat in the armchair next to her and was fully absorbed in the documentary on television. A woman was sitting at the dining room table doing her nails.

"Mr. Ward…."

"How did Becky get here?" asked Tom sharply.

"Tom…." said Gillian in a soothing voice.

"My brother happened to walk past your house this evening when your daughter was ringing your doorbell, beside herself and crying," explained Gavin. "She was coming from a friend of hers, if I understood right. And no one was at home. He didn't want her to just stay there in the snow, so he brought her here."

"But I said right away that he should leave a message with you," the woman said.

Becky opened her eyes and looked at her parents in surprise. Then she jumped up and squeaked with joy. "Dad!" She threw her arms around him.

"That was nice of you, Mr. Segal," said Gillian to Samson, who was standing shyly behind her. "My daughter was supposed to be staying at her friend's house. Otherwise of course one of us would have been there."

"I had a massive fight with Darcy," explained Becky. "So of course I didn't want to stay."

"Does Darcy's mom know you went home?" asked Gillian.

"Yes, I told her."

"And she did not think to check that we would be home?" asked Tom, dumbfounded.

"She has fifteen children staying over," reminded Gillian. "She probably doesn't have a moment to think!"

"Still…it's not on that…."

She wished Tom would just stop blaming everyone. She felt bad enough as it was.

My daughter could not get in because I was in bed with my lover.

And it was true: unlike Tom, she had not said she would not be at home. Becky had been sure she would find her mom at home.

A dangerous stranger could have come and abducted her….

"I liked taking care of Becky," said Samson. "You kn-know, I like children."

"Yes, thank you," said Tom, who finally, reluctantly, realized that Samson Segal had not done anything wrong. "I-if you need me…I've got time."

"My brother-in-law is unemployed," injected the woman pointedly, waving her hands about to help her nail polish dry more quickly.

"Thank you," repeated Tom. He wanted to go home. He found the whole situation unbearable, Gillian knew that. The shrill woman with her dark red fingernails, stuttering Samson Segal, his tired and run-down-looking brother, the stuffy living room, the blaring television. He was angry, and it was clear to Gillian that his anger was directed mainly at her. Because she had not been there. Because she had allowed the situation to arise.

He maintained a stony silence on the short walk home. He did not say anything when they got in, either. Only later, when Gillian had put Becky to bed and had a shower, did he suddenly say, "I don't like him. If you ask me, he's got more than one screw loose."

He lay in bed, holding a book but not actually reading. He was just staring at the wall.

Gillian was standing in the middle of the room, combing her wet hair. "Who?"

"That Segal chap. With the funny name. Samson Segal. Something odd about him."

"Why do you say that? He's shy and inhibited, but he's very friendly."

"He's not normal," insisted Tom. "Who lives like that? He's in his mid-thirties at least. Can barely say a word without getting himself tied up in knots. There's no woman in his life, and—"

"How do you know?"

"I can feel it. He's too uptight for a woman. So where does he make up for that? With children?!"

Gillian shook her head. "That's unreasonable, Tom. You were being unreasonable earlier, too. Mr. Segal did just what a good neighbor should do. He helped our family out of a difficult situation. Now you make him sound like some child molester. I'm happy he was there at the right time. It could have been anyone else—and that thought makes me feel queasy."

"Right," said Tom. He put the book down and sat up. "I think that is just what bugs me so much: why did he just *happen* to pass by yet again?"

"'Yet again'?"

"Don't you remember last Saturday? When we left the house. He was standing on the pavement right by our hedge. What was he doing there?"

"No idea. He was going for a walk. Maybe he just stopped now and then to look at the houses. His sister-in-law said he was unemployed, after all. He must spend all day hanging around the neighborhood. He doesn't have anything better to do."

"It's our house he's hanging around!" said Tom.

"Because you saw him one Saturday?" retorted Gillian, although she could not help starting to feel a little uneasy. She was remembering Tara's last visit. When she accompanied Tara to the door, Samson had just been going past. Tara had remarked that he had been around when she came. Samson Segal did seem to be crossing the Ward family's path quite a lot recently.

It might still be coincidence.

She slipped into bed and pulled up the covers. She suddenly had to think intensely about John. It was just a few hours since she had slept with him. And now she was lying next to Tom again and they were being ratty with one another because the evening had given both of them such a shock.

That is how it feels like to have a double life, thought Gillian. On the one hand, passionate sex with a thrilling and rather puzzling man in an almost-bare London apartment—and then back to the well-kept little house in Thorpe Bay with the usual marital strife and worries about their child.

"Becky has to learn not to just go off with strangers," said Tom. "I really thought she knew that by now!"

He was not going to let it rest.

Gillian rolled her eyes. "She has now. But he's a neighbor—if a slightly distant neighbor. She had seen him around, in any case."

"So what? Often it's just such neighbors, people that children trust, who are the problem."

"I'll have a good chat with her about it tomorrow," said Gillian.

And I won't see John again, she swore to herself. I can't let such a situation arise again.

She did not only mean the fact that her daughter had been locked out and unable to cope. She meant all the lying. The rush to get home. Feeling ashamed and needing to shower.

Probably she was not made out to live a double life.

She suddenly started to cry quietly, subdued, into her pillow. She thought how it had been in bed with John. How wild. How tender. She thought about his bare apartment that stood in such stark contrast to her own house with its little turret and bay windows.

She longed to be back there.

She was going to call Tara the next day and tell her everything. Well, almost everything. She would leave out the dark side of John's past. John would simply have always had his own company. And as Tara had not lived and worked in London eight years ago, she did not know the Burton case. But the *Burton case* was not the problem.

The problem was Tom and Becky and their life together.

She had to talk to someone. She needed advice about what, for heaven's sake, she was to do.

She started sobbing when she thought that Tara would probably not be able to help her this time.

Monday, December 21

1

"JUST A FEW days until Christmas and we're sitting here after a second gruesome murder, without the faintest hint of a clue," said Peter Fielder, glumly. "Out there, a killer is on the loose who murders women in complete depravity, and we aren't any closer to catching him."

He was sitting in his office, at his usual ungodly early hour, surrounded by the special silence of an almost empty large building. Christy McMarrow was there, of course. She was sitting opposite him and had brought them coffee. The two of them were exhausted—completely shattered, in fact. The weekend, inasmuch as "weekend" is a synonym for *free time* and *sleeping in*, had not lived up to its promise at all. Not after a real estate agent had called the police from a remote house in a wood beyond Tunbridge Wells on Thursday evening because in the house's bathroom he had found the body of one of his clients. She had obviously been dead for a good week. The tea towel stuffed deep into the dead woman's throat had caused the inspector on the scene to phone Detective Inspector Fielder at Scotland Yard immediately. With Christy, he had fought through the heavy snow in the godforsaken wood that same evening. In and around London, traffic had been thrown into chaos, but somehow they managed to reach their destination. What they saw there was as horrific and disturbing as what they had seen in Carla Roberts's apartment. However, in addition there was the fact that the house was so isolated.

"You'd go crazy out here," Peter had said to Christy. He was perplexed that some people chose such strange places to live.

In those first hours, Luke Palm, the London real estate agent, was the person who gave them important information about the murdered woman. Fielder found him sitting, ashen, downstairs in the living room. An attentive policewoman had poured him a cup of tea from a thermos, but it did not look as though he had drunk even a sip of it. He held out his brimful mug carefully, as if he were expecting someone to take it away again. Fielder could see that he was making gulping sounds and wetting his lips repeatedly.

He told Fielder what he knew of the dead woman. That she was Anne Westley, in her late sixties, a widow for the past three years. That she and her husband had bought the house as a home in which to enjoy their retirement, but that her husband had died as soon as they had finished renovating it. That Anne had finally not been able to bear its isolated location any longer and so had asked him, Luke Palm, to arrange for it to be sold. That she had also asked him to look for an apartment for her in London. After a while, it had seemed odd to him that it had become completely impossible to reach her, although he had found people seriously interested in buying the property and had several times left a message with the news on her answering machine. That is why he had driven over. And then to find….

At this point in his account, he began to shake so much that his tea spilled onto the floor. Fielder carefully took the mug from his hand, although Palm barely registered that Fielder had done so.

"Was there anything specific that made you worried?" he asked cautiously. "You couldn't reach her. I understand that. But for you to drive out here…it's not exactly around the corner from where you live. Was there anything else? Something that made you uneasy? It could be important."

Palm thought, but he could not remember anything. "No, I'm afraid not. I mean, it was rather unsettling to know that a woman who was almost seventy lived out here all on her own. But I wasn't thinking about a crime. I was worried that she might have had a nasty fall and be lying somewhere in the house, unable to reach the phone. No one would have known."

"Mrs. Westley didn't mention that anything odd had happened?"

"Something odd?"

Fielder was thinking of the elevator movements that Carla Roberts had noticed shortly before she was murdered. "Something that unsettled her?"

"She didn't tell me about anything."

"Why had she decided to sell now? Just before Christmas, in the middle of winter…. Is that a normal time for people to move?"

"It is actually rather unusual," Luke Palm had to admit.

"What reason did she give you?"

"That she felt lonely out here. She had felt lonely for far too long. She didn't exactly say that directly, but, reading between the lines, you could sense that she had endured it for so long out of loyalty to her late husband. All this was his project, really. She felt bad about getting rid of the place once he was dead and gone. But the time had come when she felt she couldn't bear it any longer."

"But she didn't mention any particular trigger?"

"No."

"My colleagues from the local branch tell me that you said you were here last week, on December 10, to look at the property. And you say that was the day she was murdered?"

"The tear-off calendar in the kitchen," Palm said quietly. "It still says December 10. So that's what I supposed."

"You didn't notice anything when you were here then?"

"No."

"Were there any other cars in the car park?"

"No."

"And when you drove away, was any car coming the other way?"

"No. I'm sorry." Palm shook his head. "I'd like to be of more help. But there wasn't anything. At least, nothing I noticed."

At that moment, Christy McMarrow came into the room and asked Fielder to come upstairs.

"The forensics team has found something," she said.

Upstairs, an officer was standing in the bathroom door and holding a clear plastic bag in his hand. Inside it was a bullet.

"He used a gun to open the door that the victim had locked herself behind. He shot the lock to pieces."

"Interesting." Fielder looked at the bullet through narrowed eyes. "At the other crime scene, there was no trace of a firearm. So make sure this one is examined thoroughly once more."

"Sir, it's already been—"

"Nevertheless. And tomorrow a team has to go back to Carla Roberts's apartment."

The investigation had been going on all weekend. In spite of searching with a fine-tooth comb, no evidence for the use of a firearm was found in Carla Roberts's apartment. The autopsy on Anne Westley had been carried out. Christy had the results this Monday morning. She took a sip of coffee and said: "The coroner confirms what the real estate agent suspected about the date of the crime. It looks like the tenth of December is the most likely date. The eleventh is a possibility too, but then the calendar suggests it isn't."

"What was the cause of death?" asked Peter Fielder. "Did she suffocate on her own vomit?"

"No. Her murderer thrust the towel down her throat with increasing brutality, but it appears it didn't make her retch. He had stopped her from breathing by taping her nose shut. So she suffocated."

"He could easily have shot her, as we now know."

"That would probably have been too quick a death for him." Fielder nodded. He looked at his notes. They had found out that Anne's husband, Sean Westley, had been a professor at University College London and that he had died three years earlier of pneumonia. Before her retirement, Anne had worked as a GP in a clinic in Kensington. The couple had not had children.

"We should ask at the clinic if there was ever a case of medical incompetence or anything negative relating to Anne Westley," said Fielder.

"You mean: vengeful parents?" asked Christy. "How does that tie in with Carla Roberts?"

"It doesn't. I just want to exclude the possibility. So we both think that we're dealing with the same murderer?"

"As we didn't go public about the cloth used to suffocate Carla Roberts, this one *can't* be a copycat crime. The two cases are patently connected. I suspect that in Roberts's case the murderer had a gun too, but didn't need to use it; but that would explain why Carla Roberts let herself be tied up by her hands and feet without a struggle: she was being threatened with a pistol."

Fielder looked back down at his notes, as if the answer would leap out at him if he only stared at them long enough.

"Where does it all meet?" he murmured. "Or is there any point where Carla Roberts's and Anne Westley's cases meet?"

"At first glance, what they have in common is their loneliness," said Christy. "Both of them lived unusually isolated lives. Both of them had lost their partner—one through divorce, the other through death. Anne Westley had no family. Carla Roberts had a daughter, but she was rarely in contact with her. In each case, the murderer could do his deed without fear of being disturbed. And could bet on it taking a while before the crime was discovered."

"But that's *all* they had in common."

"That's a lot. It might be just that the murderer wanted that opportunity. Never mind which woman and her life history—just that situation."

"Right," said Fielder. "The chance principle. I can see that that makes sense in the Westley case. That there was a psychopath, hanging around in the woods, lurking in wait. It would have been easy for him to find out that a woman lived there all on her own and that no one came by regularly. But how would he have found out that Carla Roberts was so isolated? No, there must be something else. Something that Westley and Roberts have in common, besides being all alone. The pensioner in Hackney who just scrapes by and the former doctor and professor's widow out in Tunbridge Wells who is well enough off, thank you very much. That's two different worlds there."

"Carla Roberts didn't always live off a modest pension in an apartment building," Christy reminded him. "Before her ex's construction company went bankrupt, he had earned a lot of money. It's possible that Roberts and Westley were part of the same social spheres in London at one point."

"And knew each other?"

"It's not out of the question, is it? For example, Dr. Westley might have been the GP Keira Jones, Carla's daughter, visited. That would be easy to check."

"Yes. Other connections will be harder."

"We've got a hell of a lot of work ahead of us."

He nodded wearily. Then he remembered something else. "The attic in Anne Westley's house…. She loved to paint. Was there any clue in Carla Roberts's apartment that suggested she shared that hobby?"

Christy shook her head regretfully. "No. Not in the slightest. Not a single paintbrush was found in the apartment, let alone a drawing or anything similar. I can ask the daughter again, but I honestly think we can forget that too."

2

MONDAY, DECEMBER 21, 10:05 p.m.

Gillian Ward is no better than Michelle Brown. Both of them are ungrateful and snooty, think they're something special, but they are rude. I brought one of them her dog back. That dog seems to be her life. (She obviously can't get a man, which doesn't surprise me, given how she is—I wouldn't want her now if she came begging on her knees.) And I took care of the other one's daughter. Her only child! And what do I get in return? A tepid "Thank you" and nothing more! Somehow she seemed almost suspicious of me. As if I had taken the girl with me for some base reason!

Her husband was even worse. Thomas Ward is the most unsympathetic man ever. He came in here on Thursday as if he was storming a terrorist cell. He just wanted to grab his daughter and disappear immediately. It was almost painful to see how difficult it was for him to thank me. Gavin always thought he was rather nice. I really can't understand that. I'm surprised the man can stand, with the weight of his arrogance. And yet he's throwing away his marriage and I bet he doesn't even realize it. He just lives for his company and his sport. Of course, everyone's life is their own, but you shouldn't forget your wife and kids in the process. One day Gillian will run away, that's crystal clear. And then he'll be left standing there stupidly wondering what he did wrong. I'll be happy when he's all alone and has to come back to an empty house. The annoying thing is that it wouldn't take him long to find a new woman. He looks good, earns well, and that's all women think about. Even if they are treated badly. Men like me, who would be nice to their wives, and give them our time and affection, we are ignored.

I know that he thinks I'm some child molester. It would be laughable, if it didn't feel so humiliating. I'd never do anything to children. I like children. I'd so dearly love to have my own. And as for Becky—I just wanted to help. What should I have done? What would

Thomas Ward have preferred? For me to leave her there in the dark and just walk on?

I saw Gillian leave in the car that afternoon. She wasn't in the office that day. I'm neglecting the other people I watch because I can't tear myself away from her. She came out of the house around 4 p.m. and she looked different somehow. She wasn't heavily dolled up, maybe she had a bit more makeup on, not too much. I think it was her aura that was different. It's hard to describe. She seemed so appealing. More appealing than I had found her before.

I started to get worried after she left. I think that if I'd had my car with me at that moment, I'd have followed her. But it was in the garage and by the time I could have gone home and fetched it, she would have been long gone. But for hours I was asking myself where she had gone. I felt jittery, plagued by dark forebodings. Something was afoot in the family, and it wasn't good. Thomas Ward had triggered it. But often things then develop their own dynamic, and it's possible that they already had in this case.

That day I walked my usual round. It was cold and snowing, but I couldn't make myself go back to my nice warm room. I wanted to know when Gillian would come home.

As the snow fell more and more heavily, I stood there watching the house. Its Christmas decorations came on automatically at some point. And then Becky suddenly appeared out of the dark. It was a little after six. I had seen her go over to her friend's house at lunchtime. Judging from the number of girls there, it must have been a birthday party. Now the party was obviously over, but Gillian wasn't home yet. That wasn't like her. She's not like that. I started to think it might be because

*of the snow. She might be stuck somewhere. It was the
first real snowfall of winter, and that always brings traffic to a standstill.*

*Becky rang the bell, but of course nothing happened.
She rang it again. She stepped back, looking up at the
façade. She rang the bell again. After a while, she hammered her fists on the door and then started to cry.*

*In that strange silence that the world sinks into when
it snows, I could hear her sobs. It almost broke my heart.*

*I crossed the street and stopped at their gate, calling
out to her, "Becky!" She spun around. I was standing
under a street lamp. She could easily recognize me. It
was lovely to see how the fear and mistrust vanished
from her face. She recognized me. The man who lived
down the street. "Hello," she said. Her voice was heavy
with tears.*

*"No one home?" I asked, although I knew the an-
swer.*

"No. No one. And I don't have a key with me."

"Do your parents know you are coming home now?"

*She shook her head. "I wanted to spend the night at
my friend's house, but we had a big fight and so I've
come home."*

*At least that was a reassuring explanation for Gil-
lian's behavior. She thought her daughter was going to
be at her friend's house all night. She could not have
guessed that Becky would come home.*

*"You know what," I said. "I think you'll catch a cold
if you stay out here much longer. Either I should take
you back to your friend's house—"*

"No!" she shouted.

*"—or you can come to my house. Then I'll take you
home later. What do you think?"*

She was unsure. Naturally. It had been drummed into

*her that she should not go anywhere with strangers,
and I was a stranger for her. But one who she knew by
sight and who she and her parents said hi to. That was,
no doubt, what decided it for her. She came with me. In
any case, she didn't have much of a choice. As she had
obviously had a complete falling-out with her friend, I
was the only option.*

*We gave her orange juice and homemade cookies. I
think she liked us. She told us about school and the party
she had just been at—and that she would not ever speak
to her ex-best friend again. It was charming. She was
looking forward to Christmas and to seeing her grandparents. She always went to their house on December
26 and stayed until the start of January. They are her
mother's parents and live in Norwich. So Gillian is from
East Anglia. That suits her. It's so open and green there.
I can imagine Gillian among the lakes and rivers of
the Norfolk Broads. I can see her in the lavender fields
and I know that summer will burn pale, silvery strands
into her long strawberry blond hair. After a day at the
beach, her skin will be covered in freckles, and the sea
wind will make her hair even more unruly and wavy.*

*Millie said I should leave a message on the family's
answering machine straightaway. For a change, that
wasn't a bad idea she had. Nevertheless, we still had
that unspeakable visit from the Wards. The way he acted
was disgusting and...yes, I'm deeply disappointed in her
too. Somehow I thought she might come by again later.
If not the next day or on the weekend, then today at the
latest. To thank me or apologize for her husband's behavior. But no. She acts as if she doesn't know me. That's
why I said at the start that she is like Michelle Brown.
I didn't hear any more from her, either. She is out and
about with her dog again; and me? For her I don't exist.*

Women don't notice me. Whatever I do for them. It's as if I were invisible. Or give off some bad odor that keeps people away. I thought Gillian was different. But she treats me like trash too.

I can't let my hate grow. Hate destroys. Destroys the one who feels it too.

Thursday, December 24

1

LOOKING OUT OF the window of the guest toilet on the ground floor, Millie could see the street. She saw Samson, who had just gone out. He had said he wanted to go into town to find a few last presents and that he did not want to take the car because he feared he might not find a parking space, it being Christmas Eve. As usual, Millie didn't believe him. By now she was completely convinced that he did not go looking for work when he left the house in the morning, and whatever he did in all the hours that passed before he turned up again in the evening, he could not be up to anything good. If it were, he would talk to someone about it. At least to Gavin, with whom he had a fairly normal relationship. She had mentioned it to Gavin a few days ago.

"What does Samson actually do all day?" she asked him casually. "He's never home, and it's far too cold outside for him to always be walking."

"He's looking for work," Gavin said. It sounded like the kind of automatic answer you give without thinking about it.

"But you don't look for work by wandering round. You write applications!"

"Maybe he's doing that. He sits at his computer for hours."

Millie would not let go. "But then he would get an-

swers in the post. Whether rejections or acceptance letters."

"Maybe he does it all by e-mail. That's possible nowadays, isn't it?"

"Yes, and so where is he during the day?"

Gavin lowered the car magazine he was leafing
through and said, almost pleadingly, "Just leave him be,
Millie. You can't stand him. I know. But he's my brother
and he hasn't done anything to you. You're searching
furiously for something to pin on him and, you know
what, the fact that you can't find anything is driving
you crazy!"

She had pressed her lips together and thought: I will
find something. Because there's something to find. You
can bet on it!

Now she was standing at the window and pressing
her nose to the pane because she did not believe him.
Although he was walking off with a certain purposeful
stride. Buying presents! Hopefully he would not buy
her one. She did not have anything for him. Gavin had
bought a book. That would have to do from both of them.

Samson had now disappeared around the corner. Millie could feel her heart pounding, but she told herself
that now was her chance. Samson was going to be out
for hours—in the shopping center or wherever he was
going. Gavin's shift lasted until the early afternoon. She
herself had managed to keep the day free.

I'll give it another try now, she thought.

She tiptoed up the stairs, finding herself rather silly as
she did, seeing as she was the only person in the house.
For some reason, she had the feeling that she should
act as inconspicuously and cautiously as she could. She
opened the door to Samson's room and stepped inside. It

was as tidy as ever. There was not a speck of dust to be seen. The bedcover was laid out inch-perfect on the bed.

That in itself, she thought, just isn't normal!

She turned on the computer. As it booted up, she looked at the window. They were really going to have a white Christmas. Since the sudden onset of winter last Thursday, when the whole region had been put into a state of emergency for hours, it had continued to snow. The roofs, fences, trees, and streets were covered in white.

A romantic image. Millie loved Christmas. What annoyed her was the three of them spending it together around the Christmas tree.

No one could be seen outside. She turned to the computer and typed in the password, holding her breath. If Gavin had given Samson any hint…but he had obviously kept mum. The magic word *Hannah* opened the computer.

Millie sat down, with her hand on the mouse. It took her a few seconds to realize that she was holding her breath. She navigated through the menus.

"Come on, come on," she murmured.

Something important was hidden in here. It had to be. And she was going to find it, whatever it took.

Ten minutes later she had it. The file was named *Diary.*

She opened it. She had her wits about her enough to hurry to the window and look out again. No one around. She was safe from unpleasant surprises for now.

Then she sat down again and stared at the screen. And read and read. She quickly realized that her search had been worth it.

Samson was crazy. He was probably even danger-ous. She had proof now, and not even Gavin would be able to deny the facts.

2

THE HOUSE WAS cold and smelled moldy. It had been empty for four days. Before that, the owner had lain dead in the bathroom for a week. Cold, damp air had blown in through the open kitchen door during that week.

Decay happens so quickly, thought Fielder. Why does it always happen so quickly?

Christy and he had driven out again to Tunbridge Wells and its silent, white woods. They had parked in the empty car park and stomped through the wood.

"Christmas should be celebrated in the woods," Peter Fielder had said, watching a squirrel shimmy up the trunk of a pine. "It's so peaceful here. So festive."

"And damned cold," said Christy.

At around two o'clock, they reached the house. The local officers had closed the shutters and carefully bolted the doors. Fielder had expected darkness and clammy air, but he was still surprised by the oppressive atmo-sphere. And by the sadness he felt as he went in. He had been on the force for decades. He had learned to protect himself from the feelings that can come with a case: the pain, anger, despair, and hopelessness. He wanted to make sure that he did not let the desolate state of the world get to him psychologically. If it did, he might as well retire.

Generally, he had a good grip on things. But out here today in this house, this isolation....

It's because it's Christmas, he hoped. It's a strange time.... "Sir?" Christy's voice cut in on his thoughts.

He pulled himself together. "Okay," he said. "I just want to look at the attic one more time."

They climbed the stairs again. They still had nothing. Nothing that brought them any closer to a breakthrough.

Christy had visited the clinic where Anne Westley had worked until three and a half years ago, but she had not been able to find anything to suggest that there had been any scandal, any trouble at all about a false diagnosis or a professional error.

"Anne was loved by all her little patients," a colleague had said, still stunned by the news of the murder. "And by the parents and everyone who worked here. I can't remember that she was ever blamed for anything."

"Perhaps a long time ago?" Christy probed. "After all, she was here for almost thirty years."

"What happened before my time I don't really know. But if anything had happened, there'd have been talk and I'd have heard about it. No, I really don't think anything happened."

Christy had gone through the old patient files in painstaking detail. They contained no Keira Roberts. Just to be sure, she had also called Keira Jones, as she had become, and asked about Dr. Westley. "No," said Keira. "I never visited a doctor by that name as a child. My doctor lived just a few doors down the road from us."

"But did your parents ever mention the name *Westley*? Could she have been an acquaintance, even if ever so fleeting, of your parents?"

Keira had racked her memory, but in the end she'd had to concede defeat. "No. I'm sorry, Sergeant. As far as I know, my parents didn't know anyone of that name."

They went past the bathroom where Anne Westley had been murdered. In spite of all his years of service,

Fielder had to turn away. The thought of the horrors the old lady had faced upset him deeply.

The studio under the roof was the brightest room in the whole house. Even on this dull December day, the light here was good. The walls were clad with wood. There were three large dormer windows facing south. Easels were dotted around the room, and finished or half-finished paintings were propped here and there. It smelled of paint and turpentine. A brightly splotched painting smock hung on the door. Light, bright colors and images of flowers and landscapes predominated.

"Definitely happy pictures," Christy stated after a first look around. "Although not really my thing."

"Hmm," went Fielder. He walked slowly from one picture to the next.

"Do you think we'll find something here?" asked Christy despairingly.

"I don't know. But I think it'll at least help me get closer to Anne Westley. The paintings are a part of her. They say something about her. If you can interpret them right."

"My interpretations might be naïve, but if I had to describe Anne Westley from her paintings, I'd say she was a cheery, stable, happy woman. Although I realize that none of those characteristics are any guarantee against being murdered."

Fielder stopped. He lifted a sheet from an easel and looked at the painting below it. "Here's something that isn't as full of *joie de vivre*!"

Christy stepped closer.

The painting really did look completely different from all the others in the studio. A black background. Two cones of light. A flickering beam from lamps or headlights. It was not painted in a careful or thorough way. Not all the details were painted in, as the artist had obviously enjoyed doing in her other paintings. This painting had been rushed. The canvas looked like it had been daubed viciously with a brush. It was a picture that, in spite of the neutrality of the subject matter, seemed to express anger.

And fear.

To Christy, it revealed more talent than the surrounding images of flowers, trees, and summery scenes. She asked herself how an image that did not show anything but two lights in the darkness could express such strong emotions.

"What is this a picture of? What's your first reaction?" asked Fielder.

Christy did not have to think for long. "Headlights. At night." He nodded, narrowing his eyes. "Do you feel like you're looking at the source of the light itself?"

"At the source of the light itself? What do you mean?"

"Well, I don't get that feeling. I feel like I'm looking at a mirror image. Not at the light itself, but at the image of the light."

"Could be. And what would that tell us?"

"I don't know yet. The beam of headlights passing across a wall?"

"I don't get what—"

"Me neither. It might not mean anything. But the painting is so different from all the others we have here. And it was covered. As if Anne Westley herself didn't want to look at it. And yet she painted it. With pretty strong feelings, it seems."

Christy agreed but didn't see how they were any nearer a breakthrough.

"Sir, this is getting so speculative. We don't know if—"

He interrupted her impatiently. "Right. We don't

know anything. But we have to start somewhere. I'm neither a psychologist nor an artist, but something leaps out at me from this painting: fear. More than anger or aggression. Anne Westley was afraid of someone or something. And that reminds me of Carla Roberts. She was afraid too. She told her daughter that, in their last call. I can see a similarity there. That's why it's important."

"But does it get us anywhere?"

He was still looking at the painting. "No idea. But if you ask me, Anne Westley knew that she was in danger. That is why she was hurrying to sell her house two weeks before Christmas. The murderer might have been hanging around for a while. And she had noticed."

"And now?" asked Christy.

He didn't reply. He tore himself away from the painting. For the moment, it was no good staring at it any more. Its effect was so intense, especially with its connection to the murdered woman, that it had seared itself onto his retina. He would carry it around with him, look at it, and hope that some revelation would come.

They went back down again. Christy glanced at the drawings on the walls, the nice carpets on the floor, and the curtains in the windows. Everything had been arranged with so much taste and care. From what the house said about Anne Westley, it seemed hardly imaginable that she could cause as much hate in someone as this crime seemed to suggest.

"I'm going to assign one or two people to look into the late Professor Westley's life and colleagues," said Fielder when they arrived downstairs. "Although I don't expect much. If it had been a personal act of revenge, then Carla Roberts doesn't fit in. And vice versa. We have to manage to find some connection between the two women. That's our only chance."

Christy touched him gently on the arm. "Okay, boss. But enjoy your Christmas first. You've earned it."

He looked at her. Asked himself how *she* celebrated Christmas. She lived alone with two cats, as he knew. Did she hang up a stocking at the fireplace? And if so, who filled her stocking?

As if she could read his thoughts, she said: "I'm going to have a cozy day tomorrow. I think I'll stay in bed half the day and just get up now and then to fetch another cappuccino. Lovely ones with foamy milk and sprinkled with chocolate. I'll channel-surf, chilling out and forgetting all these terrible crimes!"

He smiled and caught himself thinking that it would be nice to share such a day with her. With television and cappuccino. Especially in bed.

He hurriedly broke his reverie with a cough. He should not think like that.

"My mother-in-law is coming to visit," he replied despondently. "Just like every Christmas."

"Is she terrible?"

"Rather confused. And up for a fight."

Christy laughed. "Keep your chin up. Somehow Christmas always passes pretty quickly."

"Let's go," said Fielder. At least this year he had this: a walk with Christy in the wintery woods.

That was better than nothing.

Tuesday, December 29

1

IT HAD SNOWED again during the night. By morning it looked as if the world was slowly disappearing under the snow. However, by the afternoon at least the main roads had been cleared. Further snowfalls were forecast for the night.

Gillian had found the festive period difficult, but had tried to make the best of it. She and Tom had planned to go sledging and ice-skating with Becky, but on Christmas morning Becky had come down with a sore throat and by the afternoon she had a fever. She was in bed for two days, and even once she was up again, she had to stay inside. The obligatory trip to Norwich had been cancelled. Although Becky had grumbled that she was too old for holidays with her grandparents, now she started to cry like a little child. Her mood plummeted so far that soon all three of them felt rotten. Gillian and Tom did their best. They cooked with her in the evening. They lit the open fire in the living room. They played cards with her or watched for the umpteenth time— resigned to their fate and Tom shaking his head constantly—*Twilight* on DVD. The Christmas lights on the tree bathed the room in a warm light, while the snow, cold, and darkness of the December nights outside all provided a perfect Christmas atmosphere. It was just what a small happy family should look like, in their warm cozy home. And yet Gillian knew it was fake—and not just because of Becky's cold. Tom was itching to get back to the office, because work was waiting for him. The Christmas rituals and the expectations of quiet time felt like unbearable stagnation to him.

And Gillian was longing for…John. She had sworn not to see him again, but she missed so much the feelings that he caused in her. It was to do with the attention he gave her. His admiration for her. Most people would be susceptible to it, she said to herself to soothe her conscience. Since she had met him, she felt stronger and less insecure. And that was what she longed for above all: the security he offered her.

She had spent a long time on the phone with Tara the very day after she had visited John. Tara had not said a word in judgment, but Gillian could read between the lines that her friend did not see a relationship with another man as the solution to Gillian's problems. And perhaps she was right.

Two days before New Year's Eve, she decided to see John. She would not go to bed with him again, but she wanted to see him. Just see him.

She said to Tom that she was going to visit Tara. He replied, somewhat gruffly, "Again! You saw her just before Christmas."

"Two weeks ago! You can't really claim we see each other too much."

"I wanted to go to the office for a few hours, actually.…"

"Becky still has a bit of fever. I don't want her to be here alone."

Tom sighed. "If only there wasn't so much work to do. Now's a good time to clear the desk of all those things I didn't get around to."

"Just today, Tom. Please give me this afternoon. Please. If Becky's fever has gone tomorrow, we'll drive to London and work all day. Okay?"

"If you say so. But please be back by seven. You know—"

"I know," she interrupted. "Don't imagine I could ever forget it. Tuesday. Club evening!"

He seemed to want to say something back, but he bit his tongue. He clamped his mouth shut. That was how she saw him as she went to the garage: standing in the door with his lips pressed tight together.

She arrived at John's house in Stratford at about four o'clock and even found a parking space not too far away. She rang the doorbell on the street, but to no effect. She rang it again and then stepped back and looked up the façade. The windows to John's apartment were in darkness. It seemed he really wasn't home.

She was an idiot. She had just not considered the option that he might not be home. What had she been thinking? That he had sat motionless in his apartment since her last visit in mid-December, waiting for her call or visit, and had not budged just in case she suddenly appeared? It must be because of the deceptive festive atmosphere in this time between Christmas and the New Year. Buildings still had to be watched this week—perhaps *especially* this week—and John had a security firm. He was simply at work this Tuesday afternoon. And she had stolen the hours, lied to Tom, and driven out here all for nothing.

She slowly walked back to her car. She could not bear the thought of just driving back and spending the rest of the day in her own living room with the Christmas tree. She still had a little bit of time left. From her parking space she could watch the entrance to John's building.

She sat in her car, burying herself deep in her coat, trying to ignore the cold that gradually crept into all her bones. It quickly got dark outside. The lights went on in many apartments. A good number of windows were decorated with candles or Christmas arches. Even this rather desolate gray street suddenly looked cozy.

She wondered if life with John would feel different from life with Tom. Whether it would feel different in the *long run*. In this street. In the almost-bare apartment. Why would a man just throw a mattress on the floor and nail a hook into the corridor wall for his coat? Why live in such a reduced way? With no woman or children. Nothing like that in his past either. Affairs, but nothing binding.

She looked up at his dark windows again. He would not get involved in anything. Not in marriage or a long-term partnership. He would not even buy decent furniture that might possibly have given him the feeling that he was settling into an apartment. The way he lived, he could get up and go at any minute. Join a ship's crew and sail the world. Emigrate to Australia and open an ostrich farm. Guide tourists through Canada's national parks.

She smiled, realizing what crazy variations she was coming up with, but her smile was weak and false. She knew that her ideas were not as mad as they had seemed at first. They arose from the image and impression he gave: of being flighty, not tied to anything or anyone, perhaps even incapable of forming ties. Untouchable and unpredictable.

A woman should never get emotionally involved with such a man, she thought. At least not if you do not want to end up falling flat on your face.

At twenty past six, she knew that she urgently needed to make a decision. She needed at least three quarters of an hour for the journey home. Tom was relying on her to take over looking after their sick daughter at seven o'clock. What was more, she was now so bitterly cold that she knew she would catch a terrible cold if she sat in her car any longer.

She got out and walked slowly and hesitantly down the street. She was still hoping that he would suddenly materialize in front of her, so that her long, sad waiting would make sense.

She almost started crying at the thought of having to drive home now. She stopped. She had reached the end of the street and was standing in front of an Indian restaurant. It looked rather rundown, but at least the light behind the dirty windowpane promised warmth. And sitting down in there would mean not having to drive home immediately.

Tom could go to the club an hour later, she thought and pushed the door open resolutely.

The place was almost empty. A man was fumbling around behind the counter with a coffee machine that looked like it had seen better days and was now in urgent need of repair. A young couple sat at a corner table, staring silently into the middle distance. A few pine branches that had lost most of their needles hung in the windows, and silver baubles swayed from the chandelier in the center of the room.

"Are you open?" asked Gillian.

The man, obviously from the subcontinent, looked up from the coffee machine and nodded. "Even if it doesn't look like that at first—yes, we are. It's rather quiet at this time of year. But then come New Year's Eve all hell breaks loose." He looked at her more closely. "Good god, you look cold. What a frosty winter this year!"

"Yes." She peeled off her coat. She was so cold that she could barely move her arms.

"Well, I would suggest you take a nice strong brandy first. And I've got a lovely warm soup. It would do you good." She let herself collapse onto a chair, feeling with relief the blood flow back into her toes as they began thawing. It was surprisingly pleasant to sit on her own in an almost-empty restaurant. She could make a bit of small talk with the owner, without the need to have a serious conversation with anyone. She could surrender to the room's warmth, eat, drink, or just look at the wall, which was all the pair in the corner were doing. Nothing was expected of her. Perhaps that was why it felt so good.

The owner brought her brandy and steaming soup. Following a whim, Gillian asked, "Do you know John Burton? Does he sometimes come here?"

The man nodded. "Of course I know John. He lives just down the block. He often stops by quickly to grab a bite." He looked at her with curiosity. "Are you a friend of his?"

For a split second, it occurred to Gillian that John's female *friends* might often turn up at the restaurant, having waited for him in vain. She wondered what the owner's image of her was: perhaps a middle-aged woman who had fallen for handsome Burton, had frozen half to death waiting outside his house, and was now hoping that he might come in here too.

She did not want to confirm that impression, so she said, "He coaches my daughter in tennis. That's how I know him."

"Well, enjoy your meal," he said and went back behind the counter.

The soup was spicy and very hot. It energized her.

When she was done, she ordered a bottle of mineral water and took a newspaper from a pile left for customers. The paper was three weeks old, but she read it properly, without skipping anything. The couple were still silent. The owner did not say a word. He had turned on the radio. Jokes were being told.

Seven o'clock passed. Half past seven passed. Eight o'clock passed.

Strange how light she felt. Just because she had taken the freedom to ignore the expectations that others had of her.

It was almost half past eight. Gillian had read three newspapers, eaten some naan bread after her soup, and drunk another bottle of mineral water. She felt good, although she knew that Tom was waiting for her at home, no doubt in a rage, and that they would inevitably have a fight. She knew that this was one of the reasons why she had gone to the restaurant and done something that was not like her at all and that she had never dared to do before: she had intentionally broken a promise. She had acted unreliably and selfishly. She had given another person—her husband—cause to worry. She was behaving in a way that she actually abhorred and would never do. But this time she wanted to do whatever it took to cause a fight. She wanted things to escalate. She was even determined to tell Tom about John.

How would he react? Dumbfounded? Aggressively? Perhaps she wanted to end their marriage.

Although she was calm and unafraid and had the feeling that she was doing the right thing, she could not shake off the feeling that something was not right. Something in the situation irritated her, but she did not know what it was.

Perhaps I'm just imagining things, she thought.

Around twenty to nine she got up, put on her coat, went to the counter, and paid. The couple had gone. She was the last and only customer.

"So, going home?" asked the owner. She sensed that he could not figure her out. Usually women who sat alone for so long would get drunk, drowning their sorrows, their man trouble, with a lot of wine or something stronger. They swayed when they finally left for home, back to an empty apartment and a cold bed. But apart from that first brandy, Gillian had only drunk water and obviously read the paper with interest.

Let him think what he likes, she thought.

She stepped outside. It was cold. Snow had started to fall again. The fresh air felt good after the muggy air inside. It was nice not to hear the fast-talking radio voices too. Gillian took a deep breath.

As she walked to her car, she looked for her key in her handbag. As she did, she suddenly found her cell and stopped. Suddenly she knew what had been disturbing her unconsciously the whole time: her phone. It had not rung one single time. And yet anyone would have expected it to start ringing every five minutes at least by a quarter past seven, with Tom trying to ask her what was keeping her. Because he wanted to go. But also because he was worried.

She took it out of her pocket, checking in the light from a streetlamp that it was turned on. She looked at the display. There was not a single missed call.

Suddenly uneasy, she picked up her pace. Was Tom so mad that he would not even call her?

It was not like him.

She unlocked her car. It was ten to nine when she drove off.

2

At a quarter to ten she turned in at their drive. In the living room, the bay window that looked out over the yard was lit up. The curtains had not been drawn, which did not put her mind to rest. Tom hated to be "sitting there for all the world to see," as he liked to say. It was just not like him to leave the light on and not to draw the curtains.

She got out and locked the car. She felt queasy. She had felt so strong sitting in the restaurant in London and putting a question mark over her life with Tom; but now that she had to actually face him, she was weak at the knees. Driving home, it had occurred to her that he might have called Tara and already found out that he had been lied to. Gillian had not asked Tara to cover for her this time. Tara might have gotten tied up in knots trying to make excuses. *Fetch Gillian to the phone*, Tom had probably said, and then Tara would have been unable to comply.

But she would have called me to warn me, thought Gillian. So that didn't quite fit either.

And would Tom call Tara? Did he even have her number? Wouldn't it be more likely that he would try his wife's cell?

She quickened her step. The sense of foreboding increased. It was snowing heavily.

She opened the front door. The entrance hall was lit up brightly. "Hello?" she called out in a low voice.

No one replied.

He's in the living room. He's had a few whiskeys, and now he's going to make a terrible scene, she thought with a sinking feeling.

"Tom? Are you there?"

There was still no reply. She peeked into the living room. It was empty. She hung her coat on a coat hook and took off her boots. She went into the kitchen in her tights. The door to the back yard was open. It was ice-cold in the room. A plate with sandwiches stood on the work top, next to a knife and a cut tomato. A bottle of wine stood next to the sink. It still had its cork in it, but the corkscrew was nearby. It looked as though Tom had been preparing supper for Becky and himself when he had been interrupted unexpectedly. And had then not eaten or drunk anything. Had he then decided to leave it all there and go eat at the club? And take Becky with him, although she was actually still too ill?

Why had he left the lights on? Why had he left the door to the back yard wide open?

Gillian left the kitchen and stepped into the dining room.

She saw the figure crumpled half over one of the dining-table chairs, half on the floor.

It was Tom. It was Tom lying on the chair, his face buried in the cushion, his legs splayed out at unnatural angles.

She moved toward him as if in slow motion.

A heart attack. He had suffered a heart attack. As he prepared the supper. He had just gone into the dining room, perhaps to get a fire going in the fireplace or to set the table, and he had collapsed.

She had always known it would happen. He had steered straight toward that fate with suicidal directness. She had not been able to reach him with her warnings and reproaches.

A throttled sound came out of her throat. God, why like this? She drives off to meet her lover and Tom suf-

fers a terrible fate like this. Alone. Without anyone to
help. He has to deal with it himself and cannot.

Where was Becky?

She pushed past the table and bent over Tom. Dear
God, let him be alive.

Carefully, she tried to turn him over and put him
down gently on the carpet. He was astonishingly heavy,
almost too heavy for her. "Tom," she whispered, in despair. She was horrified, stunned. "Tom, say something, please. Tom! It's me, Gillian! Tom, please turn
around!" She put her hand on his head and with her fingers touched her way around to his face. Suddenly she
had wet, sticky fingers, and she pulled back and looked
at them in disbelief. She sank to her knees.

Her whole hand was covered in blood.

Her brain tried hard to produce some logical chain
of thoughts, but it moved more sluggishly than she had
ever felt it move before. As if her mind did not want to
reach the conclusion it was going to be forced to accept in the end.

He could hardly have injured his head on the cushion that his face was pressed into. He had hit his head,
struggled to his feet, and made it to the table, where
his legs had then given way.... Somewhere in the room
there must be blood, perhaps on the mantelpiece or one
of the door jambs. She looked around in a frenzy. She
could not find the place where he must have hit his head.

Where was Becky?

Becky must have noticed that something was not
right. At some point, she must have come downstairs
to see why her father had not called her for supper. She
must have found him. What would a twelve-year-old girl
do next? Run out to find help. Ring the neighbors' bells
like mad until someone answered. Paramedics should be

here, an ambulance. How could Tom just be lying here like that? Perhaps he had been here for hours.

Why was the kitchen door onto the back yard wide open?

She suddenly had a new thought, which bathed the scene in a completely different light.

She jumped up.

Where was Becky?

She ran out of the room and bounded up the stairs. Upstairs, all the lights were on too.

"Becky!" She roared her daughter's name. "Becky! Where are you?"

Becky's room was empty. The Barbie dolls with which she only played rarely in secret nowadays were strewn across the floor. The pad of drawing paper and a number of paintbrushes lay on her desk, alongside an open box of paints and a jar filled with water. The wardrobe door was open. Most of Becky's jumpers, skirts, and jeans were on the floor. It looked as though they had been snatched from the drawers in a mad rush. Gillian pulled back the bedsheet, then looked under the bed, then behind the big box of toys. Nothing. No sign of Becky.

She sobbed without noticing that she was sobbing. Her husband lay dead in the living room. He might have been killed by a burglar. And her daughter had disappeared from the face of the earth. Apparently in panic, she had just left everything. Whatever had happened, it had caught Tom and Becky completely by surprise.

They had been having a completely normal evening, and suddenly someone had disturbed the peace of it, entering their house ready to be violent. To do anything. It felt to Gillian as if she were in a terrible nightmare which, to top it all, she did not understand. She just knew it was horrific and unreal and should end any minute—except that if there was one thing that was clear to her in the confusion, then it was that there would be no merciful moment of waking up. The horror would only increase.

She ran into the next room, which was the master bedroom. The lights were on here too. The wardrobe doors were open, but the room was empty. *Why were the lights on everywhere? Why had someone searched all the cupboards?* Becky had been in her room—painting, it seemed. Tom had realized that his wife was going to be late and had—no doubt grinding his teeth—started to make the evening meal. Why was the light on in their bedroom? Why in the upstairs bathroom too? Why in the guest room? She ran into all the rooms. All were lit, but all of them were empty. No trace of Becky.

Taking two steps at a time, she ran up the stairs to the attic. In the attic there was a little room that they used for storage, and a bigger room where Tom had hung a swing from the beam and put gym mats down on the floor. When Becky was younger, she had rollicked about up there with her friends when the weather had been bad outside or the yard too muddy. Even its light was on.

Gillian was breathing heavily. "Becky! Becky, please, where are you?"

She was about to run downstairs, because it had occurred to her that she had not looked in the cellar yet, when she heard a noise. It sounded as though it was coming from the nearby storage room.

She spun around. "Becky?"

Then she heard a sob clearly. "Mommy!"

In a flash, she was in the storage room. It was a terrible mess in there. She had wanted to tidy it up for ages, but recently she had not had either the time or energy.

Suitcases and travel bags were piled up, as well as old boxes, Becky's old toys, magazines that someone had once thought they might want to look at again, a few old pieces of furniture, and rolled-up carpets. It was impossible to make heads or tails of it all.

"Becky?" asked Gillian fearfully.

The lid of a large suitcase rose slightly. Becky's face appeared. Strands of her hair fell in a jumble across her forehead. Her eyes were red and swollen from crying. Her skin was pale and covered in red blotches.

"Mommy!" Her voice croaked. She had still not gotten over her throat infection.

Gillian stumbled over the mess underfoot, knelt down beside the suitcase, and lifted the lid, wrapping both arms around Becky. "Becky! For God's sake…what happened? What on earth happened?"

"Mommy, my legs! My legs hurt so much!"

Gillian rubbed her daughter's legs vigorously. Becky must have been lying in the suitcase in a completely cramped position, possibly for hours. It was no wonder that all her bones ached.

"That will go away, darling, it'll be over soon. What happened?"

Becky looked around, wide-eyed with fear. "Is he still here?"

"Who?"

"The man. He did something bad to Daddy and then he looked all over the house for me. Maybe he's still here."

"I don't think so. Who was it?"

"I don't know. I don't know! I didn't see him, and he never said anything at all!"

Gillian could see that the pupils of Becky's eyes were

unnaturally dilated and stared in a frozen way. They needed a doctor immediately. They needed the police.

She lifted Becky up. "Is that okay now? Can you walk?"

Becky suppressed a moan. "Yes. No. It's…okay." Her face still contorted with pain, she leaned on Gillian, who was trying to push the junk to the side with her foot in order to make a little pathway for Becky and herself. Somehow they reached the door.

Becky shrank away from the dazzlingly bright light in the stairwell. "Are you sure he's not here anymore?" she whispered.

Gillian nodded, calmer on the outside than she felt on the inside. "I've gone through the whole house. There's no one here."

She had not been in the cellar. Of course their house would have to be one of the ones that had a cellar. Gillian had always been pleased it did, because it meant extra space. Right now she wished things differently.

But why would someone hide down there?

A murderer waiting for Becky to appear from her hiding place. Becky, who could be dangerous for him. Who could identify the culprit.

They hobbled down the stairs. Gillian steered Becky into her room. "Lock yourself in here now! And don't open up until I tell you to, all right?"

Becky immediately grabbed ahold of her mother. "Mommy! Don't go away, please! Don't leave me on my own!"

"I have to call the police, Becky. And the emergency services. Please wait here! And lock the door!"

"Momm—"

"Please!" Gillian could hear how her nerves made her voice sharp. "Do what I say, Becky!"

She drew away from her daughter. It was clear that Becky was on the point of getting hysterical and before she could, Gillian had to get her to safety and tell the police.

"Into your room, Becky! Right now!"

Becky looked at her mother. Her face was still as white as chalk, apart from the feverish blotches. That frozen stare.

"Where were you, Mommy? Where were you all evening?" Gillian did not answer her.

Thursday, December 31

HE WAS OUT of breath when he arrived at the front door, although he had made an effort to walk normally. He had been afraid of drawing a policeman's attention if he tore through the dark streets like a madman. He did not know how quickly the wheels turned. Was there already a search warrant out on him? Did every policeman already have a photo and description of him? Was a manhunt already in full swing?

He wiped his hand across his brow and realized in surprise that his face was wet. And it was a cold night, almost ten below zero Celsius.

It was half past ten. Another hour and a half until midnight. But all over the city, rockets were already going up and spraying their wild, colorful patterns across the dark sky. Here and there, groups of happy people, some of them rather drunk already, were roaming through the streets, although not *all* that many people. It was just too cold. Whoever could do so was staying inside.

He looked up at the façade. A townhouse in the center of Southend. All the floors had lights on, apart from the top floor. Loud music blared from somewhere or other. Of course. Who went to sleep early on New Year's Eve? People were partying, meeting up, dancing, having fun.

If they were not being hunted by the police.

He hoped that Bartek was home. And that the party noises reaching down to the street were not coming from his apartment. What if there were now thirty people up there in a party mood? He hesitated, but then pressed the doorbell after all. He had no choice. He needed a hiding place; and if he looked for one outside, he would freeze to death on this icy night.

It took a long time before the door buzzed. Samson pushed it open and started up the stairs to the third floor. He had been here a few times. He could not remember that the few stairs had ever been a struggle before. Now he had to stop again and again to catch his breath.

He was completely exhausted, mentally. His nerves were shot. It seemed like that affected his breathing.

Bartek was standing on the half-landing by his apartment, peering down. A hubbub of voices and dance music flooded the stairwell.

It *is* his party, thought Samson despondently.

Bartek looked first shocked and then embarrassed as he recognized the late guest. "Oh, Samson, nice of you to come by!" he said slowly. "We have a few guests over and…well, I meant to invite you too, but you don't like parties, so I thought that maybe…."

Samson climbed the last steps. "Bartek, I need help," he said.

"You look terrible." Bartek pulled the door almost shut behind him. "What happened?"

"The police," said Samson. "The police are after me."

"What?"

"Millie reported me to the police. And Gavin warned me. And now…I don't know where to go."

"God," said Bartek. He did not seem nearly as cool as normal. In fact, it looked like the situation was a bit much for him to deal with.

No wonder, thought Samson. He has the apartment full of guests. All he wants to do is have fun, and now I turn up with a story that must sound completely absurd.

"What do you mean she *reported* you?" asked Bartek. "Why can she report you?"

"I'm in it deep," said Samson and thought he was understating the situation. He had never been in it as deep as this before in his life. "I told you that I...well, what I do all day."

"That you...watch women?"

The way that sounded! Samson himself thought the phrase sounded highly suspicious. *You watch women.* The words conveyed an image that had nothing to do with what had actually happened, but that was just his problem. His hobby was so strange that he could only hope that regarding the recent events, he would just be considered a harmless freak.

"I wrote it all down," he explained quickly. "My observations and thoughts and so on. And I saved it all on my computer. Millie spied on me. She cracked my password, read it all, and printed it out. For her, it's proof that I'm dangerous."

Bartek shook his head. "Well, it's not exactly normal what you do."

"The day before yesterday, a man was murdered. In our street. Shot. In his living room."

"I read about it," said Bartek. "But why—?"

"Since then, Millie must have been nagging Gavin, telling him that they should take my notes to the police. He tried to talk her out of it, but in the end Millie always does just what she wants. So this morning she marched down to the nearest police station with all the materials and declared to them that she thinks I am a suspect."

"But I don't think the police would—" Bartek started to say, but he was interrupted. The door opened and a young woman wearing a short black dress and daringly high heels looked out.

"Ah, there you are, Bartek! I've been looking for you everywhere!" She looked carefully at Samson. "Hello."

"Hello," said Samson. He barely knew Bartek's fiancée Helen. Twice when he had visited Bartek, he had said hi as she rushed past the two of them. She obviously could not remember who he was.

"My friend Samson," explained Bartek.

"Oh, yes. Hello, Samson. Why are out here? The party's inside!"

"We're just coming," said Bartek. "Samson has a little problem to work out."

Helen laughed. Samson realized once more that she was very attractive. As good-looking as Bartek. One day the two of them would have beautiful children.

"All right. Well, once you two have sorted out the problem, come inside," said Helen, disappearing back into the apartment.

It was apparent that Bartek was starting to get impatient. "Well, like I said, Samson, I think—"

"Wait," interrupted Samson. His friend had to understand why the situation was such an emergency. "The man who was killed two days ago…was the husband of the woman I like so much. I told you about her. You know, the family I've spent the most time…watching. That's in my notes too."

"Shit," said Bartek.

"And then there's something else—"

"Christ!"

"I…let loose with a really hateful rant against the guy. In my notes. Because…I was really annoyed by him just before Christmas."

"Why were you annoyed?"

"Because he…was so rude to me. I had taken his twelve-year-old daughter home, and—"

Bartek looked at him in horror. "What?"

Put with everything else, it sounded terrible, thought Samson, absolutely terrible. But his friend could not think that he…God, why did everyone immediately see him as a pedophile?

"No," he said, despairingly. "It was an emergency. She was locked out of her house, both her parents were away, and as I was just coming by, I—"

"You were hanging around outside the family's house again," stated Bartek. The expression on his face said it all. *Why did I have to befriend this idiot, and why am I standing here and letting myself get drawn into this miserable mess?*

"I couldn't leave her outside in the snow. But when her parents fetched her, her dad acted as if…as if he thought…."

Bartek sighed.

"I wrote in my journal that I hate him. And now he's dead and…well, the police are going to find it odd that I was watching the family."

"I can't believe it," said Bartek. "I just can't believe it! God, I told you that you had a screw loose doing all that. No wonder you got yourself in hot water! You're sure that your sister-in-law went to the police with your notes?"

"Gavin told me this at lunchtime. He was in quite a state, both because he had not been able to stop her and because of the whole situation."

"I can understand that," murmured Bartek.

"Then I drove off in my car in a panic. I drove around aimlessly all afternoon. In the end, it occurred to me that it could be dangerous to carry on. I mean, they must have my license plate number by now too. I left the car over at Gunners Park and walked back into town, taking a hundred different detours. Bartek, I've been walking for hours. I'm exhausted. Can I stay here?"

"No way," said Bartek. And, seeing his friend's shocked expression, he added, "I mean, that would be stupid. The police will want to know the names and addresses of your friends, and your sister-in-law will give them my name. They'll figure out right away that you're hiding here."

"But I have to stay somewhere!"

"Do you have some money?"

"A hundred pounds in cash. That was all I had in my account."

"Okay," said Bartek. "Okay." It was clear that he had only one objective right now: to get rid of his friend for now and then think what to do next.

"Listen, that's plenty enough for tonight. For a little inexpensive B&B. Find yourself a room. And call me tomorrow. Maybe I'll have thought of what to do by then."

"A B&B? Isn't that dangerous?"

"I'd say it's not half as dangerous as my apartment," said Bartek. Samson nodded. He realized that Bartek was right.

Bartek glanced back through the door, where they could hear music, laughter, and the clinking of glasses continuing unabated. "Samson, I have guests. I have to go in. We'll talk tomorrow, won't we?"

"Will you help me?"

"Of course," said Bartek, but Samson had the impression that Bartek would have said anything to him at that moment. He wanted nothing so much as to end the wretched scene.

"Bartek," said Samson pleadingly. "Please believe me: I have nothing to do with all of that. I didn't kill

Mr. Ward. I could never kill anyone. Or attack or hurt them. I'm innocent."

"Of course I believe you," said Bartek soothingly. He sounded like a doctor speaking to a patient who was *noncomposmentis*.

Samson closed his eyes for a second in exhaustion. "I really didn't do it."

"Till tomorrow," said Bartek and disappeared into his apartment. He closed the door firmly behind him.

Samson turned to go. His feet were hanging like lead weights. Gavin had advised him to go to the police. "You'll only make it worse if you run away. If you haven't done anything, you'll be able to tell them that. Hiding won't help. At some point they'll find you, and then it'll look *really* bad."

Gavin was undoubtedly right, and yet.... Samson was not brave enough. He was afraid. He was petrified and only able to follow his first instinct to find somewhere safe.

But where would he be safe?

He slowly crept down the stairs. Eleven o'clock. Another hour, and then the new year would begin.

From its first second, it promised him nothing but a nightmare.

Friday, January 1, 2010

1

DETECTIVE INSPECTOR PETER FIELDER knew that his wife often had to be very patient with him, but the gruesome series of murders had taken a surprising turn on December 31, of all days, so there was no way he could spend January 1, which would be followed by a weekend, at home in front of the fire. Even if it would have been better for his marriage.

So he had arranged an extra meeting at the Yard for that morning. After taking much time and effort to scrape the ice off his windshield, he had driven on that bitterly cold, dark morning to the office. He was tired, because he had seen the New Year in with his wife and a couple they were friends with. But he knew Christy would make him a cup of coffee that would bring him back to life. He did not know anyone who made coffee as perfectly as Detective Sergeant McMarrow. Apart from that, she was one of his most intelligent and clever colleagues. Peter Fielder knew that Christy could be dangerous for him. He himself was shy in such matters and would never make the first move. He knew that. But it could be tricky if she ever tried to get closer to him.

The meeting was tough. Everyone was tired, hung over, and not particularly motivated to be there. Detective Constable Kate Linville chipped in that they knew who the culprit was, they just had to find him.

"Oh, right?" asked Fielder. "And who's the culprit?"

"Samson Segal. I thought that—"

"I think we should be careful," Fielder interrupted her. "I admit that when you read Samson's notes, you quickly figure out that he's not quite right in the head. But at this point, that's all we can say."

"He was aggressive about Thomas Ward," insisted Kate.

"And said nothing about Carla Roberts and Dr. Anne Westley."

"He wanders around all day and spies on strangers. Especially women. It wouldn't surprise me if it was him going up and down in the elevator in Hackney!"

"We'll check that," Peter Fielder assured her. "But as long as we have no results, let's keep wild speculation in check, Constable Linville!"

Kate Linville went pink. She was no longer one of the youngest. She should have been promoted long ago, but she remained a constable, as if she were something left to get dusty in the corner. She was a reliable and dutiful member of the staff, but she did not have the slightest sense when it came to criminals, had little understanding of human motivation, and rarely made a constructive suggestion. It was more typical that she would jump to conclusions about possible culprits. Possibly, Fielder suspected, in order to have something to say in meetings.

They had to take things one step at a time. A forensics team was out in Thorpe Bay and had collected a number of Samson Segal's fingerprints. These were now being compared with the few unidentified fingerprints in Carla Roberts's apartment in Hackney and the multitude of prints in the elevator, as well as with the prints in Anne Westley's house. If there were any matches, that would be a great step forward.

At the end of the meeting, Fielder had sent Constable Linville off to talk to Millie Segal once again. Millie was the woman who had turned up in the Southend-on-Sea police station with her brother-in-law's computer notes and claimed to have uncovered a dangerous killer.

"It was him! He killed Thomas Ward. And who knows who else. Read this, and you'll see you are dealing with a psychopath."

Fielder concentrated on the jottings strewn around on his desk. He had scribbled them on various pieces of paper, according to a system that no one apart from himself could see or understand. The whole story was getting more and more complicated, and he felt that he was light years away from a solution. No one had been able to give him any really good leads in the meeting, but perhaps he was asking too much of his team on New Year's Day. Christy was in the next room on the phone. The others had either gone home or were working on the tasks he had given them.

He had time to brood on it. He had the whole long, cold day. The name *Thomas Ward* jumped out at him from his notes. He had circled it in red pen and put a question mark next to it. How did Thomas Ward fit into this series of murders of old women who lived on their own? At first glance—and at second and third glance—he did not fit in at all. Thomas Ward was a man. He was anything but on his own. He had been killed, although his young daughter had also been in the house at the time. He had been found within a few hours by his wife. He had not been suffocated with a cloth stuffed down his throat.

He had been shot. His murderer had fired two shots at him. One bullet had grazed his temple and caused a lot of blood loss, but he had not died of that. The second shot had destroyed his carotid artery. He had not had a chance. Nor would his chance have been any better if he had been found sooner.

It was standard procedure that after the bullet had been analyzed, a computer search would be carried out to ascertain whether the weapon and ammunition had been used in other crimes. The Southend police had had an unexpected match: Thomas Ward had been killed with the same weapon that Anne Westley's murderer had used to shoot his way into her bathroom.

So the case had landed on DI Fielder's desk. And to complicate matters further, when strange writings surfaced written by a Samson Segal from Thorpe Bay, who lived near Thomas Ward and obviously had a bone to pick with him, they had also been forwarded on to Scotland Yard.

That was the reason for the extra meeting on January 1.

At the end of which they were all still as confused as before. What did Thomas Ward and the two murdered women have in common?

Christy McMarrow had expressed the key question. "And what if Ward was not the target? What if the culprit actually meant to get his wife? And didn't know that she wasn't at home?"

Fielder nodded thoughtfully, while he drew another circle around Thomas Ward's name. On December 30, a day after Ward's murder, he had talked to Ward's wife. She had been able to answer his questions calmly. According to what he heard, it was indeed the case that Ward normally went out to his tennis club on Tuesday nights. Normally he never came home before ten or ten-thirty. Anyone who knew a little bit about the Ward family's habits would have assumed that Gillian Ward would be at home, not her husband.

If she had not tried to see her lover that evening. She had told him that too. It had not been easy for her to tell him, but he did not have the impression that she was withholding anything.

Gillian Ward.

He had noted her name too, and circled it a few times. And he had drawn an arrow from her name to another name that he had written in black and underlined repeatedly: *John Burton.*

That had really amazed him. Bumping into Burton unexpectedly like this. In connection with a murder case.

Detective Inspector Burton. His former colleague. Who had ruined his Met career in such idiotic fashion. Burton, whom Fielder had never been able to stand, although he had found it difficult to justify his aversion. Sometimes he suspected that he just did not like the man because he drifted through life footloose and fancy-free, just as Peter Fielder sometimes dreamed of living but never had dared to. Burton had found a young woman attractive and had rushed into a fling without thinking of the possible consequences. When the situation escalated and he had almost no choice but to resign, he had not taken it in his stride but had left his colleagues with the nasty feeling that he was leaving them behind with their monotonous daily grind and their career ambitions, while he was stepping out into freedom and independence. In a moment that had in fact been the greatest failure of his life, he had acted like a winner, not a loser.

Maybe that was what really got my goat, thought Fielder. He immediately pulled himself together: be careful, stay objective! You'd like to get your own back at Burton, of course, but don't let that cloud your judgment.

And now Burton had gotten involved with Gillian Ward, whose husband had just been found murdered. Fielder found it all extremely odd. Burton had, after all, the suspicion of past sexual harassment hanging over him. Even if all the reports had absolved him of any guilt and the Crown Prosecution Service had not pursued the case.

Christy entered the room. "Some news: Samson Segal's car has been found. Gunners Park, out in Shoeburyness. No sign of Segal himself. And I talked to Forensics. No matches yet. The prints in Samson Segal's room don't match any in Roberts's apartment or in the elevator. They're still working on prints at Tunbridge Wells."

"In any case, I think we'd be rash to think of this Segal as the murderer and that—"

Christy interrupted him: "Sir, excuse me, but I know what you're thinking. You think it's Burton, so Samson and his odd notes are just in your way. But why would John Burton—"

"—kill Thomas Ward? He was having an affair with his wife."

"And that's why he'd kill the husband? If he wanted a future with Gillian Ward, she could have gotten a divorce!"

"Maybe he wanted to kill Gillian. From what she said, he didn't know that she was going to visit him that evening or that she ended up hanging around in the Indian restaurant in Stratford. He thought she was home."

"What? And didn't think her daughter would be around?"

"He coached her at tennis. It's possible that she had

told him about the planned holiday with her grandparents, isn't it?"

"And why would he want to kill Gillian?"

Fielder stood up and stepped over to the window. Low clouds hung above the city. "Don't forget, Sergeant, that Burton has already been accused of a sexual crime. What exactly do we know about him? Maybe he's highly dangerous. Disturbed, perverted, what do I know? He got away relatively unscathed last time, but still he decided to leave the force pretty quickly. Why? To stop any further investigation? To stop things from surfacing that could have been awkward for him?"

"What things?" asked Christy.

"No idea. Burton is messed up about sex."

"Sir, I'm not going to defend him. John and I were a team back then. We worked well together. I know his strengths—and his weaknesses. He can't keep his fingers off pretty women, but that doesn't mean by a long way that he is *messed up about sex*, like you say. None of us believed for a moment that he had actually raped that rather hysterical young woman. The prosecutors didn't believe it. The report writers, all independently, didn't believe it. And of course he couldn't stay. Because all his male colleagues, at the very least, here at the Yard made it clear that they wished the whole drama on him. And because it was obvious that the incident would follow him around for his whole life. A high-ranking inspector doesn't cut a particularly convincing figure if every criminal he catches, or the criminal's lawyer, can ask him with a grin if he is the cop who was once investigated for rape. He didn't want that. I can understand him completely."

"Christy, perhaps you aren't completely objective about Burton. I know you appreciated him as a policeman. But that doesn't change the fact that he's turned up in a murder investigation and that we have to check up on him and how he fits into all of this."

"Good. Let's look at *all of this,*" she said. "Why Carla Roberts and Anne Westley? Not exactly Burton's typical prey, are they? One in her mid-sixties, the other almost seventy. He certainly didn't bed them."

Fielder continued to press his point: "Burton certainly doesn't have an alibi for the time of the Thomas Ward crime."

He had sent an officer to talk to John Burton. John had claimed that he had been in his office on Tuesday afternoon. He had met a customer who wanted to protect his mansion with a comprehensive security system and needed to be advised. The conversation had gone on until six o'clock. The customer confirmed this. However, John had been alone after that, immediately starting to produce a concept for his customer and to calculate the costs. He had also been on call until nine o'clock. Then he had been relieved by a colleague and, as he stated, had gone home. Unfortunately for his alibi, there had not been a single call that evening. Nothing had happened. That meant that between six and nine, John could have driven out to Thorpe Bay and back to London without anyone being any the wiser.

"Not everyone without an alibi is guilty," pointed out Christy. "And Burton wouldn't be stupid enough to leave when he was on call. Too many things could go wrong."

Fielder turned away from the window. "I'm not saying it is Burton," he said. "I'm just trying to not get too focused on this Samson Segal. It's just a feeling.… Everything about this man, or at least what we know about him, seems too…obvious to me. Maybe it's just the feeling that we're being handed the culprit on a plate. Suddenly this woman appears and claims casually that her brother-in-law has a neighbor's life on his conscience while handing over a pile of papers that practically proves her thesis. That sets alarm bells ringing for me. It's a reflex; I can't help it."

"He's disappeared. That doesn't exactly look good for him. Or suggest he's innocent," said Christy. She shook her head. "I know what you mean, boss. But sometimes that's how it works out. You get your man because someone who knows him, and had been suspicious for a long time, just can't keep quiet any longer. And you have to admit that Segal fits our profile of the killer perfectly. He has massive hang-ups about women, as his sister-in-law says and his notes confirm. He has wished for years for a relationship and has always been rejected. Sometimes he writes hateful rants about women. He stalks women, noting every detail about their lives. And about their families. He knew that Thomas Ward is never at home on Tuesday evenings. He knew that Becky Ward should actually have been at her grandparents' house. He had all the information he needed."

"Not all of it. He obviously had no idea about Gillian Ward's affair with another man. At least he didn't know anything specific."

"Of course people try to hide such things as best they can."

"Admittedly. But would he, because of his intense observation of them, not have noticed that the daughter was home?"

"She didn't go out because of her sore throat. He wasn't seeing her, and so he must have assumed she had gone off," suspected Christy. "She goes to her grandparents' every year between Christmas and the New Year. Everyone who knew the Wards knew that."

"But all those people don't have the odd character traits that Samson Segal does."

"So, let's say he thinks Gillian Ward is home alone. Does he force his way in so he can kill her? The woman he worships?"

"Who doesn't pay him any attention," added Christy. "Doesn't even notice him. And she didn't defend him when her husband barked at him. He felt like she treated him *like trash*, that's what he wrote. He was expressing the hate that he feels. He *had* worshipped her, but then it changed: he had been bitterly disappointed by her." Fielder rubbed his hands over his face. He was tired and impatient, and last night's champagne was not helping.

"And how do Westley and Roberts fit into this theory? One living in Hackney, the other in Tunbridge Wells?"

"He had a car. Those distances were hardly insurmountable for him."

"Then he would have mentioned them in his notes. No, Sergeant, there's too much that doesn't fit in," said Fielder, shaking his head. "Even the chancy theories we already have are now collapsing. At least Westley and Roberts had something in common. They both lived on their own and had been pretty isolated since their retirements. Gillian Ward, on the other hand, is married, has a daughter, and works."

"That means," said Christy, "that we have been focusing on the wrong common denominator. The fact that they live on their own doesn't seem to be the decisive link between the victims. There must be something else. Something we've missed."

"We have to go deep into Anne Westley's past," said Fielder. "And Carla Roberts's. And Gillian Ward's. That will be easier, because she's still alive. Yes, we should start with her."

"And we should make sure we find Samson Segal," said Christy. "He's important! Either he's guilty or he's an interesting witness. He observed the Ward family and sniffed around their lives. He might have noticed something decisive."

"The sister-in-law is just being questioned again," said Fielder. "Maybe that will give us some clue. It's terribly cold outside. Segal must have found a warm bolthole."

"We'll get him," said Christy.

He looked at her. He could feel her conviction that they had the killer.

But he still could not believe it.

2

SHE HAD THE feeling that she had just been sitting on the sofa for close to three days, staring at the walls with no understanding of what had happened in her life. What was not right about it. She would cook (for Becky, really), tidy the apartment, shower in the morning, and put on clean clothes. She would fill the dishwasher and empty it again. Every evening, she would take a strong sleeping pill, lie down on the sofa, and sink into a numbing black abyss, from which she woke in the morning without feeling refreshed. She prepared breakfast, toasted bread, cut fruit, fried eggs.

Tara had already complained. "Gillian, there's nothing left for me to do! I want to take care of you, but I have the feeling it's the other way around!"

Gillian had looked pleadingly at her friend. "Let me do something, Tara. Otherwise I'll go crazy."

Tara concurred immediately. "Of course. I understand."

In that horrific night, Gillian and Becky had gone to stay at Tara's apartment, along with Chuck, their tomcat, whom Gillian had found in the end after a desperate hunt, shivering and confused a few yards farther down the street. He must have run out of the open kitchen door in panic when the horror and violence descended on their house. A friendly and very sensitive policewoman had explained to Gillian that the house had to be cordoned off as a crime scene. "We can't let any clues be destroyed. Do you know anyone who could put you up for a few days?"

Gillian had thought of her parents first, but they lived too far away. Then Tara occurred to her. She had called her friend and explained to her what had happened. At first, there had only been a silence on the other end of the line. After a long while, Tara had said, utterly stunned, "*What* happened?" And then, the next moment, she showed that she was a woman who dealt with this kind of situation regularly at work. She had acted calmly and decisively. "I'm on my way," she said. "I'll fetch you and Becky. Of course you can stay at my place as long as you like."

They had been there since that night. In Tara's beautiful old apartment in Kensington. A Scotland Yard detective inspector had come to talk to Gillian, and she had told him everything she knew. She had even told him the whole truth about her relationship with John. A policewoman had talked to Becky in the presence of Gillian and a psychologist. Becky, Gillian knew, was an important witness. She had not seen the culprit, but she had crept downstairs when she heard a loud thud and crash from downstairs and heard her father shout "What on earth do you think you're doing?"

Then there had been two shots. Becky had seen, looking through the dining room door from her vantage point on the stairs, her father fall onto a chair.

"Did you think about running over to him?" asked the policewoman.

Becky shook her head. "No." It sounded apologetic. "I knew someone was there. I'd heard my dad talking to someone. I'd heard someone shooting. I…was so afraid. I just wanted to get away. Away!" She had gone white as a sheet. "I should have helped him. I should have gone over. I should…."

The psychologist stepped in quickly. "Absolutely not, Becky. You couldn't have done anything for him. You did the right thing to get yourself to safety."

"I just wanted to find out what had caused Becky's sudden instinct to hide," explained the policewoman. It sounded like a justification. "Unfortunately, everything she saw, heard, and felt that evening is important to us."

But nothing Becky told her was really useful. She had been painting, had been so engrossed in it that she had only realized a stranger was in the house threatening her father when his voice had risen.

"When I saw Daddy collapse, I got really scared. I was standing on the stairs and I slipped. That made quite a loud noise, and in that moment I knew…I knew somehow that the person who had done it now knew I was in the house. I lost it a bit, I was so afraid. I ran upstairs and looked for a place to hide."

She had remembered the suitcase in the storage room in the attic, because she used to hide in it when she and her friends played in the house. She had lain there, with cramps in her arms and legs and barely daring to breathe, and she had heard the culprit comb the whole house for her. He had run from one room to the next, thrown open wardrobes, pushed furniture aside.

"When he came upstairs, I almost died of fright. I thought he would find me immediately. He was making a lot of noise, and he threw boxes around in the room I was in. I thought I'd be dead any minute."

"But you saw nothing at all?"

Becky shook her head. "The suitcase lid was closed. It was dark inside. Completely black."

The policewoman wanted to know if Becky had heard the doorbell ring at an earlier point, but she could not remember. "I don't think so. I don't know. But I think I would have gone downstairs if I'd heard it."

On this New Year's Day, Tara and Becky, who still looked rather drugged and listless, had gone ice-skating in Hyde Park. Tara had tried to persuade Gillian to go with them, but she had refused. "No. You two go. I'll be happy to be here on my own."

Soon after the two had left, Detective Inspector Fielder had called and asked if he could come by. She would have preferred to fob him off with some excuse, because she felt so tired, burned out, and empty; but she knew that she had to pull herself together. The man was doing his job, and he needed her support. It was important that they find Tom's murderer.

Now Fielder was sitting opposite her in an armchair in Tara's living room. She had made coffee, and he was grateful for the cup she poured him. He looked very tired. Probably he had been partying the night before.

What a terrible New Year's Day, thought Gillian. From where she was sitting, she could see the balcony and the gray sky. Chuck was sitting at the window. He too was looking out, his eyes following the birds that sometimes landed on the railing and looked at him cheekily.

Detective Inspector Fielder was just expounding his theory of how the culprit had gotten into the house. "If we assume that he didn't ring the bell, and—following on from that—that no one opened the door for him, then it could be that he found a much easier way in. We've had a look. From the street, as I'm sure you know, you can look through the little window in the front door all the way to the kitchen and see if the door to the back yard is open. That works even better in the evening, when everything inside is lit up. We suspect that your husband had opened the back door. Maybe he just wanted to let some fresh air in. Because there is nothing on the door to suggest it was forced open. The murderer, who might have planned on ringing the bell, saw his chance, ran around the house and entered the kitchen from the back yard. That's why Becky didn't hear anything."

"Are there any footprints?"

He shook his head regretfully. "By the time the police arrived, several more hours of snow had fallen."

"But why?" asked Gillian. "Why? Why would anyone want to kill Tom?"

He asked a question in return. "Do the names Carla Roberts and Anne Westley mean anything to you?"

Gillian needed a few seconds to understand the full amplitude of what he was saying. "Do you think there's a connection…?"

"So you know who the two women are?"

"From the papers. I don't know them myself."

"You'd never heard of them before? Your husband never mentioned them to you?"

"No. Never."

"Dr. Anne Westley was a doctor in London. You never visited her with Becky?"

"No. Like I said. I don't know her."

Peter Fielder took a sip of coffee and gently placed his cup back on the table. He looked at Gillian with a serious face. "The weapon. The pistol that shot your husband. It is almost certainly the same weapon that was used against those two women."

"Were they shot too?" asked Gillian. In the newspapers there had only been speculation about the causes of death, as the police had not revealed any details. For this reason, Fielder did not want to go into specifics with Gillian.

"It appears that they were at the very least threatened with the weapon," he replied evasively. He didn't want to mention that the culprit had shot the lock to pieces of the door to the room in which Dr. Westley was hiding.

Gillian found it all rather strange. "But why should someone who killed two old women then kill a man in his early forties? Nothing was even stolen from our house. It doesn't make sense!"

"Nothing makes any sense yet," said Fielder, with some resignation apparent in his voice. "At least, we haven't found a link yet. There is a strong possibility that…." He was trying to find the right words. He did not want to just blurt out his suspicion without finding a way to soften it somehow.

Yet she guessed what he wanted to say. She could see it. "You think Tom was not the intended victim? You think it was *me*?"

He seemed relieved that she had said it. "It really is just a hypothesis. But it is the case that your husband would not normally have been home that evening. Just like your daughter. Anyone who knows your family a little, or who had researched it, could have assumed you'd be home on your own."

"He looked in the kitchen—"

"Yes. But he didn't see anyone, because it appears your husband was in the dining room. His murderer just saw the lit-up kitchen and the open door. He came inside and suddenly there's a man in front of him instead of the woman he'd expected. Of course, he had no sensible explanation for why he had crept into this man's dining room with a pistol. He can only kill him—so that he can't be identified by him later. And then to his horror, he hears a sound on the stairs. There's someone *else* in the house. Someone who might have seen him too. So he hunts like mad for that person. Thankfully, he didn't find her." Gillian groaned and buried her face in her hands. "If he'd found Becky...."

"Becky is very lucky. She was also lucky that the murderer obviously got jittery about sticking around at the scene of the crime to carry on looking for her. He gave up. Your daughter has a guardian angel, Gillian!"

She lifted her head. "But why me? Who would want to kill me?"

"We've been asking the same question for weeks in the Roberts and Westley cases," said Fielder. "And if we consider you alongside the two murders, and put your husband's murder down as a terrible and unplanned mistake, then that leaves us with two carried-out murders and one attempted murder whose motives are as yet unknown. Mrs. Roberts and Dr. Westley must have died in horrific ways. At first we thought the culprit must be full of aggression for all women and had just chosen Roberts and Westley because the two of them, living in such isolated circumstances, were easy prey. They were both found a week after their murders, and even then only by chance. But you don't fit that pattern.

So it must be something else that you and the other two women have in common."

"But I don't even know them!"

"Your lives might still overlap in some way."

"Oh, god," mumbled Gillian. "What a nightmare."

"What do you know about Samson Segal?" asked Fielder. Gillian gave him just the answer he had expected after reading Segal's notes.

"Segal? That guy who always hangs around our house?"

Maybe Christy was right, he thought suddenly. But before he could ask anything else, the doorbell rang and Gillian stood up, murmuring an apology. When she came back, she was not alone.

John Burton was following her.

3

SAMSON SEGAL ALMOST jumped out of his skin when someone knocked on the door of his room. As the dive where he had holed up definitely did not offer room service, he assumed it was not someone from the hotel.

He asked hesitantly, "Who is it?"

"Me. Bartek. Open up!"

With relief, Samson unlocked the door. He had called Bartek that morning, but had only gotten through to his answering machine. He had explained where he was and asked him urgently for help with money. After that, he had sat on the worn-out mattress, stared at the square of sky visible from the window, and hoped that his friend would hear his message sometime that day. His paltry hundred pounds would not last long. When he had turned up in the night and asked for a room in this place that could scarcely be called a hotel, the woman at reception, who stank of alcohol and cigarettes, had taken thirty pounds immediately and said that she also wanted to be paid thirty in advance for the next night. That meant he only had money for three nights.

"Thirty pounds?" he had asked in horror, and the woman had immediately turned nasty.

"What world do you live in, young man? One where things are free? Well, wake up and smell the coffee! And that price includes breakfast, so stop grumbling!"

Not that he had yet tried the breakfast. He felt paralyzed. It felt impossible to leave the cold damp room with its grotty furniture for even a moment. He knew that the security provided by the four rickety pale green walls was only deceptive, but the world outside seemed like shark-infested waters to him and he didn't dare go out.

Bartek looked terrible. Samson saw that as soon as his friend stumbled into the room. He had dark rings under his eyes and his lips were ashen. He must have been partying well into the night. He looked tired and hung over. Under normal circumstances he would no doubt have stayed in bed until evening. Instead he had to help a friend in trouble.

Samson felt guilty immediately. "Bartek! Thanks for coming!"

Bartek looked around the room. The hotel was right next to the Southend railway station. It was an old run-down building with low ceilings and creaking floors. The windows were tiny, the carpets disgusting. You could see that lying in the bed in Samson's room, you would sink down to the floor. There was one armchair. A small chest of cheap wooden drawers. A sink on the wall. You had to cross the hallway to get to the bathroom.

It was utterly wretched.

"God," said Bartek. Then he raised his shoulders, shivering. "It's cold in here!"

"The heating doesn't work properly," explained Samson.

"Oh, man," said Bartek and dropped down into the armchair. "Samson. This is a bloody mess! The police were just at my place."

"What?"

"And not just any old Southend bobby. *Scotland Yard*, you understand?"

"Christ!"

"A policewoman. Detective Constable Linville. She had just spoken to your lovely sister-in-law, who had given her the tip to visit me. She said what good friends we are and that we meet every week in the pub and who knows what else! And so the policewoman rushed over to my place. Helen and I were still in bed."

"Did Helen say I went to your place yesterday evening?"

Bartek shook his head. "No, thank god! Although we hadn't agreed on that. She was completely shocked to have a policewoman suddenly standing in our apartment and asking about you. But she's a clever girl. She just kept quiet."

"What did you say?"

"That I had last seen you before Christmas. And that I had no idea where you were, of course."

Samson relaxed a little. "I'm really grateful, Bartek."

Bartek shook his head again, as if he wanted to reject Samson's thanks, as if he wanted to keep Samson as far from him as possible. "Then I listened to your message on my phone. That's careless, Samson! Don't do that anymore! Don't leave messages on my voicemail. Nor on my landline's answering machine. In fact, don't call me at all from now on!"

Samson felt himself go weak at the knees. Without anywhere else to sit, he settled on the mattress, which sank down toward the floor with a sigh. "But I need your help, Bartek! I can't do it on my own!"

"Nor can you do it with me," said Bartek. "You have to face the situation." He fished around in his trouser pocket and pulled out a few crumpled notes. "Two hundred pounds. I can't give you any more. I can't do anything else for you."

Samson leaned forward and took the money. With it, he would be able to stay here for almost a week and a half. As long as his picture did not appear in the papers. Then it would become dangerous to stay in any one place for more than a few hours at a time.

"Thanks, Bartek, I know that for you it's—"

"It's completely dangerous," said Bartek. He sounded angry. "I don't have English citizenship, understand? I'm starting my life here. I work hard. I want to get married. Helen and I want to buy an apartment. We want to have a child. Do you know what it would mean for me to end up in a murder investigation? If they have a warrant out for your arrest and I help hide you? You might go to jail for a few years, but I might get deported. I might be back in Poland, and everything I've worked so hard for would suddenly be all over. You might wreck my whole future!"

"But it wasn't me, Bartek. I haven't harmed anyone!"

"Then don't run away! Go to the police!"

"It's too late now! I've already run away!"

"You can explain that—panic, confusion. You realized how suspicious you must look, so you ran away, scared."

"They won't believe me."

"They won't be able to prove you did anything, if you haven't done it!"

"But you know what it's like. They need a culprit, and I'm perfect for them. They don't really care whether or not I—"

"Oh, stop it," said Bartek. "They can't just put you in prison for no reason. They have to have proof. And if you didn't do it, then they've got a problem." He got up. "I'm not going to get drawn into this anymore, Samson. That was the last thing I'll do for you. I can only hope I haven't messed up my life by doing this much. From now on, you have to get by on your own. I promised Helen too. She's going crazy. I've never seen her so mad."

Samson got up too. "It wasn't me," he replied. It was already sounding like a stuck record to him.

"Then you've got nothing to be afraid of," said Bartek.

"Nor you," said Samson. "Because you're not helping a killer. You're helping someone who's innocent."

He could see the doubt in his friend's eyes.

He thought to himself, sadly: He isn't certain.

4

THE TWO MEN stood facing each other in silence for a few seconds. Both of them were surprised and unsure at first how to proceed.

Then Fielder said, "Hello, John. I hadn't expected…."

He did not finish his sentence, but of course John chimed in. "Hello, Peter. What didn't you expect? That we would ever see each other again?"

"That we would see each other again during a murder investigation. I didn't expect that," said Fielder.

"Your people have already checked on me," said John.

Fielder smiled at him in a friendly way. "Right. And found out that you don't have an alibi for the time of the crime. Of the murder of Thomas Ward."

The way Fielder emphasized the last sentence made John narrow his eyes. "What other murder should I find an alibi for?"

"You're not a suspect," said Gillian. Fielder saw that her hands were trembling slightly. "They also checked on me. That's normal, isn't it?"

"Of course," said Fielder.

"What other murders?" insisted John.

"Tom was killed with the same weapon that was used when two elderly women were murdered," explained Gillian. "You know, the ones in the papers. That's why all three crimes are probably by the same killer."

John raised his eyebrows. "The same gun?"

"Right," said Fielder. He observed John closely and saw that John immediately had the same thought that the police had been talking openly about: that Tom had been in the wrong place at the wrong time. That the killer had meant to kill his wife. Fielder could read that realization in John's eyes. He thought: either he's a *damn* good actor, or he really had nothing to do with the crime.

John turned to Gillian. "Gillian...."

"I know," said Gillian. "I might have been the target. I'm a woman and I was supposed to be alone that evening. I fit the pattern better than Tom."

"We don't know that for sure," said Fielder. "But it would be better if you were to stay here for a while. Even after the crime-scene tape comes down." He turned abruptly to John. "How did you know that Mrs. Ward was at her friend's house?"

"I texted him this morning," explained Gillian before

John could answer. "Right after Tom's…death, I didn't want to see him; but by now…." She shrugged her shoulders helplessly. "I'm not in the best of states," she added quietly. "And I have to seem like I'm on top of things for Becky. Tara, my friend, is very caring, but I think she probably has an issue with the fact that I wanted to meet John that evening. She doesn't say, but…to her, it would definitely have been better if I had left Tom for good, if I was no longer happy with him. I always think that her secret opinion is that only bad things happen when people deceive each other and aren't honest."

She swallowed. Her face trembled as she tried to hold back her tears.

John went over to her and put his arm around her shoulder. The two men looked at each other over her head. They both thought the same thing. You did not have to be a psychologist to understand that Gillian was projecting on her friend the thoughts that were torturing her all the time: her almost unbearable feelings of guilt. "You can't think like that," said Fielder. "It's not about whether you acted morally toward your husband or not. We're dealing here with a cold-blooded killer who, for some reason we don't know, targeted your family. If we're talking about guilt, then just about that person's. The culprit will be up before a judge one day, hopefully—not you, Mrs. Ward!"

She had wiped a few tears from her cheek. Now she lowered her hands. She had pulled herself together. "And do you think it could be Samson Segal?" she asked, coming back to the topic of conversation that John's appearance had interrupted.

"Who is Samson Segal?" asked John immediately.

"He lives on our street," said Gillian. "And he…he has been acting a bit strangely. Tom was pretty angry with him." She looked at Peter Fielder. "How did you find out about him?"

"We were tipped off," said Fielder. "But I have to add that we have absolutely no idea whether he is involved or not. What do you mean, *strangely*, Mrs. Ward? And what did you mean earlier when you said he *hangs around your house*?"

"There came a time when we realized that we see him almost every time we leave the house or look down the street. He would either just be passing by or be standing around.... Tom noticed him before I did. Tara noticed once too, when she visited me. After the two of them pointed it out to me, I realized that I'd been bumping into him a lot." She shrugged her shoulders. "But I didn't find him threatening. He seems to me to be a nice, if shy, man. A harmless eccentric."

"Apparent harmlessness can be deceptive," explained Fielder. "I've met hardened criminals that look so harmless that every grandmother in the world would trust their savings book to them."

"Just before Christmas, there was one incident," said Gillian. She talked about meeting John and that she and Tom had arrived home late, that Becky had left her friend's sleepover and that Samson Segal had taken her to his and Gavin's house. And that Tom had been aggressive toward him, whereas Gillian had felt grateful. Peter Fielder already knew the story from Segal's notes, but he listened with interest. He felt it was important to find out that Thomas Ward had indeed acted inappropriately toward his neighbor. Segal had clearly not imagined this or exaggerated it. He had helped the Wards' daughter in an emergency and in return had been treated shoddily by her father.

"Do you know why your husband reacted the way he did?" he asked. "What did he have against Segal?"

She thought, trying to recall the evening and their conversation. Oddly, it all seemed so very far away. As if years had passed, not just two weeks.

"I don't think he could put his finger on it," she said in the end. "He just didn't like Samson Segal. He was shocked to hear that the man, who was almost a stranger to us, had taken our daughter to his house. He immediately assumed the worst, but in fact it was all quite harmless. Samson Segal's brother and sister-in-law were there too, and Becky had fallen asleep in front of the television in the living room. I was embarrassed at Tom's rudeness. But that evening he said that he had often seen Samson Segal outside our house, and so it wasn't a coincidence that he had been there just when Becky got home and no one answered the door for her. It all seemed highly suspicious to him."

"We know that Becky had told Segal about her holiday plans in Norwich at her grandparents'. He could assume she had gone to visit them," said Fielder.

"Have you questioned this Mr. Segal?" asked John.

"No," said Fielder. "That's the problem. He seems to have disappeared."

"Disappeared? Fled?"

"Yes."

John whistled quietly through his teeth. "I understand. That doesn't exactly prove his innocence."

"If he is innocent, that wasn't the cleverest move," Fielder agreed.

"He hung around the Wards' house," said John. "He had a reason to be really angry with Thomas Ward. Is there any possible connection to the two murdered women?"

Peter Fielder shook his head. "As far as we can see—no."

He had the impression that John could see that he was not showing all his cards, but that John also realized that he would not find out more by asking questions. The man had been a really good investigator once. Very intuitive and capable of understanding what was not said.

Could he be a murderer?

You have a problem with women, Fielder thought, I'd bet anything on that. Not as obvious and classic a problem as Segal's, but you are a little unbalanced. Who throws away a promising career because he can't keep his hands off a young woman? Why are you obviously incapable of having anything like a normal relationship? Why this relationship now with a married woman, the mother of one of the children you coach? The wife of a murder victim. That's the decisive factor. "Thomas Ward's death associates you with a horrific series of crimes, John. If you had anything to do with them, I swear I'll find out and put you behind bars. It will be an enormous pleasure!"

He was scared by the strength of the feelings his former colleague caused in him. He saw the hint of a smile playing in the corner of Burton's mouth and had the unpleasant impression that his expression mirrored some of his emotions.

He forced himself to act calmly, returning to the topic of Becky's planned trip.

"Which people knew that Becky would be gone after Christmas? We cannot exclude the possibility that the culprit was banking on that fact—that your daughter would not be home."

Gillian shrugged. "It would be easier to ask who *didn't* know. I think everyone in her class at school

knew. Perhaps some of their parents. Almost everyone
we know, too. My friend Tara. Diana, the mother of
Becky's best friend Darcy. Various people in the neighborhood knew. It seems Samson Segal knew. For years,
Tom and I have driven Becky to Norwich on December
26 and returned, ourselves, two days later. My father
then brings her back before school starts. It's always
been like that. The cleaners that have worked in our
house knew. Our work colleagues knew. So, pretty much
everyone."

"I see," said Fielder.

"Before you ask: I knew too," said John. "In the last
coaching session before Christmas, we talked about the
children's holiday plans. Becky told us about hers."

"Excuse me, Mrs. Ward," said Fielder. "But I have
to ask: does Becky know about your relationship with
Mr. Burton?"

She shook her head. "No," she whispered. And she
added, "At least, I hope that she doesn't suspect anything."

"I suppose a lot of people also knew that Mr. Ward is
always at his tennis club on Tuesday evenings?"

"Yes, almost as many people knew that."

"Did you know?" Fielder turned suddenly to John.

"Yes. Gillian mentioned it to me once."

And you are much too clever to lie to me, thought
Fielder. You'll be nice and cooperative about everything
I can check. But that doesn't mean that you aren't a
lying bastard.

He held out his hand to Gillian. "Goodbye, Mrs.
Ward. Are you planning to stay here? Can I reach you
here?"

"Yes."

"It would be good if you…were not to leave the apartment too often. And were just a little bit careful. Toward

everyone." He would have liked to have made it clearer that he mistrusted Burton and that she would do well to stay away from her lover, but he could not express his suspicion as openly as that. He could not prove anything against John.

"I'll be careful," promised Gillian. Her fingers were ice-cold. "And I'll not be going out much anyway. I want to spend a lot of time with Becky. She needs me."

"We'll have to talk to Becky again. Gently, of course. But it's possible that she might remember more from that evening. She had a terrible shock and might have repressed some things. Everything that she gradually starts to remember could be of importance."

"Of course," said Gillian.

She accompanied Inspector Fielder to the door. After he had disappeared from view down the stairs, she closed the door very carefully and drew the chain across. When she went back into the living room, she found John crouched down, stroking her purring cat, who had left his place by the window.

"He's suspicious of me," he said. "Inspector Fielder. He never could stand me, and to find me caught up in this crime is music to his ears."

"He seems to me to be competent and objective," said Gillian. "He won't let any personal feelings guide him."

John stood up. "Do *you* think I could have done it?"

She looked at him in amazement. "Of course not."

He moved closer to her. His voice was tender. "How are you? I didn't have a chance to ask you yet, what with my lovely ex-colleague here. You look pale."

She had been holding herself together the whole time. For Becky's sake. But also so that she did not fall victim to her own feelings. Victim to her horror, her shock, her mourning, her guilt, and her fear. But now, as he talked gently to her, the protective wall, which she had put up around her heart or soul or whatever the pulsing, glowing heart of her pain was, broke down.

She started to really cry for the first time since the unbelievable happenings of three nights before, not just the few tears into her pillow at night, barely daring to breathe for fear that Becky, sleeping next to her, would hear. Now her tears flowed freely. She was crying, trembling, letting John wrap his arms around her and pull her to him. She could feel the wool of his sweater against her cheek, his heartbeat, his breath as his chest rose and fell with a peaceful rhythm. It was the powerful, secure embrace of a man who was used to keeping calm and never letting the circumstances around him get to him.

The embrace could have consoled her.

She only realized that she did not feel consoled after she had let go of him and disappeared into the bathroom to blow her nose, wash her face, and wipe off her smudged makeup.

She looked at herself in the mirror and could not understand. She could not understand why she still felt so cold and hopeless. Why she had felt so alone in his embrace.

Perhaps she could never be consoled again. She broke down in tears again.

PART II

Sunday, January 3

1

SUNDAYS WERE WORST. It was not that they passed in an essentially different way from Mondays or Thursdays. But a leaden calm settled over the city on Sundays, at least over this rather soulless apartment building in Croydon where Liza lived. Even where you saw people and heard noises, realizing that you were not alone in the world, a thick blanket seemed to cover and suffocate every living thing. It was as if nothing moved. Sundays were dead days.

She had once read that most suicides occur on Sunday afternoons, and she had no doubt that that was true. There was also an increase in suicides around the New Year. She believed that too. Oddly, Christmas did not see a rise. But she also understood that. People with troubles could deal with the peaceful message of Christmas to some degree. But the popping corks and blaring music of New Year's Eve's enforced cheer just rubbed salt into wounds. That was when the pain was no longer bearable. And New Year's Day bathed the pain in a pale winter light. It hurt. The New Year began as wretchedly as the old one had stopped, and in its turn it would end just the same.

So people preferred to end it straightaway.

Liza had not fallen off any of the cliffs. Christmas, New Year's Eve, New Year's Day.

She would not throw her life away on this sad, empty, dead Sunday afternoon.

She told herself to keep going. Somewhere in one of the apartments below, someone was playing the piano. The piece sounded vaguely familiar to her, but she could not place it. It was just a short passage, actually. At the end of every attempt, the piano player would make a mistake and start again from the beginning. This had been going on for two hours now. The player must have the patience of an angel.

Or be a simpleton.

Apart from the piano, nothing else in the building could be heard. Most families must be out on walks. Outside, the sun was shining, the snow was glittering, and it was icy cold. Just the day to go on a long hike and then warm up later in a cozy living room with a glass of mulled wine and a nice evening meal.

At least she could do that: she could cook something nice. It was not the same if you had not gone for a walk beforehand, but it was something you could look forward to.

She looked at the clock. Not yet four. A little early to be thinking about an evening meal. Nevertheless, she went into the kitchen and looked in her fridge. She had a few things she could use: meat, potatoes, carrots. She could make an Irish stew.

Suddenly she felt sick. She slammed the fridge door and straightened up. She had lost her appetite completely.

She left the kitchen. She would not eat anything. More than two months had passed since she had broken down that evening in the Kensington Hotel's ladies' room. Nothing had been the same since. Her whole life had changed. She wondered if she could still talk of a *life*. She was practically not moving any more, just drifting like a captive animal through her apartment in this anonymous apartment building. She had lost a lot of weight, although before it happened—in her other life—she had already been too skinny. Too often she felt like she did just then: hunger, a need to cook, and then some memory of a situation, image, moment that made her feel sick and killed her appetite. She would abandon what she had been doing and, at most, just dissolve an aspirin in water. Just to be safe. Because she knew that this feeling would be followed by a migraine, forcing her into a darkened room, where she would lie for hours with a wet cloth on her forehead, trying to endure the attack. Sometimes she managed to pre-empt it.

Once again she went into the bathroom, took a pill from the mirrored bathroom cupboard, threw it into her toothbrush glass, and poured in water. In the mirror she could see a creature with pale skin and gray lips. She turned her head a little, looking at herself in three-quarter profile. She looked like a wreck, but she still had beautiful hair. It was blond, long and a little wavy. There were moments when she thought it possible that she might manage to find the normality that other people experienced. But of course that was not true. Not as long as she locked herself in this apartment and barely ventured out. Not as long as she avoided all contact with other people.

On a day like today, with the snow shining in the sun and the cold air burning on her skin, she would have given anything to be able to go out. Just to walk briskly through the park, hearing the snow crunch underfoot, watching the children build a snowman, looking at the dogs chasing each other boisterously.

But it would not have been a good idea to do that.

Just to leave the apartment for fun. Two or three times a week she went out to do her shopping. That was something she *had* to do. And then there were her expeditions, when she visited the part of town where she used to live: to see Finley. At least for a moment.

Without that, she would not have been able to bear it all. She would have just sat in a corner and died.

She drank the water with the dissolved aspirin in little gulps. She forced herself not to let the bad, painful thoughts gain the upper hand. They could plunge her into panic.

Because she could see no prospects for the future. That was the worst of it. There was no saying how long she would be here in Croydon. There was no point to it, no hope. She might have to sit there for five years.

It could also be for ten or fifteen years.

She put down her glass and went into the living room. She lowered the blinds on the big window that faced south.

She could not bear the sun any longer.

2

SAMSON'S HEART PLUMMETED when he heard a knock at the door. Since Bartek had come on New Year's Day, he had harbored the fear that his friend would rat on him. Bartek had said how scared he was of being drawn into an ugly incident, and Samson had felt the real force of that fear on Bartek. In addition, Bartek had mentioned his fiancée's anger and fear. Samson could imagine that Helen was putting pressure on Bartek. *Go to the police! Tell them what you know! You can still get out unscathed! You're mad to help that madman. And we don't even know if he is innocent.*

In essence, Samson was waiting for the police. He knew that it would be cleverer of him to find a new place to stay as quickly as possible and not to tell Bartek where he was going, but he was too exhausted. In any case, it was only a matter of time until he would have to give up. His money was running out. His mental energies too. It would probably not be long before he would stroll into the nearest police station and give himself up.

Nevertheless, he started to shake all over now that someone was really wanting to come in. It was one thing to play out the final move in his head, where he could still control the timing and sequence of events more or less, and another to think there were a number of policemen outside his door right now, clicking open handcuffs, ready to arrest him.

"Who is it?" he asked. His voice sounded thin and shaky.

"John Burton. I'm friends with Gillian Ward. Could you let me in?"

A friend of Gillian's? How on earth did Gillian know where he was?

Confused, Samson opened the door. The man standing in front of him looked vaguely familiar to him, but he could not figure out from where.

"Can I come in?" asked John.

Samson nodded and stepped aside. He closed the door quickly behind John, asking: "Who are you?"

"God, it's cold in here," said John. He kept his thick winter jacket on. At that moment, Samson realized where he had seen him: in the Halfway House. With Gillian.

"You're a friend of Gillian's," he said, rather lamely.

"Yes, like I said," confirmed John. Without waiting to be invited, he sat in the armchair. "No doubt you're wondering how I knew where you were. I talked to your sister-in-law. She told me about your friend. The Pole. The police have already visited him too."

Millie, of course. She must have melted like butter with the attractive Burton suddenly in front of her. And she had outdone herself in giving him all the advice and help she could.

"Your friend gave me this address."

Great! Bartek was sending anyone over who asked after him! Why not just publish the address in the paper?

"If I were you, I'd get out of here as soon as possible," John continued. "That Bartek is scared silly that he might get involved in something that gets him deported. His fiancée is getting hysterical. The next time a policeman turns up there, the two of them are going to spill the beans. I'm sure of it."

"I don't know where to go," whispered Samson.

John looked closely at him. "You're in a difficult situation. You don't, by any chance, have a watertight alibi for the time of Thomas Ward's murder?"

"When was that?"

"Between seven and seven-thirty on Tuesday, December 29."

Samson shook his head in despair. "I only got home at nine. But I don't think anyone even noticed that. My sister-in-law was at work, not home, and my brother was already asleep."

"Where were you until nine?"

It probably doesn't matter who knows, thought Samson. Probably nothing in my life matters.

"I followed Gillian Ward in my car that day. I had

seen her leave home in the early afternoon in her car. I was sitting in my car at the time. So I drove around a bit...."

And watched people, John completed Samson's sentence in his head. Segal was an oddball.

"So you followed Gillian? Why?"

That was hard to explain. Maybe he did not even understand it himself. He certainly could not explain it rationally. On the level of vague feelings, he knew what was wrong with him, but what were the words for it?

"I didn't want to pester her," he started. "I've never pestered her. I just...wanted to be a part of her life. No, not a part of it. But experience some of it. Have part of it inside me. Yes, perhaps that's it. Be a part of it but *inside me.*" He paused and looked unhappily at John. "I can't explain it."

"I think I know what you mean," said John. "Unfortunately, it all sounds a little...neurotic. Obsessed, even."

He paused. "Mr. Segal. I'm afraid it's not just about Thomas Ward's murder now. You must have read in the papers about the brutal deaths of two single women in Hackney and Tunbridge Wells in the past six weeks?"

"Yes."

"The problem is...the gun that shot Thomas Ward is the same one that was used in the other two cases. You see what that means?"

A dawning understanding could be seen in Samson's sad, incredulous eyes. "The same murderer? In all three cases?"

"That's what the police have to assume."

"And they think it's me?" Samson looked at John in horror. "I'm s-supposed to have shot three people?"

John shook his head. "No one is saying that outright yet. There are too many inconsistencies. But I know that, based on the evidence so far, the police assume that the culprit is a man who has a disturbed relationship to women. And from your notes, which the police know about, the police conclude that you have—well, at least a certain…problem with women."

Samson nodded. That was undeniable.

"Did you follow Gillian all day?" asked John in a level voice. "On the twenty-ninth of December?"

"No. I lost her. On the A127. She was going fast. There was a lot of traffic—suddenly she was gone."

John nodded. It was easy to lose someone from view on that freeway.

"And then? There's a big gap between then and nine p.m."

"I didn't want to go home. I don't like it there."

"Why not?"

He thought for a minute. "I'm restless," he said. "I'm so restless. And I don't know where to go. I don't have a job. I can't find a girlfriend. I don't have anything. My life is completely empty."

John waited for Samson to continue. Samson stared at him. *If only I looked like him. If I only had his aura.*

The realization came over him suddenly, with almost physical force, that this man was in an intimate relationship with Gillian. He was not just *a friend*. He was her lover. They were having an affair, and had been having it when Thomas Ward was still alive. In fact, he had felt that when he saw them together in the pub before Christmas. He just had not realized. No doubt he had suppressed what he really sensed: the unbelievable tension between the two of them, the sexually charged atmosphere.

You desire her, he thought. A feeling of animosity swept in a wave over him and took away his breath for

a few seconds. You sleep with her and you don't care
that she has a family, a husband, a child, that you are
breaking it all up. Although, of course, now the husband is dead—how practical—and there's nothing in
your way....

Suddenly a question occurred to him: in these circumstances, John Burton must be of interest to the
police too. After all, he was in a relationship with a
woman whose husband had been murdered.

Couldn't he be in hot water too?

"Who are you?" he asked again. "I mean, apart from
a friend of Gillian's?"

John smiled. It seemed that he was well aware of sudden aggression in Samson's tone.

He stood up. "Samson, I worked in Scotland Yard
myself once. I still have a few good contacts. I've been
in touch over the last few days, so I know a few things
that aren't public knowledge yet."

"I see," said Samson, once again intimidated and
submissive. He did not understand anything, actually.
An ex-cop. Why wasn't he with the police anymore?

"Among other things, I know more or less what is in
your...diary, if we can call it that," continued John. "So I
can imagine you are at the top of the police's list of suspects. You shadowed women, mainly single women, for
months and noted down every detail of their day. And
then there's that bizarre story about the young woman
whose dog you took in order to try to gain her friendship when you returned it."

Samson could feel his cheeks burning. He had
thought the plan was so clever. Now it just sounded sick.

"I was trying to get to know her better," he murmured.

"Yes, but that's a pretty unusual way of going about

it, to put it mildly," said John. "Added to that the fact that it didn't work, and you let out a lot of hatred in your rant about her. She's on vacation until mid-January. Otherwise she would have been put under police protection. *That's* how serious it is."

Samson looked around desperately. "But I would never…yes, I was angry with her. But I'd never attack her. I've never attacked anyone. Or threatened them. They'll never find anyone who has seen me act aggressively!"

That is one of your problems, thought John. The lifelong suppression of your aggression. Every police profiler would put that on the list of the culprit's expected character traits.

He did not say so. Samson seemed to him like a trapped animal. He should not make things worse.

"The way you wrote about Gillian Ward, it sounded almost like you were worshipping her. You got carried away with really strong feelings…."

Oh, right? Samson thought, his hackles up. So we see eye to eye on that, then?

"The police think Gillian might be in danger. And I fear it too. And that is why I wanted to meet you. And I want to know what you were doing when Thomas Ward was murdered. So?" John steered the conversation back to its starting point. "What did you do when you lost Gillian?"

"Nothing," said Samson. "Nothing that I can prove. I drove around near here. I sat in two or three pubs. Drank tea. It was cold."

"Which pubs?"

"No idea. Somewhere in Wickford. In Raleigh. I was sad and confused. Just drifting. I wouldn't be able to find the places again. Let alone find witnesses who saw me. I was just thinking about Gillian, wondering where she had driven. Asking myself why my life hadn't worked out. And then at some point I drove home."

John looked at him questioningly. "I've got something to tell you, Samson. It is suspected that Thomas Ward's murderer actually wanted to kill Gillian. Being a woman, Gillian fits the series of murdered women better. At least better than a man does. And it appears that everyone around her knew that Thomas Ward had his tennis club on Tuesday nights and that he almost never made an exception. Anyone with a fleeting knowledge of the family would have assumed that Gillian would have been at home on her own. And you knew the family pretty well. You had been finding out about them for months."

"But I knew that Gillian wasn't home!" said Samson, with a glimmer of hope. "I was following her!"

"That doesn't let you off the hook yet. Because of course you might have assumed she had returned later on, once you saw that the light was on in the house. And of course it's just a hypothesis: that Thomas was not the intended victim. You might just as well have killed him in the grip of some crazy ideas about his wife."

Samson crumpled. "But why would I have killed the other two women?"

John shrugged his shoulders. "Rejection. Your basic problem."

"They were far too old for me!"

"Beggars can't be choosers. I'm not saying that was the case, understand. I'm just explaining what scenarios could be thought up."

"What do you want?" asked Samson quietly. "To take me to the police?"

"What I mainly wanted was to get a sense of who

you are. I'm not going to turn you in. I just wanted to meet you."

"So, do you think I'm innocent?"

"Let me put it like this," said John. "If I thought you were clearly guilty, I *would* tell the police. Understood?"

Samson nodded anxiously. So was he the culprit in Burton's eyes, or not?

"My fear," John continued, "is that the police arrest you and you look so suspect that they charge you. It's a possibility. Perhaps there wouldn't be enough evidence to find you guilty, but the case might still go on for a good while. Meanwhile, the murderer is free and no one is even looking for him. I don't like that idea one bit, since Gillian might well be on his hit list. It's not in my interest to help the police find the most obvious solution to the case and so to delay the capture of the real culprit."

"It really wasn't me," said Samson. How often had he said that already? How often would he have to say it before he could prove it?

John nodded. "They all say that. And I was a policeman for a long time. I've met murderers who seemed as harmless and friendly as you and yet have committed horrific acts. While there are some people you would immediately assume capable of anything, and they couldn't hurt a fly in reality. It's difficult. Who we are isn't always written on our foreheads."

"And what should I do now? Bartek told you at once where I am. You yourself say he'll tell the police, the next time they visit him. I'm not safe here. And my money has almost run out."

"Stay here in your room for now," said John. "I'll think of something."

"Can I reach you somehow?" asked Samson.

John went to the door and opened it. "No. Wait for me to get in touch."

"Please—you'll come back?"

"You'll hear from me," promised John.

Thursday, January 7

1

"Do you have time tonight?" asked John. He was sitting at the steering wheel of his car and had just stopped in front of Tara's apartment building.

Gillian, who was sitting next to him, shook her head. "Becky needs me. And…I don't want her to get the feeling that we're always seeing each other."

The police cordon had been lifted on the Ward family home, but Gillian had decided not to move back for now. The terrible event was still too close, too present. Gillian could not imagine that Becky could manage to live there this soon; she was not sure if she herself was ready either. She had just wanted to fetch a few things: clothing, laundry, books. John had offered to go with her. She was grateful that she did not have to go back to her house alone. Nothing seemed to have changed, and yet it was no longer the home she had made with Tom, where they had lived with Becky as a family. The Christmas tree was still standing and shedding its needles in the living room. In the fridge, the food was going bad. The Christmas lights and window decorations looked like relics of a long-ago time. A time of order, stability, familiarity, and normality.

That time would never return.

"Will you be able to keep the house?" John had asked when the two of them were standing in the dining room, looking apprehensively at the scene of the crime and the chair that Tom had fallen onto before dying.

She shrugged. "The question is whether I *want* to live here. Or whether I can."

"What's going to happen to your company?"

"We've got good staff. At the moment, things are proceeding as usual without needing much input from me. Of course I'll have to make a decision soon. I'm the only boss now. But I don't yet know if I'll be able to carry on with it all."

Then she had collected her things, moving more and more frantically, because she suddenly could not stand another moment in the house. She took a deep breath once she was back in the car.

"It was worse than I thought it would be," she said.

John helped her carry the two laundry baskets full of objects up the steps to Tara's apartment. Then he said goodbye. When Gillian opened the door to the apartment and stepped into the living room, she found herself facing her daughter's hate-filled eyes.

"Why send him away? Do you think I'm stupid? I know you were with him again."

Tara, sitting bent over a pile of folders at the table, looked worried. "She looked out the window. She saw you and Burton down there." Gillian tried to stroke Becky's hair, but her daughter ducked away.

"He's my *tennis coach*, Mom! Can't you keep your hands off him? And he you?"

"Becky, he was just helping me fetch a few things from our house. I didn't want to go by myself. I was glad he went, too."

"Don't you have anyone else? Tara could have helped!"

"Someone had to stay with you," Tara put in helpfully.

"I can stay on my own for a few hours. Anyway, *I* could have come with you."

"No way," said Gillian. "Becky, you experienced something terrible in the house, and it wouldn't be good if you—"

Becky's eyes shot daggers. "Oh, please, Mom! So worried for me. As if you were thinking about me! If you cared about me, you'd stop fucking around with John!"

"Becky!" said Gillian, stunned.

"Now, Becky, you're making some heavy accusations there," said Tara. "And you shouldn't use such vulgar words."

"So what should I call what my mom and John are doing? What they are *doing* is vulgar, Tara. That's why I don't need to find a nicer way of putting it."

"We don't do anything," said Gillian. "He's a friend, Becky. Nothing else."

Becky was enraged. "Stop treating me like a baby! You still haven't told me what you were actually doing the night that Dad got murdered. And I know you're too much of a coward to tell me."

"I did tell you. I was in a restaurant. On my own. I wanted to have space to think."

"You, in a restaurant!" spit Becky. "On your own! You *never* go out on your own. You met John. Probably you went to bed with him while someone came and shot Dad!" Her voice broke over the last words. In spite of the anger in what she said, she was primarily feeling pain, despair, and a terrible stunned shock at what had happened. The fear of death that she had endured for hours was still deep inside her. She was a child. A disturbed, fearful, and deeply sad child.

"Becky, let's—" said Gillian, stepping toward her, but Becky turned away and ran out of the room. The bathroom door slammed shut behind her, and you could hear the bolt being turned in the lock.

Gillian and Tara looked at each other.

"Maybe you shouldn't deny it," said Tara. "The thing between you and John. She's got good instincts, so she *knows* there's something between the two of you that isn't simply friendship. Anyone can feel that. By denying it, you're just giving her the feeling that you're lying to her. That's not good for your relationship."

"But if I admit it, she'll hate me too."

"Something terrible has just happened to her. Her father has been murdered, and she herself escaped the killer by the skin of her teeth. She has nightmares. Her sheltered world has suddenly collapsed. And her mother...."

"Yes?" asked Gillian in Tara's pause. "What about her mother?"

"I think she feels that you let her father down. That he died because of that."

"I couldn't know—"

"Of course not. But try to imagine what is plaguing Becky. Her mother is in bed with her good-looking coach while someone else breaks into the house and shoots her dearly beloved dad. Who is she going to hate if not you? The unknown, faceless culprit?"

"I wonder how we are going to survive this whole situation," whispered Gillian.

"It will take time," said Tara.

Gillian sat down in an armchair and buried her head in her hands. "I've never dived head over heels into an affair. Really, I haven't. Never done it just for the hell of it. Over the last few years, Tom and I had drifted pretty far apart. I felt very lonely in my marriage."

"Unfortunately, John is not exactly the most likeable man," Tara said. "Maybe I'm being unfair, and I've only met him briefly, but to me he seems *too* attractive, too sure of himself, as if this is all routine for him. The eternal seducer who never really commits to anyone. I hope you won't one day feel more lonely with him than you did with Tom."

"I don't know where we're going," replied Gillian defensively, but Tara's comment got to her. Her friend had said just what Gillian herself sometimes found unsettling and hard to understand: John's strange life. His abandoned career. The fact that he had never been able—or wanted—to have a long relationship. His almost-unfurnished apartment, as if he was afraid of setting down roots.

Suddenly she felt the need to talk about it. Tara was a lawyer. But also her best friend.

"By the way, he wasn't always the head of a private security firm," she mentioned, apparently casually. "He worked for Scotland Yard before that. He was a detective inspector."

"Really? And why did he stop working there?"

Gillian hesitated, looking at the floor. "There was a stupid incident. He had an affair with an intern. And the young woman reported him when he wanted to end the affair. For sexual harassment."

She looked up when she realized that Tara had not replied. Tara was looking at her in amazement.

"What?" Tara finally replied.

"There was an investigation, but the prosecutor didn't press charges. Several reports found John innocent. The young woman kept contradicting herself. John was completely innocent."

"Oh, of course. Naturally she reported him without any reason!"

"She got hysterical because John wouldn't help her when she failed an exam. She lost it completely. So he decided to end the relationship. That just made her more angry. And then…well, she got her own back on him."

"Gillian, I know about such cases. If the case was investigated and the whole thing landed on the prosecutor's desk, then there must have been at least circumstantial evidence against John, supporting what the young woman said."

Gillian regretted having mentioned it. She had hoped Tara would be supportive, but it was clear that Tara would only feed her fears and doubts. And because she had always suspected as much, she had not brought up the story until now. If only she had kept quiet.

"When John wanted to break up, they had sex again, but—"

"Really? So she could prove his sperm."

"Yes. But he never denied that he—"

"Let me guess," said Tara. "All he wanted to do was end the relationship, but this young bit was so incredibly attractive that he jumped into bed with her again. With her consent, of course, because although he wants to leave her, she can't think of anything better than a quickie with him. Afterward, she is annoyed that he still decides to end it, so she runs—the evil, vengeful little monster that she is—right to the police. At least he'll end up in jail and lose his job! That's how he told it to you, isn't it?"

Gillian rubbed her forehead. "Not those exact words, of course, but that was the gist of it, yes."

"That is always the gist of it," said Tara. "At least in the culprit's statement. You can't imagine how often I've heard that story, Gillian. If that story were to be believed, the crime of rape doesn't exist. It's just something that a few particularly nasty women have thought up to get at men who cross them."

"She injured herself to fake injuries caused by him. Several independent reports confirmed that. Tara, you can't claim there was a conspiracy hatched by all the report writers to clear John's name of a terrible crime!"

"In cases like these, there is rarely real evidence," replied Tara. "Neither for one side nor the other."

"I believe him," said Gillian. "He acted like an idiot. He knows that. But he didn't force anyone to do anything."

"And you know that for sure? You know him so well?"

"I can't imagine anything else," said Gillian, realizing immediately how lame that sounded.

Why have I gotten drawn into this conversation? Why is this whole day so crazy? Why is first my daughter, and then my best friend, having a go at me?

"What do you want, Tara?" she asked.

Tara took a deep breath. "I'm sorry. I got carried away. I don't want anything, Gillian. I'm just surprised that you…."

"Yes?"

"I couldn't start a relationship with someone who has that suspicion hanging over him. It would just seem too risky to me."

"So you're saying that even if John is innocent, he'll never have the chance of living normally again!"

"There's no need for *you,* of all people, to give him that chance…."

"Why not me?"

"Aren't you at all afraid?"

Gillian shook her head. "No."

"All right!" Tara said, raising her hands in defeat. "It's just…. Probably my imagination is running away with me, but John…I mean, I've only seen him two or three times, when he came to pick you up, but there's something aggressive about him. He takes what he wants. At least, that's what I see in him. Gillian, I'm sorry. I can't stand him. And what you've just told me only strengthens what I felt about him right from the start. I don't trust him. I'm surprised that you do. But everyone's entitled to their own opinion. And no doubt my job has made me more suspicious than I should be."

"You don't think…he might have something to do with Tom?" asked Gillian after a silence in which she tried to digest what she had just heard.

"No," said Tara. "I don't. I just think he's not good for you. I think he's brutal. That he is emotionally stunted. And that worries me." Now the two of them were silent, exhausted by their argument.

In the end, Gillian stood up. "I'll go see how Becky is." As her daughter was not going to let her into the bathroom any time soon and as she knew that, she realized that she was just looking for an excuse to get away.

She just wondered if it was Tara she was getting away from. Or from herself.

2

DETECTIVE INSPECTOR FIELDER was surprised when the caller was put through to him. She had called the switchboard, and he had not expected to hear from her.

Keira Jones. Carla Roberts's daughter.

"Mrs. Jones!" he said. "It's good to hear from you!"

Keira's voice sounded tiny and shy. "Good evening. I hope I'm not disturbing you?"

"Not at all. How are you?"

"Not great, to be honest," said Keira. "My mother's apartment was opened up again. I've started to sort things out. I had to do it sometime. And…it's very difficult. So many memories return."

She was silent.

"I can well imagine," said Fielder. "It's a difficult time for you. A murder is different from a natural death. The violence is against the family members too."

"I'd been in so little contact with my mother these last few years," said Keira quietly. "And today, when I went through her things, I was suddenly so close to her. I was a child again. She was my Mommy, the person who was always there for me…." She stopped, swallowed.

"I understand," murmured Fielder, empathizing.

Controlling her emotions, she said: "So, the reason I'm calling is that I found a letter in my mother's mailbox. It had obviously just arrived today. I didn't recognize the name of the person who sent it—a woman in Hastings. I read the letter. The woman didn't seem to know that my mother isn't alive, but I suppose the murder wasn't given the blanket coverage in papers down there in Sussex that it had here. And of course only a few papers mentioned my mother's name. I don't know, but maybe the letter contains something important."

"What does it say?"

"Nothing that is obviously a clue. But you were looking for people who were in touch with my mother, and it seems there was a group…that I had no idea about."

"What kind of group?"

"If I read the letter right, then until about three quarters of a year ago, my mother went to a kind of self-help group once a week. For women who live on their own. Either divorcées living on their own or widows. They met to talk about their lives, to meet people in a similar situation. My mother never told me about it."

Fielder thought for a moment. It was a lead. It might not help. Carla Roberts's murder might have nothing at all to do with that self-help group, but at least it offered the chance to talk to people who had known her. People other than her old colleagues from the drug store.

Perhaps it would reveal a new line of inquiry. Fielder just had to be careful not to expect too much. He had already understood that there was no free lunch to be had in this case.

"It's clear from the letter that your mother left the group three quarters of a year ago?" he asked.

Keira hesitated. "If I've understood it right, then the woman who wrote the letter was the group's initiator. It appears that she left London for Hastings for personal reasons last April, and that the group fell apart as a result. She writes that she's sorry the group didn't manage to keep going without her. She asks how my mother is doing. She's been worried about her. She just wanted to hear from her."

"I see. It's good that you called. We've found it hard to find people she was in touch with. I'll have the letter collected from your house. Could you please give me the sender's name and address?"

"Of course. The woman is Ellen Curran." She dictated the address. Then she added: "You'll tell me how things develop?"

"Of course," Fielder assured her.

After saying goodbye to Keira, he immediately asked Directory Inquiries for Ellen Curran's number. Why not try her right now? It was half past six in the evening. Even if she had a job, he might be able to reach her now.

Mrs. Curran picked up the phone on the seventh ring.

She was completely out of breath. "I've just gotten in," she said by way of apology after Fielder had introduced himself. She added in alarm, "Scotland Yard? Has something happened?"

"Sadly, yes," replied Fielder. He told her briefly about the murder of Carla Roberts, although for now he did not mention that they might be dealing with a serial killer. Ellen Curran was horrified. She had not known anything about it.

"That's awful! Oh, my Lord! Do you know who did it?"

"We're still in the dark," Fielder had to admit. "The investigation hasn't been helped by the fact that Carla lived in such isolation. It's been hard to find out much about her life. Let alone to discover possible enemies. Luckily, her daughter found your letter in her mother's mailbox when she went there to clean out the apartment. Your group is one of the few leads we have."

"I can't believe it," said Ellen. "Who on earth would have wanted to kill Carla, of all people?"

"*Carla, of all people?* Was she so popular? Or why is it so surprising in her particular case?"

"She wasn't particularly popular, but nor was she unpopular. She was almost invisible sometimes. A wallflower. Quiet, modest, reserved. But always ready to help people out. No, I can't imagine that anyone held a grudge against her."

"How many women were there in your group?" asked Fielder.

"Five. Six, including me."

"You started the group?"

"My husband left me three years ago. The classic story: he found someone younger. For a year, I thought the tragedy would kill me. Then I decided to get a grip.

I found a job and started this circle for women who had experienced something similar. Sometimes it helps to talk to other people who know just what you feel."

"I can understand that. So you started the group two years ago? And you moved away nine months ago. That means the group ran for a year and a quarter?"

"Yes."

"Was Carla Roberts there right from the start?"

"No. At the start, only three women met up. Carla joined us after about six months. A little later, the fifth woman joined us."

"How did Carla Roberts find you?"

"Not the usual way. I had a Web site: that's how the others got in touch."

"And Mrs. Roberts…?"

"Carla didn't have a computer. Nor the Internet, obviously. Somehow she'd missed that development. But a year and a half ago, a magazine ran a feature on us."

"Which magazine?"

"*Woman and Home*. You probably don't know it, Inspector, it's—"

"My wife sometimes reads it," said Fielder. "I know the one you mean." A classic women's magazine. Fashion, beauty, diet, advice, celebs.

"Right. So Carla read the article," said Ellen. "She got in touch, and that's how we met."

"Did you get a lot of approaches after the article? Maybe threatening letters from men who saw divorcées as gold-diggers or parasites?"

"No. We were sent some letters, but almost all were from women. Positive reactions."

"Was there a forum on your Web site?"

"Yes."

"But you didn't get aggressive posts there either?"

"No. But actually, there were very few comments there. We were just a small group."

"Were the names or even the addresses of the five women who had joined you given on the Web site?"

"No. I'd never have done that. No one could find out who we were."

"Is the Web site still online?"

"No. I met someone and moved to Hastings to be with him. There's no reason now for the site."

"Why did the group break up after you left?"

"That was a pity," said Ellen. "It's like that sometimes, isn't it? You don't always realize at the time, but it seems that most groups have someone at the center of things. In this case, it was me. After I left, the others couldn't agree on things, like the dates on which to meet. Often there would be just two of them that turned up…so it fell apart. One of the women wrote to me in September to say that she had lost touch with all of them. I found that a real pity."

"How often had you been meeting?"

"Every Thursday. At my place."

"This New Year, did you write to all of them? or just to Carla Roberts?"

"Just Carla."

"Why? Her daughter says you sounded worried in your letter. Why were you worried about Carla?"

"I hadn't heard from her in a long time," said Ellen. "After my move, I'd received the odd e-mail from the others, although very rarely now. But Carla hadn't been in touch at all. Neither with a letter or a card. I thought: it can't hurt to ask how she's doing."

"Mrs. Curran," said Fielder. "Carla Roberts was killed in such a way that we can assume the murderer felt a strong hatred. It wasn't a burglary. It wasn't primarily a sex offense either. The culprit must have been bottling up an enormous amount of aggression. We don't know if the aggression was aimed at women in general, or at Carla in particular. So I'd ask you to please think very carefully whether Carla ever mentioned, in your meetings, anything from her life that could have a bearing on this case. Perhaps some event, some person, anything in her life that might explain such a hatred."

Ellen Curran did not say anything for a long while. She appeared to be thinking hard.

Finally she said "I'm sorry, Inspector. I really can't think of anything. Carla never spoke much. If she ever said anything, then it was about her husband. He had cheated on her for years and, in addition, ruined the family and then disappeared. *She* would have had reason to hate *him*, not the other way round!"

"I'll need a list of your group's members," said Fielder. "Could you give me that? Names and addresses if possible?"

"I've got a list somewhere. I could e-mail it."

"I'd be very grateful." Fielder gave her his e-mail address. Then he added: "Was there anyone in the group who was friends with Carla? In spite of this extreme shyness she seemed to possess? Someone who she was closer to? who she trusted?"

Ellen thought. "I wouldn't say friends, but it seemed to me that she was a little closer to one of us: Liza Stanford. The two of them often sat next to one another. Sometimes they whispered to each other. But whether or not they ever met outside of our meetings, I don't know."

She paused.

"Liza was our exception," she went on. "That's what we always said. You see, she wasn't divorced or widowed or alone for any other reason. At the start I didn't want to allow her to join the group. She was married. But she was unhappily married. Neglected. She often thought it might be better to start over again. She wasn't brave or decisive, and she hoped that we might help her. In the end, I decided that she did in fact belong in our group somehow. That's why I let her take part.

"By the way, she was the last one to join us and the one who was absent most often. That annoyed me."

"Did she then leave her husband?"

"Not while I was still there, no. Whether she has since, I don't know."

"Did she ever talk about her marriage problems?"

"She was very vague about them. No, she didn't really say. I had the impression that she was well off, didn't know what to do with her life, and so got depressed. And, of course, her husband was to blame because he didn't pay her enough attention. But if you ask me, something wasn't right about that woman. I sometimes thought: poor husband! I wouldn't want to be married to her."

"What wasn't right?"

"I don't know. It was just an impression she gave. She seemed so utterly neurotic to me. Someone who wanted help but couldn't accept it. Maybe I'm being unfair. I've got little patience for these rich, bored wives who nurture their problems so that they have something to keep them busy."

Fielder made a few notes. Then he fired off one last, hopeless question. It would be nice if....

"Do the names Anne Westley and Gillian Ward mean anything to you?"

"No," said Ellen Curran.

Saturday, January 9

1

THE TRAVEL TRAILER was barely five yards long and three yards wide. Samson had to admit that its gas heaters made it nice and cozy. It was rather sparsely furnished, but it was definitely possible to live here for a while if you lowered your expectations. It contained a convertible sofa, a table, two chairs, a kind of cooking corner with a gas cooker, and a sink with a tap linked up to a tank. There was a cupboard on the wall, in which he found plastic crockery and some foodstuffs: instant coffee, tea, powdered milk, a few packages of spaghetti, and jars of tomato sauce. A shower and a toilet were squeezed into a tiny corner. Samson hated the crampedness of it all. Just like he hated cleaning out the toilet, filling the tank, eating spaghetti every day, being stuck in this tiny space.

But he had no choice, and he knew that he should count his lucky stars. A police cell would be much worse.

John Burton had brought him here. Samson hated him really too, but he had to be grateful. John was the only person who had taken care of him—who might even be convinced of his innocence. Although John had never said as much. Samson had asked him repeatedly about it, and John had just answered: "Until something is proven, I'm not going to believe anything."

Samson realized that he could not hope for more than that at the moment.

The flu was going around John's company, and he was having problems keeping all their sites manned. The trailer, which was a base for watching a construction site, was currently empty.

"You can stay here," John had said. "As long as it's this cold and snowing so much, nothing will happen over there at the site. No one will come around. In any case, it's a lot safer than that bed-and-breakfast in Southend."

Samson had been relieved to say goodbye to the wretched dive. It had been starting to get to him, but now he had been here for three days and had the feeling that he had jumped from the frying pan into the fire. The shabby railway-station room had been desolate, but at least you could see the hustle and bustle of life on the street below the window. You did not have the feeling of being completely excluded from the normal world, which was just what you felt here. A construction site somewhere in the south of London, where tower buildings were to be built, far from anything else. There was not even the most basic infrastructure. When Samson drew the trailer window's grubby, yellowing curtain aside, he saw the shells of unfinished buildings, towering up like ruins against the gray winter sky. He saw a few cranes and many carefully locked containers. These containers—or rather what they contained: tools and spare parts for machines—were what the company was being paid to guard.

At least it had snowed so heavily that everything lay under a white blanket of snow. Rain and drizzle would have been worse, turning everything into a muddy brown mess. But even so, the isolation and emptiness of this place was deeply depressing. Sometimes a bird would cry. Samson had not seen people a single time. The whole absurdity of his situation was crystallized in the fact that on the one hand he desperately wanted someone to appear, while simultaneously knowing that if someone did, he would be frightened to death. In his position, people meant danger. He should be happy that he was sitting here in relative safety in the back of beyond.

But for how much longer? How long would it last? How long could he endure it?

Today he had set off on a walk. He had walked the perimeter of the enormous building site and thrown his old bread crusts to the birds. He had breathed in the bracingly fresh air and recognized that he could not manage to keep going out here much longer. He was in a deep mental crisis, probably already in a deep depression, and with every hour that passed he only sank further in. He started to think that the police might not be his greatest enemy, but that the real danger came from inside, from his melancholy, his despair, his lack of any hope. The worst thing was being unable to see any end to it. A few times since the previous night, he had thought that death—in spite of the horror it caused—would also be a relief. He understood that the risk lay in such thoughts: the risk that one of these cold, snowy January days, or an equally cold, dark, and snowy day in February, he would be hanging from the trailer's ceiling because he had no longer been able to bear the bird cries in the silence and each day's emptiness.

Returning to the trailer, he heard a car engine and saw headlights shine up the dirt track that led to the building site. After a short moment of shock, he relaxed. He recognized the motor's sound.

It was John's car.

Yesterday he had not come, and today Samson had been hoping all day for him to turn up. It was crazy. He could not stand the man, plus he knew John was sleeping with the woman he himself dreamed of. But in his complete isolation, Burton was the only person he could hope for. The only one who spoke to him. The person who was his only remaining contact with the world. He hated him and simultaneously desperately wanted him to come. That longing made him despise himself too.

He stood waiting on the trailer's steps. Burton parked, got out, and walked over. Large and broad-shouldered in his black leather jacket, he had a gray scarf flung casually round his neck.

Of course Gillian went for him. The knot grew in Samson's throat.

"You went for a walk?" asked John. He had a pile of magazines and newspapers in the crook of his arm. Handing them to Samson, he said, "Here. Something to read. You must be bored to death, right?"

"It's very quiet out here," admitted Samson.

John took a few steps to his car, opened the boot, and took out two large bags. "Food. And a few bottles of beer. Alcohol doesn't solve anyone's problems, but sometimes it helps in bearing them."

"I don't actually drink alcohol," said Samson. He immediately regretted opening his mouth. John had meant well.

John shrugged. "I'll leave the bottles here. You might change your mind."

"Yes. Thank you." Samson had opened the trailer's door by now. "Don't you want to come in?"

"No time. I've got to meet someone."

"Gillian?" Samson's question slipped out.

John shook his head. "No."

"How…is Gillian?"

"I'd say: pretty much what you'd expect in the circumstances. She still seems quite traumatized to me, but she isn't apathetic. She's trying to take her first steps in this new life. She's arranged for her husband's life insurance policy to be paid, has talked to the bank about the mortgage, and has gone in to the office. Oh, yes, and she's sent her daughter to visit her parents in Norwich."

"She sent Becky away?"

"It's not that she sent her away. They were arguing constantly, and she thought it would be good if they each had some space for a while. School starts again the day after tomorrow, but Becky isn't ready to carry on as normal yet. Gillian got her excused for the whole of January—and organized a therapist in Norwich for Becky to visit. The kid needs professional care. I think Gillian did the right thing."

Of course, thought Samson with animosity. Tom is dead and Becky is visiting her grandparents; now your path's clear. All running like clockwork, right?

But of course he did not express his thoughts.

Instead, he asked: "And what about the case? Anything new? any developments? a lead?"

"Not that I know, unfortunately," said John with regret. He looked at his watch. "I've got to go. I'm sorry, Samson. I know it's damned lonely out here and you feel rotten, but I can't do any more for you right now than to come now and then and make sure you have the basics."

"And that's a lot," murmured Samson. "Thanks, John."

He watched John walk back to his car and get in. He was driving back to real life. To a meeting, a meal, to voices, laughter, lights, and company.

Good-looking John Burton. Whose presence shouted

out the fact that he would always land on his feet. Whatever fate held in store for him. Whatever traps lurked along the way.

While I always lose. And people can probably see that. And there's little that makes a man more unattractive than a big sign on their forehead saying *I'm a loser!*

He picked up the shopping bags that John had put down in the snow and stepped into his murky accommodation.

Perhaps he would drink a beer this evening.

2

ON HIS WAY back into town, John thought about Samson. The man was mentally close to the breaking point. He could feel it clearly: Samson would probably not be able to stick it out much longer. John was sure that Samson was already toying with the idea of voluntarily turning himself in to the police. The only thing holding him back was the certainty that a prison cell was not going to improve his situation. He might not be alone in prison; but for someone like Samson, that only contained new horrors. He had always been dominated by others, serving as a lightning rod for other people's aggression. Samson might be crazy, but he was not stupid. John was sure of that. Samson had a pretty clear image of himself and of the situations he found himself in. He knew that for him, prison would be a hell he could not even imagine.

John thought about his own motives, too, as he joined the heavy traffic going into town. By hiding Samson, he was committing an offense. The police would only have to interview Samson's only friend in the world, the Pole quaking in his boots, one more time for them to find out that he, John, had been there a few days ago too and had heard where Samson was staying. He should have gone to the police immediately with that piece of information. Fielder was out to get him, and this would give him the perfect opportunity.

Detective Inspector Peter Fielder. He was probably one reason why John had gotten involved in the story and was taking this dangerous path on the edge of an abyss. He had not had too much to do with Fielder in his police days, but it had been enough for the two men to form a deep dislike to each other. Not that they had ever had a real fight or confrontation; there had just been a heartfelt sense that they would not get on at all. John thought DI Fielder was boring and conventional, possessed mediocre talent as an investigator but would climb the career ladder because he always stuck to the regulations, was highly reliable, and never antagonized the people important for his career progress. John's colleague at the time had been Sergeant Christy McMarrow, the woman Fielder was hopelessly in love with. Everyone knew it, but Fielder probably thought that he had been clever enough to conceal his feelings. It had been the most popular topic of gossip in every hall. Everyone had smirked to think of the pining policeman. In the end, the topic had run its course, even for the most hopeful romantic and the most fervent gossips: there was no development beyond John's worshipping of her. John could have guessed that from the start. Fielder was far too square, too conventional for actual adultery.

And even when John's departure meant that Fielder, so to speak, inherited Christy, romance did not bloom.

John knew that Fielder despised him because there were few middle-class virtues that John had adopted, and yet that Fielder simultaneously envied him because he lived out what Fielder denied himself. It had been the same for many of his colleagues. John was rather unpopular with other men: because he was good-looking, had few scruples, was completely independent; and because he could have almost any woman he was attracted to. Most of his colleagues had been all too happy to see the intern put him in such an awkward situation, but he had managed to turn the tables. He had left the service of his own volition and had happily started his own company. He knew that he had given his colleagues the feeling that *they* were the real losers.

He saw a space and parked. It was still some distance from the restaurant he was going to, but around here empty spaces were as rare as water in the desert. At the moment, they were even rarer, as the snow cleared from the roads was piled high by the roadsides, taking up valuable space.

The Italian restaurant welcomed him with warmth, candlelight, a smell of pasta and herbs, the hubbub of voices, and the sound of glasses clinking. Saturday evening. It was rather full, but John could see from the door that his date was there. She was sitting near the back, at a table off to one side.

Clever girl.

Perfect for what they had planned.

She had seen him now too and waved at him. As he approached through the rows of tables, he could see that she was glowing with happy expectation. She had something for him. She could not wait to see his surprise and to hear him praise her.

Detective Constable Kate Linville. Thirty-five years old. Looked at least forty-two. Light brown hair, pale face. Features that were not easy to remember. Her little eyes always looked a little swollen, as if she had gotten blind drunk the night before and barely slept, which was definitely not the case: her eyes just had that unfortunate form. Kate was repeatedly passed over by men, and her police career had not exactly taken off. Why she had ever chosen that career in the first place had always been a mystery to John.

She had been one of the women in Scotland Yard who had fallen for John. For a long time he had not known it, or even imagined such a possibility. But one day when he was at the photocopier, she had come up with a document she wanted to copy and, after waiting silently for a while, she had asked him suddenly, "Would you like to catch a film with me this weekend?"

Her voice had trembled and her lips had been pale. Looking at her in surprise, John had realized that she had been hoping desperately for such as an opportunity for months, that she must have practiced that sentence *ad infinitum.* And he had recognized something else in her eyes: that she longed for him, that he was the hero of her daydreams, and that in her mind there was a world where he and she had experienced wonderful things together. He had recognized how monotonous her life was, with its quiet evenings and empty weekends. He had seen the desperation that gave her the courage to ask him.

Would you like to catch a film with me this weekend?

He had found a polite excuse to let her down gently and, as he expected, she had never again dared to approach him with any similar request.

But now, wondering who he could ask for information, he had remembered her. She was not adventurous, and what she was doing was risky: she could lose her job or face disciplinary action. But he had guessed right. She was so utterly alone that she had not been able to resist the temptation of getting a date in this way. Even a second and third date, perhaps. And with the man she had pined for all those years. Her desperation was greater than her caution. John had speculated as much and had not been wrong. This was their second meeting that day. And she had no doubt been sitting there for half an hour waiting for him.

"Hello, Kate," he said when he reached the table.

"Hello, John," she replied.

"I'm sorry I'm late. I had to park quite far away. It's not easy around here. Did you come by car?"

She shook her head. "By train. I wanted to be able to have a glass of wine."

He sighed, but just on the inside. He had offered to come out to Bexley, where she had been living for ages, but she had insisted on meeting in town, saying she also had some urgent shopping to do. If it got rather late (and he knew from their first meeting that she would try to stretch things out as long as she could), then he could not in good conscience let her take the train. Was she hoping for that? That he would take her home? Or that he would offer that she should stay at his place?

He sat down and took the menu that the waiter held out to him. Kate waited until he had chosen something and they had both ordered before leaning over and whispering, "There's news!"

He smiled at her. "Pray tell!"

"Well, we found out something from Carla Roberts's life. She was in a kind of self-help group. For women on their own. Divorcées, widows, and such. They met once a week and tried to…well, somehow to come to terms with their situation. The group stopped meeting nine months ago, but the group's initiator got in touch and told DI Fielder about it. There was a woman in the group who was…well, friends with Carla Roberts might be an exaggeration, but at least closer to her. Liza Stanford. Who didn't live on her own, by the way. But she wasn't particularly happily married."

"I see," said John. He noted the name mentally. "How many people were in the group?"

"Six women. Fielder has all their names. Anne Westley is, unfortunately, not one of them. That would be too perfect. But Stanford...we struck gold with her!"

"How so?"

"Well, Christy had the idea yesterday. Our clever Christy McMarrow," Kate said with some bitterness in her voice. She had never been able to stand her. Christy too was a single, but out of choice and happily. Christy never had difficulty in getting a date for the weekend. And their boss worshipped her too. "So, Christy took the names of the group members to the clinic where Dr. Anne Westley had worked and compared it with Dr. Westley's patients. And what name did she discover?"

"Liza Stanford," said John. "As you said, you struck gold."

"Right," confirmed Kate.

She was silent for a minute, as the waiter had brought a carafe of wine and a bottle of water. He filled their glasses and then left. "Liza Stanford has a son," Kate reported. "Finley Stanford. She had been to Dr. Westley's clinic four or five times with him. Of course the boss is in seventh heaven. Because he had been looking like crazy for some point where Carla Roberts's and Anne Westley's lives cross. He assumes it's no coincidence that they both knew Liza Stanford."

"It probably isn't," said John. He tried to sort the different questions and thoughts that were suddenly whizzing through his head. "Was there any problem with the son?" he asked. "In medical terms, I mean. Something serious?"

Kate said no. "It was always just little things. A throat infection. Measles. A sports injury. Nothing spectacular. Nothing that would suggest any motive for a crime against Westley."

"And what about Gillian Ward? Does she know the woman too?"

Kate pulled a regretful face. "Of course that was immediately checked too. That would have been nice and tidy. But no. She had never heard the name. Fielder tried to find out if her husband might have been in contact with her, either through work or sports. But that's harder to ascertain, of course."

"Did you visit Liza Stanford?"

Kate looked as though she had been waiting impatiently for this question all along. "Here's the best bit," she said. "Fielder naturally went to see her *immediately*. Yesterday, late afternoon. Or rather, he tried. And found out that she disappeared. Almost two months ago!"

"Disappeared?"

"He found her husband. And guess who it is? *Stanford.* Logan Stanford!"

"Oh," said John, surprised. "'Charity' Stanford?"

"That's the one. The legendarily rich lawyer with his showy Hampstead mansion and his friendly contacts to everyone, including the Prime Minister and the Queen for all I know. Who is always appearing in the gossip mags in connection with his charity balls. That's the one. And he told Fielder that his wife had disappeared mid-November."

"Aha. And Stanford found that normal? Or did he do anything about it?"

"As far as I know, it's all a bit mysterious," said Kate. John understood from Kate's phrase that she was not completely in the loop in this regard. "Stanford didn't do anything because it appears it wasn't completely unusual for his wife. To disappear now and again, I mean. He admitted to Fielder that his marriage isn't particularly happy, which matches what we heard from the women's group. Liza Stanford was thinking about separating from him. The image we can gather of her is of a rather depressed, nervous woman who regularly takes time out to try to figure out what her future should be. In those periods, she has no contact with her family."

"What is the real problem with the marriage? Was Fielder able to find that out?"

"I don't know that," admitted Kate. "You know, it's only Christy that he really talks everything through with. I just find out what is discussed in the general meetings, and we just had a short chat about this latest development last night."

"The son. What's he like? Was he at home?"

"Yes. Finley is twelve years old and was sitting at his computer when Fielder arrived. He doesn't seem very chatty, but then boys his age never are. But he seemed fine. He didn't seem disturbed to Fielder. He seemed like the situation wasn't unusual for him."

"Hmm," thought John. "What do you mean? What do *you* think of the situation?"

"Me?" asked Kate in surprise. She obviously had not expected John to seriously ask her about her opinion. "Well, in all honesty, I can't quite make heads nor tails of it. A wife and mother who disappears for weeks on end and her husband and son just carry on as if nothing has happened. I mean, especially if she is depressed, they should be worried, shouldn't they? Even if she has always ended up coming back, I'd imagine that the moment could come when she'd do something stupid. She could have killed herself, and her family wouldn't even know!"

"And she was in touch with two women who have been murdered, one right after the other. However Fielder sees it, it can't be a coincidence," said John thoughtfully.

He played with his wine glass, then drew back his hands as the waiter stepped up to the table and laid a large steaming plate of pasta in front of each of them. For a few minutes they ate in silence, which suited John fine. It let him follow his thoughts.

He could not judge whether Stanford could be taken at his word. He would have had to talk to him himself to know that. Yet the story was certainly odd.

If I want to carry on with this, then I'll have to talk to him.

As if she could read his thoughts, Kate looked up from her spaghetti and asked, "John, I know it's none of my business really, but…why? Why do you want to know all of this? Why don't you just let Fielder do his job? Why do you want to do your own investigation?" He had said at the start that he knew Gillian Ward, whose husband had been murdered, and given that as the reason for his interest. He had left unmentioned the fact that he had a relationship with her—or had had? He did not know quite where they stood right now. He had just told her that he had coached Gillian's daughter at tennis. His instinct told him that Kate would have closed up like an oyster if he had said more than that. She was just talking because she had her own hopes.

"It's fun," he said. To his astonishment, he realized as he said it that this answer was the absolute truth. Apart from everything else, it really was *just fun*. His connection to Gillian had been the initial trigger, but now his hunter's instinct had been awoken. He was trained to do what he was doing now, and he felt how much he had missed this work. Not the office hierarchies and intrigues, the waiting for promotion. But work. The work itself.

"And you know what," he added. "I know the Ward family. I like the daughter a lot. The girl's been traumatized. Maybe that's what's made me mad with whoever did all this."

He could see that he had convinced Kate.

"Two more things I didn't mention yet," Kate said. "They've also been withheld from the media for now. We know that Carla Roberts felt threatened in the weeks before her death in a vague way. She told her daughter. She lived on the top floor of an apartment building and she had noticed that the elevator kept coming right to the top. But that no one ever got out. That scared her."

"I suppose the elevator was investigated? It couldn't have been a purely technical fault?"

"No, it couldn't. And now Fielder has the idea that Anne Westley might have felt threatened. Why else would she suddenly want to sell her house and move to the city just before Christmas? After she had put up with living out there for years."

"In what way does Fielder think she was threatened?"

"Well, he found a picture in her house. Anne Westley had a studio in her attic. Painting was her hobby. Watercolors. Her favorite motifs were flowers and trees, sunny landscapes. Positive, colorful pictures. But there was one that didn't fit in at all."

"In what way?"

"I haven't seen it myself, but Fielder described it. Pitch-black night. Two glowing points in the darkness. He interpreted them as a car's headlights. He wondered if she had seen them in the time just before her murder. The lights of a car appearing out there near her lonely house. Again and again. Without anyone appearing. Just the car, coming and going. Like the elevator in Carla Roberts's building."

"Not a bad link," said John. He had to admit it was a pretty creative connection for Fielder, who was not the most imaginative guy. "Both women were terrorized in a planned way. With Carla Roberts, it's clear when that started. If it started about two weeks before her death, then—"

"—then that fits in pretty much exactly with the time when Liza Stanford disappeared," Kate completed his sentence.

The mysterious, invisible woman. But another name came to mind involuntarily for John: Samson Segal. Who had spied on a variety of people. Had he gone up to the top of the building with the elevator? Had he haunted the empty woods around the old lady's house?

"So both women were harrassed, it seems," said John. "But you talked of *two* things that you hadn't mentioned yet?"

She smiled, suddenly coy. "Later," she said.

After two forkfuls of spaghetti, she said: "Fielder hasn't said this directly, at least not in our group meetings, but things leak out. You know that he's also toying with the thought that *you*...might be somehow mixed up in this?"

"I know. But that's absurd. And, in my opinion, he won't have anything to hang that idea on. I know the Wards. But not the two dead women. However he turns it around, he won't find a motive," said John.

"I'm taking quite a risk here," said Kate. "I know."

"Still, I'm glad to!"

He gave her a reserved smile. He could not afford to give her too much reason for hope. By now it was crystal-clear to him that she had not come by car for one reason only: she wanted to get into *his* car. And, if possible, his apartment.

"Some people would think that what I'm doing here is stupid," Kate continued.

"I don't think it's stupid," John reassured her. "And you can trust me completely. No one will ever find out about our meetings and chats."

He steered the conversation skillfully to a neutral topic. He could see Kate's strategy. By stressing how far she was sticking her neck out for him, she hoped to gain his admiration and recognition. At least his thanks. He was supposed to feel obliged to her, and she was going to try to take advantage of that feeling.

He told her about the company he had built up, the places they guarded: construction sites, supermarkets, petrol stations, sometimes private homes too.

"And four of my staff are bodyguards. They are in such high demand that I really need to expand in that area, but I'm not sure yet."

"Why not?" asked Kate.

"I don't like to tie myself down," John said. "When I founded the company, it was a temporary solution. That I could give up at any time. The bigger it grows, the less mobile I feel I am."

"Is that why you're still alone? I mean, why you don't have a wife and kids? Because you don't want to tie yourself down there either?"

"Maybe," he said vaguely. He took a sly look at his watch. Kate could not miss that last train.

"I'd like that. A family," Kate said dreamily.

"Not the easiest thing in your line of business."

She shrugged. "Other people manage it."

"True." Somehow they had wandered onto treacherous ground. He motioned to the waiter, mimed that he wanted to pay. He felt his throat constrict, seeing Kate's desiring gaze on him. She had not given him all this information without expecting something back, but thankfully they had not agreed on its price. If she were not to get what she had hoped for, that was not his fault.

When he had paid and the two of them were standing in the dark street, he said "I'll walk you to the bus stop."

"Thank you." She sounded frustrated.

They walked silently along. In the end, she said in desperation, "I don't absolutely need to get home, John."

He stopped. "Kate…."

"Tomorrow is Sunday. I'm not on duty. We could have breakfast together…."

"I'm sorry, Kate. That's not possible."

"Why not? Is there…do you have a girlfriend?"

"No. But at the moment there's no space for a woman in my life."

"I don't want to tie you down, John. We can see what develops. And if nothing develops…well, that's just the way it is."

Empty words, he thought. If he were to put his money on just one thing, then it would be that he would never shake off a woman like Kate if he gave her an inch. Let alone spent a night with her. Kate was the kind of woman who would start stalking him if she was rejected.

"It just won't work, Kate. It's nothing to do with you. Just with me."

"I thought…."

"What?"

"Oh, nothing." What could she say? That she had thought his interest in her was more than a simple need to obtain secret information? He could see just how she felt in that moment: like an idiot.

Yet he still risked a question. "You said you had something else for me?"

She looked at him blankly. Thought about it. In the end, she realized that she would look even more ridiculous if she now sulked because she had been rejected. That would show with complete transparency what she had been after and how disappointed she was.

"Yes. There was one more thing. With regard to the murder of the two women, one vital detail wasn't made public. The way the victims were killed."

"So they weren't shot?" He had always suspected as much, because there had been talk of particularly gruesome crimes.

"In Westley's case the culprit shot the lock off a door to get into a room. But apart from that, the gun was evidently just to make them do what the culprit wanted. There are no signs to suggest that they struggled when the murderer tied their hands and feet with masking tape."

"And then?"

"He stuffed a tea towel in their mouths. Rammed it right down their throats. That made Carla Roberts retch. She died choking on her vomit."

"And Anne Westley?"

"He had to give her a helping hand. She didn't die easily. He finally closed off her nostrils with masking tape too, and she suffocated."

"Oh, God," said John.

Hate, he thought; an unbelievable, mad hatred. It was not just a matter of killing the women. It was about making them die a painful death.

"But Thomas Ward was actually shot?" he asked,

just to make sure. Although he was sure that Gillian, who found her husband, would have told him if it had been any different.

"Yes. And that supports Fielder's theory that Thomas Ward wasn't the intended victim. The murderer was expecting a woman. Suddenly he was face to face with a man. And not just any man. Thomas Ward is tall. Athletic. In shape. Ward would no doubt have defended himself a lot more than the two elderly ladies, if he hadn't been shot immediately."

"And in both of the women's cases it was just *tea towels*?"

"Yes."

"Did they belong to the victims? In other words, were they just what was nearest at hand for the murderer? Or did he bring them with him?"

"They belonged to the victims. In Carla Roberts's case, her daughter identified the towel. In Anne Westley's case, identical towels were found in a drawer. The murderer seems to have taken advantage of what he found there."

They arrived at Charing Cross station as her train arrived. "Well, then," Kate said. Her complexion looked even paler than usual.

"Safe journey," said John. "And—thank you!"

She was hurt and did not turn around before getting onto her train. She chose a seat where he could not see her.

He guessed that she was probably crying.

Sunday, January 10

FOR THE FIRST TIME since Tom had been murdered, she had entered the house on her own. John had accompanied her the last time, but this time no one stood at her side.

It was smelling worse and worse in the rooms. A lot of food urgently needed to be thrown out.

Gillian took her suitcase up to the bedroom immediately. It looked just as it had when she left the house on December 29. The bedspread lying tidily on the bed. A book, a thriller she had started to read, lying open and spine-up on her bedside table next to the crumpled pages of *The Times*. Several sports magazines on Tom's side. One of his sweaters on a chair in the corner, and a tie on the wardrobe door.

All his things, thought Gillian. There's probably little point in holding on to them.

She decided to unpack her own suitcase later. For now, she just opened the side pocket and, fishing out her toiletries bag, took it to the bathroom. She put her toothbrush in the cup for toothbrushes and placed her comb on the shelf in front of the mirror. She tried to filter out the view of Tom's things. His shaver, aftershave, mouthwash, cleaning solution for his contact lenses. A few of his black socks were hanging off the large woven laundry basket. Although she had tried to prepare herself for this, Gillian felt the same bewilderment she had felt on her last short visit at seeing this unaltered normality. A Sunday morning in January. Snow and low clouds outside. Inside, dirty laundry and abandoned books and magazines that looked like they were just waiting to be read again, come evening. Everyday objects all around. The house did not look like the scene of a bloody crime. It looked like a normal house.

Gillian felt that she had two possibilities open to her. She could sit and stare at the walls, letting the invisible horror work on her until she started to scream. Or she could dive into the activities that the house was crying out for after her long absence.

She decided on the second option.

She spent the next four hours bringing order to the house. She washed mountains of laundry, putting it in the dryer and hanging it up in the boiler room. She went through the fridge, throwing out most of what she found. She put two bags of rubbish in the garbage can outside. She took the decorations off the Christmas tree and carried the needle-shedding monster outside onto the deck. She took the Christmas lights down from the windows, putting them away in their cardboard boxes and then storing them in the attic. She got rid of Chuck's cat litter, because he had gone to Norwich on Friday with Becky and would only return in a few weeks. She cleaned the bathrooms and kitchen, vacuumed and aired the entire house, and put fresh sheets on the beds. Lastly, she got a fire going, brewed a large pot of coffee, and sat down with a sigh in a comfy armchair. The house smelled good, it was warm, the crackling logs gave the place a cozy feeling. The coffee was hot and strong.

Three o'clock.

What should she do for the rest of the day?

She lit a cigarette, but then thought better of smoking in the living room and stubbed it out.

She knew it was dangerous to just sit around. She had cried in John's arms, but she had not really broken down after finding Tom murdered in the dining room. Her instinct told her that she would, sometime. The breakdown was lurking out there, just waiting for a suitable opportunity. Until now, she had been able to keep it at arm's length, especially because she had barely been alone for a moment. Tara and Becky had been there. They had only disappeared for the occasional hour or two at most, in which Tara aimed to take Becky's mind off things. On those occasions, she had often had John near her. In addition, there had been all the conversations with the police.

She was now completely on her own for the first time. In a big, empty, silent house.

Probably it had been a mistake to return.

She was drinking her fourth cup of coffee when her phone rang. It was John.

"Hi. I wanted to ask how you are doing."

"Pretty good. I cleaned the house, washed oodles of laundry, and am just treating myself to a nice coffee." She sounded so falsely cheerful that it pained her to hear herself. "And how are you?"

"You cleaned the house? Which *house?* Are you home again?"

"Yes."

"Why? Just to clean it?"

"I've moved back. This morning."

"But why?"

"I live here. At least until I find somewhere else. I can't avoid my own home forever."

He was silent for a moment. "What happened?" he asked quietly in the end.

She gave up playing hide-and-seek with him. Why

shouldn't he know? "I had a fight with Tara. On Thursday evening, after you left. And since then…I haven't felt comfortable in her house."

"What did you fight about?"

"We talked about you. Becky had made an ugly scene because you and I had met again. After she stormed out of the room and locked herself in the bathroom, for some reason that I myself no longer understand, I was stupid enough to…tell Tara that you'd been a policeman. And why you aren't any more."

"Aha. And she took that badly," John supposed.

"She was horrified. Sexual harassment is, of course, a term that isn't particularly well received by most women. I explained the circumstances, but she could not understand that I believed your side of the story without any reservations. She certainly can't understand why I keep on meeting you."

"I see," said John.

"It wasn't that she kept harping about it after that," Gillian continued. "It was more that we avoided the topic completely. But I didn't feel comfortable around her after that. I was always nervous when you called. And so I waited to call you until she would leave the house. All in all, it was a stressful and unpleasant situation. And the other thing is…."

"Yes?" asked John when she hesitated.

"The thing is, I need to start *living* again. I can't just sit on Tara's sofa forever and wait for my future to open up before me. After all, Tara works all day. I'm mostly on my own when I'm at her place."

"But you're on your own in your house too. And I don't think that's good for you."

"In my current situation, I don't think anything is good for me."

"Let me come and visit. Or come and visit me. Please."

"Not today, John. I have to find my own path."

He could understand her, but.... "Listen, Gillian. There's something else too. Apart from your difficult mental situation. You know, there's the theory that your husband's murder was a mistake. That you were the real target."

"I know. That's not news."

"Gillian, the murderer didn't get what he wanted. And we don't know that he won't try again."

"I'm not going to open the door to anyone. I'm not going to leave the garage door open. The house is secure, John. We've got an alarm system. I can turn it on at night."

"I don't like the fact that you're on your own."

"I'll be all right."

"Call me, if anything happens, okay?" She promised she would.

After they finished talking, she started to stare at the wall again. She asked herself why she was feeling such a strong reaction to the idea of being near John. When she was at Tara's house, in the days after the murder, she herself had made contact with him, wanted him near, and hoped to find consolation and support from him. Then something had changed. Inside her. For hours she had sat there and brooded over what had happened. Over how she had first fallen into a depression, then rushed into an affair, and why Tom was dead now. The terrible realization she came to was that she saw everything in an exaggeratedly dramatic light, and that this had set in motion a bad chain of events. She had been hurt by Tom's withdrawal from her; but if she had looked closely, she would have seen that he had never left her. She had let Becky's aggression and stubbornness drive her crazy, when she could have just waited for Becky to grow up a bit. Nothing had happened in her life that did not happen in thousands of other women's lives.

And if she had not still—*still*—been that girl with the low self-esteem, she would have been able to see everything differently. All those years ago, she had gone from the security of her parents' house much too quickly to marriage with Thomas Ward. From the first time they met, he had always been there for her. She had always felt safe with him. Much of what she had elatedly seen as her emancipation from her parents had really been an emancipation supported by a strong and self-confident man. When work started to demand more and more of Tom's time and he barely took the time in his busy schedule to breathe, she had reacted like a neglected child and thrown herself into the arms of the first man who came along. John appeared, desired her, admired her, gave her a feeling of warmth and self-confidence. But life could not go on like that. She had understood that, despite all the pain, mourning, and sense of guilt over the past few days. She had to learn to assert herself, however hard and bitter that path might prove.

Her cell rang again. This time it was Gillian's mother, of all people, reporting that, given the circumstances, Becky was doing all right, that Becky and her grandfather had just gone swimming, and that she would go to her therapist for her first session the next morning, on Monday. Then she wanted to know when Tom's funeral was.

All that's coming too, thought Gillian, exhausted.

"I don't know yet, Mommy. They're still doing the autopsy. I'll let you know in good time."

"What a horrific tragedy," her mother said. "I'm just

happy you can stay at your friend's house like this! I wouldn't have had a moment's peace otherwise."

Gillian decided to let her continue to believe she was at Tara's house. She knew she would never hear the end of it if she told her otherwise, and she did not feel that she had the strength to face that now.

"Say hi to Becky from me," she said before they hung up. "Ask her to call me, all right? I'd like to hear her voice."

Just after half past three. The long silent afternoon lay ahead of her. She stood up, putting on her boots, coat, scarf, and gloves.

Luckily, it had snowed heavily in the past week.

She would shovel the snow from the driveway. Perhaps after that, she would be too tired to have a breakdown.

Monday, January 11

1

"CAN YOU REMEMBER anything else about Liza Stanford?" asked Christy. She could see that she had chosen a terrible time for her third visit to the clinic where Anne Westley had worked. It was the first Monday morning after the Christmas holidays for many schools. The waiting room was jam-packed. Christy had heard that two of the doctors were out with the flu themselves. The two remaining GPs, a nervous young man and a woman, looked like they would be the next to be laid low by the flu. They were working at full speed to deal with the horde of patients. Now Christy had appeared right in the middle of the chaos to once again start asking urgent, detailed questions about their patient Finley Stanford and his mother. She had come at a very bad time. They would have liked to show her the door with a few polite phrases, but they recognized that she was just doing her job.

"Could you come by later?" the receptionist had asked somewhat testily, but Christy had shaken her head in a friendly but decided manner.

"Unfortunately not. Believe me, I wouldn't bother you if I had any other option."

The woman, whose name badge on her lapel revealed her name to be Tess Pritchard, said she could answer a few questions. She led Christy into one of the sick doctors' empty consulting rooms and sat down behind the desk, offering Christy one of the chairs in front of it. Asked again about Liza Stanford, she nodded.

"Oh, yes. I remember her well."

"Why? What did you notice about her?"

Tess snorted contemptuously. "Her wealth. And her arrogance. That woman had no lack of either."

"You mean it was easy to see that she was rich?"

"You'd have had to be blind not to see it. Always wearing chic clothes. Expensive jewelry. Enormous Gucci sunglasses. A Hermès handbag. And her Bentley outside. She parked right outside the clinic once, so we saw it."

"I see. And she was…arrogant?"

"We assistants were beneath her," said Tess. "She barely managed to open her lips to us. Her dignity didn't allow her to talk to us. I expect she talked more to Dr. Westley. She will have had to, if she wanted to explain what was wrong with her son."

"But you were never there at the consultation?"

Tess shook her head. "No. Not me or anyone else. It wouldn't be normal. Unless someone is needed to assist the doctor. That wasn't the case here: there was never anything seriously wrong with the boy."

"What was your impression of Finley?"

Tess thought for a moment. "A nice boy. I thought he was friendly. He was quiet, but not in a snobbish way like his mother. Just shy. A reserved child."

"*Unusually* shy? *Unusually* reserved?"

"No. We see them all here, as you can imagine. Some children race around the waiting room like spinning tops and their parents can barely get them to sit down. Others, the ones who don't like going to the doctor and who feel unsure of the whole situation, tend to clam up and withdraw into their shell. Finley was in that group, the ones who are reserved. But still absolutely normal."

"He started coming to the clinic quite late on, didn't he? And if I understood the files I was able to see on Friday, then he only came five times altogether. Until his ninth birthday. He was never seen here when he was little, was he?"

"No. He was seven when he came here for the first time. As far as I can remember, he had developed bronchitis after a cold and it just wasn't going away. So, nothing major."

"Finley was pretty healthy, on the whole?"

"Yes. The things his mother brought him here for were harmless-enough illnesses. Sometimes he wasn't even ill at all."

"Did Dr. Westley ever say anything about Liza Stanford? An anecdote? Let something slip? Anything?"

"No," said Tess. "She was very strict about confidentiality. At least to us, working in the clinic. She never mentioned anything about patients or their parents. Certainly not about Stanford. She will have noticed how we bitched about her, and she would have been sure not to get involved in that. Not to fan the flames, as it were."

"Could she have talked about her to the other doctors?"

"Maybe," said Tess hesitantly. "But the two doctors here today weren't working at this clinic when Dr. Westley was still here. She did talk a lot with Dr. Phyllis Skinner."

"One of the doctors with the flu right now?" Christy supposed.

"Right. If she talked to anyone here about a patient's case, then it would have been with her."

"Can I have Dr. Skinner's address? I must speak to her urgently."

"Of course," said Tess, ready to help. She looked at her watch. She could hear her phone ringing, the doorbell ringing and ringing.

"Sergeant, I don't want to be rude, but...."

"I'm almost done," promised Christy. "Just two more quick things. To check that I've got the facts right. Finley was here from age seven to nine. He came five times. Now he's twelve. That means he hasn't come here for the last three years?"

"The last three and a half years, in fact. That's right."

"So his mother and he stopped coming after Dr. Westley retired?"

"Yes."

"And secondly. We have a statement saying Liza Stanford suffered from depression. Depression that meant she sometimes disappeared completely for periods. That she would leave her family and be untraceable. Did you know about that?"

"No," said Tess, astonished.

"You never noticed any depression?"

"Well," said Tess. "Frankly, I'd eat my hat if she was depressed. The way she behaved certainly put *other* people into depressions. That's all. She herself...well, you can't see inside people, of course, especially if they refuse to talk properly to you, but I just can't imagine it in her case. From my dealings with Liza Stanford, I'd completely exclude that possibility."

"Thank you for your time," said Christy.

2

THERE WERE THREE women left on Christy's list of people to visit: the three members of Ellen Curran's women's group apart from the murdered Carla Roberts and the missing Liza Stanford.

Ellen Curran had e-mailed all the group members' names and addresses, but Christy had soon found out that she would only be able to talk to one of the women. The other two had gone off together in December for a tour of New Zealand. They would only be back in England in February, and attempts to reach them had, as yet, gone unrewarded.

Which left Nancy Cox, who sounded nice on the phone. "Go ahead and come over this morning," she had said to Christy. "I've been enjoying my retirement for a year now. I've got time."

The rush-hour traffic was starting to thin out as Christy drove across town. She remembered her conversation with Fielder on Saturday. She had wanted to know what kind of person Logan Stanford was, as she only knew him from the media. Fielder had hesitated a good while before replying.

"To be honest, I don't like him," he had said in the end. "But of course that can't influence the investigation in the slightest. He is just so damn rich, and he really lets it show. I've never liked people like that. What's more, he's a classic hotshot lawyer. You feel he'd sell his own grandmother. That he doesn't mind stretching the truth or evading taxes or slapping injunctions on anyone who crosses him. You know what I mean?"

She had laughed. "Yes, I do. But be careful what you say. Especially about tax evasion!"

"I'm just telling you this as an impression, Christy. No idea if it's true. But with him you can imagine it."

"And his wife's disappearance really doesn't disturb him?"

"He's used to it, he says. He's just as used to her suddenly appearing again. That's why he's not too worried."

"Does that sound normal to you? I mean, even if

you're used to it…. Someone who is so depressed that she disappears for weeks…. That's not right! He can't just ignore it. Surely he'd try to help her."

"He seems pretty emotionless to me. And very focused on his career and appearance. Of course, we don't know how much he might have tried to help her in the past. Partners can fail with their depressed other halves. They can exhaust their energies and in the end accept how things are, just hoping that things will turn out more or less all right."

Now, while driving, Christy suddenly had another thought. The receptionist at the clinic had rejected the idea that Liza Stanford suffered from depression. And it was clear that the family was swimming in money.

A lawyer's wife, thought Christy. Stacks of money. Expensive jewelry, designer clothes. The Bentley. Such a woman might disappear for other reasons for weeks on end. To give herself a real makeover, maybe. Brazil, for example. Maybe she is sitting in a São Paulo clinic, getting liposuction, tighter eyelids, smoother skin, and Botoxed lips. No one likes to talk about that. Her husband could have banned her from talking about this extravagant hobby, and the best idea that he could come up with that they could use rather than the truth was to say that she suffered from depression. Harmless possibilities like this should not be ignored, Christy thought.

At the same time, she understood Fielder's line of thinking. "We have two murdered women, and the woman who links the two has disappeared without a trace. Something fishy there, Christy! I know that crazy coincidences can happen, but then I want proof that it's just coincidence. Don't forget: the Stanfords' marriage was not a happy one. If a married woman joins a group of *single women*, in order to build up courage to make a decisive step in that direction herself, then their marriage was in serious trouble. We're in the dark! What if Carla Roberts urged her friend to finally leave the ice-cold lawyer, and that really got Stanford's goat? A divorce could have cost him a lot of money. Money that he might not have. The family lives in a showy house, drives showy cars, and likes to show off in general. Isn't it often the case that such homes are built on wobbly foundations? Maybe they've got an enormous mortgage on the house. Maybe the cars were bought on credit and they're just barely keeping up with the payments. A divorce would be the last straw. Stanford might have hated that group his wife went to—especially Carla Roberts."

"And what about Anne Westley? and Thomas Ward? or Gillian Ward?"

Fielder had not had any answers there. Neither had Christy. Nancy Cox greeted Christy at the door of her small terraced house in Fulham and led her into her living room, where a large pot of aromatic coffee awaited them. She was a delicate woman with friendly eyes and short gray hair who came across as very warm-hearted. Two sleeping cats lay on her sofa. A snowman stood in her yard.

"My grandchildren were here for the weekend," she explained, seeing where Christy's gaze had landed.

What Nancy said about Liza matched what Ellen Curran had already said, while not completely matching the picture the receptionist had drawn.

"Arrogant? I never thought so. Yes, she was always wearing the latest designer apparel, and the jewelry she wore on one hand was probably worth more than the money I get for my pension in five years. But that's not what makes people happy, is it? She seemed sad to me. Worn down."

"What did she say about her marriage? She wanted to leave her husband, didn't she?"

"You know what? I always thought to myself: she'll never leave him. She just wants to make sure she could. Hard to say what exactly she held against her husband. She barely said anything. She and Carla Roberts were both very quiet. While the other four of us never stopped babbling on."

"Carla Roberts...."

Nancy looked concerned. "Do you know now how she was killed? I couldn't believe it, when I read it in the papers. You never think something like that could happen to someone you know. I was stunned!"

"Although Carla and Liza said little—they must have said something now and then?"

Nancy thought for a moment. "Yes, sometimes Liza said she was unhappy in her marriage. Her husband only thought about money, prestige, keeping up appearances. He's often in the papers because of all those charity events. But that doesn't mean he cares properly for his wife, now, does it? I think she felt utterly alone, even when he was home."

"Do you know if he accepted the fact that she took part in the group?"

"I don't think he knew about it. She had told him vaguely about a self-help group. He probably thought it was pretty silly but harmless."

"Did Carla tell her to leave her husband?"

"I don't know. Sometimes the two of them talked quietly to each other, but who knows what about." Nancy looked guilty. "Honestly, I found them both rather boring. The rest of us were having a fun time while those two wet blankets.... At some point I stopped paying much attention to them. Liza was often absent, anyway."

"Did she say why?"

"Social obligations. That wasn't surprising, given her husband's position. But it still annoyed Ellen a bit."

"There's no chance that her husband stopped her from coming at all, is there?"

"No, of course not. But I'm just repeating what she said. We didn't dig any deeper."

"Did Liza ever mention her son's GP? Dr. Anne Westley?"

"No. Why?"

Christy did not respond to the question. "And what did Carla Roberts talk about?" she asked. "When she talked."

"Well, Carla had real problems," said Nancy. "She was a broken woman. Her husband gone off with the secretary, the company bankrupt. Carla had lost everything overnight. Their house was auctioned off.... Suddenly she was working in a drug store, unpacking boxes and stocking shelves, to make ends meet. At least until her retirement, when she became completely isolated. She just could not come to terms with it. And her daughter, who was the only person she had left, had an increasingly separate life."

"Yes, the daughter didn't take much care of her mother."

"Well...." Nancy shrugged. "That's young people today. They're all thinking about their lives, their future. When my husband told me he had another woman and wanted a divorce, I fell into a black hole, believe me. And I didn't see my children much then. They had their studies, their friends...weekends with a bawling mom were not top priority."

Once again, Christy thought she had made the right

choice in not going down the traditional route of having her own family and children. She often had the impression that all children today were completely selfish.

She finished her coffee, took her card out of her pocket, and pushed it across the table to Nancy.

"Here, take this. Call me if you remember anything else. Anything that Carla or Liza said or just mentioned by the by. Anything could be important."

"I'll see if I can come up with anything more for you," promised Nancy.

3

THE PROPERTY WAS unusually large, even for Hampstead. As John was aware of house prices in different areas of London, he had an idea of what the Stanfords must have coughed up for the place. The house was quite far back from the street and difficult to see through the tall old trees that stood close together and that even at this time of year, without their leaves, formed a rather hermetic wall. John checked quickly to see which way was south and realized that in the summer, the trees must swallow up all the sunlight. The house must be constantly in shadow. John wondered how someone could pay a fortune for a mansion with park-sized grounds and then live in the same gloom they could have acquired cheaply with any basement apartment. Suddenly he was not particularly surprised that Liza Stanford was said to suffer from depression.

He was about to ring the doorbell, which with a CCTV camera was just beside the wrought-iron gate, when he saw a boy who looked to be about twelve or so approaching through the snowy yard. The boy was not walking on the carefully cleared drive, but was stomping his way through the snow. He was pulling a sled behind him, a kind of red plastic saucer topped by a small molded seat. John remembered the wooden sled he had had as a child. So much had changed since then.

The boy opened the gate and simultaneously noticed the man who was standing there and waiting. He jumped.

"Hi," he said uncertainly.

"Hi," said John. "I'm John Burton. And you are…?"

"Finley. Finley Stanford."

"Hello, Finley. I wanted to visit your mother. Is she in?"

"No."

"Do you know when she'll get back?"

"No."

"Where is she?"

"I don't know."

"You don't know?"

"She disappeared," said Finley.

John looked at him with a pretense of surprise. "Disappeared? When did she disappear?"

"On November 15. It was a Sunday."

"Ah. So she just packed her things, left, and didn't come back? Or what?"

"No. Mom and I had been watching TV that Sunday afternoon. She drank tea and I drank hot chocolate. And we ate cookies."

"Just you and your mom? Not your dad?"

"He was in his study. He had work to do."

"Got it. And then?"

"Dad left because he had to meet someone for supper. A client. My dad's a lawyer."

"I know."

"Mom and I didn't have supper, because we were still

full from the cookies and chocolate. I played a little on my computer. At nine I had to go to bed." Finley suddenly stopped and looked suspiciously at John. "Why do you want to know?"

"I know your mom well. I need to talk to her urgently, so it's important for me to find out what happened."

"Well," said Finley, "I don't know that either. The next morning, Dad woke me and said that Mom had left in the night, but that she would be coming back. I just went to school like normal. I was really hoping she would be there when I came home from school, but...." He shrugged.

John looked closely at him. The boy was pale and delicately boned. He was obviously worried about his mother, but not mentally unstable. He seemed calm, maybe even a bit too calm. In his time as a coach, John had worked with many children from difficult families, and he had noticed sometimes that children from particularly hopeless situations conveyed a strange peacefulness, which was actually an expression of the child's complete withdrawal from everyone else. Some children from intact families were much more conspicuous in their behavior than some of those where you later heard that the mother drank and the stepfather was violent. John had found that children whose behavior was conspicuously inconspicuous could well come from a home that was an unmitigated disaster.

He wondered whether he would have characterized Finley as conspicuously inconspicuous if he had been completely unprejudiced.

"What school do you go to?" he asked.

"William Ellis School. In Highgate."

"Do you like school? Do you have many friends?"

The boy thought about the question briefly. "Yes,

it's okay there. I don't have many friends. But I *like* to be on my own."

"I understand," said John. Then he carried on from where he had left off: "Did that happen in the past? That your mom would just disappear and no one would know where she'd gone?"

"Once. About two years ago. But then she came back ten days later."

So Mrs. Stanford's disappearance was not as normal as Stanford had represented it to Fielder. She had disappeared a single time and for a limited length of time. This time she had been gone since November 15. Without a trace. It was now January 11. Almost two months had passed.

"The police asked about her too," said Finley. "On Friday. An inspector from Scotland Yard was here. But you're not from the police, are you?"

"No, Finley. I'm not from the police."

"So why all these questions?" said a sharp voice from behind him. John turned around. Without his noticing, a man had walked over from the house. Jeans, sweater, carefully combed gray hair. Logan Stanford.

"Mr. Stanford?" asked John.

"What do you want?" asked Stanford without introducing himself. "What do you have to talk about with my son?"

"He knows Mom," said Finley. "He has to talk to her."

"Oh, right? What about?"

"That's private," said John.

"Who are you?" asked Stanford. His voice was calm.

"John Burton."

Stanford looked at him. John could imagine him in court. He did not look particularly friendly or unfriendly. Very objective. Very much in control of himself. It was impossible to see what was going on inside him. He was completely impenetrable.

John decided to be direct with him.

"Mr. Stanford, the police came here on Friday. About your wife. You know why."

"Who are you?" repeated Stanford.

"Two women have been killed. And a man. The man's death doesn't seem to have been planned. The murderer's target was the man's wife. A coincidence saved her, but it's possible that she's still in great danger. You want to know who I am? I'm a very close friend of that woman. I care for her. I want her to be safe."

"I understand. But I can't help you."

"I suppose Detective Inspector Fielder explained the circumstances to you. You will know why the police wanted to see your wife: she's the only link between the two dead women that has yet been found. It's really important that I speak to her."

"I don't know where she is."

"And you find that normal? Not to know anything about your wife's whereabouts for two months?"

Stanford shrugged. "What I find normal is my business, Mr. Burton."

"Your wife suffers from deep depression, am I right?"

"Mr. Burton.…"

"At least that is what you told the police."

"You've hit the nail on the head right there, Mr. Burton: I only talk to the police. Not to some complete stranger who intercepts my son in our yard and interrogates him with the sole excuse that he is a friend of the wife of one of these murder victims. Our conversation is over."

The two men looked at each other for a moment in silence. John understood he would not get anywhere with

Stanford right now. Stanford was not going to waver, could not be provoked, certainly would not let slip some unguarded comment. John would not get a sliver of a lead from him.

"Goodbye, Mr. Stanford," he said.

"Goodbye," replied Stanford. He put his arm around his son's shoulders.

John turned around, crossed the street, and got into his car, which he had parked on the other side of the road. He was sure that Stanford would note down his number and immediately check to see if John had given his real name. He would probably try to find out more about him.

So what?

He was not planning on giving up. There was another possibility still—the boy. He had to go to school, and Stanford could not have him watched around the clock. William Ellis School, Highgate. It shouldn't be difficult to find Finley there.

The boy was Logan Stanford's Achilles heel. Not only because John could reach him, but also because he knew a lot. He had learned to accept things, to bottle them up inside, and to play his parents' game: that they were an intact, successful, happy family.

Perhaps the most deceitful bit of acting the city had ever seen.

1

GILLIAN HAD THE impression that since the day she had found Thomas dead in their dining room, she had not had a moment's rest. That was almost literally true, discounting the nights when she took a strong sleeping pill and collapsed like a felled tree, waking the next morning from the depths of the narcosis without—fortunately—the slightest memory of any disturbing dreams. Her nights were utterly black and utterly empty. When she got up, she felt like a hamster about to get on its wheel and run itself to exhaustion. The caged hamster runs from the boredom and isolation of its prison. Gillian was running from the moment of finally understanding what was happening.

At some point, she would no longer be able to run.

She had cleaned out the house. She had bagged up and taken Tom's clothes to a charity shop, got rid of the clothes Becky had long outgrown, and sorted out her own old, no longer used clothes. She had fetched old newspapers and cardboard boxes from the attic and put them in the recycling bin. The cellar still contained the furniture from the beginning of the marriage. They held so many nostalgic memories that Gillian had never been able to separate herself from them; now they too were put on the list of objects she would throw out.

In the cellar she had found many flattened cardboard

boxes from the time when Tom and she had moved into the house. She lugged them upstairs, assembled them, and started to pack. Books, china, framed photographs, candlesticks.

By now, the house looked like a move was imminent. Realizing how hungry she was, she took a pizza from the freezer and put it in the oven. While waiting for her food, she booted up her computer and Googled for a real estate agent in Southend or London. She did not know anyone in the business, and she could have gone for the first name she saw, but then she saw Luke Palm's name and it rang a bell with her. The name had been in one or two newspapers. Palm was the man who had found Anne Westley murdered. She wondered if he might be the best option for her. She would be able to tell him openly why she wanted to sell the house without him falling off his chair in shock or showing no understanding or being greedy to hear the details. In a way, he was a part of the whole thing. Since the brutal act had occurred in her life, Gillian sometimes felt as if she were afloat on a floe of ice far from normality and from people who had never experienced such violence. She saw Luke Palm as another person adrift on an ice floe. She trusted him more than other people.

She dialed his office number and was put through immediately by his secretary.

"Hello, Luke Palm here."

"Hi, this is Gillian Ward." She paused slightly and waited to see if he reacted in any way, but Palm obviously did not know her name. He must have read of Tom's murder in the papers, although only one of them had actually given Tom's full name.

"I'd like to sell my house," she continued. "Out here in Southend, the Thorpe Bay part of town. I'd like ad-

vice on what price I should put it on the market for. I've
no idea about the state of the market right now."

"No problem. I can visit any time. When would be
good for you?"

"Would tomorrow be all right? Tomorrow afternoon?"

"I'm afraid I've got a few appointments tomorrow.
Would half past five be too late for you?"

"No, that would be perfect."

She gave him her address and telephone number.
After she had said good-bye, she carried on sitting at
the dining table for a few more minutes, looking out at
the yard, which lay deep in snow. It looked like it would
be her last winter here.

I'm really going to do it, she thought. I'm really going
to do it. I'm going to burn all my bridges.

A few hungry birds fluttered around the bird feeder
next to the cherry tree. They flew off in disappointment
when they realized it was empty. Gillian could not stop
herself seeing in her mind's eye a scene from Becky's
birthday two years ago on November 22. Becky had
wanted so much to have the bird feeder, and had gotten it. Gillian had stood at the window and watched
as Becky and Tom put it up that very same afternoon.
Becky's cheeks were glowing with joy. Tom had enjoyed doing something with his daughter. The two of
them had looked so happy, so harmonious. Just watching them had made Gillian feel all warm. She could still
feel some of that warmth now—and that was dangerous.
Much too dangerous.

She shooed away the image.

Once again she saw the empty back yard in front of
her, buried under a carpet of virgin snow. No longer

with a husband laughing and talking to a child. Just the hungry birds.

I must buy bird food, Gillian thought.

2

SAMSON CLOSED THE DOOR of the trailer carefully behind him and put the key in the pocket of his parka. The cold outside made him shiver. A bright blue sky, sunlight, and deep snow whose surface sparkled and shone. At least minus ten Celsius, thought Samson. He couldn't remember ever having experienced a winter as cold and snowy as this. No, the last few years had only brought nasty, wet weather. No one had thought they would see another white Christmas in England. Or see children pulling sleds behind them as they stomp toward the nearest hill for an afternoon's fun. Samson could remember doing that when he was very young.

But that had been a long time ago.

He had a bag of bread crumbs with him. He wiped the snow off a half-finished section of a wall and shook the crumbs out onto the bricks. He knew that as soon as he moved away a little, the birds would descend like a black cloud on the wall. He had fed them regularly over the last few days. They were his only company out in this desolate place. Their hungry cries almost broke his heart.

"From now on, you'll have to manage on your own," he said quietly. "I can't cope out here any longer."

He planned to make his way across the fields to the outskirts of London, find a phone booth, and get John Burton's address either from a phone book or from directory assistance. He needed a new place to stay, and

Burton was the only person who could help him. If he could not find Burton, then it would have to be Bartek, although he could imagine that if he turned up, Bartek would either faint or chase him away. Samson's brother Gavin would be the last resort, because of Millie. But to be honest, he would rather starve or freeze to death than return to that hellcat's den. He would end up in a police cell, he had no illusions there; it was just a question of how long he could put it off. And by now he had long reached the conclusion that time in a cell was not the worst of all imaginable evils. Being alone had almost broken him. He was setting off now to find John in order to save his life. A few more days in the trailer on the abandoned building site, and he would have committed suicide.

It was half past one. On the horizon he could see the silhouettes of the houses on the edge of the city. It was not clear what part of London he was looking at. He guessed that he had an hour and a half's walk ahead of him until he reached a residential area. He did not mind. He had always liked to walk, he was wrapped up warm, and before he started he had strengthened himself with a meal of the canned food. Nothing could go wrong on the walk.

He just needed to find somewhere to sleep before night came. The temperature plummeted at nights to around minus fifteen.

He set off. It was not easy to walk, because he sank deep into the snow with every step.

I'm going to feel it in my legs tomorrow, he thought.

He turned around just once. The cranes and the incomplete walls of the buildings towered up against the unearthly blue sky. His trailer looked small and insignificant beside them, almost lost.

The birds fluttered around the wall, fighting for the bread.

3

JOHN HAD BEEN parked opposite the school since three o'clock, keeping a close eye on all the gates. A few pupils had left the red brick building with its white window frames. Others had gone in, but Finley was not one of them. The school backed onto the meadows and fields of Hampstead Heath, the edge of which contained tennis courts, sports facilities, and various buildings belonging to the school. Even if Finley had a lesson in one of those buildings, John supposed that he would have to come out the front when he went home. The bus stop was a little farther down the road. He assumed that Finley would go there in order to get home.

John was hopeful.

He was less upbeat when he thought about his company. The last few days' research had had a decidedly negative effect on his presence in the office. He had capable employees, but it was important for the boss to hold the reins. And that was not happening right now. What is more, he felt guilty about Samson Segal. He should have popped in and seen him ages ago. The poor fellow was so utterly alone out there and no doubt near to despair. John felt responsible for him, but instead of looking after him, he was playing the role of a private detective out to find a disappeared woman and waiting for hours for the right leads to materialize. The thing was that a real private dick was normally paid for his work, while he was neglecting the work that paid his bills.

Never mind. What he had started, he would finish.

At around three-thirty things started to happen. A trickle of pupils left the school, soon followed by a horde. The peaceful, snow-covered street was suddenly unrecognizable. Shouts, laughter, and screaming filled the road. It was teeming with children and young people. John got out of his car and concentrated on looking at them. He hoped he would not miss Finley in the crowds.

At the same time, he kept a close watch on the street and other parking cars. He did not rule out the possibility that Stanford himself would come to pick up his son. John was not afraid of meeting him, but he knew that his chances of talking to Finley on his own would be close to zero if Stanford found him here at the school gates. If that happened, Stanford would probably not leave his child unaccompanied for a moment in the future, even if it meant hiring a bodyguard.

However, John could not see Stanford anywhere. Good. The man had to do some work for all that money of his, after all.

Finley appeared in front of John so suddenly that John almost started. Unlike most of the others, he did not come out in a big, noisy group, but he walked out on his own. He recognized John and went over to him. He just looked at him with his calm, gentle eyes. "Hello, Finley," said John, scanning the area again from the corners of his eyes. Still no Logan Stanford in sight.

"Hello, Mr. Burton," said Finley. "My dad said I shouldn't talk to you."

"Yes, I expected he would. And I know that I'm asking a lot when I ask you to ignore that. But it's important. It's about your mom." Finley looked torn. He did not want to do what his father had expressly forbidden, but he was also a child who missed his mother.

"You don't know my mom?" he asked.

"No," admitted John. "I don't know her. But it's important that I speak to her. It's important for someone else, who I do know well."

Finley shrugged. "I don't know where she is."

"Do you have a photo of her?" John asked.

Finley nodded. He slid his rucksack off his back and put it down on the snow, so that he could rummage around in it. After a minute, he pulled a photo out of a wallet. "That's her."

John looked at the picture. A beautiful woman, as he saw immediately. Long blond hair and large eyes. A finely chiseled face. But he saw too a harassed expression, fear in her eyes. Signs of depression? Or very specific fears that were poisoning Liza Stanford's life?

He gave him back the photo. "She's very beautiful," he said.

Finley nodded. "Yes."

"Is your father in his office?"

"Yes. He's just coming back this evening."

"Were you going to get on the bus?"

"Yes."

"If you like, I'll take you home. And we can talk a bit on the way."

Finley shook his head firmly. "I never get into a car with a stranger."

"Okay. You're right. But would you give me five minutes of your time to talk here on the street?"

"My bus leaves in ten minutes," said Finley.

"All right, then. Finley, you know, it's almost impossible to believe that someone disappears *without reason*. Certainly not a mother. She had to leave behind what is dearest to her in all the world—you. A woman would only do that if she was under some enormous pressure."

"Yes," said Finley.

"Your father told the police that your mother has always suffered from depression. Do you know what depression is?"

"When you're always sad."

"Right. Is that something people could say about your mother? That she is always sad?"

"Yes," said Finley seriously.

John tried another tack. "The reason why depressed people are sad is often hard to see. They might feel there is a reason, but for us on the outside it can seem that there's no reason. As if the sadness was just there, like a runny nose or sore throat. A kind of illness. Even when everything in these people's lives seems fine and people might say *Why is so-and-so always so sad?* Is it like that with your mom?"

"You mean that no one knows why she's sad?"

"Yes, that's what I mean."

"It's not really like that," Finley said quietly. He was no longer looking at John.

"So you know why she's sad?" insisted John. Finley nodded.

"And do you know why she went away?"

Finley did not say anything. He was looking fixedly at his boots. John could see that the veins under the pale white skin of his temples were twitching slightly.

"Can you tell me?" Finley shook his head.

"But it might help me to find her."

Finley's eyes started to wander around. It seemed that he was hoping for something to come to his aid, although he himself had no idea what it would be.

"Did your parents often fight?" asked John.

Finley looked as if what he wanted more than any-

thing right then was to run off. John understood that he
would not be able to keep the boy there another minute.

He had had an idea about a faint chance to find Liza.
He just needed one piece of information from the boy,
and he would not get it if he continued to be so insistent.

He changed the topic abruptly. "Do you do anything
outside school?" he asked casually. "After school, I
mean. Do you have a hobby? Rugby? A musical in-
strument? Anything else?"

Finley looked surprised and relieved at once. "I play
tennis on Wednesdays. And I've got a piano lesson on
Thursdays."

"You play tennis? That's great. I coach children in
tennis in my free time."

"Really?" Finley looked at him with respect.

"Yes. Really. Are you any good?"

"I'm okay."

"Do you play at school?"

"Yes."

"And the piano lesson—is that here too?"

"No. I've got a private teacher. Near the Hampstead
tube station."

"I see. I suppose your mom used to take you there,
am I right? And now you go on your own?"

"Yes. My dad doesn't have much time."

"Of course. Finley—thanks for talking. I hope you
can still catch your bus."

"Goodbye," he said uncertainly.

"Goodbye," said John. He watched the boy walk
away. As he walked, he hunched his shoulders forward.
He looked as if he were carrying an invisible load.

Certainly not a happy child. A child who was well
provided for, who was supported in so many ways, who
had a giant, well-equipped playroom waiting for him

at home. But a sad child with neglect written all over his face.

It was clutching at a straw, but it was the only chance John could see. If Liza Stanford was still somewhere nearby, occasionally she would try to check up on how her son was doing. Or she would just try to see him, to make the separation from him bearable in some way. John harbored a small hope that Liza would sometimes hang around those places where she knew Finley would appear at certain times, in order to catch a glimpse of him. If he was lucky, he would manage to recognize her. He could either talk to her or follow her.

It was just a chance, nothing more. And it meant that he would have to twiddle his thumbs for whole afternoons. He had not asked Finley what time he had tennis and piano lessons, as he did not want to draw attention to his interest. That meant he would have to keep watch from early afternoon. It would eat up his time—and not be at all pleasant in this cold.

He looked at his watch. He wondered if it was still worth going in to the office to see if everything was going well. In the end, he decided to work things out on the phone—and to visit Gillian instead.

4

CHRISTY MCMARROW WAS sitting in DI Fielder's office. The day before, on Monday, she had told her boss about her conversations with Nancy Cox and Tess Pritchard, the receptionist from Anne Westley's former clinic. Fielder himself had wanted to try to talk to Dr. Westley's confidante Phyllis Skinner, and had succeeded.

"I spoke to Dr. Skinner," he said. "I'd have preferred to see her in person, but she's in bed with a terrible case

of the flu and isn't up to having visitors. She remembers
Liza Stanford. She describes her in a similar way to the
receptionist: showy, arrogant. Icily distant. She says that
Anne Westley hadn't mentioned anything particular
about her until shortly after she retired, three and a half
years ago. Then one evening Anne called her, Dr. Skinner, and said she had a problem with the mother of one
of her patients, or rather ex-patients, as she had stopped
working two or three weeks before. With Liza Stanford."

"Ah!" said Christy, sitting up straighter.

Fielder waved his hand dismissively. "Unfortunately,
it peters out there. Dr. Skinner was just packing, as she
was off on vacation the next day. She had no time to
talk. Anne Westley could tell on the phone that she was
stressed, so, without even hinting at anything else, she
suggested that they could meet and talk about it when
Dr. Skinner got back. But the house-warming party for
the Westleys' newly renovated Tunbridge Wells house
was planned for just a few days after Skinner came back
from her vacation. A day before the party, Anne Westley's husband fell off the roof, contracted pneumonia in
the hospital, and died. So whatever Anne Westley had
intended to tell her former colleague, it was completely
forgotten in the ensuing tragic sequence of events. Neither of the women thought any more about it."

"They never took up that conversation later?"

"No. Unfortunately not."

"Bloody hell," said Christy with some force.

"I know," said Fielder. "But moaning won't help us
now. What my call has made even clearer is that Liza
Stanford has an important part in the whole affair. She
knew two of the murder victims, and one of them had
some problem with her. And now she's disappeared.
She's mixed up in these cases. We don't know exactly

how or why, but I bet she's the key to them. Or at least, that she'll be vital in our finding the key."

"That means we must find her."

"Yes."

"What can we do? Put her husband through the third degree?"

Fielder nodded slowly. "He's a tough nut to crack. Pretends that he's friendly and cooperative; but if he doesn't want to talk, he doesn't talk. And he's got connections."

"Which he'll use, of course."

"Of course. We have to be careful. He'd lodge a formal complaint before we know it, something like that, at the highest level."

"Still," said Christy, "at the moment he's our only chance."

"We could also report Liza Stanford as a missing person and look for her."

"He won't allow that to go through unchallenged," she said.

"You're right," admitted Fielder. "Especially as we can only speculate vaguely at this point. We don't have many hard facts. His version is that his wife has taken herself off to a secluded spot for a while because of her depression, that she does this often, and that there is no reason to be worried. That does not justify any search." Both of them were silent. The case was getting them down. In the end, Fielder asked: "What about Samson Segal? Any sign of him?"

"He's still in hiding," said Christy. "He was my favorite suspect, but I'm not so sure now. Maybe he really is just a harmless crank driven right now by panic and the thought that he could blamed for something he didn't do. He's the living embodiment of the opposite of

Stanford: he's someone who never knows how to make life easier for himself."

"It would be interesting to know if he knows Liza Stanford."

"He didn't mention her in his notes."

"We still shouldn't rule it out. We have to find him too, urgently."

"And John Burton?"

"Keep our eye on him," said Fielder. He added: "I've asked to see the files of his investigation back then."

"There was no court case," objected Christy. She had come to think that she could not remind her boss enough times about this. "The charges didn't stick!"

"Still. I just want to have another look."

"And I—"

"And you try your luck with Logan Stanford. Maybe you'll be luckier with him than I was," said Fielder.

She rolled her eyes. She had guessed that Fielder would put her on to Stanford, on to the man they wouldn't get anything out of.

"Will do," she said, resigned.

5

THE FIRST THING he saw as he came up the drive was the wide-open front door. In view of everything that had happened in the last few weeks, he felt an icy hand grip his heart as he feared for the worst. He stood still, wondering how best to act. But that same moment, he saw Gillian come around the corner from the back yard. She had obviously not been outside long, because she was not wearing a coat or scarf. She had just put on her fur-lined boots to trudge through the snow. She was holding a plastic bucket in her hand. She jumped when she saw she had a visitor, but then relaxed when she recognized who it was. Not that she seemed particularly pleased to see him, as John noticed.

"Hello, Gillian," he said.

She smiled, politely rather than warmly. "Hello, John."

He approached her and gave her a kiss, but she turned her face so that his lips only brushed her cheek.

"It's probably rude to come by without warning, but I was in the area...." he said.

That was not true. He did not have coaching on Tuesdays. He had absolutely no reason to drive out to Thorpe Bay. None, except to see Gillian. But luckily for him, she did not question him.

"Come in." She stepped into the house ahead of him and put the bucket down by the door. "I've just fed the birds."

"Aha." He looked around. Boxes were piled up along the walls of the hallway. From the clear marks on the walls, he could see that pictures had been taken down too.

"What's going on?" he asked.

"I've packed some things already," said Gillian. She disappeared into the kitchen. "Would you like some coffee?"

"Yes, please." He looked around, still shaking his head. The signs were clear: Gillian was preparing to move out.

He stepped into the kitchen. Outside, it was almost dark, and yet through the glass of the back door he could still see the bird feeder on its pole. He turned to Gillian, who was busy with the espresso machine. "Why don't you go out the kitchen door when you want to get to the back yard?"

She paused. "No idea," she replied. Then added: "I've

got a problem with leaving the back door open. Even just for a minute. That's where the...murderer came in. It's just...impossible."

"But you can't then leave the front door open instead—that's not logical!"

She turned the machine on. "Logical? *Everything* in my life has been *completely* illogical for a while now."

John moved closer to her. "Gillian! What's up? What does this mean...you suddenly packing up? Are you moving out?"

"Yes. I'm selling the house. A real estate agent is coming tomorrow."

"Isn't that a bit rushed?"

"Should I live in this house, and bring up my daughter here, where my husband was murdered?"

"Where do you want to move to? Do you want to rent an apartment somewhere here?"

"I'm not staying here. I'm moving back to Norwich."

He looked at her in horror. "Norwich? Why?"

"That's where I'm from. That's where my parents live. As a single mother who has to work, I'm going to have to let other people help me take care of my daughter. Better them than strangers. I need my family nearby in this situation—and they don't happen to live here."

"But this is your house. Becky goes to school here. She has her friends here. You have a company in London that supports Becky and you. That's all *here*!"

"I'll sell the company. It's doing well, so it won't be too difficult. Add to that the money from the sale of this house, and I'll have a tidy sum. That will give me time to find work. I'll find a way somehow."

"You've got it all planned out perfectly," said John in amazement. Steaming, the coffee poured into the two cups that Gillian had placed under the spouts. She added frothed milk and put them on the table. Cautiously, John took a first sip. He still burned his lips, but he barely noticed. He looked at Gillian, who was bending over and examining her cup, as if the cappuccino held some fascinating secret. He could have sworn she was still suffering from shock and that this was the reason for her ghostly pale skin, her somewhat mechanical way of speaking, and her unnatural calmness. She had not combed her hair, so she looked as though she had just gotten out of bed. Without her makeup, she looked younger than usual. And so fragile that he wanted to take her in his arms and hold her tight, but he figured that was the last thing she wanted right then.

"Life goes on," she said.

"Yes, but do you have to make such momentous decisions now? And must you do it at a time when you can hardly think clearly about everything? Gillian, it's just two weeks since you found your husband here. Two weeks! You can't have dealt with your feelings yet. You can't even have begun to. And yet you're changing your whole life!"

"It's my way of beginning to deal with it."

She was not the woman he had known. She was so rigid, brittle with him. He felt an increasing despair as he realized that he could not really get close to her. Whatever he said, he would not be able to touch Gillian inside.

Nevertheless, he tried. "I can understand that you don't want to live in this house anymore. You're quite right. It's full of terrible memories for you. But you can move to another house in Southend. Or find a pretty apartment for Becky and yourself, but don't uproot yourselves completely right now!"

She looked suddenly tired. "John, please. I don't want to discuss it. It's all decided."

He would have liked to grab her by the shoulders and give her a good shake. He was surprised that he suddenly felt himself confronted by such strong emotions, by his *own* strong emotions. He was not like that. He was not familiar with the situation. He had rarely experienced a woman withdrawing from him, unless the woman was completely disillusioned about him and the way their relationship was going. But in those cases he had, inside himself, already distanced himself from them and so had created the conditions for their frustrations. This time it was different. This time he would have begged her not to go.

"And what if you moved in with me, Gillian?" he exclaimed, before immediately correcting himself: "What if you and Becky moved in with me? And your cat?"

She looked up in surprise. At least he had managed to reach her—she was amazed.

"With you?"

"Why not? It's a new city, new surroundings—what you are looking for. And I'd help to look after Becky."

She almost laughed out loud. "John! You can't even bring yourself to furnish your apartment, that's how afraid you are of settling down. Do you really think you would cope with a woman, her child, and her cat moving in with you?"

He knew that her question was a fair one. And yet he also knew that his answer was the absolute truth. "Yes. I could cope with anything, if it's *you* moving in."

She shook her head. "John—"

"Please. Consider it."

"We barely know each other. We've gone to bed a few times. Nothing more than that."

There was a desperate look in his eyes. He knew that his suggestion that she could move in had come too quickly, had rushed her. Her husband had just been murdered. Gillian had not yet gotten to grips with that. And he was planning a life together! He was acting like an oaf, but he was suddenly afraid…terribly afraid that he could lose her forever.

"If that's how you see it, Gillian," he said, "then yes, it was nothing more than that. But now I love you, Gillian."

It was clear that this was all too much for her. "John, it's just not possible. Please understand. When I cheated on Tom with you, I was just acting like a little kid. A kid who is begging for attention, affection, and a feeling of security, who thinks she can't live without them. And then this terrible tragedy occurred. I can't just carry on as if it hadn't happened. Do you understand?"

"Yes. What happened to your husband is horrible. I can understand that you have terrible feelings of guilt. And that you need to analyze the motives that pushed you toward me. Maybe you're right about them, but…I still think we belong together. And I know I love you."

"I just can't—"

"It's the first time I've said that to a woman," he interrupted her. "It's the first time I've felt that for someone. Please, whatever you're thinking, don't throw my feelings back in my face."

They looked at each other.

After a while, Gillian said, "I don't want to hurt you. But I'm going to Norwich. To my family. To the rest of my family."

Shit. Damn it. Okay. He was not going to get down on his knees and beg.

Overwhelmed and stunned by the pain that was suddenly welling up inside him and that felt as if it would soon become unbearable, he still dared to ask: "Is there anything that would make you mine?"

She turned her eyes away. "No," she said.

Wednesday, January 13

1

THE BEAUTIFUL WEATHER was almost over. It had been snowing since early morning in big, heavy flakes that came down from the sky like an almost impenetrable curtain.

John had gone in to his office that morning. At least he had managed to deal with some deskwork that had been waiting for him. He had a headache, although he had already taken three aspirin tablets that morning for it. After visiting Gillian the previous afternoon, he had gone to the Halfway House and gotten completely smashed. He had hoped the alcohol would save him from the thoughts that would not stop going around and around in his head.

What the hell had gotten into him?

A woman had never hurt him. In particular, *breaking up* with a woman had never hurt him. Until now, he had always experienced the opposite. He had always gotten into relationships reluctantly. At some point, the women had demanded more than he had been willing to give— living together, marriage, children—and at that point he had said good-bye. Each time, he had had the unpleasant feeling that he was hurting someone who had not done anything to him, and yet he had also been relieved that he was escaping a situation that threatened to tie him down and corner him. He liked his freedom. He found occasional affairs a nice change; but beyond that, he did as he pleased. He had thought he was incapable of firming lasting ties, for whatever reason. He was not the kind of person who would reflect in depth about his childhood and youth, certainly not with a psychotherapist, to find out the reasons for his character. As he saw it, it did not matter at all whether his father or mother had done something wrong years ago, or whether for mysterious reasons things had taken a turn for the worse somewhere in his adolescence. You could not change things now. Things were the way they were.

For the first time, he suddenly saw the possibility that things were not just the way they were. That everything could be quite different.

John Burton was faced with a shattering realization: he had fallen in love with a woman. He was so deeply in love that the thought of losing this woman was almost too much to bear. He had pleaded with her to stay and been rejected out of hand. Shocked, he had to face the fact that his feelings were not reciprocated—or, rather, were *no longer* reciprocated. It looked as though he would not be able to win this woman's love. As if there would be another breakup in his life, and this time it would not be his choice. And this time he would suffer like a dog.

He had no experience in dealing with such a situation, and so his first reaction was to withdraw. He got plastered to take the edge off the thoughts that were torturing him.

Around half past nine, he had set off for home. By car, although completely unfit to drive. He knew it was a miracle that he was not stopped by a patrol car, especially as he drove in an aggressive and challengingly careless manner. He had put all the rage he felt for Gillian into his driving. As he later told himself, the fact that he actually arrived safe and sound at his front door was more to do with luck than anything else. He had stumbled up the stairs and collapsed onto his mattress without even getting undressed.

He would have slept through half the following day if his alarm had not gone off. Its excruciatingly loud beeping at half past six penetrated John's alcohol-soaked dreams and forced him to get up, in spite of his throbbing headache and parched mouth. His clothes and the bed itself stank of the pub, frying fat, and alcohol. Disgusted by himself, he had crept into the bathroom and taken a long shower. Three cups of coffee and the three aspirin later, he was somewhat ready for work. By the time he was sitting in his office, he was feeling quite a lot better. He had never drunk as much alcohol as he had the night before, and he swore he never would again. He might have lost his driver's license and been taken to court, and all because of Gillian. Because she had rejected him.

Never again. Never again would he let a woman make such a fool of him.

Around midday, he felt uneasy. He had enough work to sit all day at his desk, but he had planned to be outside the William Ellis School at three o'clock in the hope of seeing Finley Stanford's mother hanging around to secretly catch sight of her son on his way to the sports club. The question was whether he, John, wanted to continue with his plan. His motive had been Gillian, the fact that she was part of these mysterious goings-on and might even be at risk. Seeing the turn events had taken, should he keep on sticking his nose into what did not really concern him, for the sake of Gillian, of all people?

In the end, he decided to go anyway. It was not like

him, he thought, to withdraw from something just because he felt offended.

He called the tennis club and, pleading a terrible cold, cancelled his coaching for today and the rest of the week. Then he put on his coat, grabbed his car keys, and left the office. A flurry of snow almost blinded him.

At three o'clock on the dot, he parked in front of Finley's school. And waited. Watched. The heavy snow did not make his task any easier.

At some point, somewhere, Finley's mother had to appear.

2

"WELL," SAID LUKE PALM. "The house is in great condition. Well maintained and with a cozy aspect. I can't see any real problems arising."

They were standing in the dining room. Outside, it was getting dark. It was snowing. It had not stopped snowing since early in the morning.

Palm had looked at everything and taken some notes. Now he nodded. Satisfied. "No problem," he said again.

Gillian could feel how tense she was. Palm's positive remarks had not changed that at all. She had not yet said the most important thing, and she was not sure whether Palm knew already or not. He had not mentioned it.

"There's something else," she said hesitantly.

"Yes?"

"You asked why I'm selling, and potential buyers will ask too. I told you that my husband had died and that I'm moving near to where my parents live. The truth is—he didn't just die. He…." She stopped speaking.

Palm nodded. "I know. When you called, I couldn't figure it out at once, but then I realized when I thought about why your name sounded familiar. It was in the paper. I know, your husband—"

"He was murdered. I found him here in this room."

Palm looked around uneasily. "I see."

"It might scare some buyers."

"We don't have to tell them," said Palm. "If someone finds out on their own and then backs out, that can't be helped. But we certainly shouldn't bring it up."

Gillian nodded. "Thank you. That's why I wanted you to deal with the sale. I thought you'd understand best. Because you too have...been burned."

The two of them went silent, thinking about the absurd connections that can bring a person into your life. Palm thought it rather odd that he was becoming a real estate agent who seemed to be specializing in houses that had been the scenes of violent crimes. Gillian thought that if anyone had told her a few weeks ago what was going to happen, she would have thought them mad: that she would sell her house and move to East Anglia and that she would find a real estate agent to whom she did not need to explain the situation because he himself had found a murder victim and been through the emotional wringer that follows such a discovery.

She accompanied him to the door, they said goodbye, and she watched him walk away. Even before he had reached the street where his car was parked, he had been swallowed up in the driving snow.

Like a curtain, she thought, shuddering.

Her gaze fell on the bucket with birdseed. She had completely forgotten to put some out today. She didn't know whether the birds would come to feed, now that it was dark, but she wanted to at least give them the chance to find something. Sighing, she slipped into her boots, put on her coat, picked up the bucket, and, going out the front door and leaving it open as usual, stomped around the side of the house. It was completely dark now.

It was not easy to make progress. The snow was up to her knees. The boots were almost no help. Her trousers were wet through. She would have to change when she got back inside. And she could see next to nothing. Turning around at the bird feeder, she could barely recognize her own house. She could just about see a diffuse light from the kitchen.

She shoveled several handfuls of seed into the feeder and was glad she had made herself come out. All of yesterday's feed was gone. There was not a single grain left.

Holding the bucket in her numb fingers, she started back toward the house. The wild whirling of the snowflakes almost made her dizzy. She felt her way along the side of the house and breathed a sigh of relief when she reached the door. A welcoming beam shone out from the door, promising a bright, dry, warm home. It was as if she had just been on an Arctic trek, even though it was only her own yard. She closed the door, keeping out the snow, the cold, and the night that was falling.

In the hallway mirror, she could see the full glory of her strange getup: a woolly cap on her head, her hair soaking wet below the cap, snow on her arms and shoulders, drenched jeans. She peeled her coat off, bent down, and pulled off her boots. Everything was wet. When she straightened up again, her gaze alighting fleetingly on the mirror, she thought she saw some movement in the background.

In the kitchen.

For a few seconds, she stood absolutely still, paralyzed. It had looked like a shadow that had flitted by for a fraction of a second. She was not sure whether she had really seen anything, it had happened so fast. Maybe it was her own movement that had made her think she had seen something.

Her heart was suddenly pounding so fast that she was acutely aware of it.

How long had she been outside? It could not have been more than five minutes. The front door had been wide open all that time. If anyone had been hanging around outside, waiting for a suitable opportunity, they had certainly found it. Five minutes were quite enough to slip into a house with an invitingly open door and hide away. And to wait for the woman to come back inside.

She was suddenly sure that someone was there. She felt it. She was not alone.

Her first impulse was to phone the police; but, looking around quickly, she saw that the phone was not on its charging station in the hall. It was probably in the kitchen. If someone was hiding there, she would be crazy to try to reach the kitchen. Should she run to her neighbors' house? *Hi, excuse me, can I phone the police from your house? I've seen a shadow in my kitchen.*

She would look like a real fool if it turned out that no one had been there.

But someone is here! I can hear him breathing!

She could barely suppress a hysterical sob when she realized that she was hearing her own breathing.

I'm going mad. And for God's sake, I'm afraid of going into my own kitchen!

She stood stock-still, almost paralyzed, utterly undecided about what she should do. She had nothing to defend herself with, should she need to.

On no account should she move away from the front door, from her escape route. But was she going to stand here all night? What if the other person had nerves of steel and also waited her out—until she made a mistake?

Maybe I'm just going loopy, she thought.

And in that exact moment, the lights went out. Everywhere. In the whole house. From one moment to the next, it was pitch-black.

Gillian screamed, and now nothing held her back. She threw open the front door and dashed outside, out into the dark and the falling snow, although she was in her socks and not wearing a coat. She would have gone out barefoot. Anything to get away. Away from the deadly trap that her house had become within just a few minutes.

She had almost reached the end of her path when a shadow appeared in front of her. It seemed to materialize out of nothing, as if it had been waiting for her. It blocked her way. She banged into it and began to scream, began to hit it with her balled fists. Fear was deranging her. She could hear her own blood in her ears, could hear herself fighting for breath and screaming. Suddenly her wrist was gripped by an icy hand and pressed downward.

"What's happened, for Christ's sake?" It was a man's voice.

"Let me go!" she panted.

"It's me, Luke Palm! What's happened?" She stopped defending herself.

"Luke Palm?" She screamed his name in a high, shrill voice. He seemed to be someone from another time.

"I think I left my notebook in your house. That's why I came back. You're shaking all over!"

Her arms felt as wobbly as jelly. "Please let me go."

Cautiously, he released her wrist, waiting to see if she would start to hit him again. But she could not move at all. She needed the last bit of energy she had possessed to not collapse into the snow and just lie there.

"Someone is in my house," she whispered. She suddenly felt too weak to speak loudly.

"In your house? Who?"

"I don't know. Someone is there. And the lights suddenly went out."

"We just went into every single room a few minutes ago. There wasn't anyone there then."

"I went out to feed the birds. And left the door open. When I came back…there was a shadow in the kitchen…." She realized that she sounded over-excited. Gradually her heartbeat slowed down, as well as her breathing. She realized how bitterly cold it was, that her feet were two clumps of ice in the snow, and that she was shivering all over with cold.

Palm could obviously see that too. "You've got almost nothing on. Come on, you have to go back inside."

"But there's someone there," she insisted.

"I'll come with you," said Palm courageously.

She stumbled along beside him toward the door. The hall was completely dark. Palm felt for and found the switch, but the light did not come on. "It must be the fuse. Do you have a flashlight somewhere here?"

After she had stopped quaking with fear, her teeth started to chatter, she was so cold. "Yes-s…in th-the dr-drawers…under the m-mirror…t-top drawer."

Their eyes had become accustomed to the dark somewhat now, and some light from the street lamps was filtering inside through the falling snow. Luke opened the drawer, found the flashlight, and switched it on.

"Where did you see the shadow?"

"In the kitchen."

Palm seemed less eager to head down into the dark room now. "Your fuse box is in the cellar, is it?"

"Yes—but do you really want to go down to the cellar now?"

"It will all be easier if we have light."

They went down the cellar steps together. At the fuse box, they found that the circuit breaker had indeed tripped. Palm reset it. Bright light immediately flooded down into the cellar from the hallway above.

"How could that have happened?" asked Gillian, confused.

"No idea. Something overburdened the system. Come on, let's go up again."

Back up on the ground floor, they found all the lights on. They looked into the kitchen. It was empty.

"I don't think anyone is here," said Palm. He tried the door to the back yard and squeaked with surprise when it swung open. "The door isn't locked! Do you know if it was locked before?"

"I don't know," admitted Gillian. "I mean, I always lock it, but I couldn't swear that I did this time."

Palm looked out. There were many footprints on the terrace and they were already starting to fill in with fresh snow. However, that was no surprise. During the viewing, which was still just a few minutes ago, Gillian and he had been outside too.

He felt braver now. Gillian suddenly felt foolish. They looked in the dining room and the living room, looked around the upper rooms and the larder, but they did not find anyone.

"I think I've acted like an idiot," Gillian said when they were back in the living room. "I really thought I saw something move, but I obviously imagined it. I think my nerves are all shot."

"Hardly surprising, considering what's happened

here. What you experienced…it would drive anyone crazy. Don't be too hard on yourself."

They stood there looking at each other. Gillian looked at Luke Palm's split lip. "What's that?" she asked, feeling guilty.

Palm felt his lip with his index finger, jumped a little, and then grinned. "You're not a bad boxer."

"I'm really sorry."

"Don't worry about that; I'll survive. Listen, don't you think you should talk to the police? They could send someone over to have a good look around."

Gillian shook her head. "I'll just look ridiculous. It's bad enough that I looked like an idiot in front of you."

He looked seriously at her. "I think that's the wrong way to think about this. You're not a woman who just gets hysterical for no reason. There's a killer on the loose, the police haven't found him, and he's been here once before. Do the police even know you are living here on your own?"

"No, they don't know yet."

"I don't like it."

"Mr. Palm—"

He interrupted her. "You probably think it's none of my business, but now that I've turned up a bit like a knight in shining armor for you, and searched the house for that shadow, I feel responsible. I don't feel comfortable driving home and leaving you here on your own."

"I'll bolt all the doors."

"You obviously left the kitchen door unlocked. That worries me. You shouldn't be here on your own."

She knew he was right. Whether or not the shadow she had seen was a flesh-and-blood being, it was not good to be here alone. She could already see what her night would be like, and every night from now on. She would not be able to sleep. She would leave all the lights on. She would listen for every noise in the house, unable even to breathe. Every creak of a beam would make her sit bolt upright in bed.

She had just seen it: her nerves would not be able to cope with the situation.

"I'll work something out," she promised.

3

HE WAS COMPLETELY frozen when he arrived home, although he had had the heating on full blast in the car on his way home. He had trudged around in the snow and stood around in the icy cold outside far too long. It felt like nothing would ever be able to remove the cold from his bones. Maybe a long hot shower. He hoped so.

Liza Stanford had been nowhere to be seen. John had sat in his car watching the school and its neighboring sports hall, but in the end he had thought that his field of view was too narrow. He had gotten out of the car and hung around all afternoon on the school grounds, especially around the sports facilities, trying not to be too conspicuous. A grown man hovering near minors could all too easily be the object of suspicion. That meant that he had to constantly change his position. At least that meant he was moving around a little. Nevertheless, the cold and damp had crept through his boots and up his legs, spreading through his body and settling in his bones.

There finally came the moment when he was utterly fed up with it. He began to question his own plan. Who was to say that Liza had any interest in her son? And if she did, who was to say that she would try to satisfy her interest by watching him on the way to an extracurricular activity? Who was to say that she was still alive? Maybe he was waiting for a ghost, while he crept around a school like some pedophile and shivered in the cold.

After he had seen Finley Stanford leave the gym at a late hour and disappear toward the bus stop, without any trace of his mother anywhere, he decided to give up. Forever. This was not his problem. Let the police get to the bottom of it. He was calling it quits, as of this afternoon.

It felt almost as if he was free of a burden when he opened his front door and climbed the steps to his apartment, taking two steps at a time to warm up. Quitting the case also meant freeing himself from Gillian. He had to do that. He was not the kind of man to spend years dreaming of an unattainable woman, like Peter Fielder with his ridiculous yearning for Christy McMarrow.

Over. Done. Finito.

He came to an abrupt stop when he saw a shape crouching on the stairs by his apartment. Samson Segal looked at him, wide-eyed and fearful.

"Finally," Samson said.

He was the last person John had expected to see here. He was, really, the last person John *wanted* to have to deal with right now. Actually, he did not want to see anyone that evening. He just wanted a hot shower, a double whiskey, and complete peace and quiet.

"Samson!" he said in amazement. "How did you get in?"

Samson got up unsteadily. John noticed how scrawny he looked. He had lost a lot of weight in the short time, barely over a week, since their first meeting in the bed and breakfast. It was clear that he was having a terrible time of it.

"One of your neighbors in the house let me in. I was

sitting downstairs, freezing to death, and he felt sorry for me and let me in. I said I was one of your colleagues and needed to talk to you."

"I see." John realized he had no choice but to invite Segal into his apartment. "Come in. The stairwell is not exactly warm. You must be half frozen to death."

Samson nodded. "I'm...not well," he struggled to say.

John unlocked the door and led him into his living room, where he forced him to sit in the room's only armchair. It looked rather out of place on its own on the wooden floor. At least the room was nice and warm. "Would you like something to drink?"

"A hot cup of tea would be lovely," said Samson.

John went into the kitchen, put the kettle on, and rummaged around in his cupboards. He rarely drank tea and did not exactly have well-stocked cupboards, but in the end he found two peppermint teabags and put them in the teapot. He put two mugs and a sugar bowl on a tray. While he waited for the water to boil, he started to think. What had made Samson leave his safe hideaway on the building site and risk appearing here? He felt he knew the gist of the answer: Samson was in a bad way, mentally, and his feeling of being lost had no doubt gotten worse on his own until he had simply not been able to bear it any longer.

I should have visited him more often. But I can't blame myself.

He suddenly had a premonition that his desire to put an end to his involvement, to return to normal life, would not be as easy as all that. Samson was sticking to him; and now that he had hidden a man the police had been hunting for two weeks, he too was deeply implicated.

He cursed as he poured the boiling water into the teapot. How could he have been so stupid? To shelter a man who was being hunted in connection with three murders and whose actions had made him a prime suspect.

You never learn to avoid problems, do you, Burton?

He carried the tray back to the living room. Samson was sitting just as he had left him. John put the tray on the floor, for lack of a table, and sat down on the wooden floor with his back against the wall. The hot shower would have to wait.

"Why are you here, Samson?"

Samson looked unhappy and guilty. "I couldn't stand it any longer. Yesterday lunchtime I set off. I locked up the trailer. Here are the keys." He fished the keys out of his coat pocket and put them down the floor.

"Yesterday lunchtime? Where did you spend the night?"

"I was here yesterday evening. I found your address in a phone book. I took various buses here and there before I got here. Then I waited around in front of your house for ages. But…you didn't come."

Of course. Yesterday evening, he had let himself get bladdered in a pub to deal with the frustration of being rejected by the one he loved.

"In the end, I couldn't stand the cold any longer," Samson continued. "I went to the tube station, where I hung around all night, changing my seat so I didn't draw too much attention to myself. I was really scared the police would find me."

"That was damned risky, Samson. You were really lucky."

"I know, but what should I have done? Freeze to death outside your house?"

"You could have stayed in the trailer."

"I can't stay there anymore. Please, try to understand.

Sitting there, I was going mad. I don't even know what's going on. Am I still a suspect? Or have they got someone else now? Am I going to have to hide out for years, or just for a short while? Those thoughts can drive a man crazy, John, seriously!"

"I can believe that."

"So I came back here this morning," said Samson. "You still weren't here. But at least the old gentleman let me in."

"So you've been sitting outside my door for six or seven hours?" Samson nodded.

John thought for a minute. "Where do you want to go now?" Fear flashed across Samson's face. "Can't I stay here?"

"It would be a hell of a risk for me to take."

"I know. But there's no one else."

"I won't just chuck you out. Don't worry. We'll think of something." John sipped at his tea as he thought about it. The hot drink did him a world of good, although he hated the taste of peppermint. The problem was that however long he thought about it, he would probably not be able to think of any other solution than to put up Samson in his apartment and to hope the police would not decide to visit him. Samson could not go home to his brother and sister-in-law, and wild horses would not drag him back to the trailer, that much was clear.

I'm stuck with him until they've caught the culprit.

He asked himself if that would ever be the case. As he knew from Kate Linville, Fielder and his team were looking for Liza Stanford too—but would they manage to sniff her out? And how long would it take?

His resolve to withdraw from the whole affair started to wobble again. Perhaps he had an overly high opinion of himself, or maybe it was connected to his aversion to Fielder, but he had the feeling that he would get to the bottom of this murky, apparently hopeless case better than the police. The question was whether or not he felt like it.

But maybe it was no longer about what he felt like doing; maybe the fact that he had harbored Samson was forcing him to make the next move.

"I've wondered about going to the police," said Samson. "At least it would all be over then. It's terrible, being on the run. To have to hide. Without any end in sight. Sometimes I just want to give up."

"Please don't do that just yet. Remember, I'm involved too!"

"I wouldn't tell anyone that you'd helped me," Samson immediately assured him.

John shook his head. Samson did not have a clue how refined and stubborn the interrogations would be, if the investigating officer was at all skilled and experienced. In the blink of an eye, Samson would have tied himself up in contradictions and would end up telling everything as it had happened, in every last detail.

"I might be on to something…." John began.

Hope immediately lit up Samson's face. "Yes?"

John waved away his question. "Don't get your hopes up yet. I have no idea if it will lead anywhere. It's good to feel we're getting somewhere. The police too. They, too, no longer see you as the only possible culprit."

"But then—"

"In your case I wouldn't come out in the open yet. Like I said, the new lead could turn out to be completely irrelevant. What's more, you've made yourself culpable by evading police questioning."

"But that's not the same as being accused of three counts of murder," said Samson.

John could not deny that. "True."

It was obvious to him that he was going to be back on the case in the morning. Finley Stanford was going to have a piano lesson. Somewhere near Hampstead tube station. At least it would be easier and less conspicuous for him to watch the area around the station than the school grounds.

"All right. So you'll stay here tonight in any case," he said. "I must have another sleeping bag somewhere. You can have it. And then we'll see how things go."

More than ever before, his intuition was telling him that Liza Stanford was the key. That if he met her, light would be thrown on the whole situation and everything would change. For the unfortunate Samson Segal too.

John drained his tea mug. He felt better. He was not freezing like he had been. It was amazing what a difference that made.

"I don't know about you," he said, "but I'm terribly hungry. As we shouldn't go out in public, my local at the end of the street is out of the question. I'll order each of us a pizza for delivery. Agreed?"

"I'm famished," admitted Samson. "I haven't eaten since yesterday lunchtime."

"Then it's high time." John jumped up. "What kind of pizza do you like?"

For the first time since John had met him, Samson gave him a wide, friendly smile.

"Hawaiian," he said.

4

WHEN THE PIZZA was delivered, it was already after eleven. The delivery man brought cold and the smell of snow into the stairwell. Tara took the two hot cardboard boxes, paid him, and went back into the living room, where Gillian was sitting on the sofa in her pajamas, dressing gown, and thick woolen socks. Her hair was still wet. She had just been soaking in the bath for half an hour to relax and warm herself up. Tara had poured an essential oil into the water. It smelled of eucalyptus and was supposed to help prevent colds. After she had heard that her friend had been running around in the deep snow in her tights, she had insisted on the oil.

"Cold feet are dangerous. And you can do without a cold right now!"

She had been relieved that Gillian had called her. Gillian had worried for a long while over the decision, but in the end she could not think of anyone else whom she could ask to shelter her—apart from John, and that would only cause other problems. She had sat for hours in her kitchen with Luke Palm, scared, panicky, but at the same time wondering whether she was reacting hysterically to something that was all in her imagination. Around nine in the evening, Palm had said that he had to go home, but that he would only go if Gillian decided not to spend the night on her own. She had understood how afraid she was and that she would not be able to bear another minute in her house. So she called Tara. Palm took her with him to London and dropped her right in front of Tara's door. His relief was obvious, and that only made Gillian more afraid. If he had treated her like a jittery neurotic who had let herself get carried away with crazy ideas, she would have felt calmer. But Palm was taking seriously what had happened that evening.

Perhaps, she thought, that's normal in a man who has found a horribly murdered woman in an isolated house in the woods. Luke Palm's perspective on reality was no doubt different now to what it had been before all these horrors.

Tara had scolded her for not calling the police immediately. "That's what you should have done! They have to know whenever something like this happens!"

"Tara, I'm not even sure something *has* happened. I thought I saw a shadow in my kitchen. But I might have been mistaken. The real estate agent and I hunted all over the house. There wasn't anyone there."

"And your hunt probably obliterated any clues that a police expert could have found. That wasn't very clever, Gillian."

"I felt so ridiculous," Gillian said quietly.

Gillian had also swatted away the idea of informing the police at least now, retrospectively, as Tara suggested. "No. Then they'll just tick me off like you did, Tara. I'm dead tired, completely *kaput*. I don't want to talk to a police officer now and be told off. I can't take any more."

Tara gave in. She had poured a bath for her friend, ordered pizza, and gotten two bottles of beer out the fridge. Gillian was glad her friend was being so uncomplicated about her return. Not that there had been any really ugly scenes, but her affair with John had created an uneasy atmosphere between them that was still in the air. Sitting now in the living room and eating their pizzas, out of the blue Tara said: "Gillian, I've wanted to say something for a while. I'm sorry for my reaction about John. I overreacted. And I shouldn't have meddled in your affairs. I was just shocked. Sexual harassment…that term pulled me up short, and at the time I didn't understand why you…well, never mind. I drove you away, and the whole time since then I've wanted to call you and say how much I wished I hadn't!"

"Well, I'm here now," said Gillian. "You see, you can't get rid of me all that easily."

"Thank God. My home is your home."

"I was suddenly so afraid. I mean, on the one hand I feel foolish. On the other hand, the police warned me too. Whoever killed Tom might have been out to get me and might strike again. Do you think that's crazy?"

Tara lowered the slice of pizza she was about to bite into. "No. I wish I did think it were absurd. I'd feel a lot better if I did."

"But…."

Tara pushed her pizza box to the side and leaned forward. She was intensely serious now—frighteningly so, thought Gillian.

"Gillian, I'm a lawyer. I'm confronted regularly with this world that seems so absurd to you right now. This is the first time you've been affected by violence and such horrors. I've got the feeling that you're trying to deal with it by putting it all down to crazy flights of fancy. But as you know, that's impossible. Your husband was real. You found him shot dead in your house. Don't underestimate these things. I can understand that you think that's the only way you can bear it all. But you'd be careless to deny the danger. It wasn't okay that you went back to live in your house. I'm bitterly sorry that I was partly to blame for that. I won't let it happen again."

"I'm safe now."

Tara pulled a face. "I'm not sure. I don't know if you're safe here."

"Why not?"

"Gillian, we don't know who is after you. But there's still that Samson Segal guy, and he hasn't been caught. Or to be precise: the police don't seem to have the faintest idea where he could be hiding. He obviously spied on you for months. Do you really believe that he doesn't know me, your friend? And that, if he does, he couldn't figure out where you might be hiding?"

"We haven't got any idea whether he's involved in this or not," said Gillian, although she herself realized that she did not sound convincing. Because they were talking about risk. And the risk remained, especially because no one had *any idea*.

"Around the New Year, when you were here with Becky, I could take whatever time off I wanted," said Tara. "But I can't right now. You're here on your own all day long while I'm at the office. I don't feel comfortable with that."

"I'm not going to open the door to anyone."

"And how long will you be able to bear that? Sitting around here from morning to night without seeing a soul, and not able to go out either, because that could be dangerous?"

"That does sound wearying," Gillian admitted. She was suddenly no longer hungry. She pushed her pizza box to the side too. She felt that Tara wanted to be rid of her, and she thought she knew the reason: Tara was herself afraid. If a killer was out to get Gillian, the killer's gun might end up pointing at the person sheltering Gillian too.

She could understand her friend. But she suddenly felt very lonely.

"What would you suggest?" she asked.

"You're welcome to stay here," said Tara. "For as long as you like. But you're not safe here. You sent Becky to stay with your parents. I think that was a sensible thing to do. It would be good if you too—"

"No!" said Gillian. She saw Tara flinch and understood how harsh her *No* must have sounded.

"No," she repeated more calmly. "Not Norwich. Not to my parents. If your fears are justified and the culprit could think I'm here because you're my friend, then he will certainly know that I've got parents. He might even know that Becky is with them. I can't put her in danger, Tara. If I run away to my parents, I might draw him there too. That's too dicey."

"You're right," said Tara, resigned.

"I'll find something," Gillian reassured her, although she actually had no idea who she could turn to. Of course she had friends and acquaintances in town. But it was one thing to meet up now and then for coffee or a meal. It was quite another thing to be put up by a family for weeks because you were on the run from a killer.

No idea how to deal with such a situation, she thought dejectedly. Tara seemed to be thinking about it too. "A hotel?" she suggested, hesitantly. "Somewhere up north. Or south of London, in the country. Maybe a B&B."

"Hmm. What would I do there all day long?"

"Well, at least you'd be safe. That's the main thing."

Gillian pondered it. A hotel, a bed and breakfast… somewhere isolated. Maybe in Cornwall or Devon. She imagined herself walking on snowy cliffs, her face reddened from an icy wind. Tara was right. At least she would be safe.

"I don't know.… It would probably be the sensible thing to do.…"

Sensible. But not particularly appealing. Gillian asked herself if she had a choice.

In any case, it should only be a short-term solution. She did not want to go into hiding for months on end. But maybe she could start to prepare for her new life in Norwich. She could take a laptop with her and look at the job ads. Research the property market. That would make her feel that she was not just twiddling her thumbs.

"We mustn't say a word to anyone about it," she said.

"No one," said Tara.

Thursday, January 14

1

FOR AN HOUR he had been watching the Hampstead tube station with its dark red-brick façade. He had also kept his eye on Hampstead High Street and Heath Street, the roads that forked away from the station. In spite of the cold and snow, the roads were full of people heading into the shops, pubs, and cafés. It would not be easy to spot the woman he was looking for among the hurrying throng: a blond woman keeping watch for her son.

Of course he was prepared for the possibility that she would be in disguise. If she, for whatever reason, did not want to be recognized, then she would probably wear a wig. So he wasn't necessarily expecting a blonde. A woman with black or red hair standing here and looking around would have attracted his attention too. But he could not see any woman *standing around*. Not one of the people pouring out of the station or in the streets was waiting around. It was cold and damp. Everyone kept moving.

The important thing now was to see Finley when he appeared and to find out which building he went into. John would have a better chance of success once he no longer had to watch two busy streets but could concentrate on a single building and its surroundings.

Maybe he would be lucky.

He had not told his guest what he was up to. That

morning, he had said to Samson that he would spend the
whole day in his office. He asked him to please stay in
the apartment and not open the door to anybody. Samson had sat on the armchair in the empty living room
and watched John go.

He won't be able to stick it out for long here, John
had thought. John stepped from one foot to the other,
breathing warm air into his cold hands now and then too.
He had forgotten his gloves. No doubt he would end up
not finding Liza Stanford but contracting pneumonia.

Around half past four, when he was already sure he
would not get lucky with a lead that day, he suddenly
saw Finley Stanford coming down High Street. He must
have gotten off a bus farther down the road. He had a
rucksack on his back, which he assumed contained his
piano music. He was walking down the road at a lei-
surely pace, if not to say dawdling. Piano playing was
obviously not one of his passions.

John was immediately wide awake. His frustration,
tiredness, and awareness of the cold all evaporated in a
split second. Now the moment had come. If Liza Stanford was to see her son, then this was the best moment.
Within one or two minutes, he would have gone into his
piano teacher's building, and then there would only be
the moment when he left the building. By then it would
already be dark.

He looked around. Up and down the street, behind
him, upwards. Was there any suspicious-looking character anywhere?

The woman seemed to appear out of nowhere. That
alone made her stand out. John had looked a few seconds ago at just the place where she was now standing,
and she had not been there or anywhere nearby. Now
she was there. A hundred yards up the road from him.

She was wrapped up warmly, which was the case for most people today. It just seemed strange that not a single strand of her hair was visible. She was wearing a shapeless woolly cap pulled low over her forehead and ears. All her hair was hidden beneath it.

Strangest of all, however, given the stormy conditions, were her giant sunglasses. They were monstrously large, covering almost her whole face. Add to that the turned-up collar on her coat and the scarf wrapped across her chin.... Here was a woman who did not want to be recognized in any way.

She was staring at a building on the other side of the road. A building with a blue façade, the ground floor of which was occupied by an antique shop. There was a narrow drive right beside the shop door, and Finley Stanford was going into it at that very moment.

Her eyes were glued to him, sucking him in.

He was sure. He was completely sure. He had her. His plan had worked. A mother's longing. And the piano lesson, which had no doubt been something just between mother and son: Liza's wish and Finley's readiness to fulfil it. Thursday afternoons had belonged to the two of them. She had dropped him off, had done a bit of shopping, and then returned a little early to listen to him for the last ten minutes of his lesson. Maybe the two of them had then gone for a hot chocolate or eaten an ice cream together in the summer.

John could feel it. He could see it in the way the woman stood there, in the sorrow in the face that even behind her glasses, scarf, and cap was not completely hidden.

He stepped toward her.

Either he had been too hasty or abrupt, or Liza Stanford like all hunted animals had a sixth sense for danger. She jumped in fright, looked around, and then retreated.

She disappeared so quickly, it was as if she had never been there.

Now John was running. He had started too suddenly, not been cautious enough. The woman lived in fear of being recognized and discovered. She had a thousand invisible feelers out and had immediately known that someone had seen her.

He stopped when he could no longer see her. It was enough to drive you crazy. She had almost been close enough to touch. He suppressed a curse and the desire to kick the nearest wall. He was furious, mainly with himself. She had gotten away, and the worst thing was that she would not appear again near her son for weeks now. Even if she were dying to see him, she would not take that risk again anytime soon.

It was no use his letting anger and disappointment get the better of him. He had to keep calm and think about it. It was possible that she had come by car. If so, she had probably parked in a side street. That meant that she would have to drive down High Street, as a lot of the other streets nearby were one-way. If he saw which car she was in, he might be able to follow her.

It was his only chance. She could just as well hide away for a few hours in one of the many shops and cafés and then head for home from a distant bus stop, if she were not walking.

He ran back to his car. It was parked on a side street in a no-parking zone. He got in and pulled as far forward as he could, so that he could watch the main road. If Liza drove by, he would pull out immediately. He only hoped no car approached him from behind, wanting to turn onto the main road. If so, he would have to drive on instead of waiting there. Lots of pedestrians crossing the side street shot him evil looks as they made

their way around his car, taking them dangerously close
to the traffic on the main road. A man banged angrily
on the hood of John's car. John showed him the finger.

Tense, he peered into each car approaching from the
left. At least it was not snowing, an almost rare occur-
rence this winter. He leaned far forward over the steering wheel, his gaze deep inside each car. The evening
rush hour had started. The cars were bumper to bumper,
beeping and braking nervously. John knew that it was
only minutes until he would be driven from his spot,
and then he would have a real problem because it was
not even possible to stop on this side of the road.

At that moment, he saw her coming in a little blue
Ford Fiesta. The woman with the sunglasses and the
woolly cap low over her eyes. It looked like she was
concentrating completely on the road and the traffic.
Another car was right behind her. It would be rash to try
to slip in between them. John could only hope that he
would not cause an accident, but he had no other choice:
he had to risk everything. When the woman was on a
level with him, he nudged out far enough to block his
side of the road. Once the Fiesta had passed, he lurched
forward. The driver of the car behind the Fiesta slammed
on his brakes so hard that his car slid and shuddered.
The driver honked his horn like crazy, waved his arms
around, and no doubt rained down a whole series of
curses on John. But John was on the road and there had
not been a collision. He could see that Liza looked in her
rearview mirror, shocked by the honking and screaming tires behind her. He hoped that she did not recognize him as the man who had suddenly started to move
toward her on the street. Not that the recognition would
have helped her much. She could hardly have escaped

anywhere, hemmed in as she was by the slow-moving column of rush-hour traffic on this winter's evening.

He had her. As far as he could see, she would not be able to lose him now. Nevertheless, while they waited at a red light, he took down her license-plate number in his notebook so that even if something unexpected happened, he would have something to go on.

He felt an almost childish joy at his success.

And a hunter's instinct. He had not known that he still possessed it.

2

IT LOOKED AS THOUGH Liza Stanford had really not noticed that she was being followed. At least, she made no attempt to shake off John's car. No quick acceleration at a light turning red, no sudden change of direction without signaling first. She seemed calm. John suspected that she had been aware of him on the street in an instinctive rather than conscious way and that she was now annoyed that she had taken flight so quickly. She probably looked forward all week to seeing her son on Thursdays, and now she had interrupted it prematurely. Probably she normally waited until he came out again. Instead, she was on her way home and wondering if she had done the right thing.

They were moving toward South London, the complete opposite direction from Hampstead where Liza Stanford's actual home was. He wondered if her car was still registered at that address. He guessed it was. It would be the clever thing to do. If a policeman stopped her for anything, the police would just end up at her husband's door, who would only be able to say that his wife had disappeared without trace. It looked as though

Liza had constructed a new, utterly anonymous life for herself.

Why? Why would a married woman and mother of a child do that?

After a while, they reached Croydon, Southeast London. In the last twenty years, numerous tower apartment buildings had sprung up here, soulless buildings that offered great opportunities for someone to hide. Liza's car wound past the first buildings before stopping to back into a parking space that had suddenly become free in a long line of cars parked along the road. John did not have it as easy. He had to drive on much farther before he found somewhere to park. He rushed back as fast as he could. Luckily, he caught up with her as she stood in front of the glass door to one of the buildings, looking in her bag for her key.

He stepped up to her. "Liza Stanford?"

He gave her such a fright that her bag fell out of her hands and into the snow. She looked fearfully at John. He could see her trembling lips and just about see her wide eyes behind her giant glasses.

He bent down, lifted up the bag, and handed it to her.

"You are Liza Stanford, aren't you?" he asked, although by now he was sure it was her. She had clearly reacted to the name.

"Who are you?" she asked in return. Her voice sounded rather hoarse.

"John Burton."

"Did my husband get you to find me?"

He shook his head. "No. It's got nothing to do with your husband." She looked confused and frightened and completely unsure about what to do.

"I have to talk to you," said John. "It's important. I

have no intention of telling anyone about you and where you're staying. But I need some information."

He could sense that she did not trust him, but that she was afraid to just tell him to go to hell, because that might just make things worse. She looked as though she really wanted to run away but knew how senseless that would be.

"Please," said John. "I probably don't need much time. It's important."

She was obviously still trying to figure out how he had found her. "You were on the street, when I...." she said.

"Yes," said John. "When you were watching your son. I thought you would come, which is why I was waiting there."

She had gone as white as a sheet. "Have you talked to Finley?" she asked.

"Yes."

"How is he?"

"Good. But he misses you, of course. And something is troubling him—over and beyond the fact that his mother suddenly disappeared. But he's...well provided for."

"Well provided for," she repeated. "Yes, I knew that. That he would be well provided for."

John could see that she was in inner turmoil. She would have liked to pepper him with questions, to find out every little bit of information about her son. But that would mean talking to him. And she was still deeply suspicious, afraid.

He risked a direct approach: "Do you know Dr. Anne Westley? And Carla Roberts?"

For the second time in as many minutes, she jumped. Then she said, "Come on. Let's talk."

She found her key and opened the door. He followed her to the elevator, and up they went.

The apartment was furnished with simple, light wood furniture. It looked a little like a friendly, clean student apartment. Nothing special, but a place where you felt comfortable. Nevertheless, there were signs that the woman who lived here had only moved in recently. There was none of that clutter that accumulates over time in a home. Everything looked too new. The objects were barely used, with no signs of wear and tear. The apartment's only personal touch was about two dozen framed photos of Finley. They decorated the window sills and shelves. Finley as a baby, Finley as a young child, Finley as he looked today. On the beach, skiing, in a rowboat, at the zoo, with friends in the yard. Normal snaps from a normal childhood.

And yet this was not normal. Not at all.

John turned around when Liza stepped into the room. She was carrying a tray with two cups of coffee and a little jug of milk. She had taken off her disguise. No sunglasses, no woolly cap to hide her hair. John saw the beautiful woman that he recognized from the picture in Finley's wallet. Large eyes, full lips. Long, wavy blond hair. She was even more attractive than he had imagined. And sadder than he had guessed.

"Why?" he asked, pointing to one of the photos of her son. "Why are you doing this to yourself? This separation from your son?"

She put the tray down on the wooden dining table.

"You asked me about Anne Westley and Carla Roberts," she said. "About the murdered women. It's about them, isn't it?"

"Yes."

"But you're not a policeman?"

"No. I'm...a kind of private eye. A crime was committed that affected someone I know personally. The crime was related to the murders of Mrs. Westley and Mrs. Roberts. That's the only reason I'm getting involved."

"I see," said Liza, although she looked rather confused.

"Do you know the Ward family?" John asked. "Thomas and Gillian Ward?"

She thought about it. "No."

"Thomas Ward was murdered too."

"I didn't know that," she said. "I read about Carla and Dr. Westley in the paper."

"Anne Westley was your son's doctor."

"Yes."

"Did you like her? Or were there any problems?"

"I liked her. Fin did too. She had a nice way with children."

He looked closely at her. "What about your relationship with Carla Roberts?"

She sat down at the table, took one of the cups, and motioned with a nod for her guest to take a seat too.

"It was not a particularly close relationship. I can't even say that we were really friends. We met in that women's group that you probably know about already?"

He nodded and sat down too, taking a sip of coffee. "Yes."

"We were both outsiders. The other women chattered away, talking about their failed relationships, the future, their plans, hopes, fears...who knows what. I'm not like that. I can't come out of my shell as easily. Nor could Carla. We tended to sit there quietly."

"Isn't there a logical contradiction there? Don't people join such groups to share things?"

"Maybe. I went because I was looking for help, and then I realized I wouldn't find it there. It was just something I tried. I missed most of the meetings anyway. That got them quite annoyed with me. But I didn't care."

"The police are looking for you," said John out of the blue.

"They won't find me. Unless you rat on me."

"*I* found you. They could think of the same thing: sticking to your son."

"I won't see him for a very long time now. I've been warned."

"Liza," John said, suddenly insistent. "The police are working feverishly on three murder cases that, in all probability, were all carried out by one person. The biggest problem had been that there was no apparent connection between the three victims. That has left the police in the dark as to the killer's motives. You are the first ray of hope in weeks: two of the victims knew you. The police aren't going to rest until they find you."

She looked at him with a serious face. "I haven't killed anyone. Not Carla Roberts, Dr. Westley, or anyone else. I've no reason to do so."

"The police might think differently. You know two women who were killed in gruesome ways, and you disappeared from the face of the earth. Your husband says you suffer from depression and sometimes disappear for longer periods. No one believes that. People think something is not right about you; and that, in connection with the murder investigation, puts you in a suspicious light."

"Perhaps. But I haven't harmed a fly. I saw Dr. Westley four or five times when I took my son to her. I wasn't at all close to her. And Carla Roberts was a completely neurotic elderly woman who might get on your nerves, but that was all. I don't kill people because they get on my nerves, Mr. Burton."

"So why *would* you kill someone?"

"I wouldn't."

"Why did Carla Roberts get on your nerves?"

"Oh, she was always complaining so much about her past. Her husband had cheated on her for years and led her family into bankruptcy. She had not seen it coming and so was always saying that now she could not trust her own perception of things. That had become an obsession of hers."

"But she was no longer in contact with her husband?"

"No. He had made himself scarce long ago. As far as I know, he can't return to England because if he did, his creditors would get him."

"Carla Roberts never mentioned that she herself was threatened by her husband's creditors?"

"No. They wouldn't have gotten anything from her, anyway." John sighed. He had found Liza Stanford, *the missing link,* as he had thought. And now he was up against a brick wall once more. The path he had followed had turned out to be a dead end.

"And what about you? You held no grudge against the two women? Against Westley and Roberts? For any reason whatsoever?"

"No," said Liza, but for a moment there was a tiny, barely noticeable trace of uncertainty in her expression and in her voice.

There's something there. Damn it, there is!

"So it's all pure coincidence? That the two women were murdered and that you disappeared at the same time, leaving your husband and your child, moving to the other end of London? Looking at distances, the victims were certainly within striking distance for you."

Liza's eyes narrowed. "Do you always have such a lively imagination?"

"The police know that Carla Roberts was happy to open the door when her murderer rang the bell. A woman living on her own in the otherwise empty top floor of a building of apartments doesn't just open the door for anyone. But if someone she knows well is at the door, then of course that's different."

Liza got up. She started to say something but at the last moment decided against it. John knew what she had wanted to say. She had wanted to tell him to get lost. And then she had reconsidered. She could not afford to annoy him. She was in his hands.

He could see the anger in her face.

He stood up too. For a few seconds they looked at each other in silence. Then he said: "Why don't you just throw me out? Why are you so scared that I'll head straight to the police and reveal your hiding place? Why, for god's sake, if you haven't done anything, are you so scared of being found? What's happening, Liza? What's happened in your life?"

She did not reply.

He tried again. "You took part in a self-help group for single women. Women who had been suddenly bereaved or were divorced and were trying to come to terms with the new situation. You explained to them that although you were married, you were thinking of separating. Why, Liza? Why did you so urgently want to get away from your husband, so much so that you are now in hiding, living incognito in this tiny apartment in Croydon?"

She still did not say a thing. He thought she was never

going to answer him and that he would have to leave without hearing another word from her.

But just as he gave up and was about to grab his car keys and go, she started to talk.

"You really want to know? What's up with my life?" She closed her eyes for a moment. "I can't believe it. After all these years, someone *really wants to know!*"

3

THE MANSION LAY in complete darkness.

There was not even a lamp lit at the gate or along the drive. Only the snow gave some light that evening. The branches of the trees bent under the weight of the snow.

Christy looked at her watch. It was six o'clock. She had hoped to find either Dr. Stanford himself or his son at home, but no one had reacted to her ringing of the bell. The darkness behind the trees that sealed off the house from the road also told her that no one was in.

Christy wondered whether she should drive to Stanford's office. She was afraid that she might miss him on the road if she did.

But to wait here, in this horrible cold? Where was the boy?

She slowly, undecidedly, crossed the quiet, snowy road back to her car. When she was about to unlock it, she was suddenly approached.

"Did you want to visit the Stanfords?"

Christy turned around. A woman was standing at the gate of the house diagonally opposite the Stanfords' gate. Christy guessed that she was around seventy years old. She had thrown a coat over her shoulders, which she clasped closed with both her hands. Christy stepped across to her.

"Yes. I have to speak to one of them urgently—Mr. Stanford or his wife. But it doesn't look like they are in."

The woman spoke in a low whisper. "No one's seen Mrs. Stanford for weeks."

"Oh, no?" Christy acted surprised. Maybe she would glean some new information. She kept to herself, for now, the fact that she was a policewoman, so as not to scare the woman into silence. "For weeks, you say?"

"Since…let me think. Mid-November, I'd say. That's the last time I saw her. She picked her son up from school. She didn't often leave the house, you know, but she would give her son rides here and there. I saw from my living room window."

"Maybe Mrs. Stanford is lying ill in bed?" wondered Christy out loud.

"Oh, come on—ill? For two months? And without a doctor coming to visit? No, I don't think so. Nor do any of the neighbors."

"What do you think? And what do the neighbors think?" asked Christy.

The woman lowered her voice even further. "There's *something going on* over there!" she hissed.

"Really?"

"You won't say you heard it from me, will you? I'm afraid of him. Everyone here is afraid of him!"

"You're talking about Mr. Stanford?"

"You wouldn't guess it to look at him. He's well-mannered, polite. Quiet. You wouldn't complain at all about it, except…."

"Yes?"

"As a neighbor, you see certain things. No one here is nosy, but you can't always look away, can you?"

"Of course not," agreed Christy.

"Well, Liza Stanford sometimes was a real mess.

She nearly always wore giant sunglasses, even when it was rainy or dark, but I sometimes saw her without her glasses too, when she came quickly to the gate, to fetch her mail from her mailbox. Often her face was beaten up. Swollen eyes, a split lip, bruises. Her neck was often bruised too, or her nose bloody. She looked as if she'd just been in a boxing match. One that she had lost."

Christy caught her breath. "And you think—"

"I don't want to spread rumors about anyone," the woman said. "But if you put two and two together.... Who was beating this woman up? Only three people live in that creepy, dark mansion: Liza, her son, and her husband."

"I see," said Christy. "It does look as if.... But then why didn't she ever go to the police about it?"

She asked the question with an intentionally fake naïveté. She was an old hand at this. She knew from long experience as a policewoman that there were a thousand reasons why women in Liza Stanford's position did not go to the police. Or to anyone else for help. In fact, the truth was that very few women ever did seek help.

"Her husband is influential," the woman said. "Lots of money, a bigwig. On first-name terms with the most important politicians in the land. Knows everyone. Probably he's good buddies with the top brass in the police too. It wouldn't surprise me. Maybe Liza just didn't think that was a way out. And scared she'd just make things worse."

"When you last saw her, was she injured then?" asked Christy. The woman shook her head. "Not that I could see. Those sunglasses—they cover almost her entire face."

The giant Gucci sunglasses.... Christy remembered her conversation with the receptionist at Anne Westley's clinic. The dark glasses that Liza obviously kept on even in gloomy rooms made her seem distanced and arrogant, making people dislike her. But she could not have done otherwise. For most of her marriage to Stanford, she probably had to hide her face as well as she could.

"And you are saying that everyone here is afraid of Mr. Stanford?" Christy checked.

The woman nodded. "It's hardly surprising. Seriously, you should have seen the woman. A husband who does that to his wife isn't normal. He's dangerous. I mean, that wasn't just a few slaps. He must have attacked her with real hatred and brutality. Something's not right about the man. His eyes stare at you, too. He seems ice-cold to me. I couldn't stand him, even though he always greeted me very politely."

"But no one in the neighborhood ever tried to do something?"

"How? She would have denied everything if she'd been asked. She also tried to hide the signs of it. And to call the police…no one was brave enough. Nor did we ever witness the incidents themselves. The house is too far back, and it has that giant yard and the trees around it. We didn't hear or see anything. If we had heard screams, cries for help, we would have known the police could catch him red-handed. But without them…. In the end, the police wouldn't have been able to do anything, but he would have found out who had reported him, and then…."

"And then…?" asked Christy, when the woman stopped speaking.

The woman seemed worried about looking ridiculous or over-excitable. "You don't know him. I was just afraid."

"Nothing unusual about the son?"

"He's a quiet and very pale kid. Too quiet and too pale, if you ask me. Certainly not a particularly happy child."

"But there was no sign that he was abused in any way?"

"No. Never. Somehow I don't think Stanford has anything against children. He does against women."

"With other women as well as his own?"

"It's just a feeling...but yes. I can't explain why."

Christy thanked her for talking and said goodbye, taking note of the house number and the woman's name, which was written on a doorbell by the gate. Perhaps they would have to talk to her again.

"You didn't hear anything from me!" the woman called after her. Christy got into her car, turned it around, and headed back into town. She called Fielder from the car phone. As she expected, he was still in the office.

She outlined her unsuccessful attempt to see the Stanford family and her conversation with their neighbor.

For a while there was nothing but a stunned silence from Fielder's end of the line.

"Unbelievable," he said in the end and then added: "Do you think the neighbor's testimony can be trusted? Or could it be that she had an overactive imagination?"

"I didn't get that impression. She really seemed to be afraid of him. And somehow it all fits together. We knew that something was up with the family. The story about Liza's depression and her regular disappearances sounded suspect to us. Now we're starting to get a clearer picture."

"Yes," said Fielder. He sounded worried. "You mean...."

"I mean that Liza Stanford is either hiding from her

husband because she thinks her life is in danger—or that she's no longer alive. That he made her disappear."

"Do you know what you're saying?"

"Of course I do. This case stinks. I've got a terrible feeling. Stanford is feared by his whole neighborhood. He regularly beats up his wife. The neighbor's description is of a psychopath, basically, and she didn't seem like a crazy old woman."

"Still. It's all just conjecture, Christy. And the claim that he has abused his wife is only backed up by a conversation with a neighbor standing in the front yard. That's paltry evidence."

"What's so paltry about it? Liza has disappeared. Two women she knew were murdered by someone who was obviously a psychopath!"

"You mean to say that Stanford…*Charity Stanford*, the guy who regularly collects hundreds of thousands of pounds for the poor…that he is responsible?"

"I wouldn't exclude that possibility. There's something odd about him. He has issues about power, which is why he beats his wife up so brutally. Maybe he thought Carla Roberts was some danger to him. Maybe Liza had told Carla about her disastrous marriage and Carla had kept on at her, saying: *Go to the police! Take him to court! If you don't, I will!* Something like that. He heard about it and flew into a rage. Like he seems to have done with his wife often enough!"

"And Dr. Westley?"

"Dr. Westley, as we know, had tried to talk to a colleague about Liza Stanford. Because there was a problem, as she said. She might have detected some signs of physical abuse. She was a doctor, she'd notice such things. Or Liza hinted at something to her. Anne Westley might not have known exactly what to do, and so she wanted to talk to someone about it. Her husband's death then pushed it all out of her mind."

"But that was over three years ago. She was only murdered now."

"Because Stanford just heard about it now. Liza might have threatened him with it in a fight. *My friend knows! And our son's former doctor!* She was scared. She wanted him to know that there were people who knew what was going on and who would look into it, if anything serious happened to her. In that moment, she hadn't realized the danger she was putting the two women in."

"And how does Thomas Ward fit into this theory? Or Gillian Ward, if she was the intended victim?"

"I don't know," admitted Christy. "But I'm almost sure that there's a connection. We just don't know what it is yet."

"We must find Liza Stanford. There's nothing else for it," said Fielder after a few seconds of silence. "With all we know, we could do worse than to check on all the women's refuges in the area. She might well have fled to one."

"She might be dead. Or in extreme danger. Or someone helping her might be in danger!"

She could hear Fielder sigh. "I know what you're getting at, Christy. But the way things are now…there's just not enough to justify arresting Stanford. We have nothing but speculation and vague statements."

"What the neighbor said was anything but vague," Christy replied, braking just in time at a red light that she had almost gone through. She felt an enormous ball of anger gathering inside her. This was what had made her drive too fast and inattentively. Fielder was trying to worm his way out of something with potentially unpleasant consequences. She knew why. Stanford's influence. The contacts and friendships of a successful lawyer and good friend to politicians. He was member of the most influential members' clubs in London. And what did the neighbor say? *Probably he's good buddies with the top brass in the police too.* That was just what Fielder was afraid of, Christy bet. He could see his career and further promotion disappear over the horizon if he took a step now and the ice turned out to be thin.

Damn it! She felt like slamming her fist down on the steering wheel. She hated these guys who carve out a position for themselves where they are apparently above the law, who hide behind their wealth, success, and influential contacts to live out their disgusting perversions, certain that no one will ever be able to touch them.

You won't manage to do that with me, Stanford, you can bet on it!

"We'll redouble our efforts to find Mrs. Stanford," Fielder said stiffly. "Until I have her testimony, I'm not going to do anything to her husband."

"And what if he finds her before we do?"

"He's not even looking for her."

"He says. Do you believe what he says? He's rich enough to set five assassins onto her. She's dangerous for him. He has to find her!"

"Don't get carried away, Sergeant. We don't know if he is looking for his wife, or getting anyone else to. We don't know if he's responsible for the murders of Roberts and Westley, let alone for Thomas Ward's death. We don't even know for sure if he's physically abusive to his wife. We just don't know! I'm not going to risk my neck for something this vague, I'm sorry."

Christy did something that she had never let herself do to her boss. Without another word or so much as a good-bye, she hung up and switched the phone off so he could not call her back. Although she guessed he would be unlikely to do so. He would be relieved not to talk to her for now.

She slowed a little and made a U-turn with a screech of the tires. She had planned to go back to the office. Now she decided to drive home and soak in the bath.

And to open a nice bottle of red wine.

Friday, January 15

1

IT WAS ALMOST half past midnight when he said good-bye. She stood at the window and, looking down, could watch him by the light of the streetlamps as he walked along the road. She wished he had stayed, but she had not dared to ask him. She would have felt safer with him around. John Burton was someone who would not let himself be intimidated or scared. He was also capable of defending himself.

Nevertheless, she did not know whether she could trust him. All evening she had been unable to completely understand his role in the whole game—in this game that was anything but a *game*. He had said he was a *private eye*, but she had felt that she would not get anything else out of him on that subject. He said just as much as he wished to say. Not a word more.

Maybe he was going straight to the police to tell them where she was hiding. Maybe he even thought that was for her own good.

Although he did not seem naïve.

He had disappeared from sight, and she turned away from the window, drawing the curtains. The apartment no longer seemed like a hiding place, a refuge to her. From one moment to the next, that had gone. John Burton had found her, which meant that anyone could find her.

She had to find another place to stay as soon as possible.

She sat down at her dining table and poured herself some more coffee. She had brewed a number of pots of coffee that evening, while she told John Burton, a complete stranger, her painful story. The physical humiliations at the start. His compulsive control of her. The years before anything physical actually happened, but in which she felt increasingly suffocated. In which she had to justify her every step, every movement, almost every thought.

"I wasn't allowed to decide anything. Not about our furniture, our curtains, our car pets, or the pictures on the walls. Not about the crockery we ate from, nor the flowers we planted in the yard. Not about the books in the shelves. Nor the clothes I wore, nor my undergarments, my cosmetics, or my jewelry. His perfectionism is sick and everything, absolutely everything, had to fit his image of the perfect house, the perfect yard, the perfect wife, a perfect life."

He had asked the question he was bound to ask. "Why didn't you leave him?"

And she had answered quietly. "Above all else, men like him do one thing. And they do it without it even being noticed. They rob their victims of their self-confidence. They destroy their souls. Suddenly you no longer have the strength to leave. You no longer believe in yourself. You no longer believe that you can do anything in life. You stick to your torturer because after destroying you, he has managed to convince you that you can't live without him."

John had nodded. She was grateful that he did not reply with some silly phrase to the effect that a pretty woman like her would have found someone right away.

She had the impression that he understood what her husband had done to her as a person.

After a long pause, John said, "When did he start to hit you?" He seemed to know that it had led to that. He knew how these things developed.

She knew exactly. "After Fin was born. He couldn't cope with the fact that I was not all his anymore. My child. Having a child gives you strength. I felt stronger after Finley was born. I don't think I acted any differently, but maybe it was visible somehow…more inner peace, happiness. My love to my little creature. He could no longer affect me as deeply with his sadistic, controlling ways, his attacks, his insults. Fin gave me a kind of inner protection. That must have made my husband furious. He no longer had total control over me. That was unbearable for him."

She described how difficult it became to hide her injuries. How she would always wear the large sunglasses when she had yet another black eye. A split lip meant not leaving the house for days. Sometimes she stayed inside for weeks on end.

She could feel that John Burton was angry. Not at her. But at men like her husband. And at the psychologies and laws that meant women like her were exposed to such helpless situations.

She felt the need to describe the full complexity of the situation—to explain why she had remained, paralyzed, in such a nightmare. "I was scared. Especially of losing Fin. My husband is powerful and influential. I always thought it possible that I would come out worse, even if I went to the police with serious injuries and reported him. He would have squirmed out of it. You know, I've been treated for depression. He would have managed to get me declared insane. Would have gotten someone to give evidence that I'd harmed myself. I would have ended up in an institution. I'd never have seen my child again."

"That's not as easy as all that," said John. "You can prove whether or not someone has harmed themselves or been harmed by someone else. I don't think he could have had you committed." *You're crazy! I'll put you in the loony bin! You won't ever get out!* To prove her fear, she had, in the end, taken off her sweater in front of this stranger. Under it, she had been wearing a top with a plunging neckline. She had heard him snatch for breath as he saw the ugly scars on her neck, her arms, her shoulders.

"He started to go at me with knives," she whispered.

"God, Liza!" Burton stood up, walked over, and embraced her. They stood like that for a minute. She could feel his strength, his calm—as if she had found safety, a harbor, a place to rest.

Until she pulled herself together, telling herself: *Don't trust any man!*

She had pulled away and put her sweater on again. He had promised: "I'll help you, Liza. Believe me, I'll help you."

"You can't help me. You can't do anything against him."

"He's managed to make you think he's invincible. I can understand that. But he isn't. He's a normal man. And laws apply to him too."

"He'll kill me if he ever gets near me again."

"He won't. He'll go to jail."

She laughed cynically. "And you think he can't organize someone to get revenge on me from there?"

"Do you want him to get away scot-free? And to stay in hiding for the rest of your life?"

"I might not have a choice."

"Your son...."

Rage flashed from her eyes because she heard a certain accusatory tone in his voice. "Now, don't tell me I shouldn't have left him! Don't tell me that! You have absolutely no idea what situation I'm in! How could I have taken Fin with me? A child who goes to school and has to lead something like a normal life. Logan would have found me immediately. I can't just go completely underground with a twelve-year-old boy. It's just not possible. I know Fin has it good with him. Logan would never touch him. He never has. As crazy as this sounds, he's a loving father. More than that: he idolizes the boy. There was no other way. Fin has his familiar environment, his home, his school, his friends. That's better for him than if he has to live on the run with me. Believe me, being separated from him is driving me half crazy. The only reason I can bear it is because I'm sure it's best for him. And because I try to see him now and then. Like today. Now I know what a risk I was taking. My husband could just as well have been waiting for me there."

"Finley misses you."

She struggled to keep back the tears. "Yes. And do you think I don't know that? Do you think it doesn't tear me apart? I could die. But I know that he's doing better than he was before. And unlike what would have happened if my husband had had me committed, I feel free now to end the situation at any time. If I can't bear living without Fin any longer, then I'll go back. In spite of everything that's waiting for me there."

"Your husband never feared that Fin would tell anyone? A teacher? A classmate or the classmate's parents?"

"My husband doesn't know the meaning of fear. At least, he doesn't know what it feels like. He only knows how to cause it. He's paralyzed Fin as much as me. Both of us always knew that things would only get worse if we told anyone. My husband didn't even need to expressly forbid us to tell anyone. We simply would never have done so. We just wanted to bear it all somehow. And to survive."

She drank her coffee, staring at the opposite wall where Finley's large eyes were looking out at her from all the framed pictures. She asked herself whether Burton had really understood. Living with a dangerous psychopath changes everything, your whole outlook on the world, especially the feeling of security and stability that you might once have had. Sometime long years ago, in another life, she had believed in the protective guarantees of law and order, justice and the solidarity of other people. She had walked on solid ground and felt safe in the society she had grown up in.

Then she had learned that she had been mistaken. There was no security, nor protection, nor justice or solidarity. There was only the law of the jungle, of the strongest, nothing else. The world was full of horrors. Only on the surface was there a semblance of balance, provided by a thin web of false systems of security. Whoever slipped through the gaps fell into an abyss. More people fell through than she had ever imagined. She had only understood this when she found herself in freefall. When there was nothing and no one to break her fall.

Burton had asked again about Carla and Anne.

Carla Roberts and Anne Westley.

A bitter and resigned smile flitted over her lips, even now as the candlelight flickered on the walls and she felt afraid that she was going to lose this refuge, which in spite of everything she had grown used to over the past eight weeks.

Carla and Anne had been her two attempts to find help. Both attempts had failed. Both women had failed her.

"Your husband didn't mind that you went to that women's group?" Burton had wanted to know.

She had shaken her head. "He didn't know that it was for women who were divorced or separated. I told him it was New Age stuff, which he found idiotic but not disconcerting. The whole thing was a massive risk, of course. He could have looked into it at any time. He didn't, though. He had too much on his plate at work. He started to get sloppy at keeping tabs on me."

"You confided in Carla Roberts?"

"I didn't tell her everything. She was always just talking about herself and her tragedy and saw me as a patient listener. But one day she and I met outside the group, at her house. I was using my sunglasses again. After Carla had moaned and complained for half an hour, she suddenly paused, looked at me, and asked: *Why do you always wear those sunglasses?*

"It was a dark, rainy day. Normally I would ward off such questions with something about my oversensitive eyes, my allergies, or conjunctivitis. But suddenly...I don't know why...I just took off my glasses and said: *That's why!*

"I was a mess. My right eye was swollen shut and bruised. Not a pretty picture."

"What was Carla's reaction?" John asked.

"Horror-struck. Good old Carla, who thought the worst a husband could do to his wife was to have an affair with his secretary and bankrupt his company. Now she was given a sense of what else went on in the world. She was stunned."

"Did she ask questions? Or tell you to take your husband to court?"

"She asked questions. I didn't tell her the full extent of my martyrdom, but I said that my husband flew into rages and that he liked to sort out his problems with me with his fists.

"She was horrified, but…what can I say? Fifteen minutes or so later, she was already back to her old themes: her cheating husband, the daughter who didn't take enough care of her, the company going belly-up, her loneliness. That's how she was. She wasn't a bad person, but she could only see herself. She wasn't able to take a step back from herself for a second. She probably couldn't help it."

"Did she ever bring it up again? Or offer you any kind of help?"

"No. But then we barely saw each other again. The group fell apart and my personal situation became more serious. I was hardly capable of social contact. I was afraid to die. I had no wish to meet Carla and have to listen to her whining."

"And you had turned to Dr. Anne Westley at an earlier time?" She had explained the situation with Westley, and he had understood why she had sounded unsure when answering his question about whether she had borne grudges against Carla and Anne. No, she would not say she had borne grudges, but both women had left her in the lurch. She was very well aware of that.

Then he asked: "Did your husband have any idea that there were two people who could be dangerous for him outside the family? Because they knew what was going on between you two?"

She thought for a minute. "I never told him. But of course he could have found out."

"How?"

"No idea. But I don't think there's much he can't do, you know. He might have known."

"And the name Ward really doesn't mean anything to you? Thomas and Gillian Ward."

"No. I'm sorry. I've never heard of them."

Then he had left. Before leaving, he had once again promised that he would help. She wondered how.

"Is there anything else I should know?" he had asked her on his way out. When she had said no, he had dug deeper: "Are you sure? Sure you've told me everything that could be important in this affair?"

"Yes."

He had left his card. In case she thought of something. Or needed his help. He did not know that she had decided long ago not to take any risks. John Burton might be one of the good guys, but she had learned to see men as potential enemies, as culprits. She thought it would be safer not to make any exceptions.

She would go into hiding, further away. She would not go near Finley for months, even if it broke her heart.

She had not told Burton everything. But had he really expected that? She did not know him. He was a complete stranger.

And he had asked for *what could be important in this affair*.

She did not know whether what she was keeping to herself was important.

Probably not.

2

HE COULD PICTURE the situation. Liza had described it with a calm voice, almost lacking all emotion.

The motherly, competent, friendly doctor: Anne Westley. The woman who was so good with children. But who also knew how to reassure a child's parent.

And Liza Stanford. She had a nasty gash at her temple, the result of a punch she had been given the night before. The punch had knocked her onto the corner of a cupboard. Her husband had not liked their evening meal. Irish stew without carrots. She had not had carrots in the house nor had time to buy any. But he had asked specifically for Irish stew, which always has carrots. She had hoped that he would not notice.

Of course he had noticed.

It had not been her choice to leave the house the next day. The wound was still bleeding. It was not coagulating. But then Finley came back from school saying that he had had a nasty fall during P.E. He had broken his fall with his right hand and not felt any pain at first. However, over the course of the afternoon the hand started to swell and the pain increased. Liza hoped that it would sort itself out, but Finley was moaning more and more and she finally saw no alternative but to find a doctor. She put a large sticking plaster on her cut, combed her hair as far forward as it would go, in order to hide her mishap as best she could, and put on her sunglasses. She would have preferred to go to an emergency room where she was not known, but Finley, now in real pain, was asking for the doctor he knew and was close to tears.

And so they ended up in Dr. Westley's clinic late that afternoon. In spite of the full waiting room they were ushered in immediately, as it was obviously an emergency.

It turned out that the hand was badly sprained. Finley was given a splint. Then Dr. Westley sat behind her desk and wrote out a prescription for painkillers. Liza sat opposite her. Finley had gone to a corner and was playing with a few Sesame Street characters that always fascinated him when they visited.

Anne tore the prescription off her pad and was about to hand it over when she stopped. "What's that?" she asked.

Liza instinctively pushed her hair forward. As she did so, a warm liquid ran along her temple and down her cheek.

Oh, no, she thought in horror.

"You're bleeding," said Dr. Westley. "Wait, let me see."

She came around from behind her desk, although Liza protested, "It's nothing…really…don't worry."

The plaster was soaked through. Before she had left the house, the cut had largely stopped bleeding. But for some reason it had started again.

Dr. Westley bent over Liza, carefully taking off her sunglasses. Her left eye had not escaped completely either, although it was less garishly colored than it would be the next day. Nevertheless, the eyelid was red and no one could miss its slowly spreading greenish color. It was hardly going to be mistaken for badly applied eye shadow. Liza listened to Dr. Westley's quick intake of breath before taking off the plaster with a skillful hand.

"Dear God," she said. "That looks bad! Have you had it looked at?"

"No," said Liza. "It had stopped bleeding, so I thought it was going to heal on its own."

"The wound looks infected. I'm going to prescribe an antibiotic for you. And it has to be dressed better. A sticking plaster isn't enough. I've got a spray to stop the bleeding."

"All right," said Liza stiffly. She did not dare to look at the doctor. Dr. Westley leaned against her desk.

"How did it happen?" she asked calmly. As if she was making a point of being calm.

Liza knew that she was repeating the worst cliché, but she really could not think of anything else at that moment: "On the stairs in our house. I've done it a few times. The stairs are very steep and I'm so clumsy." She gave a fake laugh but her wound hurt so much that she grimaced. "I'm always doing stupid things. The bottom of the banister has a wooden ornament and I fell right onto it. I'm lucky I didn't lose an eye. So silly. I really have to learn how to be more careful, but even when I was at school, during P.E. I was always…"

She stopped talking.

I'm talking too much, she thought.

"Mrs. Stanford," said Dr. Westley, who was still standing up, leaning against her desk, "please look at me."

Hesitantly, Liza raised her eyes. She felt naked and exposed without her usual enormous dark glasses. She knew she must look terrible.

"Mrs. Stanford, I don't want to meddle in what is not my business. But I want to say that you…that people can find help in any situation. Sometimes people think their situation is completely hopeless. But it's not. There's always a way out."

Liza looked the gray-haired woman right in the eye. She could see the woman was affected and shocked.

She knows. She knows exactly what happened.

She said nothing, then looked away.

"I'll look after your wound," said Dr. Westley after a while. There was a certain resignation in her voice. "Is that all right?"

Liza nodded.

She let the doctor dress her cut, while Finley continued to play in the corner without even looking up. It did not escape her attention that Dr. Westley was also throwing concerned glances at her child. She was obviously annoyed that Finley had not reacted when his mother had the blood rinsed from her face and was bandaged. Liza wondered if Dr. Westley would reach the obvious conclusion: that Finley often saw his mother in an injured state and that he had learned to cut himself off inside, because he would not otherwise be able to bear it.

Dr. Westley had not said anything else. But when Liza finally left the practice, she thought: Perhaps she will get in touch again. Perhaps she will offer me her help. She knows what happened and she was pretty shocked.

She didn't know if the idea of an insistent doctor was something that scared her or gave her hope. Probably both. She was afraid that everything could get worse if someone meddled. And yet at the same time she felt certain that things could not go on the same forever, although she herself was not strong enough to take any decisive steps. Now and then over the following days, she imagined that someone else would take on her case and get *things* started, which could only really mean: report her husband. The thought filled her alternately with hope and panic. She went on a rollercoaster emotional ride until at some point she realized that nothing was going to happen. She never heard anything more of Dr. Westley.

"And that was the end of it as far, as I was concerned," she had said to John. "I wasn't going to get any help from Dr. Westley."

A thousand thoughts raced through John's mind as

he drove through the city at night, repeatedly needing to check that he was not breaking the speed limit. He felt agitated. There were too many disconcerting possibilities opening up.

One was the fact that he had suspected Stanford in the murders. But should he consider Liza a suspect too?

The woman had been through hell. The scoundrel she was married to had let loose a sadism on her so extreme that John was shaken to the core, and as an ex-policeman he had seen a lot and was not easily flappable. The man was sick, without a doubt. But was he a murderer?

How deeply had it embittered Liza that she was not given any help by the two women who knew about her problem? Had she expected a sisterly solidarity and not understood why it was not given? She had told him about it without any emotion. She had even denied holding a grudge against the women. Her voice was level and calm as she talked about it. John Burton could remember questionings where the person opposite him had sounded just like that—and later turned out to be a downright liar or even murderer.

One thing was sure: Carla Roberts and Anne Westley would both have opened the door to Liza and let her in.

Had Liza gone underground to start a campaign of vengeance? He smacked his hand down on the steering wheel. Damn, he was getting deeper and deeper into this case. First Samson. Now Liza. Both were sought by the police. Both were suspects. He knew where both were staying.

With all that he knew, he should have gone to the police long ago. He was making himself culpable. He was heading for a catastrophe with his eyes open.

He was dead tired and yet buzzing with adrenaline. He knew this odd mixture from his days as a policeman.

He had experienced it especially during tiresome sur-
veillance work. Utterly worn out and in pain from the
effort of keeping his stinging eyes open too long. And
yet at the same time sensing the danger that was imminent, keeping every fiber of his body awake and tense.
He thought it must be similar when you were on drugs.

He turned into the street where he lived and immediately looked up at the windows of his apartment. He
was relieved to see that they were in darkness. Samson
must have gone to sleep already, thank god. He had no
inclination to get into a nighttime chat with him.

He parked his car, stomped through the snow, unlocked the building's front door, and climbed the stairs,
swaying with exhaustion. When he entered the apartment he peeked into the living room. He could see the
vague outline of Samson's body. He was wrapped in
his sleeping bag on the camping mat, breathing evenly.
Luckily, he had not woken up.

John went to his bedroom, pulled off his clothes,
and let them just drop to the floor. Collapsing onto his
mattress, he suddenly remembered Gillian with painful
clarity. He had not changed the sheets since her visit,
and he convinced himself that he could still smell her.

He buried his head in his pillow. He had to tear this
woman out of his heart, whatever it cost. He did not
want to suffer and mourn her, give himself over to despairing thoughts.

He would change the sheets first thing in the morning. No sooner had he made this plan than he fell asleep.

3

"I'LL DO IT," said Gillian. She and Tara sat opposite each
other in the kitchen, eating breakfast. Outside the win-

dow, it was still pitch-black. "I'll find a room somewhere and go off the map for a while." She had lain awake all night, thinking. She felt safe in Tara's apartment, but she realized that she could be mistaken, and above all she understood that she could not be putting her friend at risk like that. It was thoughtless of her to move in with someone and to assume that nothing would happen. And it could be just as fatal for her to go back to her own home. She still did not know whether anyone had been there or not. Tara was right: it was foolish of her not to have called the police immediately. At least they would probably have been able to say whether or not she had imagined the intruder. At the moment, she was completely in the dark.

Can't be helped now, that was the conclusion she had come to, tossing and turning on the sofa. But at least I should act sensibly now, she had thought.

"Are you sure?" Tara replied. She still looked rather sleepy. It was half past six in the morning.

"Yes, I'm sure. Until we know whether or not someone is out to get me, and until we know the reason for what's happened, we shouldn't take any chances. Not with my life or yours. It's better if I disappear for a bit."

"I think you'll be able to come back soon. The police are working 24/7 on the case. They'll find the guy."

"I'm going to start to think about my future," Gillian said. "I'm taking my laptop with me. I'll look online for a job and an apartment in Norwich. Everything here will carry on just fine without me. I'll send the real estate agent a key, so he can start to show people around. If I have to go to Norwich, for a job interview for example, I'll just drive over. No problem."

"Sounds good," said Tara. "Listen, I have to go to the office now, but it's Friday. So I can leave work early.

How about if I drive you to Thorpe Bay this afternoon, so you can pack everything you need? From there, you can set off in your car."

Gillian protested. "I can't accept that, Tara. You've got too much on your plate right now. Let me take the train."

Tara shook her head. "It'll take you forever. I can drive. Really, it's no problem."

She finished her coffee and stood up. "You'll wait here for me?"

"All right. Thanks," said Gillian.

She hoped she had made the right decision.

4

JOHN WOKE UP because even in his sleep, he had sensed that someone was suddenly in his room. Startled, he sat up in bed hurriedly and found himself looking at Samson Segal's smiling face.

"Did I wake you?" Samson asked, concerned.

John stopped himself just before replying in annoyance that Samson seemed to *want* to wake him; why else would he be creeping around his room?

"It's okay. What's the time?" he asked.

"Almost eight o'clock."

"Oh, damn it," said John. "I should be in the office already." He looked at his alarm clock on the floor next to his mattress. In his tiredness last night, he must have forgotten to turn it on. That had never happened to him before.

"You were really late last night," said Samson. "I waited until half past nine, but then...."

"It was a long evening," said John. He stood up and

looked out the window. Day was breaking. The apartment smelled of fresh coffee.

"I've made breakfast," explained Samson. "I've been out already. I bought a loaf of bread."

"You're supposed to stay inside!"

"But then we'd have had nothing to eat. Yesterday evening too...." He stopped talking, embarrassed. John ran his hand through his tousled hair.

"I'm sorry. I should have thought of that. I'm coming for breakfast soon."

John disappeared into the bathroom, had a quick shower, and decided to skip his shave. He pulled on a pair of jeans and a sweater and went into the kitchen. As there was no table in the kitchen, Samson had put the plates, cups, bread board, and toaster on the work surface and brought up an old barstool. He poured the coffee and gestured to the stool. "Sit down. I eat standing up."

"Me too," said John. "So you can sit down."

Samson continued standing up, but he put his cup of coffee on the stool.

It would not be a bad idea to invest in a table sometime, thought John.

He was torn over the question of how much to tell Samson. Normally he never shared his thought processes with others until he had come to a conclusion that satisfied him. He had always been like that, even when he was in the police. But, on the other hand, Samson was not stupid and he had been watching the Ward family for months. Maybe he would remember some important detail if John shared what he knew.

"Does the name Stanford mean anything to you?" he asked. "Logan Stanford?"

Samson looked thoughtful. "Stanford...the lawyer?

The one who has so much money and is always organizing charity events? He's in the papers a lot. Just before Christmas, he put something on in Thorpe Bay… in the golf club, I think. A tombola game or something."

Interesting. At any rate, it was a connection. Stanford had been to Thorpe Bay. Near Gillian's house.

"But you don't know him personally?"

Samson laughed. "No. Someone like him would not even notice me! I don't mix in his circles."

John decided to pass on at least some of what he had found out. "His wife, Liza Stanford, was in contact with the two murdered women. Carla Roberts and Anne Westley."

"Really? How do you know that?"

"It doesn't matter how. I do. And it's important to know whether she or her husband was in contact with Gillian Ward."

"Ask her!"

"I asked Liza. She says that she's never heard the name Ward. You don't know anything about that, do you, by any chance?"

"No, I'm afraid not," said Samson, confused. "I'm guessing you're wondering if I ever saw Stanford visit the Wards? No, I didn't. I mean, I just know his face from pictures in the papers, but I think I'd have recognized him. But I don't know what his wife looks like."

"Very attractive. Tall, slim. Long blond hair. She always wears large sunglasses. She's a woman who stands out."

"No," said Samson. "I'm sorry. Gillian rarely has visitors. Actually, only her best friend visits her. And sometimes mothers who bring or pick up Becky's schoolmates. No one else."

"I see," said John. That matched what Kate had told

him. Gillian had told the police that she did not know
Liza Stanford. Fielder and his team were now sifting
through Thomas Ward's professional contacts and those
from his tennis club. John did not think the solution
would be as simple as finding Stanford in the same tennis club or among Ward's clients. That would have been
so quick that Kate would have already known about it
when they met. It would be much harder to find the connection—if there was one.

Charity Stanford was a brutal murderer. John did
not find it hard to imagine that, not now that he knew
how the elegant gentleman beat his wife when he was
unhappy about something. Yet too much was still un-
explained. Kate had said that Carla and Anne might
have been terrorized and intimidated in subtle ways for
weeks. Carla had talked openly about some strange happenings, while the interpretation of Anne's last picture
suggested something similar. It was almost unimaginable that Stanford had gone to an apartment building
on many different days and taken the elevator to the top
floor to scare an old woman living on her own. It did
not fit John's image of him, nor did he have the time to
do so. Nor would he drive around in the woods at night
to scare his son's doctor. If Stanford had murdered the
two women, then he had just one motive: they knew too
much and that's why he had to silence them. That could
have been done quickly, without all the drama that had
obviously accompanied the actual murders. And the
gruesome, painful method of suffocating the women
seemed very strange. The hate…. Would a man do that
if he were just wanting to remove a danger? On the other
hand, Stanford was a sick and evil sadist.

Liza…. She certainly had reason to hate Carla and
Anne and to enjoy an act of vengeance. Yet it was dif-

ficult to imagine this worn-down, fearful, desperate woman in that role. However, he knew he should not exclude the possibility. Especially because Liza was very pretty and because she, as he clearly felt, woke his protective instincts, he should be careful not to let himself be influenced.

"Was Mrs. Stanford involved in the crime?" asked Samson.

"I don't know." John played with the slice of toast on his plate. He too had not eaten since lunchtime yesterday, but the hunger he had felt when he had gotten up had already gone.

As he looked at the breakfast Samson had made, another thing occurred to him: What did Liza live off? She had to pay the rent on the apartment, to eat and drink. Gas for her car wasn't cheap. Apart from that, the apartment would need to be rented in a name that passed all the checks, and she would hardly have used her own. Landlords wanted to see people's papers. How had she solved that problem?

So much new information had come at him the previous evening that he had not thought of this obvious question. If he had understood Stanford's personality type, Stanford would have blocked her use of their accounts. So it was unlikely that Liza was using their credit or debit card, apart from the fact that it would have been dangerous and allowed her location to be traced.

And that led to his next question: *Who was supporting Liza Stanford?*

Damn it. He should have thought about that earlier. "You're deep in thought," Samson said.

He nodded distractedly. Was there a crazy but possible connection here? Could Gillian or her husband be behind this? Gillian would not have told the police, as it could have put Liza in danger. Was that what had made the Wards a target for the murderer—who in that case could only be Logan Stanford?

And why only now? Anne Westley had represented a danger for three years. Maybe Stanford had just heard about her, for whatever reason. And it was *only now* that the situation had gotten worse. Liza had gone into hiding. Stanford might have had the feeling that things were getting out of control.

He had chosen the solution he knew: violence.

"Do you think you're closer to solving the case?" Samson asked timidly.

John replied honestly. "I don't know. In one way, yes, but everything just seems to be getting more tangled. I can't really make heads nor tails of it yet."

"You're my only hope," Samson blurted out. His face was blotched red with excitement. "Please, stick at it. You're the only person who can get me out of this mess."

"The police won't cut corners either, Samson. They don't want to arrest the wrong person."

"But I don't trust them." He looked pleadingly at John. "Please help me. I can't stand it any longer. I've got no home. I'm desperate. I just want to live my life again. Only that. Just live my life again."

John bit back the comment that in his eyes, Samson's life was not the most appealing place to return to. Sure, he did not know much, but what he knew did not sound enticing: a man who lived with his brother and sister-in-law, was unemployed, and had the highly eccentric hobby of spying on other people and finding an obvious satisfaction in identifying with their lives. His own sister-in-law had snooped around on his computer and taken his notes to the police, delivering him to the lions. The Segal family did not seem a harmonious place.

And yet: it was Samson's life. And even if he was unhappy in it, it was the life he knew. The life he had learned to deal with. Which he somehow coped with. It was familiar to him.

Compared to the existence of a man on the run from the police, who had no idea when that circumstance would end, it seemed like paradise.

"I'll do what I can, Samson," he promised. "You can be sure that—"

At that moment, the phone rang.

John excused himself and left the kitchen. The cordless phone was on a pile of books in the living room. The number on the display seemed familiar to him, but he could not think whose it was.

"Hi, it's Kate here," said a woman's voice on the other end.

"Oh…hi, Kate." That was why he knew the number. He was surprised that Kate Linville was calling. That evening at Charing Cross, he had thought he would never hear from her again.

"How are you?" she asked stiffly.

"I'm fine, thanks. And you?" *What does she want?* he wondered.

"Fine too. John, I had actually decided not to go out of my way for you again. The whole thing is just too risky. It could end badly for me."

"I promised that I'll never let anyone, under any circumstances, know that you gave me information. You can rely on that. I know that I've got a bad reputation, but I've never broken a promise."

"I didn't want to insinuate that you would. But there's still that risk."

"Of course. With everything we do in life."

Kate hesitated, then carried on. "I don't know why I

think I should warn you, but…,well, I'm not completely indifferent to you."

"'Warn' me?"

"Maybe it's no big deal. But Fielder asked to see the file that was opened on you. I know because I had to ask the Crown Prosecution Service for the file."

"The file from the investigation?"

"How many files do you have? I mean the one about rape," said Kate smugly.

"I see. So he's not excluded me completely yet." It was not as if this information came as a complete surprise to John. Fielder could not stand him, and he was at sea with the present case. As John knew, Stanford was on Fielder's radar. However, John also knew that this fact was playing on Fielder's mind. If he just went for Stanford now and in the end it turned out that he had made a mistake, he would find his career starting to stall. If he still had a career to work on. Fielder did not like risks. He was scared shitless. He would have done anything to be able to quickly come up with another culprit before he had to go after Stanford.

"All right," he said. "Thanks for telling me, Kate. Fielder is flailing about—let him. The whole affair wasn't taken before a court. He won't be able to construct anything on it."

"Right," said Kate. "I just wanted to let you know. By the way, I could see on the cover of the file that you're obviously the man everyone wants to see. Fielder was the second person in just a few days to ask for your file."

The names of the people who had asked to see the file were always noted, with the date of the delivery, on the file's cover.

"Really? Who else?"

"There was a request from…wait, what was the name…."

He could hear a rustling. Kate was leafing through her notes. He wondered. Stanford, no doubt, he should have known. Of course he had taken down his number plate, knew who he was, had gotten his own investigation started, and now he had unearthed this old story. As a lawyer with top-notch contacts, he would have found a way to see the file.

He must have acted quickly.

"Let me guess: Logan Stanford."

"No," said Kate. "It was a woman. Who works for the Crown Prosecution Service. Wait, here it is…Tara Caine. Public prosecutor."

"No way!" he exclaimed.

The pieces of the puzzle were fitting together. Gillian's sudden rejection of him. Her wish to go back to Norwich. Her complete withdrawal from him. She had fought with Tara after she told her the details about his past. She had even moved out of Tara's apartment. But Tara had obviously not given up. She had mounted a campaign against him. Had obtained his file, gone through it with a fine-tooth comb to find moments that cast him in a bad light, and then no doubt enjoyed describing them to her friend.

And in the end, she had won. Gillian had lost her nerve. She had given up on the relationship that was just beginning and gotten as far away as possible. John could imagine only too well what Tara had said: *You've got a child! You've got a daughter just going into puberty. Do you want to be with a guy who's been investigated for rape? You realize you're putting your daughter in danger? Never mind that the investigation was shelved, where there's smoke, there's fire. They just didn't have enough proof to take him to court. That doesn't mean he's innocent!*

He could not suppress a groan. She was a viper. A damned viper.

"John?" asked Kate. "Are you still there?" He pulled himself together.

"Yes. Still here. Thank you, Kate. I really appreciate your telling me all this. So, Tara had already returned the file?"

"Yes. Before Christmas, in fact."

"Okay." Something about this information niggled at him, but he could not immediately see why.

"Caine," said Kate. "Hasn't that name cropped up somewhere before?"

"Yes. She's friends with Gillian Ward, the wife of the third murder victim. Which will be why she's gotten involved and would like to see me as one of the suspects."

Then he remembered something else. "Kate, could you do me a favor? I've got a car's license number here. It would just take a call—I need to know what name the car is registered under."

After a short pause, Kate said, "I can do that."

He took the piece of paper on which he had noted the number of Liza's car from his pocket and dictated the number to Kate.

"All right," said Kate. She waited for a moment. John had the impression that she was waiting for *him*, for something that would give her hope. The offer of a meeting that weekend or just some warmth in his voice that she could hold on to.

"All right, speak soon," he said.

"Speak soon," she replied and slammed down the receiver.

He could only hope she would still help him with the number plate.

5

THE CELL PHONE RANG. Gillian recognized John's number on the display and hesitated. Then she decided to take his call. John had not done anything to her.

"Hi, John," she said.

"Hi, Gillian." He sounded relieved. He had probably been afraid she would see his number and not pick up. "How are you?"

"Fine."

"Really?"

"Yes." Then she corrected herself, "Well, *fine* is maybe stretching it after everything that's happened. But I'm getting there. Life goes on."

"Are you still sorting things out in your house?"

"Not right now." She thought for a minute and then decided not to come clean with him. "I'm not at home. I'm at Tara's house again."

Silence from John's end.

"Well, then my chances are pretty slim," said John in the end.

"John…."

"She's utterly set against me. And by now, all her reservations about me have no doubt convinced you too."

"We didn't even talk about you again. I moved back to her house because I didn't feel safe in the big house on my own." She did not mention the events of the evening two nights before. After all, she still did not know whether it was all in her imagination or not. "I just have to see how I can best cope. You probably think I'm haring around in a crazy zigzag. Maybe I am. But I haven't found a straight path yet. Nothing in my life is like it once was."

"Can we meet?" It sounded almost like begging.

"No. It's—"

"Please, Gillian. Just to see each other. To have coffee together. To talk about unimportant things. I promise that I won't pressure you toward a life together. I just want to *see* you."

"It won't work, John. I'm leaving London. In a few hours."

"You're already going to Norwich?"

"No, not yet." She stepped over to the balcony door, looked out over the snow-covered railing into the anthracite-gray London sky. She asked herself, not for the first time in her life, how people managed to survive January. "I'm going to disappear for a bit. Find some hotel in the country. Hope that everything gets cleared up soon and that I can try to construct a halfway normal life."

He won't know where I'm going, she reassured herself. I myself don't yet know.

He sounded confused. "A hotel? Why? In the country? Where? Which hotel?"

"That's not important. I'm just going to stay for a while, sort my life out, and then try to find my feet."

"Why don't you stay at Tara's place?"

"It's just better like this."

"Gillian," he implored. "Something's not right! What are you hiding from? Or whom? Why did you move back out of your house although you were busy enough planning your move? And why leave Tara's house? To go to some anonymous hotel. Why, Gillian? It feels to me like you're running from something!"

"I've got to find out where things go from here, John. That's all."

"But you won't find it out by constantly changing where you stay. Is Detective Inspector Fielder behind this? Does he want to make sure you are safe at an unspecified location?"

"The police know nothing about this."

He was silent for a while. Then he asked quietly: "Are you hiding from me?"

"Why should I hide from you?"

"Because she—Tara—has stirred you up against me. No idea what she's told you. But I heard today that she asked to see the file that was opened on me back then. And she won't have done that just out of idle curiosity."

Gillian was surprised. "The file of your investigation? She didn't tell me that."

"You were probably not to know that she was spying on me. But she definitely had my file in her hands. And I'm sure she would have studied it carefully."

Gillian turned away from the window.

She's my friend. She would do something like that.

She said it out loud. "She's my friend, John. She was probably very worried and wanted to see for herself what happened back then. Because of her work, she can easily access such files. Isn't it normal for her to do that? I'd probably have done the same in her place. But believe me: she never told me. So probably she didn't find anything she hadn't already known."

"Nor could she have. They had nothing, absolutely nothing, to cobble together a case from. Because nothing had happened."

"I have no doubts about you there, John."

"So, where do you have doubts about me?"

"Nowhere. I told you what my problem is: I have to stand on my own two feet. I have to find my own stability."

Both of them were silent.

"Well," said John in the end. "Take care."

The resignation in his voice was easy to hear.

"Will do," said Gillian. She snapped her phone shut without any further goodbyes.

She looked uneasily at the clock. It was just nine. So many hours until the early afternoon when Tara would return. She had packed all her things.

She had nothing to do but wait.

6

JOHN HAD FINALLY gone in to the office, although he had feared he would not be able to concentrate or think straight. But work was piling up. He had lost enough time over the last few days, and the alternative would have been to sit at home with gloomy Samson in his apartment, not knowing what to do next.

For a few hours he managed to plunge into his familiar daily routine. That soothed his fraught nerves. He had to produce work schedules for the coming weeks, answer questions, write invoices, deal with one employee who was giving his notice. He barely noticed the time pass. When he got up to make coffee, he realized it was already half past three. Apart from him, there was only the person on phone duty in the office. Friday afternoon. Everyone left as early as possible for the weekend.

He had not eaten a thing since nibbling at the toast that morning. He noticed how hungry he was. Perhaps he should get a burger instead of just coffee. He pondered for a minute, then decided to drive home. He had made headway today. And Samson was no doubt sinking deep into depression. It'd be better not to leave him alone for too long. John was not unafraid that Samson, that strange man, might do something stupid.

No sooner had John left his office than the bad feeling returned that he had been able to escape for a few hours. Liza and Samson were two big issues. And he was worried about Gillian, because he had the impression that something was not right. He had sensed her fear. That, plus the fact that she was obviously running away, disturbed him. The feeling grew that he was just treading water and did not know what to do next. He had found Liza and spoken with her, but it had not led to the breakthrough he had hoped for. In fact, he had not made any progress at all.

There's something I'm missing, he thought. From his time in the force, he knew that things can sometimes be staring you in the face and you do not see them because you are incapable of peeling their silhouette from the surroundings and so of seeing their importance.

Maybe that was the case here. Maybe the solution was right in front of him and he was unable to see it.

He saw a McDonald's and went through the drive-in, buying cheeseburgers and fries for Samson and himself. When he got home and ran up the stairs, he realized that the bag of food already felt cold.

Samson was sitting in the armchair in the living room, reading a book. John could see immediately that he was not doing well. He had an unhealthy color to his cheeks and red eyes. He looked pained. He was on the verge of a mental breakdown.

Something has to happen soon, thought John.

"Here," he said, handing him the bag. "I missed lunch and you can't have found anything in my rather empty fridge. You'll feel better after eating something."

"Thanks," said Samson quietly. It did not sound as if he believed John.

Just when they were starting to eat, the phone rang. John answered immediately. It was Kate.

"Sorry, John. I didn't manage to do what you asked until now. It's been a hell of a day."

"No problem. Have you been able to find out who owns the car?"

"Yes. And it's really strange."

"Strange? Why?"

"Because it's someone we've already talked about. The car is registered to the lawyer Tara Caine. Coincidence?"

"That's…unbelievable," said John slowly.

"Is there anything I should know?" Kate asked. "I've been very open with you!"

"I know. I just can't say anything right now. I can't work it out yet. I have to order my thoughts." *Tara Caine!*

He would have expected anything but….

"So, when you've ordered your thoughts, remember me," said Kate rather sharply before hanging up. John could guess that the next thing she would do would be to find Tara Caine's personnel file and trawl through her life, at least her professional life. She would not find much. She could not make the connection to Liza Stanford without further information.

Samson had stopped eating. "What's up?"

John pushed the burger he had started back in its carton, no longer hungry. Tara Caine. Liza Stanford was driving a car that was registered to the lawyer. And John would have put money on it that the car's rental contract was also in Tara's name. Was Tara pulling the strings here? Supplying Liza with an apartment and a car, supporting her with money, and enabling her to go into hiding?

He thought furiously. What conclusions should he draw?

"What do you know about Tara Caine?" he asked. "Gillian Ward's best friend."

Samson thought. "The one who often visited her in Thorpe Bay? Not a lot, I'm afraid. I was just an outside observer. The two seemed to be really good friends. Gillian was happy when she came. They hugged. But as to what they talked about—no idea!"

"Gillian is staying at Tara's apartment right now."

"That doesn't surprise me. It's natural that she can't deal with living in the house her husband was murdered in, isn't it?"

"Of course. The question is—is the missing link perhaps not Liza but Tara?"

Samson looked utterly mystified. "You're talking about Liza Stanford? The lawyer's wife? The one you mentioned to me this morning?"

"Yes. I can't go into details now, Samson, but somehow I'm a bit worried." John grabbed the phone and dialed Gillian's cell phone. Gillian did not answer, but her voicemail came on. After a short pause, he left her a message.

"Gillian, it's John here. I'd like to talk to you. It's very important. Please call me back quickly. Thanks!"

"Is Gillian in danger?" Samson asked wide-eyed. He pushed his food away. He had obviously lost his appetite too.

"I don't know. Honestly. No idea. It's all very strange."

"But Tara isn't a danger to her, is she? Her best friend?"

"I hope not," said John. He grabbed his coat, which he had thrown onto the windowsill. "I have to go. I have to talk to someone."

"Can't you do that by phone?"

"I don't have a number for this person. And it's better...." He didn't finish the sentence. Explanations would have taken too long and would no doubt have left Samson more confused than enlightened. Because what John had said was true: he still could not figure out the connections. But he had a bad feeling. A very bad feeling, in fact.

He was going to drive out to see Liza Stanford now. She was the only person who could give him answers to a few urgent questions.

7

IT WAS FOUR O'CLOCK by the time Tara got back home. She had bought plastic-wrapped sandwiches and a few bottles of mineral water.

"I don't know how far you're driving today," she said. "But at least you won't starve on the way!"

"You're fantastic, Tara," said Gillian gratefully. She was relieved to finally see her friend. Sitting alone, doing nothing, in an apartment that wasn't hers for hour after hour, had increasingly unnerved her. She had read every magazine she could find, had leafed through a number of books, and in the end cleaned the bathroom, which was actually in urgent need of cleaning. Then she couldn't think of anything else to do and so had just looked out the window at the snow floating down, which had stopped at some point.

"Nothing you wouldn't do for me," said Tara, looking down at her clothes. She was wearing a light gray trouser suit and stiletto heels. It was a mystery how she had managed to clamber over the piles of snow along the roads. "I'm just going to change."

Ten minutes later, the two women were sitting in

Tara's car. Tara was wearing jeans, a warm coat, and waterproof boots. Gillian had put her travel bag and the bag of food on the back seat.

Hopefully I'm doing the right thing, she thought.

They made slow progress. The Friday afternoon traffic had plunged the city into the usual chaos. They only started to speed up when they reached the freeway.

"We'll be at Thorpe Bay soon," said Tara. "And by the time you get going, the worst will be past. Do you know yet where you're going?"

"This running away. Right after that...thing that happened at home, I just wanted to get away. To your place. And until this morning, I was sure it would be better to leave London. But now I don't know. Maybe I've been too hasty. Maybe I'm just going a little crazy. About... nothing!"

"Thomas, lying murdered in your house, is not *nothing*," Tara reminded her. "And what happened recently—"

"I don't know *whether* anything happened," Gillian interrupted her. "That's the thing. I just don't know! It seems more and more likely to me that nothing happened. A shadow! If I try to recall it, I can't even see the *shadow* anymore. It was a fraction of a second—probably just in my imagination."

"But perhaps not. Perhaps something would have happened to you. You might just be really lucky that Luke Palm went back to your house," Tara replied.

Suddenly the glass under Gillian's cheek seemed colder.

...that Luke Palm went back to your house...

I didn't tell her the real estate agent's name, thought Gillian. That was her first, almost intuitive, thought.

Then her reason kicked in: Or did I mention it? Sometime in the last two days? During our chats?

She could not rule it out completely, but she was almost sure that she had not. She had not wanted to admit to Tara that she had turned to the real estate agent who had found Anne Westley dead. As his name had been mentioned in the media on many occasions, Tara might have recognized it had she said it. She had been embarrassed to explain how she was on an ice floe, adrift from other people who had never experienced violence and crime, and that Luke Palm had a similar shadow over his life. She wanted to keep it to herself, although she would not have been able to explain exactly why. Perhaps it had something to do with the devastating wound she had been dealt, deep inside her, the evening she found Tom and wandered through her house looking for her child in a panic. She did not want to show anyone, not even her best friend, how much it had disturbed her.

Never mind, it's not important, she thought. But she could not stop the thought niggling away at her: *If I didn't tell her the real estate agent's name, how does she know it?*

She remembered that evening. In her mind's eye, she saw herself come rushing out of the house after she had thought she had seen a shadow in the kitchen and then the lights had gone off. She had run outside, through the snow, in the dark, in her tights, and at her gate had banged into a large shape, which she had started to hit with her fist, full of fear and blind horror. The person she was hitting had grabbed her hand and held it tight.

"It's me. Luke Palm!"

And she had screamed. "Luke Palm?" A high-pitched, loud scream full of fear.

If someone had been in the house or yard, the person could have heard it.

This is absurd, she thought.

She looked at Tara in profile. Her straight nose, her full lips, her high forehead. She was such a beautiful woman. Rather strange that she had never had a man in her life.

How on earth does she know the name?

She thought about all the conversations she had had with Tara since Palm had taken her to Tara's house that night. She was pretty much sure that she had only ever spoken to Tara about *the real estate agent*. She had only mentioned him briefly.

The real estate agent, who is going to sell the house for me, had just gone. Luckily he came back, because he'd forgotten something. He reset the circuit breaker in the cellar and looked around the house with me. But we didn't see anyone.

"Are you all right?" asked Tara now. She had looked over at Gillian. "You've gone pale. Aren't you feeling well?"

"No, I'm fine." Gillian tried to smile. It was obviously not a convincing attempt, because Tara said, "Really? You seem upset."

"I'm just not sure I'm doing the right thing," said Gillian. "It just seems so crazy to sneak away to a place I don't even know. That's a pretty dramatic step to take."

"Staying here could turn out to be a far more dramatic step," said Tara. "If the murderer tries anything again."

They had reached Thorpe Bay. Quiet roads. Quiet houses. Yards deep in snow. Children were sledding on a hill in a little park. Until recently, all of this had been normal life for Gillian.

Now nothing was normal any longer. Now she was about to run away.

And she felt a prickle at the back of her neck. An underlying nervousness, a suspicion that, as strange as it seemed to her, she could not silence.

There was a voice inside her which told her quietly but insistently: *Just get away! Something's wrong! Make sure you get out of Tara's car. Make sure you get far from her!*

Maybe I mentioned the name sometime, Gillian thought in despair, and I just can't remember!

Maybe she was in such a mess now that she saw ghosts wherever she looked.

Tara turned into Gillian's drive. The car's wheels crunched through deep snow.

"Here we are," she said.

She looked at Gillian. And Gillian saw it. She saw it in her eyes. A strange look. Unnaturally large pupils.

Tara's eyes were glassy.

Suddenly Gillian was afraid. And she knew one thing: Tara could not be allowed to see it. To notice Gillian's suspicion, fear, and confusion.

"Okay," she said as casually as possible. "Then I'll just go in quickly, pack a few things, and go. You should get going, Tara. It's quite a drive."

"I'm not in a hurry," said Tara. She opened her door and got out. "I'll come with you."

Gillian got out too. She was holding the front door key in her hand. Her hand was trembling, and she hoped that Tara could not see it.

Tara went around the car, moving as if everything was normal.

And what if I'm just going mad? thought Gillian.

Probably I'm on the verge of a nervous breakdown and just seeing things.

At that moment, her phone rang. It was in her handbag, which was still in the foot well of the passenger seat.

Gillian immediately turned around, but Tara held her back. "Leave it. You can call back later. Don't waste time now." She had that glassy look again.

Gillian felt perspiration on her forehead. "All right," she said. She thought her voice sounded funny, but Tara did not seem to notice.

They trudged slowly over to the house. Gillian opened up and stamped her shoes free of snow. She heard Tara do the same behind her.

She felt her heart beating loudly and fast. She was sweating profusely now. She did not know if it was just chance that Tara was sticking close behind her like a second skin. Unimaginable that she would be able to go anywhere on her own, or even make a call. And what was she to say to the person on the other end of the line? *I'm in my house with my friend. I've got a bad feeling. Something's not right with her. Of course I might just be imagining it, but fear is eating me up and I think I need someone's help.*

There was only one person she could call. One person who would not think she was crazy and would rush over: John. She only had to say: *Please come!* And he would come.

But there was no way of calling secretly. Tara was as close behind her as a shadow.

The toilet, Gillian thought. She can't follow me there.

There was a toilet for visitors on the ground floor. With an outside window. She could try to climb out and run down the road. She could ring a neighbor's doorbell and ask to phone.

Tara could hardly stop her.

"What's up?" asked Tara. "Didn't you want to go upstairs and pack your things?"

She turned to Tara. Hoped that she did not look as bad as she felt. "I just need to go to the loo," she said apologetically. "Would you wait a minute?" Tara stared at her.

At that moment, the phone rang. The two women jumped. Then Gillian reached out her arm.

Tara stopped her. "Let it ring. It'll just hold us up!"

After the sixth ring, the answering machine, which was also in the hall, came on.

8

SAMSON WAS NOWHERE near an understanding of the direction things had taken, and John had left the apartment so quickly that he had been unable to ask him a single further question. Confused and uneasy, he was left in the bare rooms.

He went over the last few minutes of their conversation once more.

Is Gillian in danger? he had asked, and John's answer had hardly set his mind at rest: *I don't know.*

And then he had asked if Tara, her best friend, was a danger to her, and this time John had answered: *I hope not.* Which was not any better.

Tara.

John's faint suggestions did not make any sense to Samson. He had been on the phone and then there had been the name Tara Caine and John was instantly buzzing. He spoke about some missing link that everyone had been looking for. Somehow it was all connected to

Charity Stanford's wife, but Samson could not make heads nor tails of that.

He tried to recall the images he had of Tara Caine.

He had watched her a number of times when she visited Gillian. It had been immediately clear that the two women were close friends. Their greeting was not exaggerated but had a real closeness that made fussing unnecessary. He had liked Tara. He kept a jealous eye over the image he had carefully constructed of Gillian's perfect, invulnerable family. The way Gillian's friend fitted into that image was important to him. Tara Caine had put him at ease. She was friendly and, what was even more essential, she suited Gillian. She seemed like a very normal woman. She was intelligent, elegant but never overdone about it, never garish or vulgar. Sometimes she had obviously come straight from work and was wearing a chic trouser suit. Sometimes she just wore jeans, a sweatshirt, and sneakers.

Fit right in, he thought. Fine. The perfect friend for the perfect woman in the perfect family.

Apparently he had made a bigger mistake than he had already realized. Thomas Ward had not been a nice man, and the Wards' marriage had teetered on the edge. Gillian had gotten involved in an extramarital affair. Her daughter had massive problems. And now something was not right about her best friend too—Samson just did not know what.

Tara isn't a danger to her, is she? I hope not.

He paced back and forth between the window and the chair in the middle of the room. The whole room smelled of cold fries. Samson looked at his half-eaten burger in disgust. It was still lying on its carton. He could not believe that just a little while ago, he had been so hungry that his mouth had watered. Now the thought of food tied his stomach up in knots.

John had said that Gillian was at Tara's house. That made sense. It must have been a nightmare for her to return to the house where her husband had been murdered. And secretly Samson had been relieved—although also ashamed at his relief, as John had been the only person to help him, to risk a lot for him—that Gillian had not taken refuge with John but instead with her best friend.

That told Samson that John and Gillian's relationship was not all that close.

John had tried to call Gillian, but she had not answered her cell. If she was in danger, she might still be completely unaware of it.

Samson had often read that someone *was tearing their hair out* and until now he had just thought that was a way of saying that someone was going mad with anger, confusion, or helplessness. Now he realized that you could actually do it. He was grabbing his hair, running the ten splayed fingers of his hands through his hair as if he could make his mind come up with one good, sensible, useful thought. Something to free him from this never-ending wait. Sitting either in unheated guesthouses or in a trailer at an abandoned building site or in an empty old apartment, waiting for something and not even knowing what that something was.

He wanted to finally do something. To finally play a part, make something happen. Be useful. Not for himself so much as for everyone else caught up in this confused situation.

For Gillian, more than anyone.

His hair was shooting out in every direction now, but he had come up with an idea. John's unsuccessful attempt to call Gillian had obviously been in the hope of warning her. Why shouldn't he try to do the same?

He could ask Directory Assistance for Tara Caine's phone number and then call her. However, that idea worried him. It was late on Friday afternoon. Probably Tara had left the office long ago and was home already. She would probably pick up the phone. She would see John Burton's number on her display. And what should he, Samson, say then?

Hi, it's Samson Segal here. The man being hunted for the murders. As you can see, I'm sitting in the apartment of John Burton, the ex-cop. Can I talk to Gillian, please?

He might possibly be able to make his call anonymous from John's phone, although he had no idea how to do that. He might even pluck up the courage to introduce himself with another name, and Tara *might* even pass him on to Gillian.

And then?

Would she calmly listen to his warning while the person she was being warned about was standing right beside her?

Still, he thought, I'll give it a go. He was feeling hot all over.

He need not have worried so much. When he called Directory Assistance, he found out that Tara Caine had an unlisted number.

Not surprising, given her job, thought Samson. Otherwise, how many ex-cons would terrorize her once they got out!

He could not just sit back down again and twiddle his thumbs. Not after he had gotten so far ahead, at least in his thoughts.

Just once he wanted to do something decisive. Be the hero just once.

He took what was left of his now-unappetizing meal to the kitchen and threw it in the wastebasket. Strangely, as he did so, he had a brainwave.

Gillian was living with Tara, but she must visit her house now and then. To water the flowers, to pick up the mail, to fetch something she needed. He knew her phone number by heart. And she had an answering machine. He had often called the Wards when he knew no one was there just to hear her voice. *We can't get to the phone right now, but please leave us a message.*

He had always hung up at that point, without saying a word. But this time he was going to speak. And even though there was no guarantee that his action would be a success, because he could not know when Gillian would actually hear her messages, there was at least a chance that it would succeed. Not just a slight chance either, he thought. And it was a lot better than doing nothing.

He went back into the living room, dialed the familiar number with trembling fingers, and cleared his throat several times.

As long as his voice did not fail him now!

9

GILLIAN AND TARA stared at the answering machine as if transfixed.

Gillian's recorded voice rang out loud and clear in the hall. "Please leave us a message."

The machine beeped.

First there was the noise of a throat being cleared noisily. A man, thought Gillian. Perhaps John. Perhaps Luke Palm, with questions about the sale of the house. Luke Palm, whose name Tara should not have known.

"Yes, hello, Mrs. Ward," a voice was saying now.

Definitely a man. Gillian thought the voice was familiar, but she could not place it immediately.

"It's me. Samson. Samson Segal."

Gillian put her hand to her mouth. Samson Segal.
That strange man who was hiding from the police. He
was calling, even daring to leave a message on her answering machine.

"Mrs. Ward, we're worried about you." Samson
sounded less awkward now. "It might sound strange
to you, and I can't explain it properly either, but...you
should be careful around your friend. Tara Caine. Something's not right. Get away from her. Please." He paused.
"I hope that you hear this message sometime soon. It's
important. Please."

With a click, the message ended.

Gillian could not move. She had the impression that
she was not even breathing.

She did not know how Samson Segal had come to call
her. She had no idea who he was talking about when he
said *we*. She was completely in the dark as to how he
had come to see Tara as a threat. But she understood
one thing: he was right. He was not just talking rubbish.
And she was not just seeing things.

"You've got loyal friends," said Tara behind her. Her
voice sounded different. Strangely lacking in emotion. It
was too level. "Nice, worried friends. How nice for you."

Gillian ran her tongue over her lips. They felt suddenly dry. She turned around to Tara and tried to smile,
hoping that she managed to do more than grimace.
"Segal is not my friend. He's disturbed. You know the
police are looking for him. I expect he wants to divert
attention from himself. He thinks his situation will improve if he spreads wild rumors."

"Interesting rumors," said Tara.

Gillian shrugged. "The man's off his rocker. I don't pay him any attention. Listen, I should hurry. I'll just go to the loo, and then—"

"What for?" asked Tara. There was something threatening in her voice and posture. "So you can escape through the window?"

Gillian tried to look calm, but she felt that she sounded odd. "Of course not; why would you think that? I just want to—"

"Forget it," Tara interrupted her. "Don't try to make a fool out of me! You're trying to get away, that's all. You're shaking with fear, Gillian. And not only since that idiot"—here she nodded at the answering machine—"was stupid enough to broadcast his warning throughout the house!"

"That's not true. I'm—"

"It happened in the car. But I wasn't a hundred percent sure then. It was just a feeling I had. If you'd been a bit cleverer, you might have gotten away with it now. But…after this clear warning…do you really think I'm going to let you out of my sight for a moment now?"

Gillian's vision flickered and she heard a roar in her ears, but she pulled herself together. She could not fall apart now. She had to keep her nerve.

"Why, Tara?" she asked. "What's happened? Have I ever done anything to you?"

Tara looked at her with interest. Gillian looked back at her uneasily. She saw her friend's familiar face. A face she had known for years. And yet it had changed completely. Tara's expression was one she did not know. And the voice was not Tara's voice. Tara's feelings could be heard in her voice: laughter, worries, joy, or irritation. None of those could be heard now. It was a strangely soulless, inhuman voice.

"You've not done anything to me personally," said Tara. "Carla and Anne didn't do anything to me personally either."

There was a hatred in her voice that made Gillian jump.

"Carla and Anne...." she repeated, dumbfounded. "You—?"

Tara shrugged. "The world's not a poorer place without them."

"And Tom?"

"Tom wasn't planned."

"Tara, I don't understand what's happening," said Gillian pleadingly. "Please explain what's going on."

Tara laughed. It was not a friendly laugh. "No, darling. I know what you're planning. You want to get me involved in a long and protracted conversation and hope that someone comes by and helps you out of the mess you're in. Forget it! We have to think what to do next. Do you know what's so tragic? I'd decided to let you get away. No idea why. Perhaps because of the time we've spent together. Maybe because I failed twice already with you."

She was the shadow, thought Gillian with horror. *And that's how she knew Luke's name. She's tried to kill me twice!*

But why? Why?

"I wanted you far away from me. I can't bear you any longer, Gillian. As you were afraid to live here, the idea of you in a hotel would have suited me perfectly. Then you'd have gone to Norwich, and hopefully we'd never have met again in our lives. But now I can't let you go. You see why."

"Please, Tara! Why?"

Tara reached into the pocket of her winter coat. In the

next instant, she had a pistol in her hand. She pointed it at Gillian.

"First, we have to go somewhere where we are safe. The guy who just called your landline might call the police next. So it's high time we left. And then I have to think about what I'll do with you." She pointed to the front door with her gun. "Let's go to the garage. You go first. If you make any unexpected movement or try to get away, I'll shoot you in the head. Got it? I won't hesitate an instant."

Gillian gulped. She felt like she was in a strange, completely unreal play. Surely Tara was about to laugh—not in that strange way, but in the friendly, easygoing way she used to—and, letting her arm drop, would say: *Gillian, don't look so horrified! Just a joke!*

I just wanted to give you a real fright. For God's sake, you didn't take me seriously, I hope?!

But she knew that would not happen. None of this was a joke. Tara had never had a predilection for macabre jokes. She actually was a rather serious person.

She meant what she said.

Gillian moved slowly toward the front door. Tara stepped to the side, to let her past. She grabbed a roll of masking tape that lay on a pile of cardboard boxes by the door.

Once they were standing outside, Gillian asked, pleadingly: "Tara, I don't know what you have against me. But whatever it is—please think of Becky. She only has me."

Tara laughed once again. It was the same creepy laughter, lacking any emotion.

"You won't believe this, Gillian," she said, "but I'm thinking of her. I've been thinking of her the whole time. Becky is the reason I've done this. You know why? It's better for some children to grow up without a mother and father. For some children, any orphanage is better. Believe me, I know what I'm talking about."

"But...."

"Just shut up and keep on walking," Tara ordered her. She pressed the pistol deep into the folds of Gillian's winter coat. If anyone had walked past, the person would not have seen it. Not that there was anyone else about. In the encroaching twilight, the street looked dead. "We'll still have time to talk. Later." Tara nodded toward the garage.

Gillian walked slowly along the path.

10

"I KNEW YOU'D come back," said Liza Stanford wearily. She had not immediately opened the door when John rang the bell. He had then spent some time pacing up and down the paved square in front of the building, hoping she would look out her window and see that it was only him coming to visit, not her husband or the police or whoever else she feared. Then he had rung the bell again, and finally she had buzzed him in. Upstairs, she had waited inside the door to her apartment, which was open just a crack.

"Would you like a cup of tea?" she asked after he had come in.

"No, thank you. Liza—do you know a Tara Caine?" He observed her closely as he asked the question.

She jumped. Her pupils widened. "Tara Caine. Yes, I know her."

"I asked you to tell me everything yesterday," John said.

"You didn't ask about her," Liza replied in a quiet

voice. She went into the living room and collapsed onto a chair at the dining table. John followed her and stood in the middle of the room.

"Your car is registered in her name. And I expect she rented this apartment?"

Liza nodded.

"She's giving you money too? Because your husband must have blocked his accounts, I'm guessing from what I know of him."

"She set up an account in my name and gave me the debit card. I take out money when I need it."

"Generous of her. She pays your rent, pays your living costs. That's not something that happens every day, is it?"

"I'll pay her everything back. We've got an agreement."

"Aha. And when will that be? And how?"

"I don't know yet. Everything had to be done so quickly.... We couldn't plan things through to the end."

"What needed to be done so quickly?"

"I had to get away. I had to go into hiding!" She had been looking at the tabletop all this time. Now she looked up at him. John saw tears in her eyes, and anger. "You can't imagine what it's like. No one can if they haven't experienced it. I've lived in fear of my life for years. I've lived with despair, humiliation, physical pain, and mental torture for years. I knew that he'd kill me one day. I just knew it."

"He wouldn't have done that," said John. "Your husband is, putting it bluntly, a piece of shit, Liza, but he's not stupid. He wouldn't have risked getting thrown in prison."

"It wouldn't have led to prison, believe me. He would have made the whole thing look like an accident. He'd have found a loophole, wriggled his way out of it somehow. That's what he's like. I know him well enough."

There it was again: the omnipotence that Liza always ascribed to her husband. To her, he was beyond all laws, untouchable whatever he did. Perhaps, thought John, the worst thing men like Logan Stanford did to their wives was to grind them into the dust and raise themselves up to the height of the heavens; worse than the physical violence was the mental violence that they inflicted on their wives. Liza was an intelligent person. Nevertheless, Stanford had managed to bring her to believe and internalize the idea that she was nothing. And that he was god. There was no point in her fighting him, because she had already lost before she even started to think about resisting him.

He shook his head. It was not the right time for philosophy. He did not know why, but he couldn't escape the feeling that time was short. That there was a danger in dragging his feet.

"Whatever you say," he said. For the moment, he wouldn't be able to make Liza believe that her husband could go to jail like anyone else. "How do you know Tara Caine?"

"I've known her since October last year," said Liza. "Since October thirty-first."

"So, not that long?"

"No. About two and a half months."

He went over to the table and sat down opposite Liza. He was buzzing, wanted to get all the information as quickly as possible, but he controlled himself. Acting aggressively toward Liza could well make her clam up completely.

"How did you meet her?"

Liza laughed. "Coincidence. My husband and I had

been invited to the seventy-fifth birthday party of one of my husband's colleagues. There was a big party in the Kensington Hotel. My husband insisted that I go, although I didn't feel at all well. My nerves were all frayed, and I had another lovely shiner. On my left eye. The swelling had gone down, but it was still blue around the edges. You don't feel too confident mingling with people when you look like that."

"Of course," said John. "But your husband seemed unconcerned about the risk that people might gossip about you and perhaps him too?"

"He knew I'd hide the bruise somehow. It wasn't nearly the first time we'd been in this situation. I've got makeup that's extremely good at disguising anything. The most important thing an abused woman can have, you know. I could hide the problem, really."

"So you went to the party...."

She nodded. "There were lots of people there. Especially law people. Barristers. Public prosecutors. Judges. My husband was always the center of things, making speeches. Showing off about his charity work. He had organized a tennis competition that summer to raise money for AIDS orphans in Africa. It had been a massive success, and so now he was bathing in the adulation. Everyone clapped him on the back and said what a wonderful chap he was...and I, standing beside him, could have puked. Really. I wanted to puke right there, in the middle of all these snazzily got-up people who were so sure they were doing good and who, in truth, were just celebrating themselves and did not realize that someone there was feeling terrible."

He could guess what was coming next. "Caine was one of the guests. And unlike the others, she noticed something?"

"I really wasn't feeling good that evening," said Liza. "I found it unbearably hot in the room, and I suddenly had the feeling that I was sweating profusely. I was afraid my makeup would run. Crazy, right? Actually, it should have been embarrassing for my husband if everyone had suddenly seen my black eye. But I just saw it as something I should be ashamed of."

"From what I know, that's the way a lot of women in your situation feel," said John.

"I ran off to the ladies' room. Luckily, it was empty when I got there. While I tried to fix my makeup in front of the mirror, I suddenly started to cry. It was a real crying fit. I was completely horrified. My makeup was running, my eyes were all blotchy…and I knew I'd have to go back to the party. But I couldn't stop. I just couldn't stop."

It was clear from her expression that she was reliving the moment—the moment that had obviously led to a big change in her life.

"Then the door suddenly opened, scaring me half to death," she continued. "It was Tara. I didn't know her yet, but I assumed that she was one of the party guests. I couldn't manage to slip into one of the cubicles in time. I screwed around with a pile of tissues, trying to pretend that I just had a cold or an allergy or something…. But then Tara was there, standing behind me, asking me if she could help. I put the tissues down. I cried. We looked at each other in the mirror. By now, almost all my makeup had come off my face. The skin around my eyes was gleaming in all its many colors. I think neither of us said anything for a minute, and then Tara said *Your husband?* It was both a question and a statement. And for the first time, I didn't try to make excuses. Didn't talk about falling down the stairs, about a clumsy collision with a tennis racket. I just didn't have the strength to try. So I just nodded. And then Tara asked: *You're Logan Stanford's wife, aren't you?* And I just nodded again."

"And that's when the plan was hatched to go into hiding?" asked John.

"Not quite," said Liza. "I told her that there was no way I could go back to the party. Tara helped me. She whisked me out of the hotel unseen, called a cab, and took me home. She paid the woman who was looking after Finley and showed her out while I was still waiting outside in the car. She made me a hot cup of tea. And I was crying the whole time."

"Then you told her everything?"

"Yes. Absolutely everything. It just all came pouring out."

"She's a public prosecutor. She should have instituted proceedings, whether or not you agreed."

"She told me that. I pleaded with her not to. In the end, she promised she wouldn't. But before she went, she looked at me and said: *Liza, I'm not going to give up until you go to the police yourself and press charges. You have to take that step. It's important—for your life and for your self-respect. Make him pay!* That's what she said."

"And then she kept on at you?" supposed John.

"Yes. She called me almost every day. She pressured me. She encouraged me. Sometimes I was happy to hear her voice. Sometimes I felt cornered. Overall…it was a comfort to finally find someone who was worried about my future. Even though it sometimes felt too intense."

"Tara got carried away?"

"Yes," said Liza. "I was amazed at how strong her emotions were. Sometimes it seemed to me that she almost hated Logan more than I did. It must have been terribly hard for her not to go after him in court immediately. But she needed my co-operation. There were no witnesses to our conversation in the toilet, and while I was unsure whether or not I'd give evidence against him, the case had no firm foundation. And it seemed immensely important to her that I take the decisive step. She was always saying that I had to defend myself. Hit back. Destroy him. I was not to be left with the feeling that she or the police had saved me. I was to save myself. *That's really, really important for afterward, Liza*, she would always say."

"The idea in itself might not be misguided," said John, "but the way you describe her to me, she seems unnaturally involved emotionally. It's almost as if...." He stopped. He would only distract Liza if he started speculating.

"What do you mean?" asked Liza.

"I just wondered why Tara Caine got so deeply, feverishly involved in your case. I have the impression that her own life experience might have played a role, although of course I have no proof of that now."

"She never talked about herself," said Liza. Her melancholy, despairing eyes suddenly looked at him suspiciously. "What's happened? Why are you so interested in Tara Caine?"

"Why did she rent an apartment for you here?" John replied with a question instead of an answer.

"Oh, everything happened so quickly," said Liza. "Mid-November, things got worse again between my husband and me. So I pleaded with Tara to help me escape. Luckily, we had already talked so much in the two weeks leading up to that time that she agreed that Finley could stay there. She was worried about Finley, but she had understood that Logan would never attack him. He idolized his son. That's the only good thing about him."

"And yet the way Logan behaved was irresponsible, horrific," John argued. "From what I saw, Finley has completely withdrawn to his own world. It's unimaginable what he has had to endure over the years. Even if he himself was never attacked—his psyche has been damaged."

"Tara comes here every few days," said Liza. "She wants me to press charges on Logan. For me to divorce him. To start a new life with Finley. To no longer hide. I know she's right, but…." She shook her head. "I'm not ready yet. And sometimes I think things are just getting worse. I just want to dig myself deeper into a hole instead of daring to come out and attack him. But Tara won't give up. Maybe one day she'll have gotten me to the point of doing it. Sometimes I think…that I'm a project of hers. She wants to achieve something. But at least for now she has brought me somewhere safe."

Not a bad term for it, thought John. A project. Maybe so. Tara Caine did not want to attack Logan Stanford directly herself, although as a public prosecutor she had many options open to her: she wanted to encourage Liza to do it. To that end, she was investing time and a not inconsiderable amount of money. Were she to be successful, however, she would easily recoup her expenses: as a divorcée, Liza would be wealthy.

However, money was not what drove Tara. John could not put his finger on why he was so sure of that: he just felt it. It was something bigger, more important, something that meant more.

"Did you tell Tara about Carla Roberts?" he asked. "And Anne Westley?"

"Yes, I told her about both of them. Tara wanted to

know if anyone else around me had ever noticed anything, and I said no, not that I knew, but that I had confided in two women in the hope that they would do something. But they hadn't."

There was something there.... He could not see it clearly, but it was as if something in his thoughts was picking up momentum, as if he were approaching some realization that would make everything clear. This is what he had been looking for, and the police too: the person who had known all three victims, who for so long had seemed not to be connected in any way. Carla, Anne, and Tom. Gillian, who perhaps was meant instead of Tom.

For the first time, he had a name, for the first time since Samson Segal had appeared—and there was at least no evidence that Samson knew Anne and Carla.

Tara Caine.

Who was obviously obsessed by the idea of helping a woman who was unable to help herself. A woman who had been left in the lurch by everyone she had turned to when she needed help.

There were still gaps. He still needed to connect some more dots before he could reach that moment of realization.

But I'm close. And somehow it's got to do with Tara Caine. And Gillian is with her!

He took out his cell. "Excuse me, I just need to make a quick call," he said.

For the second time that day, he selected Gillian's mobile number. Once again, no one picked up his call. Once again, her voicemail came on after a number of rings.

He left a message again: "Gillian, it's me, John. Please call me back. It's important. Please call!"

"What is it?" asked Liza, hearing the urgency in his voice.

He waved her question away. "That's a long story. We might have a big problem on our hands."

John knew that the moment had come for him to talk to Fielder. He had information that he should not withhold, and the police had the means to deal with this situation. He would not be able to keep Liza out of it. Perhaps not his former colleague Kate either.

Maybe he should stop worrying.

He stood up. Before he went to the police, he would drive to Tara Caine's apartment. Maybe the two women were still inside and Gillian was just not answering the mobile because she could see his name displayed and was afraid he would try to force her into something.

But he did not really believe that. When they last spoke, Gillian had said she was about to leave London. It was now Friday evening. She must have been on the road for hours. Was Tara with her?

He had another idea. "Do you have any way of phoning Tara?" he asked.

The apartment did not have a landline, but Liza had a mobile. She found Tara's number and handed the phone to John. "Here's her mobile number. I don't have another one."

Almost predictably, no one replied. There was not even a mailbox turned on. John swore quietly to himself.

"Please stay here, Liza," he asked as he walked toward the door. "Don't try to find somewhere new in a hurry, anything like that. Please stay. I might still need you."

He hoped she would not make him swear he would not go to the police, but she didn't even think about that.

"Where would I go?" she asked, apathetically. "I can't decide anything without Tara anyway."

"I'll be in touch," he promised and went out.

He listened to her close the door and turn the key twice in the lock as he ran down the stairs.

11

IT WAS HOT in the car. Tara must have turned the heater up to high. The thick woolen blanket lying on top of her did the rest. Gillian had the feeling that sweat was pouring down her body. The wool scratched her face, too.

The fear of suffocating came, flooding her in waves of panic. She needed all her mental strength to overcome each wave. With this heat, with a heavy blanket over her head and body, with her mouth gagged shut with masking tape, she could not let herself lose control.

She had begged Tara to leave the masking tape off. "Please, please. Please, Tara. Don't do this to me. I'm afraid. Please!"

She had sworn that she would not make a noise, but Tara was having none of it. "You'd promise me anything now. Forget it, Gillian. I'm not going to take a risk, certainly not for you!"

In the garage, sheltered from prying gazes, she had wound the masking tape several times around Gillian's head. It was stuck fast to her hair, and Gillian could imagine how painful it would be to remove it. Although at the moment that was not her worry. She was not getting enough air, was scared she would suffocate. Scared she would throw up. For that reason alone, she had to control her panic. She tended to be sick when she got too worked up.

She had been made to cross her hands behind her

back. Then Tara had taped her wrists together too. "Where's the car key?" she had asked.

Gillian could only make vague sounds, but she had nodded toward Tara's parked car. Tara understood. She went out and fetched her friend's handbag and, back inside the garage, rummaged around in it. Tara found the key, took it out, and put Gillian's handbag back in her car. Gillian remembered her cell, which someone had tried to call half an hour earlier. She would not have another chance to answer the call.

Tara opened Gillian's car and ordered her to sit on the passenger seat. Then she locked the car. Gillian tried desperately to free her wrists from the masking tape, but she did not manage to loosen them even a little. Then she tried to unlock the door with her hands tied up, but that did not work either. She could only sit and wait.

In the rearview mirror, she could see Tara get into her own car, start the engine, turn the car around, and back it as far as she could into the open garage door. She realized that she was going to be transferred. Of course Tara would have preferred to drive all the way into the garage and do everything behind a carefully closed door, but there was not enough room inside. Tom's big BMW took up most of the space.

Tara got out and opened up the trunk. She pulled Gillian out of her car.

"Get into my trunk now," she ordered. "And no tricks."

Gillian, helpless and with the gun stuck in her back, climbed into the Jaguar's trunk. There was not much room. She had to pull her knees up to her chin in the fetal position.

She was fighting back tears as she felt Tara also tying her ankles roughly together. For a short moment, she thought about defending herself. Tara had put the pis-

tol down and was standing bent over the open lid of the
trunk. A well-aimed kick to her groin would immobilize
her for a moment. But then? With her hands tied behind
her back, would she be able to run outside fast enough?
Her former friend would quickly recover and only need
seconds to grab her gun. Gillian was in no doubt that
Tara's threat was serious. A shot in the head. Like Tom.

It seemed too risky to her. And then her feet were
tied too, and it was too late. Her real chance had been
earlier, when she had felt it was all wrong and known
that she should get rid of Tara. She would have managed too, if Samson Segal had not had the unfortunate
idea of warning her. How on earth did *he* come to suspect Tara? *How* had he figured it out? And he had said
we. Who was he in cahoots with?

Tara took a thick woolen blanket from the trunk of
Gillian's car and threw it over her.

"So you don't freeze to death," she said. "Who knows
how long we'll be on the road."

Gillian was again on the verge of tears, and not just
because the thick blanket made it difficult to breathe.
A memory of earlier, happier times was also welling
up in her: the blanket was originally from the car Tom
had owned as a student. The old rust-bucket would only
start with a lot of coaxing, and foam was spilling out of
the torn upholstery on the back seats. That is why Tom
had spread the blanket over those seats. They had just
gotten to know each other and were so in love that they
were walking on air.

One day in May, they had driven to the sea and taken
a swim. Gillian remembered the ice-cold water and the
fresh spring air. She had splashed around for too long.
Afterward she was so cold that her teeth chattered, her
lips were blue, and she shook all over. Tom had fetched

the blanket from the car and wrapped her in it, then put his arms around her and tried to give her some of his body warmth. They had sat like that on the beach of the isolated bay for hours. Crabs were digging into the sand, seabirds were pacing around, and slimy green seaweed was lying in glittering streaks over the low rocks. The sky was mirrored in the puddles left by the last high tide. Strangely, the situation seemed astoundingly romantic to Gillian, a pure happiness that she knew she would never forget. When, years later, Tom did not want the old blanket in his fancy BMW, Gillian had put it in the trunk of her own car.

While Tara closed the lid of the trunk, moved her car forward a little, and then got out and closed the garage door, Gillian thought that, even if she survived this whole story, she would never lead a *normal life* again. These experiences would be too heavy a burden. They would never go away. Just like the memory of Tom and the sea and that cold day one May. Now other images were layered on top: Tom murdered and strangely contorted on his chair in the dining room. The evening with Luke Palm, when she thought she had seen someone in her house.

Samson Segal's voice on her answering machine. Tara's dead eyes.

From now on, that would be her reality.

She would have given anything to go back to the normality she had known, to that very world she had found hard to accept. She just wanted to have her life back. Her life as it had been. That was all she wished for now.

When the car started up again, Gillian wondered what her chances were, and her conclusions were not rosy. When would she be missed? Her parents and Becky would probably call at some point and then, after the second or third try, they would wonder why she neither picked up the phone or called them back. And then? How were they to find her?

Luke Palm would try to get in touch too, at the latest when someone was interested in the house or there were questions about this or that detail. At least he knew that she had moved back to her friend's house, although he did not know the name or identity of that friend. But he did know the address—he had dropped her off there. Would he turn to the police because her disappearance seemed strange to him?

And then?

She had told John that she wanted to withdraw to a hotel in the country. If he told the police, they might not even investigate her disappearance. Everyone would assume that she had done as she said and did not want to be disturbed. Exactly what was to be expected from a traumatized woman whose husband had just been murdered. And yet her car was in the garage. But would anyone even check her garage? She also could have taken the train, which would make sense given the weather conditions.

There was one ray of hope: Samson Segal, the idiot she had to thank for her current precarious situation. For some utterly incomprehensible reason, he had come to the totally correct conclusion that Tara Caine was a danger to her. But what would he do with that knowledge?

What was Tara up to? She could easily have shot her right there in the house. Was it a good sign that she had not? Not necessarily, Gillian realized in despair. Tara was not stupid. She had heard the warning on the answering machine. She knew that Luke Palm knew where Gillian had taken refuge that night. Neighbors might also have seen Tara and Gillian's arrival at Gil-

lian's house. If Gillian's corpse were found in the house
in the following days, Tara would certainly be interro-
gated thoroughly. The situation would have become extremely difficult for her. No, Tara wanted to do just what
she had said: find a safe place and then decide what her
next step was to be. The chain of events had gotten out
of control. She had said Luke Palm's name by mistake,
and now Samson had called.

Since then, she had more or less confessed her guilt to
her former friend. The obvious conclusion to be drawn
from that was that she did not see Gillian as someone
who was going to have the chance to tell anyone what
she had learned.

*She can't let me get away, thought Gillian. She can
just try to make me disappear in a way that doesn't im-
plicate her. That's what she's up to.*

With this thought, her breathing immediately became
more labored. The blanket seemed to press on her face
like a lead weight, the masking tape suffocating her not
only directly by covering her mouth, but by the nauseous
smell of its sticking surface. The car started, stopped,
started again. Urban roads. Early Friday evening. They
would proceed at this stop–start rhythm at least until
the edge of town. There might be traffic jams on the
freeway too. The heavy traffic also made her feel sick.
The heat, the smell, the car juddering forward: all these
things churned up Gillian's stomach. She felt lucky that
she had barely eaten anything all day. Nevertheless, the
sick feeling was just going to get worse.

Don't think about it, she told herself, calling up all
her strength of will. Focus on something else.

She could hear the muffled voice of a radio presenter.
It was the weather report. It was going to be very cold
in the coming days. No more snow was expected, but

he recommended that drivers stay at home if they could. The Highway Agency was still struggling to free the roads from the last cold snap.

Then music came on.

Gillian thought she could even hear Tara humming along with the melody.

You always get a second chance, she thought; make sure you're ready to use yours.

She had to immediately brush away her next thought: *Silly saying, that thing about a second chance. There's no guarantee you do.*

Sometimes you don't even have one chance.

12

HE HAD EXPECTED that no one would be home at Tara Caine's apartment. Nevertheless, he had rung the bell a few times, and then stepped back to the road and peered up at Tara's balcony. Just darkness behind Tara's living room windows. The smaller windows beside the balcony must be part of her apartment too, and they too were not lit.

This was the moment to involve the police.

John got back into his car.

He thought of the evening he had driven Gillian back here, just over a week before. She had fetched a few things from her house and was confronted for the first time with the place where her husband had been violently killed. John had helped her to carry her things upstairs, but she didn't want him to go inside. He had understood that Becky was there, disturbed and confused by the murder. And keen of hearing. That it would be best that she not see another man at her mother's side so soon after her father's death, even if only as her mother's helpful friend. That she would have sensed that there was more to it. At least Gillian had expressed that worry, and John had respected her concern.

Now, looking up at the dark apartment again, he thought that maybe she had not just been thinking about Becky. Maybe she had already had a funny feeling about Tara. Maybe Tara had already started to plot against him.

No, surely not. It was only that night, he remembered, after he had left her there, that Gillian had first told Tara about the events that had led to his leaving the force. Afterward, the two women had argued. Tara had expressed her complete incomprehension of Gillian's involvement with a man whose earlier life was stained with the word *rape*; a stain that, in spite of all efforts to remove it, had never disappeared completely. Tara must have argued very forcefully, because right after that, Gillian had sent Becky to her grandparents in Norwich and had returned to her own house—contrary to the advice of someone who meant her well.

Why could he not shake the feeling that he was missing something at just this point?

I told Tara that you'd been a policeman. And why you aren't any more... .

He could hear Gillian's voice in his head. He had asked her why she was going back to her house, and she had tried to explain it to him. She had felt uneasy because it had to do with his past and because she had to confront him with the fact that the incident was still sticking to him, causing mistrust and prejudice, and that it probably always would.

She was horrified... .

Something was not right with that.

She was horrified... .

What had Kate told him? Tara Caine had requested his file and read it—back in December! She had returned it, according to Kate, before Christmas. That meant that on that Thursday evening about a week ago when Gillian told her about the investigations into his past, she had already known about them. In great detail, because she had had access to the whole file. If she *was horrified*, then she just pretended to be so. She must have acted out her horror for Gillian's benefit.

Why?

Maybe she wanted to hide the fact that she had been snooping. John supposed that the mention of the name Burton might have rung distant bells for her because of a conversation with a colleague or something overheard in a corridor. She had done her research…and kept it to herself. At that point, she must have assumed that Gillian had no idea of his past. As a best friend, would it not have been normal for her to tell her what she had discovered immediately? She was obviously not convinced of John's innocence. She certainly still saw him as a danger. Why had she said nothing at first and then acted all surprised?

John knew that none of that was enough to construct anything that really implicated Tara. A whole series of harmless explanations for her behavior was imaginable. The fact that she was helping Liza Stanford did not automatically make her a suspect either. However, the accumulation of strange events did alarm him.

And he was worried by the fact that the two women had suddenly disappeared without a trace.

Making his mind up immediately, he turned on the engine and did a risky U-turn on the road, as cars around him beeped.

He drove toward Scotland Yard.

Saturday, January 16

1

CONSTABLE RICK MEYERS had expected a quiet Saturday morning shift at the station. He was on duty, but he expected that not much would happen and he would have time to finally catch up on some of the paperwork that had been piling up on his desk. The snowy world outside was quiet and peaceful and shone in innocent white. Perhaps it was the weather that suggested that nothing would happen that day. In any case, he was royally annoyed when his boss turned up and shoved a piece of paper in his face.

"We've got something to check. From Scotland Yard in London. It's about a Mrs. Lucy Caine-Roslin. She lives in Reddish Lane."

"Reddish Lane. In Gorton?"

"Yes. I'm afraid you have to drive out there."

"What's it about?" Meyers asked. He had just gotten going on his reports.

"Her daughter might be there. That's what we need to find out. She's got some big questions to answer."

"The daughter?" Meyers was not there yet.

"Yes. She's gone missing, but they have to question her urgently and it's possible that she's driven to her mother's house. The daughter is named…" His boss paused, looking at his notes, "Tara Caine. She's a public prosecutor in London."

"Public prosecutor? Really? And she's from there?"

"Seems so."

"And why don't we just call this Lucy Caine-Roslin first?" asked Meyers as he slowly stood up. He could guess that his boss had already considered that and that there was some reason why they could not. So his idea was not going to save him a trip to one of the less pleasant parts of Manchester to find some old bag.

"They've already tried repeatedly. No one answers the phone. There's no choice: you have to drop by. We can't ignore Scotland Yard."

At least there was not much traffic, it being early on Saturday morning, and the roads had been cleared. Rick Meyers made good progress. Nevertheless, he could have done without this chore, and not just because it delayed his other work. No policeman liked to drive to Gorton, in the south of Manchester, even if it were only to find some old biddy. Any apparently harmless job in that area might end in disaster. Gorton had nicer and less nice spots. The less-nice places had many condemned houses where junkies lived. The junkies did not dither around if they saw a chance to get some cash for their next hit. Whoever moved here was at the bottom end of the social ladder and could not go down any further. Violence was rife, and the police were seen as unwelcome intruders here. And Meyers was not a hero. He often wondered why he was stupid enough to earn his money working for the police, of all people.

This morning he asked himself the same question and, as always, had no answer to give.

The appearance of the streets changed slowly. You did not suddenly arrive in Gorton; the area announced itself gradually. The houses along the roads gradually became shabbier. The green areas grew more infrequent until they disappeared completely. Then came an industrial area that looked abandoned and that looked wretched even under a thick layer of snow. Then a discount clothes store that, this morning at least, no one seemed to have found their way to.

A scrapyard. Right next to that, a row of terraced houses gradually crumbling away. Only the rubbish— some of it in trash bags, some of it just thrown out of windows—revealed that the houses were inhabited.

Then there were the tenement houses. Walls scrawled with graffiti. Broken window panes. One house's front door had been torn off. More and more rubbish, dirt, and neglect. Meyers knew that there would be many needles in the trash. Annoyed, he looked at a small child playing on the road in spite of the cold and dirt—the child was not being supervised and was in real danger. Its parents were probably sleeping or drunk or stoned—or all three. The child was still beaming. Even in this terrible environment, he was obviously happy that it had snowed. Just like any other child.

Meyers felt sad.

It was a mystery to him how a girl from here had made it as a lawyer in London. A tough cookie, no doubt.

Reddish Lane was long. Meyers was relieved to see that the house he had to visit was not on one of the worst stretches. On the ground floor of many of the houses on that stretch, there were shops and businesses of varying sizes. Although some of them had obviously given up and were either boarded up or had their shutters down permanently, most of them kept on bravely. The area seemed to be anything but well off, but it was not utterly neglected.

It could have been much worse, he thought.

Mrs. Caine-Roslin lived in a small detached red brick house. It had a tiny yard around it. At the back of the yard, a somewhat dilapidated shed was visible. The house itself seemed solid enough. Only when you looked closely did you see signs that nothing had been done to maintain it for a long time. The window frames needed to be painted, the gate repaired, and some of the roof tiles replaced. Like so many houses in the street, the ground floor was a shop front, now closed with blue shutters. A sign said that this was a bicycle repair shop. The sign was old and the lettering was hard to decipher, worn as it was from the years of wind, rain, and sun. It did not look like there was a workshop here anymore.

It was actually questionable as to whether anyone still lived in the house.

Rick Meyers parked at the side of the road, got out, and looked doubtfully at the upper-floor windows. He could not see a light on, but then it was also no longer dark. There were at least curtains in the windows, and he thought he could even see one or two potted plants. Yet a strange lifelessness hung over the house and the yard, although perhaps that came from the obviously abandoned business on the ground floor.

Meyers trudged through the snow that no one on the property had shoveled away. Perhaps Mrs. Caine-Roslin no longer lived here. Perhaps her daughter had taken her to London long ago and found an old people's home for her. Strange that she was still down on the electoral roll here. But sometimes these things happen.

And the daughter had disappeared and was being hunted by Scotland Yard.

Odd, no two ways about it.

There was a door that led to the lower rooms, but entry had been blocked by nailing two crossed boards over the door and frame. Beside the door, a steep flight of steps led up the outside wall. There was another door at the top. It did not look like it was blocked.

There was such thick snow on the steps that Rick Meyers had trouble climbing them. On one side there was a wall, but there was no hand railing on the other side, nothing to hold on to. No one had removed the snow from the steps for weeks. Rick Meyers wondered how an old woman had managed to navigate the steep, snow-laden steps. Surely Lucy Caine-Roslin had to go out sometimes and get food? The fresh snowfall made it impossible to tell when someone had last tried to climb up or down the steps. But if he, as a relatively young man, was having difficulty, how was a woman coping who must be at least in her mid-sixties? He felt it was increasingly likely that no one lived here.

Finally reaching the top, he knocked on the wooden door. It was black, and the paint was starting to peel at the edges.

"Mrs. Caine-Roslin? Can you please open the door?" He listened carefully. "It's Constable Meyers here."

No movement from inside. He knocked again, more forcefully this time. "Please, Mrs. Caine-Roslin. Police! I'd like to ask a quick question."

There was not a single sound.

Meyers tried the doorknob. To his surprise, it turned. The door opened inward. It had not been locked.

He gagged as the disgusting smell of decay hit him from the hermetically sealed apartment.

"Bloody hell!" He felt around in his pockets for a tissue but could not find one. He looked for a window that he could throw open. The kitchen window was the closest option. Meyers pushed past table and chairs, turned the handle, and leaned far out. Cold, fresh winter air in his face. It was only a minute since he had trudged through the snow down there, but it already felt to him as if he had not breathed that wonderful air for an eternity. As if he was already a part of the stench that permeated the apartment.

His fingers, which were still searching through all the pockets of his uniform, finally found a balled-up old tissue and fished it out. Meyers hated what he would next have to do. But he was a policeman. He had to get to the bottom of whatever horror awaited him in the apartment.

He took a deep breath and then, pressing the tissue over his mouth and nose, he turned away from the window. He looked around the kitchen. It looked clean and tidy, although there was a thin layer of dust on all the furniture. There were two plates on the table on which the unidentifiable remains of a meal were rotting away. They were covered with a blueish-white growth that no doubt added to the smell in the apartment, although they surely weren't solely responsible for it. Two half-full glasses of wine and a bottle of wine stood next to them. It was an expensive wine, as Meyers could read on the label. Whatever had happened with Lucy Caine-Roslin—and it was clearly nothing good—had interrupted a meal. A meal where she had obviously not been alone.

He discovered a brown paper bag on the sideboard. The bag carried the name of a Chinese restaurant. Someone had visited the old woman and brought a take-out meal to her. And then…?

He left the kitchen. He knew that the real challenge still lay ahead.

He found Lucy Caine-Roslin in a child's bedroom. Or at least, it seemed to *once have been* a child's bedroom. Or a teenager's room. It contained a sofa-bed covered with a flowery patchwork quilt. Curtains of the same pattern on the windows. A wardrobe, of which one door stood open, revealing two pullover shirts on hangers. A few posters on the walls, including one of Cat Stevens, Meyers thought. There was also an armchair on which some magazines and paper with scribbled notes were strewn. Along the wall were wooden shelves. A number of books for children and young people—as could be gathered from their titles and bright colors—were lined up on the shelves, carefully held together with plastic bookends. Meyers thought later that this was what had immediately told him it was a young person's room: the books and the picture of Cat Stevens on the wall.

Lucy Caine-Roslin was lying on her back in the middle of the room. She looked like a darkening, bloated shell of what had once been a person. The cold, dry air in the barely heated apartment had preserved her better than would have been the case in less favorable circumstances. Her face was relatively well kept, but Meyers could not bear to look at her eyes—or what was left of them. It was hard for him to keep his composure.

Normally he would have assumed that the old woman's death was, while unfortunate, at least of natural causes. She might have started to feel ill after her visitor had left and before she had been able to clean up the kitchen. However, this assumption was contradicted by the fact that there was something large and—at first glance—unidentifiable stuck in the dead woman's mouth. Controlling himself, Meyers walked over and crouched down over the stinking corpse. A cloth. A large checked cloth. It might be a tea towel.

Someone had stuffed it violently down her throat.

And blocked off her nostrils with several strips of masking tape. He got up again, stepped over to the window, and opened it too.

He leaned far out and took another deep breath of fresh air.

Lucy Caine-Roslin's death was not in itself news: an old woman who had been lying dead in her apartment for weeks without anyone noticing. Her isolation was tragic, but not unusual. Many people, especially older people, had no family left, so when they died, no one noticed. In Lucy Caine-Roslin's case, it seemed a little strange, as she still had her daughter in London. Perhaps the daughter had broken with her life in Gorton. Meyers turned back from the window and looked at the room. Like the rest of the apartment, it was friendly and clean, although it was also clear that the family had never had much money. The furniture was simple, the curtains and blankets no doubt sewn by the mother. Was this the house in which the public prosecutor had grown up? Her life today probably looked rather different.

But Lucy Caine-Roslin had not just died of a heart attack. Someone had stuffed a tea towel down her throat. Maybe she had choked to death on it. It appeared that she had been murdered. An old woman, who obviously had nothing of value. Who would gain from killing her?

Meyers remembered his task. The daughter. He had been sent here to find her daughter.

Although he assumed that he was in the house by himself, he checked all the rooms just to be sure. The house was larger than it appeared from the outside. It contained a living room, a dining room, two bedrooms, and a bathroom. It was all spotlessly clean. A teapot and teacup stood on the living room table. There were brown stains in the cup, left by the tea that had either evaporated or been drunk. There was a doily, with a needle still sticking into it, lying on the armchair. Wilted African violets stood in pots on the windowsills. Although it had been too much for Lucy Caine-Roslin to maintain the outside walls and yard, inside she had kept everything shipshape.

But back to his job: the daughter was certainly not at her mother's house.

Meyers pulled out his phone. Now he had to ask for backup. Lucy Caine-Roslin had died without anyone noticing, but now her death would be thoroughly examined. That was all they could do for the old lady now.

2

SHE HAD FALLEN ASLEEP, as impossible as that seemed to her. Her exhaustion had got the better of her horror, sick feeling, and nervous confusion. She did not know how long she had been asleep. A sudden jolt, followed by the sound of spinning wheels and the screaming engine, had woken her.

She's stuck, she thought.

She. Her best friend. The person she trusted. Someone she had known for years and who suddenly seemed like a complete stranger to her.

She could hear Tara get out and slam the door behind her. Suddenly the trunk opened. Ice-cold air flooded inside, penetrating even the suffocating, hot blanket. Then the blanket was removed. Gillian immediately scrunched her eyes closed. The bright daylight was hellishly painful after all the hours in the dark.

"Okay. This is where we stop," said Tara. "The snow's too deep. Get out!" As she spoke, she drew a knife, letting the blade spring open, and cut the tape binding Gillian's ankles.

"Out!" she ordered again.

Gillian tried to sit up and groaned in pain. She had

been immobilized in an uncomfortable position for too long, lying on the hard floor of the trunk, shaken and jolted in a car struggling to make progress on almost impassable roads. She could now feel all her bones, all her joints. Her whole body hurt. She had no idea how she was going to move. When she finally managed to open her eyes and blink at her surroundings, she saw Tara as a large, dark shadow in front of the open trunk. The sky was dove-gray above her. Behind her, there was a snow-covered expanse—and nothing that looked like a house or a hamlet.

We're far from anybody's home. We're completely alone.

"Come on," Tara hurried her.

As Gillian was still unable to move, Tara bent over and grabbed her under both arms and dragged her out. Tara was surprisingly strong. As Gillian could not hold herself up on her own two feet, she fell down lengthwise in the snow. It was soft and cold, but after a second she could feel the hardness of the tiny crystals. They cut painfully into the skin on her face. Moaning unintelligibly, she first lifted her head, then started to pick herself up. As her hands were still tied, it was hard for her to gain her balance.

Tara helped her to her feet. "Don't worry, your muscles will relax. We've still got quite a hike ahead of us."

Gillian fought the dizziness that came over her as soon as she got to her feet. She realized that she was terribly thirsty. She had not drunk anything since lunchtime the previous day. Add the masking tape over her face and the heat of the car, and she now felt completely dried out. She tried desperately to communicate this to Tara. She knew she could not go on without having a drink first.

Tara seemed to weigh up her options before grabbing at Gillian's face and pulling the masking tape down with a sudden yank. It was wrapped several times around her head and stuck to her hair, so it did not come away completely, but at least she managed to pull it down so that it hung below Gillian's chin.

"Water," Gillian croaked.

Tara opened her driver's door and fetched a bottle of mineral water that was in a bag on the back seat. Because her hands were tied, Gillian could not take the bottle, so Tara unscrewed the cap and held the bottle to Gillian's lips. She drank greedily, like someone dying of thirst.

"Please," she said when she was done. "Please don't tape up my mouth again."

"Feels pretty stupid, not getting much air, doesn't it?" Tara replied, and it almost sounded sympathetic. "Okay, I'll tell you what. I'll leave the tape where it is. No one here to hear you if you scream, anyway. Still, if you try anything, like trying to call for help or running away, I'll wrap your face with so much tape you won't see or hear a thing. Got it?"

"Yes," said Gillian. She looked around. Snow-covered hills as far as the eye could see. In the distance, a wood. They had come on a road that had been cleared of most of the snow and was just covered in a thin, hard layer. There was no village to be seen. Tara was right: she could scream as much as she wanted; no one would hear her. And running away: how far would she get? Tara would have caught her immediately. Her hands tied behind her back, she would not be nimble on her feet. She had no chance.

"Where are we?" she asked.

Tara opened her big handbag and put in some supplies: a loaf of bread and two bottles of water. She put her pistol in her hand.

"The Peak District," she said. "In other words, in the middle of nowhere."

The Peak District. It stretched over several counties, almost touching Manchester to its northwest.

Manchester.

Tara was from Manchester.

"You know this area?" asked Gillian uncertainly.

"You could say that. We're near the hut. The perfect place. No one will find us there."

"What hut?"

"Stop asking questions," Tara said. "Start moving!"

"Which way?"

"This way." Tara gestured across the fields with her pistol. "There's a footpath here, even if it's hidden at the moment. Just go straight ahead."

After the fields came the woods that Gillian had seen when she opened her eyes. Gillian let herself nurture a little hope. If there was any chance of escape, then surely in a wood. Unlike the treeless plain on which the two women were standing at that moment, it would offer hiding places. And a hiding place was the only hope for Gillian, handicapped by the tape as she was. But she was also under no illusions. She would have to be very lucky to trick Tara.

And even then she would only survive if she managed to find a village or at least a farm as quickly as possible. It was bitterly cold. It was unlikely that anyone could survive more than one night in the open air.

She took her first trudging steps. In places she sank in up to her knees. She once again realized how difficult it was to keep her balance in the deep snow with her arms tied behind her back. She could hear Tara breathing behind her. It was not an easy walk for Tara either. She was lugging the bag of supplies, holding a gun in her other hand, and probably not risking a moment's lack of concentration. Not that she would think that Gillian, hands tied and scared, was particularly dangerous, but neither was the situation risk-free for her.

Gillian stopped at one point. She had the feeling that she had been walking for hours. "Could we rest a bit?" she asked, turning to look at Tara.

Tara shook her head. "We have to make it to the hut in half an hour. We can do it."

"Tara, could you at least explain why—"

"No," Tara interrupted her. "I'll spare my breath. You should too. There's a real climb ahead. It would be stupid of us to waste our energy. So shut up and keep going."

Gillian did as she was told. She fought against a despair that wanted to take over. The cold air stung her lungs. The snow blinded her eyes. Exhaustion seemed to want to push her down toward the ground.

She walked on.

3

"WHAT I NEED from you," said Detective Sergeant Christy McMarrow with a cold voice, "are convincing explanations."

They were sitting in her office in Scotland Yard. It was Saturday morning. Fielder had driven to Croydon to talk to Liza again. He had visited her the night before. Two of his people were getting in touch with Logan Stanford, others had driven out to the Ward family's house in Thorpe Bay, while yet others had gone to Tara's apartment in Kensington. Constable Kate Linville had indeed dug up information on Tara Caine right after her call with John. For once in her career, she had really shone. She was able to provide the important information immediately: that Tara Caine had only one living relative, her mother, who lived in Manchester and might be able to say something about her daughter's whereabouts. Everyone was amazed that Kate had already looked up Tara Caine at a time when she was not on the radar of anyone else in the team. Kate explained that her suspicion had been aroused after seeing Tara's name on John Burton's file. She enjoyed showing this investigative flair that no one would have expected of her.

After many attempts to contact Mrs. Caine-Roslin by phone, they had finally given the local police station in Manchester an urgent request to find the old lady and see if her daughter was staying with her.

John was relieved to see the police apparatus swinging into action. The previous evening, they had questioned him for hours. Of course they were happy that he had found Liza Stanford, but they had reacted with utter skepticism to his suspicions regarding Tara Caine. Fielder had visited Liza later that evening and had a first conversation with her, but everything relating to Tara Caine and Gillian Ward was put off until the next morning. John had the clear sense that they found his theories, for which he had no supporting evidence yet, pretty far-fetched—even if they now, the morning after, were looking for Tara.

But a whole night had been wasted, a night in which John had not been able to sleep for a moment. He had paced up and down in his apartment and smoked two packs of cigarettes. Early the next morning, he had returned to Scotland Yard and had demanded to know what would happen next.

Christy McMarrow had time for him. It was easy to

see what her job was: to find out who had leaked information to him. John refused to reveal his source. In his opinion, it was of no importance.

He and Christy had worked together for years. They liked each other. Sometimes they had gone for a drink together after work. Back then, Christy was one of the first to tell whoever she met, whether or not they wanted to hear, that the accusations raised against John were all rubbish. John had hoped he could make her understand the current situation. But Christy barricaded herself behind a stony façade and did not appear to want to make any allowance for their earlier friendship.

He tried one more time. "Christy, I—"

She immediately interrupted him. "I still haven't gotten an answer to the question of how you stumbled upon Liza Stanford's name. The only possibility I can see is that you've talked to Keira Jones, Carla Roberts's daughter."

"No, I haven't."

"Who, then?"

He could feel a rising impatience. "Christy, does that really matter? We've got other problems. Gillian Ward has disappeared. Caine, the public prosecutor, too. Caine—"

"—need not have anything to do with the crimes," said Christy. "Your theories are pretty wild, John. 'Bizarre' would be an understatement. From what you yourself have said, Gillian Ward was planning to 'find herself,' or something, in a secluded hotel."

"No, I didn't say '*find* herself.' I felt like she was trying to *hide* from something."

"Whatever. So now you see her disappearance as dangerous—and at the same time, you seriously think a public prosecutor is the likely serial killer?"

"I've simply pointed out that she is the first person we have found who knew all the victims. And I'm uneasy about the fact that she has disappeared without a trace. With Gillian. You too considered Gillian to be at risk. Fielder told me that himself."

"Well, I think—" Christy started, but at that moment the phone on her desk rang. Christy listened and then said, brusquely, "I'll take the conversation in your room. Just a moment." She got up. "Excuse me for a minute. I'll be right back."

She left the room. John stood up and walked over to the window. He was buzzing with impatience. The police were starting to move, but much too slowly for his liking. And it was just like Fielder to give one of his most capable colleagues the job of questioning his arch-enemy. As if there were not more urgent tasks for Christy in these hours!

Five more minutes, he told himself. I'll give this stupid meeting another five minutes, and then I'll go looking for Gillian myself.

Christy came back in when his five minutes were just up. She looked very tense. John understood immediately that she had been given some disturbing news. He moved toward her, but she walked past him and took her seat behind her desk. She did not seem to mind whether John sat or remained standing.

"How did you come to suspect Caine?" she asked.

John shook his head, astonished. "I explained this last night. She's Gillian Ward's friend. So she knew Thomas Ward well. And she heard about Carla Roberts and Anne Westley from Liza Stanford. So she knew all three victims. She asked to see the file on me last month but then acted to Gillian just last week as if she had been unaware of my past. I know that's not enough, but something says to me that—"

"Gillian Ward's car is in her garage in Thorpe Bay," Christy interrupted him. "Tire tracks in the driveway indicate that another car was there recently. And that car wasn't Gillian's or her husband's car."

John went pale. "You know that Caine drives a Jaguar."

Christy nodded. It was clear that the police had already found that out. "Yes. And before you ask: yes, it could be a Jaguar's tire tracks. We know that." She hesitated for a minute. "Our team has listened to Mrs. Ward's answering machine," she continued. "There was a very odd message on it."

"Did you enter the house?" John knew that in the short space of time available, it was hardly likely that they had obtained a warrant. Something had made the situation so precarious that they had overlooked that little slip in procedure. "What happened?"

"DI Fielder's orders." Christy hesitated again. "The police station in Manchester called him. Caine's mother, Lucy Caine-Roslin, was found dead in her house. It looks like she was murdered."

"Fuck!"

"It looks like it was done by the person who killed Roberts, Westley, and Ward. That's what certain things indicate."

A tea towel in her mouth? John had it on the tip of his tongue, but he managed to bite it back. If he had given that away, Christy would have known for sure that his informant was from the Yard. He should not put Constable Linville at any greater risk than he already had done.

Instead, he asked: "What about the message on Gillian's answering machine you just mentioned?"

"It's from Samson Segal." Christy gave him a piercing look. "From the man we're hunting."

He did not bat an eyelid. "Really?"

"Yes, really. He addresses Mrs. Ward directly and warns her about Caine. He sees her as dangerous. And not just him. He says *we*. He and *someone else*, whom he doesn't name, are worried about Mrs. Ward. He asks her to be careful. Do you have any idea who this ominous other person could be?"

"No."

She could see right through him. From working with her, he knew that she was clever and had real intuitive capabilities. "Where's Samson Segal, John?"

"How should I know?"

"The police are looking for him. Anyone hiding him is culpable."

"I know. I was a policeman long enough."

"John…."

"Christy!" He went up to her desk and leaned forward with his hands on the desktop. His face was close to hers. Around her eyes he could see the lines that had become noticeably deeper over the last few years. "Christy, now don't expect me to believe that you still seriously suspect Samson Segal! The man is harmless! He got carried away in his crush on Gillian Ward and crept around her house, but the only crime he's committed is an occasional unchaste thought or two. He's odd, a strange man, a wretched case, but not more than that. Don't waste your valuable time hunting him. Don't you understand that?" He stood up straight. "Gillian has disappeared. Tara Caine can't be found either. Gillian had been living in Tara's apartment. So it's possible that the two women left London together. In Tara's car? To Thorpe Bay, perhaps? After all, at Gillian's house there are the tire tracks that might come from Caine's car. But where would they go next? Toward Manchester? Tara Caine's home town. And something must have gone badly wrong there, because Tara Caine's mother is dead now and—"

"Mrs. Caine-Roslin wasn't killed recently," said Christy. "The coroner's report isn't in yet, but my colleagues in Manchester say that she had definitely been dead for long time when she was found. At least eight weeks."

He stared at her. *What had happened? Why did it happen?*

"The motive," said Christy McMarrow. She seemed to be speaking more to herself than to John. "What is Caine's motive for all of this? I just can't see the thread running through it all!" She rubbed her eyes. They were red and tired. "I just can't follow the thread," she repeated.

"You have to find her!" John urged her. "I'm afraid that Gillian's life is in danger. I have just as little clue as you about her motives, but we'll have enough time later. Let's assume that Tara Caine killed Thomas Ward, and let's assume that Gillian was her real target. If so, Caine has gotten just what she wanted: she's got Gillian in her power."

"We'll put out a call to find Ms. Caine's car," said Christy. "Maybe the women are traveling in it. And one other thing, John: I appreciate that you want to help with advice on what we should do, but believe me, we know. We aren't looking for your help here anymore." She looked coldly at him.

He could sense anger rising in himself. Until this moment, it was despair and exhaustion that he had felt. Despair because he feared he would not manage to save

Gillian. Exhaustion because the last few days had sucked all his energy out of him. But now the two emotions turned to anger. He asked himself who Christy McMarrow thought she was. She was giving him a dressing-down, treating him with scorn, although he had given Scotland Yard everything they needed to know. He had used Kate Linville to obtain some information from the police systems, but *he* had drawn the right conclusions, *he* had found out that Caine knew all the victims in the series of murders and so was just the person whom Detective Inspector Fielder had been searching for so desperately. He had done a good job, and Christy knew it.

"Why, Christy?" he asked quietly. "Why are you so hostile to me? What have I done to you?"

Now he had gotten through to her. She gave up her pretense of icy distance. She stood up, came around the side of her desk, and stood right in front of him. A tiny, plump, furious person. For the second time in just minutes, John could see clearly on her face the furrows from the constant strain of the job.

"What did you do to me?" she repeated. "You disappointed me bitterly, John Burton, bitterly! You were one of the best policemen in the Met. You were brilliant. I loved working with you. We were a damn good team. You were my hero. I looked up to you. I thought we'd be a team forever and solve more cases than anyone else in the Yard. My career plans were bound up with you. And then you go and do such a stupid, pointless thing. With an intern! You risk your whole career just because you can't keep your hormones under control! When it happened, I just couldn't grasp it. I still can't!"

"I couldn't guess the girl would go berserk."

"But you should have known you were playing with fire. You were her boss. She should have been off limits for you. You normally understand what people are like, but you couldn't see she was a real neurotic because you had the hots for her. Everyone else could see that she was. She was attractive and at the same time completely hysterical, but of course you just had eyes for her pretty face and big chest. You were blind to the rest. You *idiot*!"

She almost spat out the last word.

He knew that everything she said was right. That just made him more angry.

"Could it be," he replied coldly, "that the real reason for your anger is that it was someone else who was the object of my *uncontrolled hormones*, as you put it? Someone who wasn't you?"

He could see in her eyes how right he had been. Then her hand smacked into his face.

"You asshole," she said.

4

WHEN THEY REACHED the hut, Gillian had already stopped believing in it. She guessed that by car they would have needed another ten minutes from where they had left it stuck in the snow; on foot it took them over an hour. It was partly because of the snow itself, in which they sometimes sank to their hips, making every single step a struggle. They had drunk almost all their mineral water. Tara did not want to give her any more, although Gillian's thirst seemed unquenchable. The dry air and the physical exertion were drying her out. More than once, Gillian thought she would be unable to walk another step.

"When were you last in the hut?" she asked once. She

was afraid that either there was no such hut or that Tara
had lost her way long ago.

"I must have been seventeen or eighteen," said Tara.
After a moment's thought, she added: "More like seventeen. I left home at eighteen and didn't come back
around here for years."

Seventeen! Tara was now in her late thirties. "Are
you sure it's still standing?"

"Some of it must be. A hut like that doesn't just evaporate into thin air."

"And you think you can find it?"

"Just follow the path. It leads right to it."

"But we can't see the path. We might have lost it
long ago."

"Don't worry yourself about that. I know just where
we are. Now shut up. Spare your breath."

After a while, they reached the woods, which did
not make their progress any quicker. The weight of the
snow had broken many branches that had now fallen and
blocked the path. Other branches hung down so low that
you had to duck constantly to avoid them. However, soon
the woods opened out into a wide field. Once again there
was no human habitation in sight, as Gillian noted with
frustration. And then, suddenly, there at the edge of the
field, sheltered by the trees, stood the hut.

"There we are," said Tara.

Gillian saw a kind of log cabin. It was larger and stur-
dier than she had imagined it would be. It was nestled
on the hillside below the woods that followed the crest
of the hill. Below it, the ground dropped steeply down
to the valley, which seemed to stretch on and on forever below them. Gillian knew that the Peak District,
which she had once visited with her parents as a child,
was beautiful country. It was a never-ending succession

of hills and valleys, woods and lakes, small stone walls and wind-bent hedges. There were dried-out streambeds on whose banks rare flowers grew, rugged rocks, and meadows with tall grasses. Here and there, charming and remote villages hugged the hillsides. The roads from one village to the next were nearly all single-track. The sky was full of wild, fast, breathtaking cloud shapes.

Now, on this day, at this time of year, everything looked different. The snow and sky merged somewhere in the distance. The clouds had joined together into one single dark gray mass, and the landscape was hidden under a deep blanket of snow. Gillian asked herself whether she should finally give up all hope of a village or farmstead, or whether she just could not see far enough because of the low clouds. Perhaps, when the weather would clear....

"There's a stream down there," said Tara. She looked down the hillside. "It's probably frozen and snowed over. I used to play there for hours as a child. I built dams, things like that. And you could wade around barefoot in the stream in the summer. Or sit in it and cool off a bit."

"You used to come here as a child?" Gillian tried to keep Tara talking. Tara looked more normal when she was talking harmlessly about her childhood. Her eyes were lively and alert, not glassy like they had been the day before in Thorpe Bay when Samson Segal's call messed everything up. Gillian understood that a lot was dependent on her not letting Tara get into that strange state again.

Tara looked around. "Yes. My father built the hut. All on his own."

"He must have been good with his hands."

"He was very good at anything that needed manual dexterity," stated Tara. She had now fished a key from her bag and was trying to unlock the door. She was not immediately successful.

"No one has been here for years," she murmured.

"Your parents don't come here often?"

"My father died long ago. I was eight when he died."

"Oh…I'm sorry."

Gillian watched Tara struggle with the lock. She felt so exhausted that she had to fight the urge to just fall down in the snow and never get up. Although Tara was distracted right now, Gillian did not even consider fleeing. Exhausted, with her hands tied behind her back, it did not seem like a possibility.

The key finally turned in the lock, and the wooden door opened with a loud creak.

"After you," said Tara ironically, gesturing for Gillian to step inside.

The musty, stale air had been sealed up in the unventilated hut for years. It hit her like a cold wall. It was too murky to see anything clearly.

It was like walking into a tomb. That was Gillian's first, disturbing impression. Tara switched on the flashlight she had brought and got to work trying to open the shutters of the two windows. They were as stiff as the lock on the door. Gillian could see two upturned sofas and, in between them, a wooden table. A wrought-iron stove. A small cupboard. And a door that seemed to lead to a further room. "My parents always slept on the two sofas," explained Tara. "I had the small room at the back."

The first shutter swung open. It was now considerably brighter in the room, which also revealed the full squalor of the place.

Moss and mold were growing on the wall. The sofas were falling to pieces, their foam stuffing spilling out of them. Some of the floor was covered in something slimy that Gillian could not identify. Perhaps lichen. Over the years, the damp had seeped in through all the cracks and, as no one had used the stove for years, the room had never dried out.

Impossible for anyone to live here. But Gillian had a feeling that Tara was not too worried about that.

The second shutter opened, failing to make their surroundings appear any less wretched.

"Do you think we could try to get the stove working?" asked Gillian.

Tara shrugged. "If there's still a woodpile behind the hut, then maybe. Although any logs will be pretty wet. Sit down," she said and nodded toward the two sofas.

Gillian hesitated.

"Sit down!" repeated Tara sharply.

Gillian sat down. The sofa gave way under her weight and she sank down almost to the floor. She guessed that there must be all kinds of creepy-crawlies in the foam filling. Maggots and worms, maybe. If they had not frozen to death. *Let them have frozen to death*, she prayed silently to herself.

Tara left the hut, but came back immediately empty-handed. "No wood there. So we can't have a fire."

What remained of Gillian's courage deserted her. Now that she was no longer moving, she was freezing, in spite of her thick coat. Tara really had found a completely remote place. No one would ever come across her here. Tara had wanted to win some time to think about her next step. In the end, she had realized that only one thing was possible: she had to get rid of her former friend somehow. Then she would go back to London alone and hope that no one noticed anything. She could tell everyone that Gillian had set off for a hotel and that she hadn't heard from her since then. She could cut Gillian's throat. She could shoot her. She could even just leave Gillian in the hut and barricade the door and shutters so she couldn't get out. It wouldn't take too long for her to starve or freeze to death. There must only be people walking through these woods once in a blue moon, so it was very unlikely that anyone would be near enough to hear her screams. Probably no one would even find her when she was dead. Tara's plan to kill her outside London and Thorpe Bay was this: no corpse, no murder. Even if people suspected her, they would not be able to prove a thing.

Gillian had to think about how to escape. That was her only, tiny chance. Somewhere there were people living, even if it had looked outside as if she was alone in the world. Perhaps she could manage to get Tara's car key too and somehow find her way back to the car. Right now, the car key was lying beside the key to the hut on the unused stove. It had fallen out of Tara's bag when she got out the bottle with the last few drops of mineral water. Almost absentmindedly, it appeared, she had put it on the stove. Yet as Tara was standing right in front of the oven, leaning against its iron door, there was no chance that Gillian could even get near it.

Tara was holding her arms wrapped tightly around her body. She was freezing, and suddenly the wind seemed to have been knocked out of her.

"We never used to come in winter," she said, and it sounded almost like an apology. "The first time in the year that we'd normally come to the hut was at Easter. Then for the summer. And not after mid-October. The nights were pretty cold then. It was often rainy, and you couldn't stay outside for long. The landscape around here is beautiful, though. Untouched nature, as far as the eye can see."

"But we're near Manchester?" asked Gillian.

Tara nodded. "In Dark Peak. The northern part of the national park."

Gillian let out a dispirited sigh. She knew that the Peak District had two parts, the Dark Peak in the north and the White Peak in the south. The White Peak was relatively densely populated, while the Dark Peak was mainly high moors that stretched on for miles without any human habitation. Hikers sometimes sought out this empty wilderness, but certainly not at this time of the year. They were at the end of the world here.

"Does your family own the land?" she asked, to keep the conversation going.

Tara laughed sarcastically. "Good Lord! My family never had much money. They really didn't. My father owned a bicycle-repair shop, and he also sold second-hand bikes that he had repaired. He kept us afloat like that, but land? We'd never have been able to afford land!"

"But...."

"Yes, the hut is illegal, you could say. The land here doesn't belong to anyone, and luckily no one ever minded. My parents once came past here on a walk—that was before I was born—and my father said to my mother that he would build her a log cabin here. Which he then did." She looked around her. A tender expression played on her features. "It was really beautiful. We had wonderful weekends here. My father did a lot with me. He built tree houses and we collected wild flowers. He played cowboys and Indians with me and showed me how to lay trails in the woods. My father gave me strength. That's stayed with me all my life."

"It must have been very tough when he died so

young," said Gillian. She surreptitiously shifted her hands behind her back. She had the impression that the masking tape around her wrists had loosened a little. Not nearly enough for her to free her hands; but if she was very patient with her efforts, she might be able to pull her hands out in the end. She just had to be extremely careful. No sudden movements. Tara could not be allowed to notice a thing.

"A heart attack," Tara said. It was as if a shadow had fallen across her face. Gillian could almost feel in her body the pain and mourning that, after all these years, still weighed on Tara. It was decades since what must have seemed unimaginable had happened. "It was a normal day. He was working in his workshop behind the house. I was coming home from school and ran toward him. He saw me coming, stood up, smiled at me, and then fell over. Just like that. He died in the hospital a few hours later." She could not keep her hands still. "God, I should have remembered to bring cigarettes. I really need one now. Shit!"

Her pain suddenly switched over into anger. In a flash. Gillian was scared. She had the feeling that Tara was an emotional powderkeg. She had never seen her friend like this in the past. Tara had always been calm and objective. Obviously she had been using a flawless mask. The elegantly dressed, smartly made-up and coiffed public prosecutor who was always in control and above things. A woman who let her reason steer her in almost all areas of her life.

When did I ever experience her excited or out of control? Gillian wondered. She remembered one time, not too long ago. She had explained John's past to her. It was not exactly that Tara had exploded, but by her own standards she did lose control. Was there some key to understanding her in that?

If only I knew!

"Tara," she said. "I'm your friend. And whatever happened—"

"Save it," Tara said coldly. "You *were* my friend, Gillian. In the past. But I was wrong about you from the start. You're a bit like my mother, and that's about the worst thing I can say about someone. My mother was a really nice woman, very friendly. I don't think anyone would have thought she was capable of something really evil. Everyone liked her."

"Your mother…wasn't as nice as everyone thought?" Gillian asked gently. She could now definitely feel that the tape was loosening. She would have liked to move her arms around wildly, but she controlled herself. As long as Tara had a knife and a pistol lying beside her, Gillian would still be in an unfavorable position, even if her hands were free.

"My mother was weak. I didn't see that for a long time, because my father gave her strength. But when he died, she showed her true colors. She went wet. Day and night she moaned that she couldn't do this, couldn't do that. Her nerves this, her health that. My father had taken out life insurance, and that kept us going for a while, but do you think my mother used the time to find a job? Or to do anything to bring her and her daughter's life back onto an even keel?

"No, she just sat in the corner and bawled her eyes out and didn't know how we were going to make ends meet from now on. I was eight! I couldn't help her. It was too much for me."

"But somehow…"

"…somehow things went on, you mean?" Tara nodded. "Yes, things went on. After my mother had bawled her eyes out enough, she suddenly had a great idea. The classic solution for a woman like her. She hooked up with the first bloke who came along. She just couldn't live without a man. And she was not unattractive back then. She was in her mid-thirties and rather pretty. She could have chosen from a whole bunch of men. Nice, friendly men."

Tara grabbed the knife, the one she had used earlier to cut through the tape around Gillian's ankles. She slowly traced its edge with her thumb and index finger. Gillian saw a fine line appear on her thumb, from which blood welled up.

"But she chose Ted Roslin. Probably because he never stopped courting her. He flattered her with all sorts of seductive arts. He gave her the feeling that she was a fantastic woman. The fact that he had nothing and had nothing going for him was lost on my mother. He swept her off her feet. They got married just before my ninth birthday." There was only a trickle of blood from the small cut at first. But the flow was increasing.

"Then came a bitter disappointment for her. I think my mother was a good catch for Ted Roslin. She owned the house and he could take over my father's bike workshop, which had always done well. But he had absolutely no interest in my mother, in spite of what he had pretended before the wedding. She just didn't turn him on. Sometimes I heard her really begging him to take her in his arms. She was always wanting to sleep with him, and he was always making up excuses. He just didn't desire her."

"Why not?" asked Gillian. "She was young and pretty—"

"He wasn't into women," interrupted Tara.

"Oh," said Gillian. "But…surely by the late seventies a gay man could be fairly open…I mean, not need to hide behind a marriage."

She was interrupted again.

"He wasn't into men," Tara explained. She looked with satisfaction at the blood that was now running warm and bright down her hand.

"He was into little girls," she said.

5

LUCKILY, THE M1 northbound was almost completely free of snow and there were no major delays. They made quick progress. The day was going quickly, and soon it would be dark. John wanted to reach Manchester by early evening. He had found two Lucy Caines in Manchester. Neither with a double-barreled surname, but he was convinced that one of the two was Tara's mother. Two addresses. That was do-able.

Samson Segal sat nervously next to him on the passenger seat. He was relieved that John had let him come and at the same time worried sick because he had no idea what would happen. After the unpleasant conversation with Christy McMarrow in Scotland Yard, John had immediately driven back to his apartment, showered quickly, found the Lucy Caine addresses, and set off for Manchester. Maybe he was making a big mistake, but Manchester was his only lead, so he decided to follow it. Tara Caine had grown up there. Maybe she still knew places to hide in Manchester or nearby. If she'd had it in for Gillian for a long time, but perhaps also knew that the net was closing in, she might have looked for somewhere where she would feel safe for now.

Samson had waited for him tensely and immediately bombarded him with questions, but John had cut him off immediately. "Are you the one who called Gillian? And left a warning for her on her answering machine?"

Samson went pale. "Yes…."

"You didn't think that one through, Samson. You really didn't. Gillian and Tara have disappeared. But it looks like Tara might have been out in Thorpe Bay yesterday—if so, then probably with Gillian. We can only hope that Tara didn't hear your message. Otherwise, the mess Gillian is in could be much worse now."

"Why?" asked Samson in horror.

John was annoyed. He should not have left Segal on his own. The man had a real talent for doing the wrong thing at the wrong time. "If Tara Caine is really dangerous, and unfortunately we have to assume she is, then Gillian's chances of getting away safely would be greater if Caine assumes that Gillian doesn't suspect anything. As soon as Gillian starts to get suspicious, then, to Caine, she's a danger."

"I wanted to warn her. I thought…."

"But you shouldn't leave a message. You have no idea who might hear it."

Samson looked as if he was about to fall into a deep depression. "I do everything wrong."

Too true, John would have liked to add, but he bit his tongue. Discouraging Samson was not going to help.

When John announced that he was going away, for at least two days, Samson jolted upright. "I'll come too!"

"No. Wait here."

"I want to come. Please. I won't do anything without clearing it with you first. But I can't wait here. I'd go crazy!"

John had hesitated, but then had agreed. Samson could do less harm where John could keep an eye on him. There were also many situations in which it could be good to have a second person around. "Okay. But I don't want you talking, all right? And you're not to do anything without asking me first."

"Like I promised. Uh…where are we going, actually?"

"To Manchester. Tara Caine was born there and grew up there. It's just an idea, born of desperation more than anything; but if Caine thinks her back's up against the wall, she might decide to flee to somewhere she knows well: her home town."

"To her parents?" Samson asked.

"It seems like she only has a mother," said John. "And the police found her dead in her house this morning. Murdered. Probably by the same person who went on the rampage down here. Maybe Tara Caine herself."

Samson was agog. "Oh, God…."

"We'd better get moving," said John.

They reached Manchester toward evening. Samson, who had been silent the whole trip and obviously deep in dark thoughts, asked: "What's the first thing we'll do when we get there?"

"We'll look for Mrs. Caine's house," replied John. "And then I'll see if I can find out anything. There must be neighbors who have known the family for a long time. Maybe there are places where she used to like to go. Tara could have fled to a place like that with Gillian."

Samson nodded. John threw him a look. Samson looked deeply worried.

He loves Gillian, thought John. He is terribly afraid

for her. "Do you think we have a chance?" asked Samson.

"I'd prefer to look for a needle in a haystack," said John. But then he added more positively: "Cheer up, Samson. We haven't been dealt the worst hand!"

He didn't say what he really thought: *Do we have a chance in hell?* At least they were lucky about one thing: the first address they drove to, in a run-down part of Manchester, proved to be the right one. A red brick house, a small yard. A sign indicating that bikes could be bought or repaired there. The only thing that really interested John, however, was that the police had cordoned it off at the gate. This had to be the place where Lucy Caine-Roslin had been found dead.

He parked his car next to a pile of snow beside the road. He and Samson got out. It was icy cold, but at least the street lamps added light. John practically never prayed, but considering that they were going to be doing a lot of driving this night, he sent up a quick prayer: *No more snow, please!*

"What next?" asked Samson. He looked over to the house on whose gate the cordon tape was fluttering in the cold wind. "Is this the house…?"

"Yes," said John. "This is it."

The house in which the public prosecutor's mother had lived and died. Was it the house in which Tara Caine had spent her childhood? He hoped so. Because only then would he be able to learn something pertinent from her neighbors.

It was a little after six o'clock. The lights were on in most houses on the street. People were at home, but they probably hadn't yet sat down to dinner. Not a bad time, in fact, for what he planned to do. "This is what we're going to do," he said. "We'll be relatively open, but not say anything about Gillian or that Tara Caine might be a bloody dangerous person. We'll just say we're looking for her. That we're friends of hers from London. No doubt, word has gone around that her mother was found murdered this morning. These things get around in no time at all. We'll say that Tara has disappeared and we're worried about her. That we'd like to know if anyone knows some special place she might have withdrawn to. Got it?"

"G-got it," stammered Samson. Standing there, pale and nervous, he did not look like the best man for the job, and John wondered whether it wouldn't be better to leave him in the car until he, John, had sorted everything out. But he might have to knock on a lot of doors before he got anywhere—if he did at all—and time was short. "You can do it," John encouraged him. "Listen, you take this side of the street. I'll start with the neighbors either side of the house and then work up the street."

"Should I introduce myself with my real name?"

"Yes. There's no nationwide search on for you. Introduce yourself as Samson Segal from London, a good friend of Tara Caine. All right?"

"All right," confirmed Samson.

John nodded at him and then crossed the street. He looked up at Lucy Caine-Roslin's house. Dark, silent windows.

Had Tara Caine killed her own mother?

He turned quickly to the neighboring house. There was no time to lose.

6

SHE TRUDGED THROUGH the snow. Darkness had fallen, and although it was too overcast to see the moon and stars, the whiteness of the snow-covered fields gave the night a little luminosity. The wind had picked up. Soon it would whip the clouds away.

She was the only person, near or far.

Knowing this gave her a sense of peace. Almost of security.

The thumb she had cut hurt. She liked the pain. She cut herself again and again. She liked to. She found a fascination in watching her blood flow. She loved its color and warmth. She loved to feel the cut part of her body beating. Like a heartbeat. As if the heart had moved and found a new place for itself. In her thumb, for example. But it could be somewhere else too. It was in her power to decide where. She could also put her heart in her foot.

She tended to cut her legs. That was why she always wore trouser suits, never skirts. She couldn't show her legs anymore.

She knew that she wouldn't get lost. She knew the area and would be able to find her way around it blind. Nevertheless, she was more tired than she had thought. It had been a long day. She hadn't slept the previous night. She had been driving north all night, spending part of it in an endless traffic jam that had formed behind a jackknifed tractor-trailer.

A little after one in the morning, she had stopped at a rest area because she needed a break. If she hadn't, she wouldn't have made it. She had seen that clearly. Of course, stopping was not without its risks. Gillian was lying in the trunk under a blanket, and Tara did not need much imagination to know that Gillian was thinking about escape. But Tara had tied her up so well that she knew Gillian would not be able to free herself on her own. And the car was locked. She had stretched out across both front seats and tried to rest. She had not fallen asleep: her makeshift bed was too uncomfortable for that, and she was too nervous. But at least she had been able to rest.

Before they drove on, she had thrown Gillian's handbag into one garbage bin and her cell phone, after switching it off, into another. No one would ever find them now.

The hike to the hut had been exhausting, and now the walk back to the car equally so. She remembered the footpaths she had taken many years ago on bright summers' evenings. Walking here and there, with a spring in her step. However simple the conditions in the hut had been, she had loved their times there from the bottom of her heart. Nature. Freedom. Back then, she wouldn't have hesitated to tell anyone that life was good.

She had not really counted on how long it would take to walk from the main road to the hut with all the snow on the ground. Nor had she realized that she would have to leave the car so far away. In actual fact, it was almost a miracle that she had been able to leave the car even this close to the hut. She had been incredibly lucky that at least the main roads around here, in this remote northern part of the Peak District, had been plowed.

She stopped for a moment, pulled her scarf up, trying to cover her face as much as possible. The cold cut her skin and hurt her lungs. It was all so tiring, for god's sake! The snow seemed to be deeper than it had been at midday. Although she must be imagining things, because it had not snowed in the meantime. She probably simply had no reserves of strength left.

It could not be much farther to her car. The thought of sinking into the soft upholstery, starting the engine, and turning on the heater gave her another boost of energy. She could not weaken now. Of course it would have been more sensible to wait until the next morning. A few hours of sleep would have worked wonders. But she was suddenly worried that she would not live to see tomorrow. It was ice-cold in the hut. The temperature outside seemed to fall lower every minute. The moldy old log cabin offered no protection from the cold. There was a real danger of freezing to death during the night.

So she had escorted Gillian outside so that she could finally pee behind a bush. Then she had tied up her feet again, closed the shutters, and carefully bolted the door. The rest was simple. Gillian would either freeze or starve to death. It was most likely that she would freeze to death before hunger became a problem. She had left behind for Gillian the meager remaining provisions: two sandwiches, some water. Mainly because she did not want to lug them around herself. They would be of little use to Gillian in any case. With her hands tied behind her back, she would not even be able to eat them. And even if she somehow managed to free her hands, she would not be able to break out of the hut.

Unfortunately, there was no other option. Gillian would die. She had become a threat.

Her thumb throbbed. Her whole hand throbbed. That was good. It spoke of life and warmth. The blood pulsed in her body. As long as it did, everything was fine. As long as it did, she was alive and breathing and could do what was right.

Things had worked out in the end, thank god. Although she had made a big mistake. Driving to Gillian's house in Thorpe Bay yesterday, she had mentioned the real estate agent's name. It was a mistake that she herself hadn't even noticed at first. She had just felt that something had changed. Gillian suddenly seemed extremely tense, restless. But she thought she might be imagining things. Or that the cause was something else: Gillian's uncertainty about her whole situation. Her fear of the leap into the unknown. She did not want to hide away from some bogeyman in a hotel. She was probably afraid of the emotions that would swamp her as she took lonely walks by the sea and thought about her life.

And Tara thought: okay, if you decide to stay in your house, I don't care. Just as long as you get out of my sight.

She had really planned to stop attacking Gillian. It was not the same with Gillian as with the two old women.

Maybe she knew her too well. Was too close to her. Maybe it was just a superstitious fear that suddenly lamed her. It had all been so easy with Carla Roberts and Anne Westley. The obstacles to killing Gillian seemed to be a warning: leave her alone!

But she probably was wrong to talk about *superstition*. It was a fact that she had twice failed to kill Gillian. On both occasions, the consequences for Tara could have been drastic. Smart people know when they are beaten.

Gillian's sudden change on the way from London to Southend had made her cautious. *Don't let her out of your sight*, an inner voice had told her, and so she had followed her into the house. Gillian had acted so innocently there that Tara thought her intuition must have misled her. But luckily, at just that moment that strange guy had called up. How stupid can a person be? He blared out his warning for the whole house to hear.

Of course Gillian had wanted to play it down. But that did not help her now—her adversary was too clever for that.

On the tediously long drive to Manchester, she had

thought constantly about two things: How had Samson Segal managed to find out that she was a danger? And who was he working with? Because he spoke of *we*.

And, secondly, why had Gillian already been suspicious? What had happened?

Somewhere near Northampton, she had found the answer to the second question. She had gone over and over in her mind the course of the afternoon, focusing in more and more closely on the time when she noticed the change in Gillian's attitude. And she had suddenly realized what it was: the name of that real estate agent. Luke Palm. Gillian had never mentioned his name. Tara had only heard it that evening when Palm suddenly returned and Gillian called out his name.

Everything had gone wrong on that day. Tara had headed for Thorpe Bay as night was falling. She had planned to ring Gillian's doorbell, just like she had done in Carla Roberts's case. She would have been let in, and that would have sealed Gillian's fate. But then she'd seen the unknown car parked in front of the house, and she immediately thought that Gillian must have a visitor, which turned out to be true. She had to wait ages until the visitor—a real estate agent, as she later found out—finally left. Gillian had stepped out into the yard, leaving the front door wide open. Tara had seized the opportunity and slipped inside, although her inner voice was telling her: *Leave it! It's too risky.* Nevertheless, she waited for Gillian in the kitchen, but then Gillian panicked and Luke Palm suddenly appeared. Tara had just managed to escape to the back yard and loop back to her car, leaving a wide berth between herself and the house.

She had no answer to the other question. What danger did that strange neighbor pose? What the hell had made him suspect her? She could not see where she had slipped up.

Never mind. She would have to deal with that later. Until now, everything had gone well. If she kept her nerve, everything would continue to go well.

She saw her car at the very moment when the desire to fall into the snow and just lie there had almost gotten the better of her. It was a small, dark shadow at the edge of the road. The wind had already dispersed the clouds enough that she could see a star here or there. But that was also why it was getting so much colder. A few more hours, and it would be a cloudless night with a sharp frost. She congratulated herself on her decision not to sleep in the hut.

She rummaged around in her bag. It was a large bag. She often used it to carry her case files. She had just thrown her keys in there when she set off in the early afternoon. They must be in here somewhere....

She found everything except her keys. Her compact. Purse. A book. A map. Tissues. Chewing gum.

But no keys.

She had reached the car. Putting the bag down on the hood, she kept on looking for the keys. She emptied her bag and spread out the contents in front of her. Finally she found a key, but from its heart-shaped plastic key fob she realized it was the key to the hut. It was not her car key, which was on a key ring with the key to her apartment.

Panicking, she turned her bag upside-down and shook it. All kinds of little things fell out—notes, broken pencils, a few coins.

She groaned. "Damn! Damn!"

She knew that she had thrown her keys into her bag.

And her bag was deep enough. The keys could not have fallen out.

She was standing on an icy winter's evening that felt like at least twenty below zero Celsius, with a strong north wind blowing, somewhere deep in the Dark Peak—beside a car that she could not drive because she didn't have the key. There was no house or farm nearby, let alone a village.

"Okay," she said out loud. "What's happened? Find out!"

Had she lost her keys walking to the car? If so, she did not have the slightest chance of finding them in the deep snow. But she didn't believe she had. Judging by the depth of her bag, they could not have just fallen out.

She repressed a budding panic. Things now looked worse for her than if she had stayed in the hut. She was in a life-threatening situation. All the more important that she keep her head.

She did what she always did when she tried to solve a problem: she called up in her mind the decisive moments, one after another.

The hut. Gillian tied up and lying on the sofa. She herself leaning against the stove. She had talked and told Gillian about the past. The key to the hut lay beside her on the stove.

Just that key?

She screwed up her eyes, visualizing the room and the situation. Oh, God, it wasn't just the key to the hut! Right beside it lay the keys to the house and car. They had fallen out of her bag when she had been getting the food out. She had caught the keys and had then put them down on the stove.

But she should have seen the keys when she picked

up the key to the hut. She would not grab one key and
simply leave the others that were lying beside it.

That meant that when she left the hut, the keys had
no longer been there. Impossible.

Gillian had insisted that she had to pee. She had
passed the stove. Had she grabbed the bundle of keys?

Maybe. How evil she was! That really could be it.
In that case, Gillian was able to move her hands better
than Tara had thought. Probably the masking tape had
come loose. Probably she had been tugging like mad at it
while she listened to Tara tell her what it was like to have
a childhood and youth with a stepfather like Ted Roslin—and while she was pretending to be horrified at it.

Tara almost laughed out loud. It was too ridiculous—
she had the key to the hut in which Gillian was locked,
and was standing next to the car that was of no use to
her now. Meanwhile Gillian had the car key, but was
stuck in the hut.

Well done! You carried that out to perfection.

Stunned, she shook the door handle and achieved an
unexpected victory: the car was not locked. She could
at least sit inside it.

In a jiffy, she gathered together the contents of her
bag from the hood and slipped into the passenger seat.
It was ice-cold in the car, but for the moment it was a
relief to be sheltered from the wind. And there was the
thick blanket in the trunk. She could hold out like this
for quite a while.

For a moment, she wondered whether she could ho-
twire the car, but she rejected the thought immediately. She had no idea how to do such a thing—or even
whether it was possible with her car. The risk of breaking something was too great.

She weighed up her chances and possibilities. Go

back to the hut? Grab the keys from Gillian? Or just wait here in the hope that perhaps a gritter would come by and be able to tow her?

You're in trouble now, Tara!

No, she wasn't. She leaned back and took a deep breath. Think it through. Keep cool. And do the right thing. That had always been her motto, and it had worked.

Her hand hurt and the night had closed in on her from all sides, bringing with it the fears of her whole life.

7

JOHN HAD ALMOST reached the end of the street without having made a single step of progress toward what he intended. People's reactions had been extremely varied. People in two apartments had simply not opened the door, although light and the noise of people moving about revealed that people were in. An old woman had peered suspiciously out from behind a chain that secured her door. In spite of John's repeated attempts to explain why he was there, she had not understood what he was talking about. Some people were actively hostile and had retorted to accusations that he had not made. "Mrs. Caine-Roslin? Yes, easy to say with hindsight that we should have noticed that she hadn't been around for weeks. But we've got our own problems too, you know! I mean, there's so much to do in your own life that you can't keep track of what other people are up to. And anyway, she had a daughter. Why didn't her daughter look after her? Good lord, I've got enough problems of my own without thinking about other people's! Did I know the daughter much? No, not at all. I sometimes saw her. With her chic Jaguar and her fine clothes. Thinks she's something special, no doubt. Apparently she's a bigwig in the London courts."

Some people were happy that someone had appeared to break the tedium of their long, lonely evening. They would have spent hours talking to John—but not about what he was interested in. He had forced himself to swallow lengthy accounts of their life histories in order to return to what he was there to talk about. "That's really interesting. But I've got to find Mrs. Caine-Roslin's daughter urgently. Tara Caine. Did you know her as a child or teenager? Can you think where she might have gone to be on her own?"

At least some of them did know Tara. The ones who had been living on that block when Tara had still lived at home. She was described to John as a very pretty, but also exceptionally thin and very withdrawn, child and young woman. She had not been close to anyone in the neighborhood. She had walled herself off from everyone.

"She always seemed so unhappy," said an old woman who said that she had moved to Gorton in 1981. "Her father had died, and her mother had remarried. The new guy was strange, somehow. Not in any obvious way. He didn't booze or cause mayhem. He took over Mr. Caine's bike repair shop and ran the business well enough. But there was something about him…I don't know. I didn't like him. No one in the neighborhood really liked him."

"What about his relationship to his stepdaughter—how was it?"

"I don't really know. I wasn't really in close contact with the family. I just know that the girl seemed unwell to me. Unwell in body and soul."

"Was there anywhere she would retreat to sometimes? To get away from what might have been a difficult family situation?"

The woman had shrugged her shoulders. "Maybe. But I don't know. I'm sorry. I'd really like to help."

He stood on the street in the dark, shivering in the cutting wind and staring at a McDonald's carton that was being blown down the pavement. An image began to form in his head. An image of how Tara Caine had been as a child, and of her path in life from an under-privileged area of Manchester via college to her highly respected London career. Anyone who started life in Gorton had the cards stacked against them. Tara Caine must have been clever, ambitious, and disciplined to make it this far.

There was an early, decisive break in her life. She had just been a child when her father died. Apparently no one liked her stepfather, although no one had any-thing concrete against him either. The family seemed to live a pretty ordered life. They owned the house, and the bike repair shop fed them all.

Nevertheless, Mrs. Caine-Roslin had ended up dead in her house. Her daughter had possibly killed four people.

She seemed unwell to me. Unwell in body and soul.

That didn't tell him anything about where she was now. Or where Gillian was.

He had reached a dead end. Time was running out, and he had not come any closer to his goal. He did not even know if he was on the right track. The only rea-son he had driven to Manchester was the fact that Tara had grown up in the city. That might be a complete mis-take. The two women he was looking for might be at the other end of England.

He raised his head and noticed someone on the other side of the street. Samson. Who was waving his arms.

With a few large strides, John was standing next to him. "What is it?"

Samson stuttered nervously. "I...I've found someone. It could be something. An old man. He's known the Caines for decades. He—oh, come with me!"

The two men ran down the road. The house in front of which Samson finally stopped was a little down the road from, and on the opposite side to, the Caines' house. It looked dilapidated and rather neglected. John felt his spirits sink. Hopefully it was not a confused old man about to tell him stories that did not make sense, stories that did not help them at all.

The man lived on the ground floor. He was waiting at his door. At least in one respect, John felt reassured when he saw him. This man was certainly not confused. He looked at his visitors with bright, attentive eyes. His face revealed him to be a clever man with much life experience.

An intellectual, thought John. Thank god.

He shook his hand. "John Burton. I'm a friend of Tara Caine. I'm worried about her. But Mr. Segal told you that already, no doubt."

"Angus Sherman," said the man, introducing himself. "Please, come in."

They were soon sitting on an ancient sofa in a warm living room, each of them holding a glass of sherry. The apartment was meticulously clean but still could not hide its resident's poverty. It was scarcely furnished. What little furniture there was of the cheapest and most modest kind. However, there were many books.

Mr. Sherman told them that he had seen Tara grow up. "I knew her father well. He was a nice man. Very special. He and Tara were very close. His early death was a tragedy for the girl, a real tragedy. No one could have imagined it. He suffered a heart attack, just fell over and died soon after. He wasn't even forty!"

"Mr. Sherman, we need to know whether—"

Angus Sherman nodded. "Of course. When your friend here," he said, nodding toward Samson, who was fidgeting nervously, "asked about a place Tara might have gone to hide away, I did remember a place. A hut."

"A *hut*?"

"A hut in the Peak District. Up in the northern part, where it's all moors and almost uninhabited. They had a hut up there."

"Out in the wilderness?"

"Out in the wilderness. Ike Caine—her father—built it with his own hands. A kind of log cabin. He built it soon after marrying Lucy. It was a present for her."

"And Tara liked to go there?"

"Weather permitting, the family liked to spend practically every weekend there. Tara loved the trips. I sometimes warned Ike: the hut was built completely illegally on the edge of a wood; the land didn't belong to the Caines and they had never received any permission to build. But Ike just laughed. *Angus, no one will mind*, he said to me. *We don't have electricity or running water. It's just a little hut by a wood. Doesn't look all that different from the roofed feeding troughs for the deer. I don't think anyone will even notice it.* And he was right: there was never any problem with it. At least, not as long as Ike Caine was alive."

"Do you think the hut is still standing?" asked John.

Angus pondered, swaying his head back and forth slightly. "Well, now…I don't know. Ike built it in the late sixties. He died in 1978. After that, the family rarely went there, I think. Although…it might still be standing, mightn't it?" He looked questioningly at John.

Thirty years. John had his doubts. But it was a straw to grasp at. The only one.

"Did you know if Tara kept on going there later?" he asked.

Angus Sherman gave him a regretful look. "I don't really know. After Ike died, I gradually lost contact with the family. The man Lucy married after Ike…well, not that I have anything specific to hold against him, but he was certainly not someone I particularly liked. And Tara wasn't the same as before. Beforehand, before her father died, she was a cheerful, open, lively girl. She laughed and talked a lot. But then she lost all her openness. She seemed to retreat into a shell. You couldn't really reach her any more. So I didn't actually know anything else about her life. Until she learned to drive, she certainly wouldn't have gone to the hut. It was much too far to get to by bike. But as to whether she later went back—no idea."

"Do you know where exactly the hut is?"

Angus got up, fetched a book from the shelf, and started to leaf through it. "A book about the Peak District…somewhere in here there's a map…unfortunately, I can only tell you the rough area…. Aha! Here it is!"

He laid the book down on the table. The three men leaned over it. It was open to a black-and-white map of the Peak District. Sherman took a pencil and circled a small area. "Here," he said. "If I understood Ike right, the hut must be somewhere here."

"Hmm," went John, sounding worried. What looked on the map like a tiny blob was, in fact, a massive area of moors, hills, and woods. It would take days to search it all.

Angus pointed to a black line. "This is a main road. It comes from Manchester. They must have taken it whenever they went to the hut. However, it doesn't go right up to the hut. Apparently they needed to take an unpaved track for the last stretch. But I don't know exactly where that is."

"There are probably dozens of farmers' tracks," said John. He rubbed his eyes. They were stinging with exhaustion.

Angus looked outside gloomily. "But in any case, it's ridiculous to think that you could reach the hut in this weather. The snow must be three foot deep. There's no way you'd get through with your car. The main road might have been plowed, but the minor roads and farmers' tracks certainly won't have been."

John and Samson looked at each other. Sherman was no doubt right.

"But in that case," said John, "Tara Caine can't have gotten to the hut. Not in her car."

"Definitely not."

Samson piped up for the first time. The stressful situation was making him stutter again. "B-but th-then we should see the c-car. It must be p-parked at the s-side of the road!"

"Right," said John, standing up. "And there must be footprints in the snow. We'll try. Thank you very much, Mr. Sherman. You've been very helpful. We'll get going at once."

Sherman stood up, shaking somewhat. "Take the book. So you can find the right road once you're in the Peak District."

John took the book. "Thank you. We'll bring it back. I don't know what we'd have done without you."

The old man smiled. "I'd do anything for Tara. If she's out there in a bad way, you have to find her! She was such a wonderful child. She was close to my heart.

As was her father. The fact that I can help her now is a real gift to me in my old age."

John nodded. He avoided looking in Sherman's eyes at this moment. If they managed to find Tara, it looked like it would be the old man's knowledge that would let them catch a four-time murderer. He did not need to know that now.

He might have this heart-breaking realization soon enough.

8

SHE HAD THE FLASHLIGHT. Tara had left it behind. So she had light, as long as the batteries held out. That was already a lot, in her position.

Her hands and feet were free. No sooner had she heard Tara lock the door from the outside than she had her wrists free of the masking tape. It was then easy to free her feet too.

She also had the key to the car. She had grabbed it as she went past it and then held it tight in her hand.

The hut was almost hermetically sealed; only tiny cracks that let the cold wind in. And icy cold. Gillian was afraid of the moment when the flashlight's batteries would run out. Then she would be enveloped in darkness. And that would be the end for her.

She had to get out. If she wanted to stay alive, she had to get out! She had grabbed the key, intending to force Tara to come back. Tara could never leave the Peak District on foot. The car would be no use to her without the key, and it was unlikely that anyone would come by. Certainly not now that night was falling. The cold, which right now was Gillian's worst enemy, was an even more deadly enemy for Tara out there. She needed the key. So she would have to come back. And then....

Yes: what then? Would Gillian manage to overpower her, a woman armed with a pistol and a knife, who would stop at nothing and had nothing to lose?

By now, a new thought had taken hold of Gillian: *I have to get out of here before she comes back!*

In the dull light of the flashlight's beam, she searched everywhere in the hut. Nothing, nothing at all that could help her. What had they used to cook with? To eat with? She had searched in vain for cutlery or a kitchen knife that she could use to arm herself. There was a shelf above the stove on which a few plastic containers stood, but they were empty. At some point someone, perhaps Mrs. Caine, had taken away all the household items because she knew that the hut was no longer going to be used. And she had been thorough. She had not overlooked a thing.

Gillian shuddered at the thought of Mrs. Caine-Roslin. Everything Tara had told her in the couple of hours before leaving made Gillian shudder. But she could not afford to think about it now. She could do that later. For the moment, she had to make sure she did not lose her strength. She had to focus on getting out. Nothing else.

She had to manage to break the lock on the door or break out through the shuttered windows. Those were her only options. Something that she could use as a crowbar would have been more than welcome now, but there was literally nothing of the kind. A few pieces of furniture. No tools, no cutlery, not even a bottle that could be smashed at the neck and made into a sharp object. The water bottles they had brought were plastic.

She looked at the key ring in her hand. It had two keys: the car key and the key to Tara's apartment. The key to the apartment was comparatively thin, with a serrated edge. It was the only object she had that was at all sharp. It might be her only chance, tiny as it was. If she had not grabbed the keys, she would have had to surrender to the fate of freezing or starving to death out here.

She pulled a set of shelves over to the door and placed the flashlight on it so that its beam shone on the lock. Then she knelt down in front of the door and examined the metal of the lock. Mr. Caine had repaired bikes and built a log cabin on his own. He'd been good with his hands. Gillian was worried that he might not have installed a simple lock. No doubt he had wanted to make sure his hut was as secure as possible. She poked around tentatively in the lock with her key. Nothing happened. Nor did she have the feeling that she would be able to make anything happen.

All right. There were still the two windows. Covered by heavy wooden shutters. Maybe she would have more luck with them.

She lugged the shelves and flashlight over to a window and examined its construction.

Square panes of glass. They were easy to open. She just had to unlatch one of them and open it. The problem was the shutters on the outside. They met in the middle of the window, where they were bolted together. The bolt was secured with a padlock which looked solid. She would have no more luck with it than with the lock on the door. Just a cursory glance told her that.

Tears welled up in her eyes, and she realized how much she wanted to just sit in a corner and have a good cry, but she forced herself to brush aside the temptation. Crying was not going to help her. It would just rob her of energy.

Focus, she told herself. *Find a way. Tara is going*

to be back at some point, because she can't get away
by car, and you need to be out and well away by then.

Tara had killed her own mother. Tara had killed
Carla Roberts and Anne Westley. She had killed Tom,
although she had actually intended to kill Gillian. She
had crept into Gillian's house a second time and waited
for her. It was only thanks to Luke Palm's unexpected
return that her attempt had failed. And until now, she
seemed to think all her actions were logical and com-
prehensible. She thought they had had to happen. She
knew that the law of the land would not see it like that,
but on the level of a higher morality, beyond any human
court, she thought she was completely innocent. It was
her complete and ineradicable belief.

He raped me for five years. Ted Roslin, my stepfa-
ther. Sometimes he would come to my bed every night
for a week. His hunger only increased the more he sat-
isfied it. He raped the little daughter of the woman he
had married—and only married because she had that
daughter. I was a pretty child. Blond, leggy. Big bright
eyes. He had liked the looks of me the first time he saw
me. In fact, as he later told me: he had become obsessed
with me. That's when he had started courting my mother.
And that had been easy. She was so determined to find
a new spouse quickly that she was more than willing to
ignore anything odd, any warning signs. For example,
the fact that Ted never got a hard-on with her. Okay,
no need to conclude from that any perverse preference
for children. But you might try to find out why, mightn't
you? But she only did that once they were married and
he couldn't get away from her as easily. Then, yes, then
she was peeved that he obviously found her about as
erotic as a dead fish. Well, at some point she realized
why. After all, he was not really trying to hide his "spe-

*cial relationship" with me. Then Mom knew what was
happening. Angry and jealous, she argued a lot with
him. You see? She was not so much worried about what
he did to me as about what he didn't do to her. But in
the end she always capitulated. Because there was one
emotion even greater than her jealousy of me and her
injured pride as a woman, and that was the fear that
he would leave her. She would not risk really annoying
him. She accustomed herself to the situation so that he
would stay.*

Gillian pulled herself together. She realized that she
had been staring at the shutters for minutes without seeing them. She had been listening to Tara's voice, which
even now, hours later, droned on and on in her head. In
spite of the delicate situation, she had listened to Tara
in complete horror as she had talked about her youth—
about the time after her father's death—in a largely monotonous tone, at times sounding almost cheerful, at
times ironic.

About her time in hell.

Gillian brushed aside the horror that arose in her
when she remembered what she had heard. She had no
time to start to deal with it now. Later, when she was
somewhere safe.

The shutters.

They were made of several boards and were attached
to the outside wall on each side of the window. The iron
hinges were screwed to the wooden shutters. By the light
of her torch, Gillian could see that over time the screws
had rusted. She tried to turn a screw by putting the tip
of the key to Tara's apartment into the head of the screw,
but it did not work. The key kept slipping out, and the
screw was so rusty that no doubt even a screwdriver
would not have been any use. The boards themselves

looked too thick and securely joined together for her to
consider breaking them.

She looked everywhere on the shutters for a weak
point. The wood had obviously never been painted, and
over the years it had turned gray. One of the hinges
caught Gillian's eye. Around the hinge, the wood had
turned a different color: not gray, but more like green,
nearly black. Gillian felt the wood with her fingers. In
this place, it seemed softer than elsewhere. She pressed
Tara's pointed apartment key against it. She really could
press it into the wood without any real difficulty. She
could sense her breathing speed up in her excitement.
Around the other hinge she could see the same black-
ish coloration; and wherever in these places she prodded with the key, she found the wood to be rotten. The
rusty screws seemed to have attacked and affected the
wood over the course of the years.

She hammered on the shutters with both fists. The
rotten spots had to give!

But they did not. Gillian's arms sank. She was breathing heavily. She did not have the strength for it.

I need a hammer.

An impossible wish. There was not even any cutlery
in the hut, let alone tools. She had looked hard enough.

So…no hammer. What else could she use? She
needed something like a battering ram, something to
slam into the old wood until, hopefully, it gave. She
shone the flashlight beam around the room. The table.
Or to be precise: the table legs. Or at least one of them.
She could use that.

She turned off the flashlight, turned the table on
its side and then upside down. Then she looked at its
wooden legs. They were screwed to the tabletop and
glued to boards along the edge of the table.

If she could prise them free of the glue with the key, she would be on the way. The single screw might not offer too much resistance. If she jerked the leg back and forth, the screw might break.

Suddenly a wave of fear and despondency swamped her, taking away her breath. The chance was so slight, the danger so great.

She pulled herself together.

She began, millimeter by millimeter, to scrape the glue out of the crack between the leg and the board.

9

JOHN WAS DRIVING. Samson sat next to him and held Angus Sherman's book on his lap. It was pitch-black outside, but thankfully the Friday evening rush-hour traffic, which had clogged up all the routes out of Manchester just two hours ago and made them almost impassable, had now ebbed. There were delays here and there, traffic lights that seemed to stay red forever and one long holdup because of a truck maneuvering in the road, but on the whole they made good progress. At the start, John swore loudly at every delay, because he had the feeling that they were in a race against time. From his years in the police force, he knew only too well how a few minutes could make the difference between life and death. But in the end he managed to calm himself down. Slamming his fist on the steering wheel was not going to help, nor cursing the driver ahead of him, who was crawling along at a snail's pace looking for a parking space. It only pumped him full of adrenaline and might lead him to make a mistake in the future.

Luckily, Samson did not talk. He concentrated on the

map, following its indications with his index finger and only speaking when they needed to change direction.

"We need to go right here, I think."

"The second exit off the traffic circle, I think."

John had retorted a couple of times: "You *think?* Or you know?" Samson's hesitancy, his wretched lack of confidence were getting on John's nerves. Yet when a short glance to the side revealed that Samson was fighting back tears, John checked his behavior. Turning his companion into a bundle of nerves would not help at all; what was more, it wasn't fair. Samson had done a good job. He had found Angus Sherman and in so doing had given them their first promising lead. He was how he was. The constant moderation of what he said with a *perhaps, I think,* or *possibly* was part of his character.

They passed the last outskirts of Manchester. Terrace after terrace of houses. A business park. A football field. A McDonald's. Then they left the lights of the city behind them. They could only see the beams of other cars' headlights.

"We're on the M60," said Samson. That was the orbital freeway around Manchester. "We come off at Stockport and take the A6 to the Peak District." He managed to suppress an *I think* that he had been about to add. "Then we go…for about five miles…."

"All right," said John. "It's going to be more difficult than it looks on the map, Samson. We have to find the right road into the Peak District—or rather, the road Sherman thinks is right. He wasn't very sure about exactly where the hut is, either."

"I know," said Samson uneasily. "Hopefully we're not too late." They left the freeway, drove down the almost-empty A6, and braked suddenly when they saw a sign for a car park for hikers setting off into the Peak

District, as well as a sign for a road leading up into the moors. John had no idea if they were right to stop, but the A road would have taken them too far south. Peak District. It sounded so harmless. You imagine a certain area with limits. But in truth they had miles and miles of meadows, mountains, and moors ahead of them. He knew that if they were unlucky, they could spend days driving around without getting anywhere near the hut.

They needed to find a way into the Peak District—and this parking lot seemed as likely a spot as any other.

Of course, they were the only people there. John stopped, turned on the dome light inside the car, and took the book.

"Probably this is the right road," he said. "I mean, this *is* this road on the map. But whether it's really the right road, who knows." The road was narrow, but it had been partially plowed. It led from the car park through a short stretch of woods into treeless fields.

Snow as far as the eye could see, which provided some help with seeing in the dark. The snow was a blessing and their only hope. John realized that there was no way they would discover the hut right beside a road. If Gillian and Tara had been able to drive to the hut by car, they would have had to give up their search now. But because of the snow, Tara would have had to leave the car beside a plowed road, and that meant that the haystack, in which they were searching for a needle, was smaller than otherwise.

A glimmer of hope. A Jaguar parked somewhere.

John kept this firmly in mind, as they pressed on into the dark, cold wilderness.

We're coming, Gillian! Please, my love, hang on!

Only when Samson glanced over at him quickly did he realize that he had not just thought those words.

He had said them out loud.

10

SHE HAD LOCKED the car from inside and then lain down on the back seat, draping the thick woolen blanket from the trunk over herself. In spite of the warm trousers and fur-lined parka that she was wearing, and now the blanket too, she was soon freezing. She pulled her legs up so far that she almost had her knees in her mouth. She held them tight in her arms. Nevertheless, she could not control the shivering that had taken over her whole body. She had the impression that the car was wobbling and shaking. In spite of her fear, she almost grinned at one point, imagining a car bouncing around in the snowy night.

But her amusement only lasted a moment. Her situation was too scary.

She was wondering constantly whether she had done the right thing. Perhaps she should have carried on walking toward Manchester, knowing she would come across people at some point—a farmstead, a gritter, perhaps even hikers or a Nordic skier. But she knew that would not happen until the next afternoon, ten or twelve hours later, and she also knew she would not be able to keep going that long. She was completely exhausted. Her legs ached. Her whole body cried out for sleep. The danger was too great that she would at some point give in to the temptation to fall into the soft snow, just to rest for a few minutes. And if she were to fall asleep then, her fate would be sealed.

She would never wake up.

So the plan to regain her strength in the car and then set out the next morning was sensible, although she had not expected it to be so cold inside the sheltered space too. Nevertheless, between the upholstered seat and the

blanket she might manage to retain some body warmth
and at least reduce the chance of freezing to death.

Outside, she was sure to die; in here, it was only a
possibility. It was the best option she had right now.

She had also toyed with the idea of returning to the
hut and fetching the damned car key, but she quickly
dismissed that idea. Gillian must have been betting on
that when she took the key. It was the only explanation.
That meant Gillian would be prepared for her if she went
back. To do what Gillian expected would be an unnecessary risk. Tara had no intention of letting Gillian, in
fear of her life, smack her over the head with a drawer
or whatever else she found. Let Gillian lie in wait for
her there until she took root. Have fun.

She could not imagine that Gillian would manage
to free herself from the hut. It was impossible. But she
had seen stranger things, so she kept her knife in her
hand as she lay on the back seat. She had put the pistol
under the floormat. It seemed too dangerous to sleep
with a loaded weapon pressed up against her body. Feeling around in the trunk, she had found some wire. She
had made a noose with it and held it in her other hand.

She thought her main difficulty that night would be
to avoid falling asleep so deeply that she would never
wake up, but now she realized that she could not fall
asleep at all. Although she was utterly exhausted, so
many thoughts were racing around in her head that she
could not relax. She had told Gillian, the spoiled daughter of caring, over-protective parents who had no idea
about the real tragedies of life, everything—about Ted
Roslin and the trail of blood she was leaving in her wake
because of her need to find inner peace. Telling Gillian
had stirred things up inside her, and now she lay there
and it was as if she could feel the hammering of her

heart all the way up into her head. So many images appeared in front of her mind's eye.

Most of them she had never wanted to see again. She tried to put them out of her mind by forcing herself to make a full, orderly plan of everything she had to do once she was back in London. There was a lot of work waiting in the office. On Tuesday, she had an important day in court, and then she had a whole mountain of files to work her way through before another court day. Just the thought of the work was too much. But she also had to find the time to visit Liza again. The woman was on her own too much. She was safe from her husband, her torturer, but now danger threatened from another direction: her longing for her child. And her loneliness and the lack of future that she saw for herself.

She had to finally press charges against the bastard, Tara thought. She had been dreaming for weeks about it. It would make her so happy. But she had to be sure that Liza would go along with it. She knew women like Liza. They were unpredictable.

She had told Gillian about the first time she met Liza in a hotel ladies' room during a birthday party. Tara did not believe in chance. It was fate that she had gone to the toilet at that moment, when Charity Stanford's wife burst into tears and tried to hide her black eye. Tara had immediately understood why Liza was crying. She would have known even if she had not seen the injury. Victims of violence recognize one another. Even if they look completely unharmed on the outside. It is something about their aura. The violence they have experienced lies on their shoulders like a coat, wrapped around them, weighing down on them. Liza Stanford's suffering had been as clear to Tara as a glaring red exclamation mark.

"But why didn't you press charges immediately?" asked Gillian. Perhaps she should not hold the question against her. How was she to know?

"*She* has to bring him down, not me. She has to take pleasure in destroying him with her own strength. That's how she'll find her way again."

God, she had talked until she was blue in the face, trying to get Liza to report him. *Press charges. Put him in jail. Destroy him. God, it's payback time for him! Show him that he shouldn't have messed with you!*

Unfortunately, Liza was a classic victim. She was paralyzed with fear and unable to make any decisions. *I will. No, I won't. I don't know. I'm afraid. What should I do?*

When Liza shared the whole of her story of woe with Tara, something strange had happened: as Tara followed Liza into the depths of despair, doors on her own horrors opened that Tara had closed so carefully years ago. They sprang open and revealed images and feelings that she had hoped she would never again have to confront. There came a time when she no longer knew who was taking whom by the hand and leading the other to a personal hell. And although she was close to despair faced with Liza's hesitation, Tara recognized that she was not a jot better. She too had avoided any settling of scores. She had buried the garbage deep inside herself and hoped it would not start to stink. Now she realized how much poison had been collecting inside her. And that someone was still waiting for her. For her to bring things to a tidy conclusion.

Not Ted Roslin. That scumbag, who had convinced himself that he *loved* the child he was abusing, had died long ago after suffering protractedly with prostate cancer and early-onset dementia.

Lucy Caine-Roslin. Her mother. The woman who had betrayed her. She had not worked things out with her, not after all these years. Sometimes she had visited her in Gorton. She had boasted about her successes with satisfaction. University. Then her excellent exam results. Her work as a lawyer in Manchester. Her rise in the Crown Prosecution Service in London. Her good income. Her status. She had driven up to Reddish Lane in her swank Jaguar and gotten out dressed in elegant clothes. She had showed her how far she had gone and thought it would bring her contentment. But she had been too cowardly to talk about what had happened. And so she had not found contentment.

She tossed from side to side on the narrow back seat, trying to find a more comfortable position, but she did not manage. She thought about the dark November day when she had driven back to Manchester.

It had been the weekend. Liza had not yet left her home, but the situation between Logan and herself was becoming acute. Tara had become aware of her own past again. Because she always heard Liza's stories. Because she could not repress everything anymore.

It was already dark when arrived at her childhood home. She did not see a light on in any of the windows. She feared that her mother might not be at home, although that was unlikely. Lucy had withdrawn a lot since the death of her second husband. She barely went out, visited nobody. She only left the house to do her shopping or to go to the cemetery once a week to visit her husbands' graves. Apart from that, she spent her time cleaning her apartment, watching romantic comedies on television, or reading the latest story about the royal family in the gossip mags. She never seemed to be dissatisfied or unhappy. As a young woman, the idea of living without a partner had sent her half crazy, but now in her old age she had had to get used to the situation. She coped surprisingly well.

As always, the house's front door was not locked. Tara found Lucy in the living room, whose windows looked out on the back yard and the workshop. Lucy was sitting in front of the television, as was to be expected. While watching television, she was working on one of the many ridiculous doilies that she placed all around the apartment. She was wearing a thick, fluffy sweater and fur-lined slippers, because it was not very warm in the house. Lucy always saved on heating costs. A pot of tea sat on the table in front of her.

Lucy had been happy to see her daughter, in the reserved manner in which she normally showed her emotions. As the dining room heating was not on at all, she and Tara set the table in the kitchen. Tara had brought food from a Chinese takeout, as well as an expensive red wine from London. Lucy's cheeks began to glow after her first sips, and her eyes shone.

"It's like Christmas," she said.

Tara leaned forward. She had taken a few sips of wine, but had barely touched her food. She was not hungry.

"Mom, I've come to talk to you about something," she said. Although she had been shivering when she came in, she realized that her whole body felt hot now. "There's something we need to talk about."

Lucy looked at her with an unsuspecting look. "Yes, dear?"

"Ted," said Tara.

Lucy looked confused. "What about him?"

"We've never talked about him."

Lucy shook her head sadly. "And now he's been dead

so many years! You should visit his grave again. I went a few days ago. I put a pot of heather by his gravestone. It looks pretty."

"I should?" Tara knew that she sounded aggressive and that was something she had meant to avoid. "Why should I visit Ted's grave? I could visit Dad's grave, but *his*? Never! Did you leave heather at Dad's grave, by the way?"

"Of course. What's gotten into you? Why are you so angry?"

"Me? I'm not angry. I'm sorry if it looked like that." Tara surprised herself. Inside, she was fighting to control an extreme hostility that she felt simply at the sight of her mother, but she was managing to sound calm and friendly. The job, she thought. She had learned to treat terrible people in whatever way was most advantageous to her, in order to get them where she wanted them. As a public prosecutor, it is pointless to go on the attack against the man sitting opposite you who beat his four-month-old baby to death and tell him what you really think of him. It was sometimes useful to listen to such people with a sympathetic demeanor so that they would break into tears and confess their crimes in between sobs, because they felt that they could confide in this motherly figure. Then she could calmly demand the maximum sentence. It had often worked.

"Mom, I just want to understand something. That's why I've come. The fact I *haven't* understood it until now is why I visit so rarely. Although I could do a lot more for you."

"I don't understand," said Lucy. She looked more alert now.

"We have to talk about everything," said Tara. "So we can have a good relationship in the future."

"We do?"

"Like I said, it's about Ted." She looked closely at her mother. "You know what he did to me."

Lucy closed up like a clam. You could see it clearly in her face. "Are you bringing that up again?"

"Again?" Tara stared at her mother. "Did you say '*again*'? When have I ever brought it up?"

"A long time ago," Lucy said, "you visited a few times and wanted to make things difficult for me…." She stood up. "I really thought you wanted to have a nice evening with me," she said, hurt. "That you missed your mother and wanted to have a chat—and now you attack me and accuse me and—"

"Sit down, Mom," ordered Tara. Her voice was so sharp that Lucy did actually sit back down on her chair. "This time you aren't going to brush me off that easily. Or run away from it. You're going to sit here and answer my questions. Understand?"

"What tone of voice is that to use with me?"

"The one you deserve, Mom. The one a mother deserves who lets her little daughter be raped for five years by her stepfather without intervening a single time. *Not once!*"

"Five years…." said Lucy. "You always exaggerate!"

"Five years, Mom. I should know. I was nine when he started. Half a year after your damn wedding. And I was fourteen when he stopped. Because I was finally, thank God, looking like a woman and he was no longer interested."

"What do you want?" asked Lucy. Her breathing had become labored. There was an unhealthy sound coming from her chest. "To give me an asthma attack? To kill me?"

"Shut up about your asthma! You never had asthma.

You always just started to wheeze when things got uncomfortable for you. But that doesn't cut it with me anymore."

"I really want to know—" Lucy started to say, but Tara interrupted her.

"No, *I* really want to know something! I want to know why you let him. Why you didn't help me. Why you didn't protect me. Why you didn't kick that repulsive bastard out!"

Lucy reached for a handkerchief. In a minute, she would start to cry. "I'm old. I've got no one in the world apart from you. And now you come here and do this! To an old woman who can't defend herself!"

"What about the child who couldn't defend herself?"

Lucy dabbed at her eyes. "Good Lord, you make it out as if…."

"Yes? As if what?" asked Tara.

"As if something terrible had happened. Just because Ted liked you. He was a good man. It wouldn't have been easy to find another husband. Who marries a widow who has a child? Without you, I'd have had more opportunities; you must be able to see that?"

Later, Tara remembered that this was the moment when she had felt a dizzy haze set in. Just a little, but she had felt something change inside her. She had not been able to see as clearly, and a quiet humming started up in her ears.

"So you think nothing terrible happened?" she asked quietly. "Do you think it's normal for a man who is almost fifty to get into a nine-year-old's bed every night? To clamp a hand over her mouth when she tries to scream? To tell her that she'll end up in an orphanage if she tells anyone? Do you think that's *nothing terrible*?"

Lucy blew her nose. She had pulled herself together. "It wasn't easy for me either."

"Oh! Really?"

"You always just think about yourself," said Lucy. "You don't care about my situation. I had to live with his rejection of me. Whatever I tried, he ignored me. He was fixed on you. He waited at the gate for you to come home from school. His eyes followed you everywhere. And I was invisible to him. Air. As a woman, I mean. I cooked for him and did his laundry. I cleaned the apartment, keeping our house nice and cozy. I took out of the housekeeping money as much as I could to buy pretty things. To look good for him. But he didn't notice. He didn't notice *me*."

The humming in her ears increased.

"You were a grown woman. I was a *child*!"

Suddenly, for just a split second, an expression of hatred was visible in Lucy's eyes. "A child! A calculating little vixen, you were! You were young—and you took advantage of that! With your tight jeans, your clinging T-shirts. You enjoyed taking my place, as if I were some old bag. I was thirty-five! I wasn't old. I was pretty. But of course I couldn't compete with you."

Tara did not notice herself standing up. The kitchen was swaying around her. It was pointless. They were not going to work anything out. Not now. Never. Her mother was not going to regret anything. She didn't even understand.

Her mother thought *she* was the victim.

"I don't think I can forgive you, Mom," she said.

Lucy got up too. She reached automatically for the tea towel hanging by the oven, as she always did, and wiped a small smudge of sauce from the tabletop.

"Forgive what?" she asked. She did not sound cynical or ironic. Not even bitter or hurt.

It just sounded like…a question.

And all Tara's pain was there once again. The feeling of having been abandoned. Her despair. Her horror. Her helplessness. All her fear. The endless torment. The ebbing hope.

She realized that none of that had ever left her. And would never leave her. She would feel completely alone in the world. That she had no one. In free fall in a hell. Betrayed by the woman who had been the first person in her life: the person who had given birth to her.

And in that moment, her gaze fell on the red-and-white-checked tea towel that her mother was using to wipe the table.

"You still have this old tea towel," she heard herself say. It was the moment when she lost control.

She had not imagined how good it would feel.

11

SHE LET OUT a cry of triumph. In the complete silence that surrounded her, it sounded louder than it probably was.

"No way!" she screamed.

She was holding the table leg in her hand. She did not know how long it had taken, but she guessed that a good three quarters of an hour must have passed until she had worked it free of the glue. Then she had rocked it back and forth for ages. And suddenly, just when she thought she had no strength left, when the sweat was pouring down her face and body, the screw gave way. Gillian could pull the table leg out of its place, as if it had been meant to slip out like that all along.

I can't believe it! It worked! It really worked!

Needing a minute to gather her strength, she sank down onto the sofa, wiped the sweat from her brow, and tried to calm her panting breath. Just for a moment. She did not have much more time. Tara might come back any minute. Tara was her greatest enemy now and the biggest danger she faced. And if Tara found her, she would not risk leaving her in a hut—admittedly, a hut almost as secure as Fort Knox—a second time and trust that the cold weather would finish her off. This time she would deal with her herself. Suffocate her with a tea towel stuffed deep down her throat. As she had done to her mother. And to Carla Roberts and Anne Westley.

Earlier, Tara had leaned against the stove and talked about the problem of failing to render assistance as Gillian sat, immobile, on the sofa. Not talked—lectured. Gillian had not had the impression that an answer was expected of her, so she had remained silent.

Failure to render assistance is not given serious enough consideration as a crime. Neither in our society or in court. Many people think it's of minor concern. The perpetrator is the baddie. The person who just watches and doesn't do anything...well, maybe they didn't act quite as they should have, but they shouldn't be put on a par with the perpetrator. And that is why the person who stands by and does nothing is often ignored. People even feel some sympathy, perhaps. After all, in all honesty, who knows how we would act in such a situation.

She stood up and grabbed the table leg with both hands. She tried to gather all her remaining strength for her first strike. She raised her arms and smashed the table leg into the shutters with all her force. Nothing moved.

Gillian paused, gathered her strength again. One

more try. *Give it all you've got, Gillian! Come on! You can do it. You have to do it.*

The next powerful blow.

She heard something crunch. Maybe something gave too, but she could not see any change.

Of course a culprit should be punished and locked up. But normally it's someone with a screw or two loose and you get the impression that the person is never going to be normal. The lives of these people, especially their childhoods, read like horror stories. Now, I'm not saying that someone is bound to be a serial killer because his mother was an alcoholic and his father abused him, but it's...it relativizes things, doesn't it? But those people who just watch and don't say anything, there's nothing you could put on the scales in their favor. In our country, parents let their children starve to death, or torture them to death, and their neighbors turn a blind eye. In our country, women are abused by their husbands and everyone claims they never saw a thing. In our country, pupils are bullied by their classmates to the point that they throw themselves under a train, but the teachers don't intervene. These things happen everywhere, all the time. And it only happens because the majority of the population is too cowardly, too uninterested, too lethargic to do anything.

What had she been thinking about beforehand? She had imagined a battering ram before she had thought about using the table leg. Perhaps she was going about it the wrong way with her little blows. Perhaps she should try to ram the table leg against the shutters one single time.

She grabbed it with both hands and, taking a run up, smashed the table leg into the shutters.

The shutters shuddered. This time she *was* sure. She

examined the hinges. There was a couple of millimeters between them and the shutters' wood now.

It might work. Perhaps she would finally be lucky this time on this terrible day. Breathing heavily, she took a short break. Her hands hurt. Just a short rest, and then she would go on the offensive again.

Tara had told her Liza Stanford's crazy story. Gillian did not know Logan Stanford personally, but she had often read about him in the newspaper. The man did not look all that nice in the pictures she saw of him, but she would never have guessed that he was so sick and violent. Gillian had always had the impression that he was less interested in doing good than in being in all the papers. But that had not bothered her. After all, the money he raised helped people in need, and that was what counted. Who cared about his motives? Certainly it was better to do good because you needed recognition than to do nothing at all.

The fact that his wife was hiding from him, that he had tormented her for years—Gillian had been astounded.

"Charity Stanford? No way! Are you sure?"

"I saw Liza. That evening in the hotel. Her black eye. And later she showed me her whole body. Scars, bruises, grazed skin. The honorable lawyer is a sadist. And a psychopath!"

"And she's let him do that to her for years?"

"Yes, these stories are always hard to believe. Almost incomprehensible. But they happen all the time. The victims don't say a word and hope that everything will improve, if they can just fit in better. If they can find a way not to annoy the perpetrator. Because that is what they believe, on some level of their consciousness: that it's all their fault. That something is wrong with them

*which forces their tormentor to act as he does. Logan
Stanford as the victim, you see? That he had married
an impossible woman. That it was Liza's fault that he
was angry and lost control."*

*"Was there no one she could have talked to about
it?...and who would have helped her to leave him immediately?"*

*"Over the course of the years, she confided in two
people. A friend, and her son's doctor."*

"And?"

"Carla Roberts. And Dr. Anne Westley."

She understood immediately. As soon as Tara mentioned the names. Carla Roberts and Anne Westley. She
understood the whole affair. Tara's motive for the deaths
of two apparently harmless elderly women.

"The two of them didn't help, right?"

*"No. Roberts was so wrapped up in her own woes
that she did not take much notice. And Westley was obviously so unsure about what to do that she ended up
doing nothing. Neither of them intervened at all. Liza
was not given the chance to accept any help."*

Failure to render assistance. The theme of the public prosecutor's life. Carla Roberts and Anne Westley
had acted like Lucy Caine-Roslin: they shut their eyes.
Anything to not take a closer look. Not to risk any awkward situation.

"And that's why you...the two of them?"

*"Believe it or not, I didn't plan to. I was pretty angry
with the two women. They had let down someone in a
real emergency, which had only strengthened Logan
Stanford's hand. But I didn't think I would kill them. I
wanted to frighten them a little. To jolt them out of their
smug, contented lives. I terrorized them. Liza Stanford
lived in mortal fear night and day. I wanted the two of*

them to have some inkling, at the least, of what that felt like."

"I see."

"It was easy to tamper with the door to the apartment building where Carla lived. I could come and go whenever I wanted, whenever I had time. It was fun to send the empty elevator up to her floor sometimes. That can wear a person down. As can a car turning up at night in the back of beyond where Anne lived. Headlights gliding across the walls of her room. An engine cutting out. But no one appearing."

"I'm sure that was effective."

"Yes, it was. The two old women certainly got nervous. But...."

"But it wasn't enough for you?"

Gillian took a deep breath. The worst of it all was that she felt weaker every minute. But she could not give up. She had gotten this far. She had a real chance now if she could keep it up.

She thought of Becky. Becky needed her.

One last, desperate try. With all her energy and all her weight, and holding the table leg in both hands, she threw herself at the shutters.

There was a deafening crack as one of the shutters broke away from the wall. It flew out, pulling the other shutter after it. The two bolted-together shutters slammed against the hut's outside wall, banged two or three times against the wall, and then hung there, immobile.

The window was open.

Gillian looked out into the night, at the snow, and needed a few seconds to realize that it had really happened. She had freed herself from an apparently hopeless situation. Her arms were shaking, her muscles screaming with pain from the unaccustomed effort.

She was free.

It was important to think about what she would do next so as not to rush into anything risky.

She stowed the valuable keys deep in her coat pocket, checking several times that they could not possibly fall out. Then she put the water bottle, in which there was still a little water, into her other pocket. It was too big to fit in comfortably and felt awkward there, sticking half out of her pocket, but it was important to have something to drink before she had to resort to eating snow. The flashlight, which had been of invaluable help already, went in the pocket with the keys. That was all she needed—at least, it was all she could lay her hands on right now.

She heaved herself up onto the windowsill and jumped down the other side. The branch of a pine tree smacked her in the face, scratching her, but she barely noticed. She landed in soft, deep snow, picked herself up immediately, and cautiously went around to the front of the hut. She peered around the corner.

There was no one in sight. The snow reflected light from the moon that shone through large gaps in the clouds. Gillian fought her way through the small wooded area and then stood still. From here, she had a good view. Behind her and to her sides lay the woods. In front of her lay the flat land that she and Tara had trudged across a few hours ago. She could even see their footprints in the snow. It would not be difficult to follow them back to the car.

What was less pleasing was that the plain offered nowhere to hide. Walking along it, she would be visible from afar as a clearly outlined dark form. If Tara

was on her way back to the hut, she would be able to
see her from a long way away. Of course, the reverse
was also true.

Gillian examined the landscape carefully once more
and considered following the edge of a distant strip of
woodland, to remain concealed under the trees. Yet that
would have meant a wide detour, making the distance
almost twice as far. And she ran the risk of losing her
way. There were no footprints to follow, and if she went
astray in those wide woods she would not survive two
days in this cold. She decided to take the same path
they had come on. She would see Tara early enough to
give her time to think about what she should do. After
all, she had one small advantage: *she* expected to meet
Tara, while Tara would assume that she was out here
on her own.

She set off, trudging through the deep snow. She
knew that after everything she had gone through, she
should really be afraid of not being able to cover the
long distance through the snow. However, the eupho-
ria of the moment of her escape had pumped a good
dose of adrenaline into her body. From somewhere or
other, she found an energy that she should not rightly
have anymore.

I can do it. She won't kill me.

Without warning, she heard Tara's voice again and
felt the shudder of horror that it had caused in her.

*"No, at some point it wasn't enough just to scare
Roberts and Westley."*

"And that's when you killed them?"

*"Yes. But at the moment I did it...it wasn't them I was
killing. They were just a continuation of a moment that
had freed me. But that hadn't satisfied me completely.
I'll never, never, never be satisfied."*

"What do you mean?"

"I mean I can't stop. When I killed Roberts and West-ley, I recognized that I won't be able to stop for as long as I live."

"Stop what?"

"Lucy. My mother. I can't stop killing my mother."

12

JOHN HAD NOT expected that a region like the Peak Dis-trict would have cul-de-sacs, but it seemed that they had landed in just such a road. They had followed the country lane for ages without seeing Tara's car, and now suddenly everything ended in a kind of turning circle. Without any warning. Dense woods lay ahead of them and to either side. And nowhere was there any sign of another car, let alone of a hut or of two women trudg-ing through the snow.

John was forced to turn the car around. But first he stopped. "All right. Looks like that's as far as we're going with this road. It must have been the wrong one."

Samson sounded depressed. "There must be tons of roads like this around here."

"No doubt. Let me see the map again."

He studied it. "I'd say we're somewhere around here. In other words, we're still in the area that Sherman cir-cled. Although pretty near the bottom edge of it. The hut might be nearer the center."

"If it is even in the area. Sherman never saw the hut himself, remember. And it's thirty years since the hut's location was described to him," Samson reminded him.

John felt like flinging the book at Samson, but he controlled himself. "Of course. He might have gotten it wrong in his mind. Or the hut might no longer exist.

Maybe Tara Caine headed somewhere completely different. She and Gillian could be in Cornwall. Or Scotland. Or in a godforsaken Welsh village. Who knows. But this hut is the only minuscule lead we have, and although I'm going half crazy thinking that we might be wasting our and especially Gillian's time here, we've got no other choice. All the other options are even more absurd."

"Of-of course," agreed Samson. "So…we'll drive back?"

John turned the engine back on. "Yes. I remember that back near the start of the lane, there was a turn-off. It seemed to head north. We should try it next."

"But it was a very narrow lane."

"It looked plowed to me. And who knows which road it might lead to. The roads here are like a spider's web— each thread is connected to all the others. At some point, we'll have tried them all." They drove on. The evening was sunk in complete darkness. Samson looked anxiously out the window, always hoping to discover some decisive clue. One thing he was sure of: their theory that the women had only taken the more important roads seemed to be true. He could not even make out any of the minor tracks for all the snow.

It's going to be okay, he said silently to himself, but he was not sure if he believed his own words.

He had not noticed that they had driven down the dead-end road for so long. In any case, the drive back seemed to take ages. They had rejected the turn-off the first time for being too narrow. They had not had any other options on their drive after that one.

"It's taking too long," John moaned through gritted teeth.

They turned into the lane. It appeared to lead to a wide, hilly, treeless landscape.

"The high moors," said John. "They start here." He cursed. "Sherman mentioned the moors. We came too far south. I should have noticed that earlier."

He braked as the road divided. They had come to a small crossroads. They could carry on straight ahead, or turn right or left.

"Shit," said Samson.

"We might as well toss a coin," said John. He peered out, trying to get his bearings. "Sherman said that the hut was built on the edge of some woodland. Which makes sense. Caine's father built the log cabin himself, and he won't have wanted to drag tree trunks over hill and dale. Where can we see some woods?"

Both men got out. The wind, which seemed strong and—at least it seemed to them—colder, made them jump.

"God, it's cold," said John. He breathed into hands that already felt frozen from the shock of the cold. Hopefully Gillian was not out in the open, somewhere in this wide expanse, far from any human habitation. You could easily freeze to death on a night like this.

"Over there," said Samson. He pointed north. "I think there's a wood on the horizon!"

The slightly darker strip running along the distant horizon could really be a wood, John had to admit. That would mean that they needed to carry on straight ahead. They could not see anything to the right or left, although that did not necessary mean that there *wasn't* a wood there. In those directions the terrain was more hilly and it was not possible to see as far. They could only see to the first large hills. What lay behind them was anyone's guess.

"Let's carry on in this direction," decided John. "Perhaps you're right, Samson, and that is a wood over there.

We can't see anything else, so—as we've done until now—we need to be happy with the tiny leads we have. Onward!"

They got back in. They drove on. Following their tiny chance.

13

SHE REALLY HAD fallen asleep in the end, although she had wanted to avoid that at all costs. She woke with a start from a confused dream. Trying to sit up, a pain in her whole body stopped her. What was it? Everything hurt—every bone, muscle, and nerve. She groaned, but then the realization penetrated her sleepy haze that she had not suddenly fallen victim to some mysterious illness. What she was feeling was the result of the cramped way she had been lying. And the terrible cold. She had the impression that she had literally frozen stiff. She could not let herself fall asleep like that again. It was dangerous. She was lucky that something had woken her.

Something? Her dream, perhaps. She had stood in front of her mother, and Lucy had been talking to her. She had spoken so quietly that Tara had not understood anything. She had only seen her lips move and strained to hear a word or two. But in vain. She had pleaded with Lucy to speak up, but Lucy had just smiled and ignored her wish. It had driven Tara crazy to imagine that Lucy might be saying something very important, the answer to all her questions, but that it would be lost because she could not hear her. Her heart had started to beat wildly. And that is what had woken her.

The thought came to her that her dead mother might have saved her from freezing to death by appearing in her dream. Was it possible? It would be the first time that her mother had ever intervened on her behalf. Tara didn't know if she liked the thought of this or not. She had waited for years for Lucy to treat her like a mother should, and now she wasn't sure if she still wanted it.

No, I don't, she decided and, ignoring the pain coursing through her body, she sat up.

And saw Gillian.

She was perhaps ten paces from the car. Not that Tara could actually recognize it as Gillian: she just saw in the moonlight a dark figure outlined against the white snow. The figure was standing there, immobile, apparently looking at the car.

It could only be Gillian. Who else would be wandering around in this wilderness?

Tara was now wide awake. She lowered herself slowly back down onto the back seat. She wondered whether Gillian had seen her, or at the least seen a movement inside the car. If so, she had not reacted at all. Because of her stiff bones, Tara had only sat up partially, and without any quick movements, so she might not have been visible from outside.

Damn it, damn it, damn it! She felt queasy just to think that she might still have been sleeping. Gillian would have been able to overpower her easily. It would have been the end of everything.

How on earth had she managed to leave the hut? The hut was so secure that it was practically impossible to get in or out when it was locked up. The only imaginable possibility was that Gillian had somehow found a tool that had helped her to break the lock or the shutters. But there was nothing inside the hut, absolutely nothing. Tara had emptied it years ago. There was no cutlery, no bottle opener, no toothbrush, nothing. The only thing Gillian had to hand were two keys. It was a mystery how she had managed to get out with them.

The keys. *The car key.* It was within reach now. If she could take care of Gillian, then she would have the key. And finally be able to leave this inhospitable place. She felt goose bumps all over as she imagined turning on the engine and cranking up the hot air. The longing for warmth was so strong, she could have cried.

But she needed to keep a clear head. She tried to fish out her pistol, but it had slipped too far forward under the front passenger seat. She could not find it. Never mind, she was a lousy shot anyway and only hit her target when it was right in front of the barrel. She had the knife in her hand, but she could not rule out the possibility that Gillian was armed. After all, she had used *something* to free herself from her prison. Nor was Tara's position on the back seat particularly good. If Gillian looked into the car before she got in....

Cautiously, Tara pulled the blanket up over herself and the whole back seat. She pressed herself as flat as she could into the soft upholstery. Of course, the blanket had been in the trunk. But she doubted that Gillian would notice such details right now. And she, Tara, had the upper hand, because she knew where Gillian was. Gillian, on the other hand, had no idea where the woman who wanted her life was. She probably thought she was on a long, arduous trek through the Peak District, heading toward Manchester.

Tara jumped when a metallic sound seemed to twitch through the whole car. What was it? Then she relaxed again. Gillian had used the remote to open the doors. Tara grinned. Luckily, she had locked the doors from the inside. Gillian would assume that the car had been locked the whole time. She would never expect to find Tara inside.

Come on, she mouthed. *Get in. Sit down at the wheel. Come on.*

She heard the crunch of footsteps on snow. She held her breath, melting into the back seat under the folds of the enormous blanket. She made herself small, invisible.

The driver's door opened.

Tara held the knife and the wire noose tightly in her hands.

14

THIS TIME SHE had covered the distance more quickly, in spite of her exhaustion. Fear had driven her. Gillian gave a sigh of relief when she finally saw the car. She was not surprised to find it, because how would Tara have started it? Her steps become slower and more cautious. As she had not seen Tara on the walk back, she had realized that Tara had not gone back to try to fetch the key, and would not. She had probably continued on foot toward Manchester.

She looked carefully at the car for a while from a safe distance. She could see many footprints in the snow. They were probably from when Tara and she had set off the previous afternoon. Although some could be fresh footprints left by Tara. She had no doubt only realized that she did not have her keys when she was standing by the car. Gillian imagined how she would have rummaged anxiously through her bag, becoming more and more panicky. It must have been a terrible moment for her. To have been so close—and yet completely helpless.

Nothing moved, so after a good while she pointed the key at the car and bleeped the doors. The lights went

on for a second and the door locks opened. If the doors
had not been locked, the sound would have been different, as Gillian knew. Good. No one had opened the car
since she and Tara had left.

She approached tentatively.

When she reached the driver's door, she let her eyes
sweep around the car's interior. She thought she would
need to use the flashlight, but by now there was a cloudless night sky, and the light of the moon, strengthened by
its reflection off the fields of snow, was sufficient to see.

The car was empty. The blanket lay on the back seat
in thick folds. She opened the door.

Knocking the snow off her boots, she got in. She sank
into the driver's seat, trying to put the key in the ignition. The first two times, she failed because her fingers
were so numb from the cold. The third time, her trembling prodding finally met with success. She turned the
key in the lock. The engine started with a splutter and
then stalled immediately.

No doubt because of the cold. Tara had sometimes
said that in really cold weather, her thoroughbred Jaguar struggled.

Come on, start!

The second attempt also failed. Experience with her
own car had taught her that in such situations, it was
best to wait a minute before trying again. Normally that
did the trick. She leaned back, leaning her head on the
headrest. She tried to calm herself down.

She was so nervous that her whole body was shaking.
She had almost managed. She had freed herself from the
most dangerous situation of her whole life. Now the engine just needed to start and she would finally be safe.

Stop trembling! You've won!

She could not shake off the feeling of a lurking danger. Something made her heart pound, sent shivers up her arms, and shot adrenaline through her body. It was almost worse than it had been before. She had felt this terrible fear and horror outside the car.

Now don't get hysterical!

She was just about to lean forward and try to start the engine for a third time when she suddenly understood. Her instinct had understood long ago, but her brain had needed a little longer: the blanket. The old, scratchy woolen blanket should have been in the trunk.

Not on the back seat!

She pushed the car door open and tried to reach safety with a quick dive from the car. At the same time a black shadow suddenly appeared and filled the rearview mirror. Gillian was a fraction of a second too late. The wire noose had been dropped over her head and was cutting into her neck. A sensation of indescribable pain. The noose was tugged tight so violently that Gillian, who had tried to get out, was pulled back. Panicking, she grabbed at the wire with both hands. The wire was suffocating her, crushing her larynx. Only a desperate rattle came out of her mouth.

"Stay still," said Tara. Her voice sounded peaceful, almost tender. "Stay still; otherwise you'll strangle yourself!"

Gillian obeyed. The pressure decreased somewhat. She could breathe a bit better once more, but her throat still hurt like hell. Tara had tugged on the noose so ferociously that the wire had buried itself deep into her skin. No doubt the marks would be visible for weeks.

If she had weeks left to live.

Her head was pressed into the headrest by the noose, forcing her whole body to stay seated too. While she struggled to breathe evenly, she swore silently at herself for being such a damned fool.

When she had still been standing by the car, trying to weigh up all the myriad possibilities, she had assumed that because the car could be *unlocked* using the remote, that Tara had *locked* it that afternoon when they both had left it. So she had been sure Tara was not in the car, as Tara could not unlock it without the key. She had not considered the possibility that the car had been unlocked and that Tara had gotten in and then locked the doors from the inside. She had just not seen that as a possibility. Worn down to the point of utter exhaustion as she was, her brain had simply not been working reliably. She had seen the woolen blanket on the back seat, and not even then had a warning light come on in her head.

Stupid, stupid, stupid woman! She groaned.

"Yes, messed that one up," agreed Tara, as if she could read her thoughts. "Sometimes people fall for the simplest tricks. But don't beat yourself up about it. Other people have done the same."

Gillian had to cough. The pain from her larynx was pulsing down into her neck and her shoulders. Her whole throat felt sore. Tara had pulled on the noose with such force that Gillian felt lucky that she had not been beheaded immediately.

"Wh—" she croaked.

"You shouldn't talk," said Tara.

Gillian heard the knife flick open. Then she felt the cold blade against her skin just below her right ear. She jerked away in despair and paid for her sudden movement as the noose cut deep into her skin once more. She moaned in pain and then went back to her previous position.

"Good girl," said Tara. "You're a quick learner. Don't try anything stupid. It won't work."

"Wh—" she tried once more.

"Wh-wh-wh-wh," Tara aped her. With the blade of the knife, she toyed with Gillian's earlobe. "Go on, talk. What do you so desperately need to tell me?"

A feeling of hopelessness and mourning fell on Gillian like lead. She had struggled so hard. And yet still lost.

Although her throat ached, she managed to form a few words in the end.

"Wh...y?" she asked. "Why...me?"

"Yes, why you?" repeated Tara. "I've told you so much about myself and you still can't work it out? You still don't get it? The mistake you made? The *unforgiveable* mistake?"

Gillian did not say anything.

In that moment she understood. Her mistake. The mistake that in Tara's sick mind must have seemed like a rerun of Tara's own story. "John," she groaned.

Tara touched her almost gently with the blade. "Right. John. He was your mistake."

Gillian coughed again. "I...think John is innocent," she blurted out. "And your colleague...the public prosecutor...did too."

Tara snorted scornfully. "Do you know who was responsible for Burton's case?"

"No."

"But I do. A nitpicker. A coward. Someone who from morning to night just thinks about how to not make life difficult for himself. You know, us prosecutors are pretty careful about pressing charges. None of us wants to lose in court. But of course we can never be a hundred percent sure. We don't know what arguments the opposing lawyer will bring. Nor which witnesses he will call on or what unexpected twists and turns the case might take. We don't know how the judge will decide. There's always some risk. And some of us are more prepared to take risks than others.

"Burton was lucky. The guy who was assigned his case is known for being so careful that he presses charges less often than any other prosecutor. He practically needs to be presented with proof on a silver platter before he will pluck up the courage to break cover. There were unresolved questions in Burton's case. You see? The fact that there was no court case doesn't mean anything. Not if you consider the lawyer who was responsible for his case."

"But—"

"No *but*!" Tara said sharply. "You want to say that you didn't know that. So what! You have a little girl. A defenseless child. And you get involved with a guy who has been investigated for a *sex offense*? You take the risk of putting this guy near your daughter? Just because you can't stand your husband but you need a man? You take your daughter's innocence, her mental and physical well-being, that lightly? And find that *normal*?"

"I—"

"Yes, I-I-I! It's always about you. You had the hots for him and you just brushed away all other concerns. Convinced yourself everything was great. He won't have done anything! Of course the girl who reported him was a liar. He's an angel! You know what, Gillian? A woman who is responsible for no one but herself can do that. Not that I can really understand that either, but that's not my business! But you have Becky. And I had decided I was going to save Becky. She should not have to go through what I had gone through. Never."

Gillian coughed again. Her voice was getting back to normal, but her throat was still on fire.

"You knew that before Christmas?" she asked. She had only told Tara about John's past in the New Year, but Tara's first attempt to kill her former friend had been carried out just after Christmas. And killed Tom, who was completely innocent. It was so horrific. And perverse. A woman running amok. And no one, but *no one* had noticed. Not even the faintest suspicion had fallen on Tara. The investigation had not left a stone unturned; meanwhile, she had been able to continue to act out her hatred and all-consuming need for revenge.

"The name Burton rang a bell when I heard it. I couldn't quite figure out why. I was in Manchester at the time that all happened. I just knew that someone at some point had mentioned his name in connection with an investigation. It wasn't hard for me to get ahold of his file. It was also clear to me that you knew too. You don't lie well, Gillian. When you finally told me the truth, I just pretended to be horrified. I'd known for a long time."

Gillian coughed again. She wished the ball of fire in her throat would go away. She wished she could stuff a handful of snow into her mouth.

"Tara, please don't carry on like this. You've killed enough innocents. The two old women in Tunbridge Wells and London…they failed Liza, but that doesn't justify murdering them. Tom didn't do anything to anyone. But after what you've told me about your childhood—I can understand why you just saw this one way to go. I really can."

"Can you now?"

"Yes," said Gillian in despair. She realized that Tara did not believe her, but she was not lying. Tara had gone through the worst hell that a child could pass through. No one had helped her. Not her mother, nor anyone near her who had noticed the changes in the girl's behavior that must have been visible. Her neighbors, her teachers, and the friends of her parents had all failed her. Gillian did not feel a grown-up woman's icy hatred and cold-blooded cruelty in Tara.

She felt the bottomless despair of a helpless child.

"I'd testify for you, Tara. Any judge who heard your story would—"

"Would what? Let me go free? How naïve are you, Gillian? Of course they'll lock me up, if they get me. They'll say that yes, my childhood was horrible, but that at the end of the day you can't just let a ticking time bomb loose on the streets. Funny old world, isn't it? Roslin didn't go to jail. Nor did my mother. Burton can waltz around the neighborhood. Charity Stanford won't be punished either, because Liza, the stupid cow, will never report him. But I…I might be caught. And spend the rest of my life behind bars. That's justice for you! And I'm not going to accept that."

The pressure of the wire on Gillian's neck increased.

For a moment she closed her eyes. Her situation was hopeless. She had no idea how she could reach Tara now. When she opened her eyes again, she thought she saw a light flash in the distance briefly. It disappeared again immediately, but before Gillian could dismiss it as a crazy delusion of her overheated brain, it appeared again. This time for longer, then it disappeared again. And reappeared again.

Gillian stared into the blackness, as if she wanted to penetrate it with her eyes. It couldn't be, could it? Probably some physical phenomenon, starlight, something reflected off the snow. Normally she would have thought she was seeing the headlights of a car. A car approaching, whose headlights rose and dipped with the gentle roll of the hills. But that was absurd. Of course there were hunters who came out here, and park rangers, and even in winter an occasional group of hikers. But not at this time of night. Even young lovers who wanted to enjoy themselves without anyone else around would never drive this deep into the Peak District at night in the winter.

Don't get your hopes up. No way is it a car. You're completely on your own with this crazy woman, and you've got a noose around your neck and a knife against your cheek. You're in one hell of a mess. That's all there is to it.

She closed her eyes and then opened them as if she wanted to force what she had just seen to happen again. And it worked. The light was there again. And now she could see that it really was *two* lights. It *was* a car out in the night.

And it was approaching.

Tara had obviously not seen it yet. She was talking about something Gillian did not understand, and then she suddenly said, "Okay. It's time." She emphasized her words with a tug of the noose.

Gillian gave out a cry.

"I didn't want to do it myself," said Tara. "You were my friend for years, Gillian. But you're a threat to me now. I'd have preferred you to have died in the hut, but since you had to break out…I didn't have any other choice but to take you out. I don't want to go to jail. You understand?"

"Yes."

"Good. Let's get out. Slowly now."

Gillian thought desperately about how she could

waste some time. Someone was driving down the road and, unless she was completely out of luck, this unknown driver, whoever it was, would be right there within ten minutes. They would no doubt be surprised to see a car standing there and, assuming the car had broken down, would stop to help.

It'd just be stupid if I was already dead by then!

There must be some topic or other on which Tara could be got talking.

I have to ask her questions, she thought, questions about the past. Someone with her life story must be burning to tell and explain some things.

She had an idea. She grasped at it like at a straw. Tara had told her how she had killed her mother. She had stuffed a tea towel down her throat and put masking tape over her nose. She had let her suffocate to death. And then she dragged her from the kitchen to her, Tara's, former bedroom. To the place of the crimes of her childhood.

The sight of the tea towel had been the trigger for the murder.

"I want to know one more thing, Tara," she said. And continued quickly, before Tara could interrupt. "That tea towel that you…that you—"

"That I suffocated my mother with? And the other two women?"

Gillian breathed out with relief. "Yes. That one. Why…why did you decide to use it? Or was it just coincidence?"

As if it mattered. But every second that she won now could be decisive. She saw the lights again. Much closer. The car had not changed direction.

"Coincidence? Nothing in this affair has been just coincidence," said Tara scornfully. Then she changed her tone. "Except for Tom…he happened to be at the wrong place at the wrong time. I didn't have anything against him."

"The tea towel," reminded Gillian.

"Yes. The tea towel. Didn't I mention that yet?" She sounded indifferent, with the strange unnatural manner she had had all day. "My mother was always a really good housewife. She was always cleaning and dusting. *You can eat off the floor in our house*, she liked to say. Her spotless, pretty house was very important to her. She had made the curtains herself, and the house was full of doilies and horrible African violets in overly or-nate porcelain pots. Yes, and she had these things within reach all over the house. These checked tea towels. So she could immediately whisk away every speck of dust or dirt." Tara paused and thought for a moment. Gillian had the impression that she was choosing her words carefully, that she wanted to be fair in her analysis of her mother. She was a lawyer, after all. She did not just make unfounded accusations. "I wouldn't say she was an obsessive-compulsive, but she was very thorough. And it increased in the years she lived with Ted. I later wondered…."

"You wondered?" Gillian prodded when Tara trailed off. *Talk!*

"I wondered if it was her way of dealing with what was happening. To get rid of the dirt that Ted had brought into our family and that she knew about. Her reaction was to have a damned clean house, and when I saw the tea towel that evening, I…."

Gillian did not dare say anything else. Tara was shak-ing. She could feel it in the noose digging into her throat.

"I thought: *Suffocate on your hypocrisy*," Tara continued. "And then, well, that's just what happened. She suffocated on it."

She suddenly sat up, as Gillian felt through a sudden further yank at her throat.

"There's a car out there," she said in shock. "Shit!"

15

"THERE THEY ARE!" said John. He braked hard. His first feeling of overwhelming relief at having found the two women was immediately mixed with the horror of the situation he found them in. They were standing near the car in the middle of the road. Tara was right behind Gillian, holding a knife to her throat. Gillian seemed paralyzed with fear.

"Oh, God!" Samson exclaimed.

John turned off the engine but left the headlights on. "You stay in the car," he told Samson. "Got it?"

"Yes. Wh-where are you going?"

John had opened the driver's door. "I want to talk to Tara Caine. And remember: don't move!"

Samson nodded. He looked wide-eyed out of the windshield at the scene in front of him. He seemed deranged. John hoped that Samson would follow his instructions and stay in the car. Samson sure had the gift of doing the wrong thing at the wrong time, and in a situation as delicate as this one he could cause a lot of trouble.

John got out and took a few tentative steps toward the two women. By the light of the moon and the headlights, he could see everything in almost brutal clarity. Tara was holding a serrated knife in her hand. He could also see why Gillian's neck was angled back and her head so motionless: she had a wire noose around her neck. Tara was holding it tight. He could imagine how deeply the wire was cutting into her skin, forcing Gillian to remain completely immobile in order not to be in more pain and danger. She was completely at Tara Caine's mercy. She had no chance to free herself.

However, the pistol that Tara Caine had shot Thomas Ward with did not seem to be to hand. She could not just shoot him.

"Not a step closer, Burton," said Tara. Her voice was clear and commanding. She was used to giving orders. She had everything under control. At least she thought so. John could suddenly imagine her in a courtroom. She probably acted just like this in court: assured of her own success. He wondered whether she had any reason to feel so sure. It did seem like she had the upper hand right now.

He stopped.

"What do you want?" he asked.

"Why do you think I *want* something?" Tara retorted.

"We can stand here for hours. But that isn't likely to help you at all."

"I can kill your friend right now. Believe me, you won't be able to stop me."

"Of course. And how would that help you? A second later, I would overpower you and then that would be it for you. Not a great outlook, I'd say."

Gillian let out a small cry of pain. John had noticed the movement: Tara had tugged on the noose. It was clear to him that for every argument he won, Gillian would suffer. He felt his fists clench involuntarily. Caine was brutal and scrupulous. A real danger.

He looked at her, waiting for her reply.

"The car key," said Tara. "I want you to throw it over to me. So it is within reach of my foot."

"The car key?"

"The car key and your cell phone. No idea if there's any reception out here, but I don't want you to call the cops as soon as I've turned my back on you."

He could see what she was planning. "You want to take my car. And Gillian. And leave me here."

"Clever boy. You'll have my car, giving you some protection from the wind. Of course you won't have the key. I've got it. It's a bloody long way to Manchester by foot, and you'd probably get lost too. But someone might come by and give you a lift. Although at this time of year, this area is a pretty godforsaken place."

He said, in a low voice, "You really believe you can get away with this? The police are looking for you all over the country. They found your mother. You are a prime suspect. You know that it will be better for you if you give yourself up voluntarily. If you let Gillian go."

"That won't help me at all," Tara said coldly. "After all the things I've done. I've not been as lucky as you, Burton. No one can prove anything against you, and your case was given to a complete idiot in the Prosecution Service. So *you* got away scot-free. It will turn out differently for *me*."

"I didn't *do* anything."

"Repetition doesn't make your statement any more true."

He thought for a minute. "Let me make a suggestion, Ms. Caine. You obviously realize that you need a hostage if there is to be the slightest chance of escaping your precarious situation. Gillian has a little girl who has already lost her father. Please don't take her mother too. Let her go free, and take me instead."

It was worth trying, but he held out little hope that it would work. Tara was clever. Just the switch here on this road at night was too risky for her. And she could control Gillian better than him. John was a whole foot taller than she was. He had police training and was a sportsman. He was not half as exhausted or frightened as Gillian. He was a much more dangerous opponent, and Tara knew it.

"Your cell phone," she said by way of answer. "And your key!" He took his cell out of his trouser pocket, crouched down, and slid it along the road to the two women. It skidded along the flat, frozen snow and stopped just in front of Tara's right foot.

"Well done. Now the key!"

John stood up again. "I left it in the ignition."

"Then fetch it. I'm not going to get into your bloody car just to find out that you've tricked me. I want to *hold* the key!"

He walked backward to his car.

She hasn't yet noticed that I've got a passenger, he thought, else she would have asked him to get out or bring her the key. Of course. The headlights are blinding her. She can't see anything behind them.

He wondered whether he could turn this to his advantage. The fact that Caine thought she just had one opponent, when in fact there were two, could have been an ace up his sleeve. If the ace was not Samson Segal, of all people.

Only when he got to his car did he turn around to open the door. As he did so, he only just managed to stifle a surprised gasp. The passenger seat was empty.

The back seat too, and the hatchback, as a quick glance showed him.

Samson Segal had gotten out of the car. No doubt through the hatchback. John would not have thought he had it in him. He must have found and pressed the release catch next to the steering wheel, then wriggled his way back, and slipped out onto the road by opening the hatchback lid a crack.

And now? What was he planning to do?

John was worried. There were a few bushes to the left and right. They were leafless at this time of year, but the snow had turned them into big fat balls of snow. He must be hiding somewhere behind them. Nothing else was humanly possible.

This could all go terribly wrong.

He had told him not to move, he thought angrily. When I catch him, he's going to get it.

"Ready?" said Tara. He took out the key.

He hoped that Samson was not planning something crazy. It was a terrible moment to start playing the hero. Samson was hopelessly in love with Gillian and no doubt he was desperate to save her, but that could only end in disaster.

I shouldn't have brought him with me. What a bad idea, right from the start.

He slowly approached the two women, holding the key in his hand. He would have liked to look around, to try to see Samson and work out what he was planning, but he did not dare. Tara Caine would have noticed that he was looking for something or someone. If there was one mistake he could not make, it was to underestimate her.

"Okay," he said. "Here's the key."

"Give it to me. Just like your cell."

He slid the key across the snow. He aimed it so that it stopped a good distance from the cell. He did not need to make things easy for her.

"You don't happen to have a pistol, do you, a souvenir from your copper days?" asked Tara.

"No."

"Take off your coat and throw it far away."

He did as she told him to. She frisked his sweater with her eyes but could not see a bulge betraying the holster of a pistol. She would have to be content with that. The circumstances did not allow for a more thorough inspection.

John saw that Tara was bending down slowly. Using the noose, she forced Gillian to do as she did. The knife remained at Gillian's throat. But a critical moment— for Tara—was coming up. She only had two hands. She had to hold the noose with one. She would need to reach for the cell phone with the other and put it in her pocket. And then she would have to stretch to reach the key. Would she put the knife between her teeth? Or in her other hand? John knew that was the moment she could be overpowered, because she would not be able to stab him. It might be the only chance he would have. He gauged the distance between himself and the two women. It was too far. He could not get there fast enough.

As if Tara could read his thoughts, she suddenly stopped before reaching for the cell.

"Back farther," she said. "Back to the car, right now!"

She accompanied her order with a tug on the noose. Gillian moaned, grabbing involuntarily at her neck with both hands. She could not get a finger between the wire and her skin. The noose was too tight.

John had no option but to obey. He stepped slowly backward. "Good," said Tara, when he was beside the car. Carefully, she transferred the knife to the hand that was holding the noose. With her other hand, she grabbed the phone and put it in her coat pocket.

Then she tried to reach the key. She could not manage; it was too far away.

At that moment, John saw Samson appear behind the Jaguar. He really had managed to creep past the women behind the bushes and go around the car, and he was now behind them, just a few steps away from them. He had everything that John would have needed to overpower Tara; above all, he was close enough to her. In addition, she did not know he was there. With a little skill, he could get even closer without her noticing him.

With a little skill....

The word *skill* seemed absurd in relation to Samson, but John clung to this tiny hope, which did exist, after all. He could do nothing but obey Tara's orders. He was forced to stand here and see what would happen next. In any case, Samson had used the time to put himself in a good position. The man was showing potential. He just could not waste this chance too.

Tara had to stand up again, pulling Gillian up with her.

She would have to take about two steps to the side, in order to reach the key. John could see the anger in her expression. She knew that he had aimed badly on purpose.

Now, thought John, now!

Perhaps the telepathy worked. Samson suddenly rushed forward. Samson, who had always acted so hesitantly and fearfully, actually shot forward. He had reached the two women in under a second, just as Tara heard or felt the movement behind her and spun around. He crashed into her so forcefully that she could not think of defending herself. She let Gillian go and fell to the ground. She still held the knife in her hand, and it would only be a moment before she would thrust it between

Samson's ribs who, overwhelmed by his own courage, was now standing there paralyzed.

But now John was there too. He pushed Samson aside and knelt on Tara's chest, disarming her with one quick, skillful movement. Then he got up and forced Tara to get up slowly, holding her arm behind her back in a half Nelson.

"No sudden movements," he warned her, "or else it's going to hurt."

She seemed suddenly to be in a daze. She did not say anything or try to resist.

She had been beaten, and for the moment she had had no idea how to get out of it.

Yet John did not relax for a second. She was still a dangerous opponent. And she had nothing else to lose.

"We're going to walk over to my car," he said. "Slowly. Step by step. Do everything I say, and then I won't have to hurt you. Okay?"

She nodded.

He would have liked to take care of Gillian, but that would have to wait. The safety of them all had to come first. From the corner of his eye, he could see her crouching on the road, no doubt just as shocked as Tara. But she had someone taking care of her already: Samson was sitting next to her and had his arm around her. He stroked her hair awkwardly. She was not crying, but she had leaned her head on his shoulder. The gesture suggested not so much a need for protection as utter exhaustion.

Samson looked lightheaded. Moved. John did not begrudge him that at all.

It might have been the greatest moment of Samson Segal's life. And he had really earned it.

Wednesday, January 20

WHEN HE TURNED into Thorpe Hall Avenue, John felt how a load had lifted from his soul. He had to grin when he realized that he—of all people—was enjoying the sight of the tidy detached houses, the pretty yards, homely streets, and parks dotted with trees. The pavements had been cleared of snow, there were snowmen in some of the front yards, and thick layers of snow covered the bare bushes and the fences. There had not been any new snow for days now, but the cold north wind had turned snow to ice. It was supposed to warm up over the course of the next week. Then the snow in all its dazzling glory would melt away. What was left would just be a dirty slush at the side of the roads and February would come with its miserable weather. But today the whole area looked like a winter fairytale.

He hoped that Gillian would not be upset with him for arriving here unannounced. She had told him that she wanted to take an afternoon train to Norwich and that she would be here until about half past two. He was hoping to be allowed to take her to the station. He had called her the day before and told her that he wanted to talk to his former colleague, Sergeant McMarrow in Scotland Yard. Gillian had asked him to please call her if he heard any news about Tara, who had been transferred to London. He had been only too happy to promise her that he would. He welcomed any opportunity to talk to her.

The main reason he was meeting Christy was to apologize to her, but Gillian did not need to know that. Of course, he talked to her about all manner of things, including Samson.

"I can't promise that you won't get in trouble," she had said. "We were looking for Segal and you harbored him. No matter how things ended, I don't need to tell you that—"

"Of course," he had interrupted. "I know."

"Of course I'll put in a good word for you. And for Segal. If I've understood everything right, he saved your bacon up in the Peak District."

"He did. I really don't know what would have happened without him."

Her eyes narrowed. "As I said recently, John, you were damned well informed. Unless you've got some supernatural powers I don't know about, then it looks like you obtained information you shouldn't have had access to. I don't suppose you're going to enlighten me?"

"No."

"I thought so," she admitted.

"What about Caine?" he asked.

"She's being questioned. We've gotten a statement from Gillian Ward that details everything Tara Caine told her. But she has also made a confession now."

"That can't have been short."

"You can say that again." Christy counted the crimes on her fingers: "Lucy Caine-Roslin's murder. Carla Roberts's murder. Dr. Anne Westley's murder. Thomas Ward's murder. Abduction and attempted murder of Gillian Ward. That's enough for multiple life sentences. Crazy, isn't it? The woman always seemed so self-controlled, so serious. But that must have made things easy for her. Carla Roberts didn't know her personally, but she probably opened the door for her because she looked so trustworthy."

John had heard the whole story from Gillian. In that night in the Peak District, she had told him everything. She had been agitated, close to despair, and—in spite of everything—had been full of sympathy for the woman who had been her best friend.

"Tara Caine herself is a victim," he said to Christy. "She experienced some terrible things. The certainty that she will go to jail for the rest of her life doesn't really make me feel good."

Christy shrugged her shoulders. "That's just how it is sometimes. When are things ever black and white? And don't forget that three completely innocent people lost their lives. Carla Roberts and Anne Westley were two completely harmless elderly women, who either failed to see or underestimated the terrible situation another woman was in; but apart from that, they hadn't done anything wrong. Thomas Ward never hurt a fly, but just happened to get in the way of a lunatic on her crusade for revenge. And as for Caine-Roslin: yes, she may have been a terrible mother, and she should have gone to jail years ago for what she did to her daughter, but Tara Caine's way to solve the problem was not right. She should not just have killed her, however much we might understand the motive. It's just not acceptable in our society."

"I know. Of course I know that."

He braked in front of Gillian's house. With its big bay window and lattice windowpanes, it looked like a fairytale gingerbread house. He could understand that she no longer wanted to live there. Apart from the fact that she had found her husband shot dead in the dining room, which must make being in that room unbearable to her, the house no longer suited her. It had been an idyllic little nest for her family and herself with its gable roof, the little turret, and the fruit trees in the yard.

That was all in her past now. In a way that could hardly be more horrific, she had become another person.

He got out of his car and walked up the path to the front door, where he rang the bell. He hoped that she had not left earlier than she had planned. But the door opened.

Gillian.

It was just after two, and he had expected to find her more or less ready to go on her trip. But she stood there in black leggings and a thick pullover, wearing slippers on her bare feet.

"Oh," she said. "I wasn't expecting a visit."

"I'm sorry for arriving so unexpectedly. I just thought…well…." He was annoyed with himself, for suddenly being as tongue-tied as an eighteen-year-old boy. "I just wanted to see you again. And I can drive you to the station if you'd like."

"Come in," she said.

He stepped inside. The packing cases were still piled up in the hall. But he could not see a suitcase or travel bag.

"I'm not going to Norwich," she explained.

"No?"

"No. I called my parents this morning. They're bringing Becky and Chuck here this weekend. At the beginning of February, Becky really has to start school, and we need some time to get used to one another again by then."

He looked at her.

"Would you like an espresso?" she asked.

"Yes, please." He followed her into the kitchen.

"What do you mean, Gillian? That Becky will go back to school *here*?"

"For now, at any rate. Until I've sold the house and found somewhere else." She filled the machine with coffee beans. "I don't want to move to Norwich."

"No?"

"No. I had a good think about it last night. And tonight. It doesn't feel right, you know. Back to my childhood home. Back to where my parents live. I thought I would find peace there, feel secure there. But now I know I won't find either anywhere. Not in the foreseeable future, anyway." She put the little espresso cups in the right place and turned on the machine. "I can't run to my family for protection." She thought for a minute and then added: "It would be completely wrong. I didn't act very grown-up before…the thing with Tom happened, and that has to change. I have to finally grow up."

"I can understand what you mean," said John. "But I think you've been very grown-up these last few days. Whatever things were like before, and however hard on yourself you are about that, during this nightmare we've all just come out of, you were strong every single minute. And very brave."

That was why when he had seen her fairytale house he had had similar thoughts to what she was saying now. The house did not fit anymore. After everything that had happened to Gillian, she had to move forward. She could not stay where she was, nor go backward.

"I'm in awe of you," he said.

She gave him his espresso. "I thought I'd look for an apartment for Becky, Chuck, and myself in London. I won't sell the company. I'll run it on my own. It will be hard work, so it's important that I don't have a long commute. After all, I'll have Becky to look after too. But it will all work out. Other single moms manage it."

"Of course it will. You'll manage." He had to take care not to let too much happiness, relief—yes, *joy*— show in his voice. She was staying! She was even moving to London. He breathed in deeply. His heart was beating fast.

She could feel what he did not express. "John…."

And he knew what she wanted to say. "I know you need time, Gillian. But perhaps we can just go for a drink. Or a meal? We can get to know each other better. I mean, until now…."

"…we've only slept together," completed Gillian, as he hesitated. "Yes, it would be nice to get to know you. But I can't promise anything, John."

"Of course not. I just want a chance. Nothing more than that." He drank his espresso and put the cup down on the table. He hoped that meetings like this one and the one the week before would not be the only ones they had: meetings where he came by without an invitation and she was polite enough to offer him a coffee before he had to say goodbye. He wanted so much more. Right now, he would have liked so much to embrace Gillian and bury his face in her hair, feel her heart beating. But he knew that the next step had to come from her. Nothing else would help.

"You'll definitely get a chance," said Gillian with a tender voice. She smiled warmly at him. "John, I owe my life to you. The police would have never found us in time. If you hadn't—"

"No!" He put his finger to her lips briefly. "No more about it! You already thanked me a hundred times the other night in the Peak District. It's all right. I don't want…."

"What?"

"Whatever the future holds in store for the two of us, I don't want it to be based on gratitude. I mean, should you call me up to agree to meet, which I so hope you will, please don't do it because you think you owe it to me. That would be terrible. Just do it if you'd really like to."

She nodded. "I *can* promise you that."

The two of them said nothing for a few moments, and then John said, "Well, I'd better go. You must have a lot to do."

"Any news about Tara?"

"She's in custody. She's also confessed everything to the police."

"I feel so sorry for her. I know that she did unforgivable things, but there's nothing I can do about it, John: I'll always see her as a victim, not a perpetrator."

"But she can't be allowed to go free. She is seriously ill and would be a danger to society. But now she can get the psychological help that she's needed for years."

"If it's possible, I'll visit her. In the future."

"I'm sure it will be possible."

"What about the woman who triggered all this? Liza Stanford?" John had talked to Christy about Liza too.

"Liza has pressed charges against her husband," he told her. "The police took her to a refuge for abused women. Her son is with her. Of course it's not easy. She has to prove that her accusations are true. Dr. Westley, who would have been a good witness, is dead. And Caine, whose testimony would have carried weight too, is now in prison for four murders. Stanford will shield himself behind armies of topnotch lawyers. Unfortunately, the cards aren't stacked against him. But we'll have to see. The main thing is, she's not going back to him. I hope so, at least."

"She was just a pebble that set a whole chain of terrible things in motion."

"Yes, she was the trigger for it all," John said. "But the pressure building up, suppressed, over the decades in Tara Caine, had reached such a level that it was bound to blow up. If Liza Stanford hadn't caused it, someone else would have. Things were going get ugly. In my opinion, it was inevitable."

He was right, Gillian knew. And she also knew that Tara would have carried on. She could still hear the shocking sentence that Tara had uttered that night in the Peak District: *I can't stop killing my mother.*

It might have seemed like a good deed when she decided to help Liza Stanford in her desperate situation, but certainly by the time she murdered Lucy Caine her crusade against a failure to render assistance had become a personal thirst for vengeance. Tara had begun to go and look for victims. She had been happy to hear about Carla Roberts and Anne Westley. Regarding herself, Gillian, Tara had needed to use rather obscure reasoning when she claimed to be protecting Becky from her mother's lover, a man who had never been convicted of anything. Probably she would have started bending logic more and more, declaring innocent people her personal enemies. And no doubt she would never again have desisted from a planned murder, as had apparently been the case with Gillian. Especially as Gillian suspected that Tara had only been ready to desist because she had already failed twice. Perhaps Tara had just had a momentary wobble in her case.

Gillian accompanied John to the door. It seemed to

him like an act of self-denial to go, but he knew it was the right thing.

"You'll be in touch?" he asked. "You'll tell me where you're moving to, won't you?"

"Yes," she promised.

He reached out his hand and stroked her cheek, then went down the path to his car.

When he turned around once more, she had already closed the door.

Nevertheless, he was happy. He was so happy, he could jump for joy.

He looked down the road and saw Samson walking toward him. Samson had pulled a woolly cap down over his eyes and was wearing a scarf wrapped several times around his neck. He was sauntering along as if he just happened to have been passing by, but John thought immediately: he's doing it again. He's hanging round Gillian's house again. As if that hadn't gotten him in enough trouble already!

"Hi, Samson," he said.

As always, when someone talked to him, Samson seemed to be taken by surprise. "Oh, hi, John," he said. He nodded toward the house. "Everything okay w-with Gillian?"

"Everything's fine."

"It's a shame she's moving so far away."

"Yes...." said John vaguely. He had no wish to let Samson know about Gillian's new plans. Let Gillian, if she wanted to. Or let Samson try and find out.

"I'm just out for a walk," said Samson. He looked anxious and worried. John looked down the road, to the shabbier end, where Samson lived.

"How are things at home?" he asked. "Your sister-in-law owed you an apology, didn't she?"

Samson shook his head. "She didn't apologize. She wouldn't do that. She just blamed me for running away. And she was annoyed because I'm back."

"She should be ashamed of herself."

"But actually it w-was good she did w-what she did," said Samson. "I mean, reporting me. Otherwise I wouldn't have gone into hiding. And wouldn't have driven to the Peak District with you. And who knows then how everything would have ended."

"If you put it like that, we really should be grateful to your sister-in-law," said John. He did not mention the fact that without Samson's thoughtless message on Gillian's answering machine, Tara Caine might never have felt herself cornered and forced to try to escape north with a hostage. He was happy to let Samson feel like a hero.

"Still," he continued. "How long are you going to put up with things as they are? With being an unwelcome guest in your own family and so dreaming your way into other lives because your own reality is so hard to bear?"

In the next moment, he regretted his words. "Excuse me. It's none of my business, actually."

"It is. I mean, don't worry," Samson said. "You're right."

John looked at him and thought of the night in the Peak District. It was very strange to imagine this awkward, stuttering, insecure man as a knight in shining armor, but luckily John did not have to *imagine* it: he *knew* what had happened. Samson had acted bravely and intelligently, with his head and his heart. He deserved another chance.

"You know what, I've been thinking," John said.

Which was not true. He had just had the thought. "Last Friday, one of my staff resigned. That means I've got a vacancy. What do you think?"

Samson's jaw dropped. "You mean that I…?"

"You've just proven that in moments of great pressure you keep calm and do just what is needed," said John. "And I can promise you that the situations my staff face are generally much less dangerous. Would you like to give it a try?"

Samson could still scarcely believe his ears. "That would be…that would be…."

"You need work," said John. "And if I can give you one piece of advice: move out from your brother's place. Ask him to pay you your half of the inheritance. If he takes out a mortgage on the house, he can do that. And then find somewhere to live near where you'll work. A small apartment where you can really feel at home. It's time…." He hesitated. He hated it when people intervened in his life, and that was just what he was doing in Samson's.

"What?" asked Samson.

"It's time to start a new life," said John.

Silently in his head, he added: *For all of our sakes.*

"You're right," said Samson. He said it confidently, without hesitating or stuttering. Standing there in the bright light of a clear winter's day, it was as if something had already changed inside him.

"Yes, you really are right," he repeated.

All of a sudden he smiled, and John understood that he was witnessing a rare moment: Samson was happy.

* * * * *